# LADY

# FLYER

Also by
HEATHER B. MOORE

*The Paper Daughters of Chinatown*
*The Slow March of Light*
*In the Shadow of a Queen*
*Under the Java Moon*

With
ALLISON HONG MERRILL

*The Paper Daughters of Chinatown Young Reader's Edition*

# LADY
# FLYER

## HEATHER B. MOORE

SHADOW
MOUNTAIN
PUBLISHING

*Dedicated to my daughter, Kara, a pilot in her own right*

*Image credits: p. 372, Nancy Harkness Love with a Fairchild PT-19A Trainer: photo courtesy of WASP Archive/TWU Denton, TX; p. 373, Robert Love and Nancy Love: photo courtesy of Davis-Monthan Aviation Field Register; p. 374, Nancy Love and Betty Gillies: photo courtesy of WASP Archive/TWU Denton, TX; p. 375 Nancy Love in a Boeing B-17 Flying Fortress: photo courtesy of the National Archives*

Visit us at shadowmountain.com

This is a work of fiction. Characters and events in this book are products of the author's imagination or are represented fictitiously.

---

Library of Congress Cataloging-in-Publication Data

Names: Moore, Heather B., author.
Title: Lady flyer / Heather B. Moore.
Description: [Salt Lake City] : Shadow Mountain Publishing, [2024] | Includes bibliographical references. | Summary: "Amidst WWII, aviator Nancy Harkness Love's passion for flying intertwines with a tender romance with aviator Bob Love. However, her dream of a female pilot squadron faces resistance from military leaders and Jackie Cochran. Inspired by Nancy's true story, Heather B. Moore's novel about this aviation hero weaves a tale of love, ambition, and pioneering courage amid wartime challenges"—Provided by publisher.
Identifiers: LCCN 2024008426 (print) | LCCN 2024008427 (ebook) | ISBN 9781639932955 (hardback) | ISBN 9781649332950 (ebook)
Subjects: LCSH: Love, Nancy Harkness, 1914–1976—Fiction. | Love, Robert M., 1909–1983—Fiction. | Cochran, Jacqueline—Fiction. | United States. Women's Auxiliary Ferrying Squadron—Fiction. | Women Airforce Service Pilots (U.S.)—Fiction. | World War, 1939–1945—Fiction. | Women air pilots—Michigan—Fiction. | Man-woman relationships—Fiction. | Houghton (Mich.), setting. | BISAC: FICTION / Historical / 20th Century / World War II | FICTION / War & Military | LCGFT: Romance fiction. | Historical fiction. | Novels.
Classification: LCC PS3613.O5589 L33 2024 (print) | LCC PS3613.O5589 (ebook) | DDC 813/.6—dc23/eng/20240315
LC record available at https://lccn.loc.gov/2024008426
LC ebook record available at https://lccn.loc.gov/2024008427

---

Printed in the United States of America
Publishers Printing

10   9   8   7   6   5   4   3   2   1

# CHARACTERS

## HISTORICAL CHARACTERS

**Nancy Harkness Love**

**Robert (Bob) MacLure Love**

Adela (Del) Scharr

Alice Chadbourne Harkness

Alice Hirschman

Aline (Pat) Rhonie

Alison Hardy Dempsey

Avanell Pinckley

Barbara Poole

Barbara Towne

Barbara (Donnie) Donahue

Barbara Jane (B.J.) Erickson

Bernice Batten

Betty Gillies

Bud Gillies

Byrd Granger

Catherine Slocum

Cecil (Teddy) Kenyon

Cornelia Fort

C.R. Smith

Crocker Snow

Delphine Bohn

Dorothy Fulton

Dorothy (Scottie) Scott

Edith Nourse Rogers

Esther Manning

Esther Nelson

Ethel Sheehy

Eugene Vidal

Evelyn Sharp

Florene Miller

Georgina Denton

Gertrude Meserve

Hannah Lincoln Chadbourne Denton

Harold L. George

Helen MacCloskey

Helen Richards

Helen (Little Mac) McGilvery

Helen Mary Clark

Henry Wilder

Henry (Hap) Arnold

Jack Ray

Jacqueline (Jackie) Cochran

Jimmy Hansen

Joe Tracy

Johnny Hammond

Johnny Miller

Joseph Choate

# CHARACTERS

Joseph Marr Gwinn Jr.

Katherine (Kay) Rawls Thompson

Kathryn (Sis) Bernheim

Mr. & Mrs. Johnson (names changed)

Lenore McElroy

Mrs. Louise Fort

Louise Thaden

Margaret (Tommy) Thomas

Nancy Batson

Opal (Betsy) Ferguson

Oveta Culp Hobby

Phyllis Burchfield

R.O. (Pappy) Fraser

Robert Codman

Robert Olds

Dr. Robert B. Harkness

Robert (Bobbin) B. Harkness Jr.

Robert H. Baker

Robert (Red) D. Forman

Samuel C. Dunlap

Suzanne (Susie) Humphreys

Teresa James

T/Sgt. Stover

T/Sgt. L.S. Hall

T/Sgt. Weintraub

Thomas L. Chadbourne

William A. Ong

William H. Tunner

## FICTIONAL CHARACTERS

Beth    Pauly    Rachel    Thad

# GLOSSARY OF ACRONYMS

**AAB:** Army Air Base

**AAC:** Army Air Corps

**AAF:** Army Air Forces

**ATA:** Air Transport Auxiliary (British)

**ATC:** Air Transport Command

**B-4 Bag:** Army-issued canvas bag

**BOQ:** Bachelor Officer Quarters

**CAA:** Civil Aeronautics Authority (1938–1940); Administration
(1940–1958)

**CPT:** Civilian Pilot Training Program

**ICA:** Inter City Aviation

**NACA:** National Advisory Committee for Aeronautics

**P:** Pursuit, or fighter aircraft

**PT:** Primary Trainer

**RAF:** Royal Air Force (British)

**RON:** Remain Over Night

**SPAR:** Semper Paratus Always Ready (Women's Coast Guard Auxiliary)

**WAAC:** Women's Army Auxiliary Corps

**WAC:** Women's Army Corps

**WAFS:** Women's Auxiliary Ferrying Squadron

**WASP:** Women's Airforce Service Pilots

**WAVES:** Women Accepted for Volunteer Emergency Service

**WFTD:** Women's Flying Training Detachment

**WPA:** Works Progress Administration

**WTS:** War Training Service (followed CTP, 1941–1944)

# INTRODUCTION

While researching and writing about the WASP aviators who served in World War II, it was interesting to discover that many of those I spoke to didn't know that women pilots flew war planes during that era. A few had heard of the British women ferrying pilots, and even fewer knew of the women who flew for the Soviet Union combat missions.

On American soil, women pilots weren't militarized, so their contributions came under the umbrella of civilian pilots. Even before the Japanese attack on Pearl Harbor, there was a pilot shortage as the US was frantically building and sending aircraft across the Atlantic to support the Allied forces. Two women, Nancy Harkness Love and Jacqueline Cochran, worked tirelessly to propose solutions to fill the pilot shortage. Their vision included establishing a women's pilot organization that would ferry planes from the manufacturers to airfields, freeing up the men to train and prepare for combat missions.

Beginning in 1940, Nancy Love persisted in her agenda at home while Jacqueline Cochran headed to England to join the British ATA Civilian Ferry Pilot Program that allowed women to ferry planes as part of the war effort.

After the bombing of Pearl Harbor in December 1941, and after the US declared war on Japan and the Axis powers, over 100,000 men and women enlisted in the military. Eventually 50 million of 132 million Americans became employed in the war effort, working for the government, and women entered the workforce as never before.

Nancy Love had a remarkable vision—one she didn't give up on. Her perseverance and leadership became the catalyst to demonstrating how women could be integrated into and valued in the Army Air Forces as pilots. Nancy wanted to see female pilots given opportunities to serve their country, and though her vision did not become widespread in the 1940s, with persistence, she became a trailblazer.

Starting in 1940, Nancy Love waded through nearly two years of setbacks before Colonel William H. Tunner approved her idea of hiring women pilots to ferry planes for the Ferrying Command, a division of the Army Air Corps—picking up the planes at the manufacturing plants, then delivering them to air bases around the country, plus other ferrying duties. This filled in the gaps that male pilots created when they left to fly combat missions.

When Nancy Love's program was finally approved in 1942, the Women's Auxiliary Ferrying Squadron (WAFS) quickly filled with twenty-eight hand-selected women pilots, who were called the Originals. These women came from various backgrounds, but all were well-qualified to transition to the larger planes and bombers coming off the assembly lines.

Jacqueline Cochran, returned from Europe, headed up the Women's Flying Training Detachment (WFTD), which trained and qualified additional women pilots to join the Women's Ferrying Program. By August 1943, the WAFS had increased to over 225 women strong. That same August, Love's WAFS combined with Cochran's WFTD to become the WASP (Women Airforce Service Pilots) (see https://cafriseabove.org/nancy-harkness-love/).

During the nearly sixteen months of the WASP Program, more than 25,000 women applied for training. Of those, 1,879 candidates were accepted into the Training Program, which was moved from the Houston Municipal Airport to Avenger Field in Sweetwater, Texas. Only 1,074 women successfully graduated (see https://www.army.mil/women/history/pilots.html).

The WASP pilots spent 1942–1944 flying every type of combat plane and delivering 12,650 aircraft to seventy-eight different bases throughout the nation while logging in more than 60 million flight miles (see https://twu.edu/library/womans-collection/collections/women-airforce-service-pilots-official-archive/history).

Women became the backbone of the progression of the war and the eventual Allied victory. They worked in factories, building aircraft, and as airplane mechanics at Army Air Corps bases. Thanks to the persistence of Nancy Love and Jacqueline Cochran, women ferried the war planes from the manufacturing floors to the air bases, where women also worked as instructors for male pilot trainees. In addition, women flew the towing targets for male combat pilot training, and they tested out planes with mechanical issues.

Nancy Love firmly believed that if women didn't learn to fly multi-engine war planes, it would create a bottleneck between the production line and ferrying the planes to the airfields. She took it upon herself to set the example that women could fly the larger, more complex aircraft. She qualified on virtually all the Army Air Force's combat aircraft, including the P-51 Mustang, P-38 Lightning fighters, C-54 transport, B-17 Flying Fortress, Consolidated B-24 Liberator, and the B-29 Superfortress. Nancy became the trailblazer for many of the WASP pilots and future pilots who would follow in her footsteps (see https://cafriseabove.org/nancy-harkness-love/; see also https://www.thisdayinaviation.com/tag/nancy-harkness-love/).

The road was rocky and full of unexpected setbacks, especially when the WASPs tried to secure militarization so the female pilots could receive the same benefits as the male pilots. Congressional bills gave the WAC, WAVES, and SPARs military status in the 1940s, but the WASP never secured militarization during the life of the program (Pearson, 140).

With the war coming to an end and male pilots returning home, authorities viewed the need for women pilots as obsolete, and the 1944 push for the WASP to militarize was shot down. The women were told to return home so the men could have their jobs back (Pearson, 140).

Nancy's belief in herself and other women pilots never faltered. Through many setbacks of family tragedy, a world war, constant obstacles and roadblocks to earn trust for women pilots, and health challenges, Nancy continued to push forward, soaring higher in order to make the path smoother for female pilots in the future.

# PART ONE

## 1927–1937

# CHAPTER ONE

"I first saw the lights of Paris a little before ten P.M., or five P.M. New York time, and a few minutes later I was circling the Eiffel Tower at an altitude of about four thousand feet. The lights of Le Bourget were plainly visible, but appeared to be very close to Paris. . . . Presently I could make out long lines of hangars, and roads appeared to be jammed with cars. I flew low over the field once, then circled around into the wind and landed. After the plane stopped rolling, I turned it around and started to taxi back to the lights. The entire field ahead, however, was covered with thousands of people all running towards my ship."

—CHARLES LINDBERGH, MAY 20, 1927

*May 1927—Paris, France*

"Do you think he'll make it?" Georgina asked, pressed close to Nancy as they watched the velvety night sky for any sign of a plane.

Nancy couldn't see anything glimmering in the Paris sky beyond the litter of stars. "I don't know, but if he doesn't, all this fuss will be for nothing."

A man in a wool coat and hat jostled Nancy's shoulder as he pushed through the crowd, trying to get a better view.

Charles Lindbergh should be appearing in the sky at any moment, flying the *Spirit of St. Louis*, that was, if all went well. A crash had not been reported yet. He was supposed to land at Le Bourget Field—right where Nancy stood with her cousin and aunt, plus one hundred thousand Parisians.

More people closed in around them. Nancy's small pocket of breathing space was officially shut off now, replaced instead with cigarette smoke and cloying French perfume. Aunt Hannah stood like a fierce sentinel next to Nancy and Georgina, acting the proper protector with her fur stole and cloche hat.

"Stay together, girls," Aunt Hannah ordered for the dozenth time, her voice pitched above the general French chatter.

Nancy and Georgina linked arms as the crowd went through another surge, and Nancy earned an elbow in the back, accompanied by a brusque, "*Excuse-moi.*" She didn't even bother turning around because it was simply the nature of the crowd.

Georgina pointed and giggled at a rather amorous couple locked in an embrace a few feet from them. Nancy wanted to laugh, too, but she didn't want to draw attention from Georgina's mother, Hannah, again. Nancy felt fortunate to have been invited along to Paris. Georgina had just turned seventeen, four years older than Nancy, and as the youngest of seven children in her family, Georgina had been allowed to invite Nancy.

Conversation rose and fell around them as flashlights strobed through the crowd—many of them pointed their lights to the sky so Charles Lindbergh could see the otherwise pitch-dark runway. There had already been plenty of false sightings. Children cheering, women swooning, excited viewers uncorking champagne bottles, men lighting cigars . . . only to be another false alarm.

"Can you stand the suspense?" Georgina asked in breathless excitement. "The entire world will remember May 21, 1927. And just think, we're witnessing this history."

"History that could end badly," Nancy said dryly, remembering the multiple other failed transatlantic flight attempts all trying for the Orteig Prize of $25,000. In 1919, Raymond Orteig had promised the prize money to the first aviator of any country who crossed the Atlantic in one flight between Paris and New York, either direction. So far, all crossings had tragically failed. "Either Charles Lindbergh will be the first man to fly solo across the Atlantic, or everyone will be mourning another needless loss."

Georgina nudged her with a huff. "Spoilsport. Mr. Lindbergh was spotted flying over England, so he's made it this far."

Flying seemed a bit foolish in Nancy's mind, even though her brother had taken some flying lessons. Plenty of pilots tried stunts that never ended well. She didn't understand the drive to put one's life in danger, although she was interested in the statistics she'd heard on the radio earlier that day.

Lindbergh had left Roosevelt Field out of New York at 7:51 a.m. He carried 450 gallons of gasoline, making the single-engine plane weigh about 2,750 pounds. He had packed only five sandwiches and brought no coffee. Since he was flying solo, he would have to stay awake for the entire trip. Thirty-two hours and counting . . .

How would it feel to stay awake that long? And how cold had it become thousands of feet above the earth, as the newspapers had reported? Had Lindbergh eaten all of his sandwiches yet? And where—

Someone in the crowd yelled, and an absolute hush dropped like a heavy paint canvas over the people who stood crushed together. The faint drone of an engine filled the air, its rumbling growing louder and closer. Suddenly, people were moving, and not in any particular direction, as they strained to catch sight of the approaching plane.

Nancy held on to Georgina with both hands, who held on to her mother. But Nancy's feet were rooted to the rutted ground as the plane in the sky circled the landing field. Flashlights clicked on in earnest now, like a horde of fireflies suddenly come to life. People aimed their flashlights toward the sky, trying to cast their own personal spotlight of history in the making. But the plane didn't descend toward the airfield; it continued to circle. What was the pilot doing? Why wasn't he landing? Was it really Charles Lindbergh after all?

"Is it really that small of a plane?" Georgina asked, wonder in her voice.

"*Regardez ça!*" someone shouted. "Monsieur Lindbergh!"

Cheers went up as the plane circled yet again, and somewhere in the crowd, an energetic song began—the French national anthem.

Nancy kept her chin raised; her eyes focused on the circling aircraft. Her pulse jarred through her, mimicking the stuttering sound of the plane engine.

Once, twice, three times the plane circled, and then it dipped. Nose first, it descended, faster than Nancy thought it should. Wasn't there some sort of brakes? People scattered, ran, shouted . . . and all Nancy could do was grip her cousin's arm and stare as Charles Lindbergh's plane touched the ground. Dust bloomed, filling the night air, and Nancy tasted grit in her mouth as the scent of engine oil seemed to seep around her. The plane bumped along for dozens of yards before coming to a final stop.

People behind, to the side, and in front of Nancy's group shifted and pressed and moved—all trying to get closer. Policemen circled the stopped plane, linking their hands to create a human barrier as they shouted in limp French for people to stand back.

The crowds broke through anyway.

Aunt Hannah's viselike grip clutched both Nancy's and Georgina's arms. "We need to get away from here," she burst out. "Everyone is going crazy."

But Nancy couldn't tear her gaze from the aviator who climbed out of the plane and waved his flight helmet in the air. She was too far away to see his face, and besides, flashlights were bobbing around, making everything distorted. It was surreal to realize that this man had just accomplished what no other person had ever done before.

"Nancy, now," Aunt Hannah demanded.

Reluctantly, Nancy turned from the man who'd made aviation history. Clutching Georgina's arm, she followed Aunt Hannah back to the train station, pushing through the tide of people moving in the opposite direction. Once free of the nearly stampeding crowd, the smoky-oil air dissipated and clean air filled Nancy's lungs.

They reached the station only to find the trains weren't running, their odor of steam and coal cinders the only thing indicating trains had been present earlier. A lone man stood on the platform, hat in hand, a gold-chain pocket watch visible on his suit vest. When Aunt Hannah approached him and inquired what was going on in her mediocre French, he said that everyone was at the field, including the train conductors.

"Ah, we meet again, Signora Denton," another male voice said in a thick accent. "I have a car that can take you to your accommodations."

Nancy turned to see a man only slightly taller than her five feet six inches. The man looked familiar, yet how was that possible? He wore a gray herringbone suit and darker-gray hat. Nancy flinched as the memory returned. She realized that the man's brown eyes were the same ones that belonged to the man who'd paid them so much attention during their time at the beach in the Riviera. Ordering them drinks, asking her aunt questions while his gaze was upon Nancy, inviting them to dinner—which they'd declined.

"No, I don't think so," Aunt Hannah cut in, her voice an octave higher than normal. "We have our own transportation, sir."

Hannah grasped Nancy's and Georgina's arms and bustled them away from the train platform.

Nancy glanced back at the man, who stood next to a sleek, dark car, hat in hand, seeming a bit forlorn. He was handsome, with his straight nose and square jaw—for an older gentleman, probably around her father's age.

"Don't look back, Nancy," Aunt Hannah snapped as their heeled boots clicked on the cobblestones.

Georgina giggled.

"It's not funny," Aunt Hannah added.

"It's a little funny, Mother," Georgina said. "Who would have thought Nancy's Italian count followed us all the way here?"

"He's not my count," Nancy protested, although it was a bit odd to see the man again so suddenly. "And everyone in all of France seems to be here—so it's a coincidence."

"Even so, there's over 100,000 people gathered here. The radio said so. And your count comes out of nowhere." Aunt Hannah snapped her gloved fingers. "Just like that. I don't like it, Nancy."

Nancy's neckline itched, and she repeated, "He's not my count." But her lips twitched as she glanced at the smiling Georgina.

Aunt Hannah led them down another street lined with shops and cafés long since closed, although the aroma of baked delicacies and creamy chocolate lingered—both tempting and tormenting.

"Now, see here." Aunt Hannah stopped just outside the halo of a streetlight. She faced them both, her arms folded. The streetlight beyond made her face an ethereal glow, but her eyes flashed as she narrowed them at Nancy. "The Italian count is no laughing matter. If he had pressed his case, I would have called over a policeman."

"He was only trying to help, Mother," Georgina countered. "You don't need to be so ultra."

Even Nancy knew not to argue with Aunt Hannah when she wore her stern expression.

"Nancy is thirteen years old, and that man is old enough to be her father." Aunt Hannah set her hands on her hips. "I saw the way he watched her on the French Riviera. Everyone saw. It was quite inappropriate and mortifying. Nancy might appear older because of her . . . shapeliness, but that is no excuse for his behavior. Do you really want your cousin to be ogled by an older man who thinks he can have whatever, or whomever, he wants?"

Georgina turned somber. "I'm sorry, Mother."

No one was laughing now. Even at the Riviera, Aunt Hannah had treated the attention as some great joke. But now, the edge to her voice held true worry.

"And you, Hannah Lincoln Harkness," Aunt Hannah said, shifting her attention to Nancy. She meant business now—calling Nancy by her full name. Father hadn't liked Mother's family's tradition of naming first daughters Hannah Lincoln, so he'd called her Nancy. And it had stuck. Mostly.

"Your mother allowed you to come on our European trip in order to broaden your education," Aunt Hannah said. "She didn't intend that education to be one of worldly men."

"Yes, ma'am."

"What do you think your parents would do in this situation?"

Nancy drew in a breath. "Father would punch the count's nose, and Mother would keep me in a locked room for the next week." It might be an exaggeration, but she knew her parents wouldn't be pleased, and now she could see that weight of responsibility upon her aunt.

"You did the right thing," Nancy continued her apology. "Thank you for bringing me and protecting me."

Aunt Hannah gave a firm nod. "Now, be prepared to walk, girls. We have a ways to go. We'll not be accepting any rides from strangers."

They set off again, and Georgina edged close to Nancy as Aunt Hannah strode ahead, seeming to keep an eagle eye out for dark, lurking forms. "Just think, if he's wealthy, you'd be set for life."

"Oh, I thought of that already," Nancy said with a quiet laugh. "But I don't really want my children to speak Italian. Maybe if he were French . . ."

Georgina giggled. Ahead of them now, Aunt Hannah checked behind her, brows pulled together.

The girls fell silent. The only sounds in the Paris streets that echoed between them were their heeled boots and rustling skirts.

It felt as though hours had passed before they arrived at their hotel, but in reality, it had probably been only a single hour. The hotel lobby was ablaze with light and abuzz with people gathered to discuss Monsieur Lindbergh's landing. No one would be sleeping tonight.

Charles Lindbergh had flown for thirty-three hours, thirty minutes, and thirty seconds. How would it be, Nancy wondered, to be the most-talked-about aviator in the world? And all that prize money was now his. Had the danger and uncertainty been worth it?

Other numbers swirled inside her head. One newspaper article she'd read the day before had reported that the single-engine plane had cost $10,580 to build, and it was powered by a Wright Whirlwind J-5 engine. Modifications had been made to the plane—ones that had proven successful, it seemed.

Lindbergh had forgone a copilot or a navigator to keep the plane lighter. He'd even left behind a parachute and radio. None of these details should be clouding Nancy's thoughts and keeping her awake long after Georgina's breathing had evened one twin bed over, but Nancy found herself curious all the same. Perhaps it was because Charles Lindbergh's flight had been successful and not a disaster. Regardless, it was a far more interesting subject to think about than an old count who kept popping up wherever she was.

# CHAPTER TWO

"We didn't fly planes in those days, we rode them. We were supposed
to get the feeling of the plane through the seat of our pants."

—WILLIAM H. TUNNER, *OVER THE HUMP*

*3 years later*
*August 1930—Houghton, Michigan*

"There's a good girl." Nancy soothed her horse, Daisy, by stroking
her sleek, soft neck. Daisy nickered a soft grunt. She'd been skittish
since the biplane in the adjacent field had started offering stunt rides for
those who'd pay the five dollars.

Nancy watched the buzzing aircraft for a few more minutes, reluctant to return home to her chores. The silver wings caught the brightness
of the afternoon sun and reflected gold and silver as the sun played peek-
a-boo in the drifting white clouds.

Townsfolk from her hometown of Houghton, Michigan, had formed
a line to take their turn in the sky. Barnstormer pilots showed up from
time to time, performing stunts for crowds willing to pay. But this barnstormer was offering rides to people.

Nancy didn't have five dollars at the ready, not since her family was
being careful with finances. The stock market had crashed the year before, and many people were struggling financially, but she didn't be-
grudge those who were paying the steep price for a biplane ride.

Nancy nudged Daisy closer, but the horse nickered her displeasure
as her shoulder muscles bunched.

"Fine, I'll check it out myself." Nancy dismounted and tied Daisy
to a nearby tree. She trekked across the field of grass and yellow-gold
wildflowers. The people in line glanced over at her, then returned to
their gawking as the biplane headed for another takeoff, leaving a smoke
trail in its wake.

"How was it?" Nancy asked a woman who'd been the most recent passenger. Over the past three years, Nancy had followed Charles Lindbergh in the news, her curiosity about flying growing.

"Stomach-curling," the woman pronounced, holding on to her gaudy lavender hat in the light breeze.

"You didn't even do the stunt route," a man said.

"I can't afford more than a penny a pound," the woman answered with a laugh. "Besides, I wanted to keep my lunch, and circling the field is fine with me."

"Wait, you can circle the field for a penny a pound?" Nancy asked. She could afford that, and then maybe she could, once and for all, satisfy her curiosity. At the very least, it would be something to tell her brother about.

The woman's cool gray eyes landed on Nancy again. "That's right, dear."

"Where does the line end?"

"There's no line, missy," an older man with a large midsection and red suspenders to hold it all together answered. "We're watching the fool's attempts. You can be next if you've got the money."

She had *some* money. Digging into the pockets of her tea-length pleated skirt, she rounded up enough change to equal her weight. At least she thought so. "I'll go next," she announced.

One of the men laughed, but Nancy didn't care. The biplane was landing again, and she stared at the rotating silver propeller and wings that gleamed bright. The pilot stopped several dozen feet from the onlookers, and a teen passenger not much older than Nancy climbed out. His freckled skin was as pale as milk.

"Who's next?" the pilot called out.

Nancy guessed that he was in his midtwenties. She stepped forward, jingling the change in her hand. "I have a dollar."

He looked her up and down, probably trying to estimate if she was telling the truth about her weight. At sixteen, Nancy had the shape of a full-grown woman. When the pilot met her steady gaze, his mouth quirked up. "Come aboard, miss."

So, Nancy did. She tugged on the extra pair of goggles and helmet, ignoring the smell of leather and perspiration. With the pilot's steadying hand to grasp, she climbed into the front seat.

"Put your toes on the brake pads on top of the rudder pedals—right there," the pilot said, pointing. "I'm going to swing the propeller."

Once the prop was rotating, the pilot hurried back and jumped into his seat, firing up the engine.

"Ready?" he asked over the grease-smelling rumble.

Nancy clipped into the shoulder harness and lap belt, pulling it tight. "Ready!" Heart thrumming in tandem with the engine, she looked over the side of the biplane as it taxied along the bumpy field, then increased speed. The brisk wind tugged at her clothing, and then her stomach dropped like a lead fishing lure as the aircraft lifted from the ground.

When her heart began to beat again, laughter bubbled through her.

"Are you all right?" the pilot called over the whistling of the wind.

"Yes," Nancy said, but the word was torn away by the wind. "Yes, I'm all right." She spoke louder this time.

The biplane circled the field, and from this height, everyone appeared so small on the ground. Like the dolls in her childhood dollhouse. But these dolls were moving and waving up at her.

Nancy grinned at the weightlessness of her body, at how her stomach felt tight like a new shoe, and at how exhilaration surged through her, making every limb tingle.

She realized the biplane was descending.

"Let's go around again," Nancy called out, hoping it wasn't too late to redirect course.

"It will cost more, and other people are waiting," the pilot called back.

He seemed to be more of a salesman than a pilot.

They dropped lower and lower. The landing wheels hit the soft dirt with a gentle jolt.

"Landed like a seagull skimming the ocean," the pilot said.

Nancy's head still hummed, and her body felt like it was floating above the ground. "How long will you be taking people up?" she asked, breathless, even though she'd been sitting.

"Until the sun sets," the pilot said, a smile in his voice. "Come up with five dollars, and I'll take you on a real flight."

"I will," Nancy said, taking off the goggles and turning to look at him. "Don't quit the day until I get back."

Once out of the biplane, she ran to her horse and made Daisy gallop all the way home, then tore through the rooms of her house. "Mother! Are you home? I need to borrow money."

She skidded to a stop in her bedroom and dug out the money from her jewelry box, where she kept her earnings.

"Nance? What in the world are you hollering about?"

She turned to see her brother, Robert, his lanky form of six feet seven leaning against her doorway.

That was right—he was home for the weekend. At twenty-one years old, he was a Harvard graduate and was doing postgraduate work at Massachusetts Institution of Technology.

"There's a barnstormer giving stunt rides," she said. "Costs five dollars."

Robert's brows pinched. "Swell. I want to go too."

Nancy straightened and rested her hands on her hips. "Then get the money." She held up two dollars. "I need three more."

Robert grinned and disappeared into the hallway. "Meet me at the front door, bossy," he called back.

Nancy didn't ask Robert where he was getting the extra money, because her heart was skipping too far ahead. He'd taken a bunch of flying lessons a few years ago and had even earned a private pilot's license, but he didn't do much with it. She'd never seen him fly, nor had wanted to go up with him.

By the time they made it back to the airfield, this time Robert driving them, he'd already argued his way into going up first. "Not only do I need to make sure the stunts are safe for my little sister, but you already took one spin around the field."

"Fine." Nancy smirked. "You can go first."

A short time later, she stood, arms folded, breeze tugging at her hair, watching the biplane containing her brother and the pilot as it dipped, looped, and rolled through the sky. Maybe Robert would get sick with so many stunts, and it would serve him right for insisting he fly next.

But when the biplane landed, Robert was all smiles. He staggered a bit when he dropped to his feet, but then he performed a deep bow to the clapping onlookers.

Nancy laughed. She hurried to the pilot, the money clutched in her hand.

"You're back," the pilot said, his smile friendly.

"I'm back." Maybe he was flirting with her, but she didn't care. She just wanted to get into the biplane again and do something more than circle a field.

After strapping in, she focused on the speckled blue of the sky above and breathed in the scent of field grass, wildflowers, engine fuel, and old leather. The pilot swung the prop and started up the engine again. As the plane bounced along the field, Nancy's pulse went up. When the biplane lifted from the ground and leveled out, her view improved. The pilot didn't even waste time circling the field like he had with Robert; he took off toward Lake Portage. Over the water that rippled gold and green in the sunlight, they did a loop, and Nancy squealed. She closed her eyes for a half second, but then she opened them again, not wanting to miss a thing.

"How was that?" the pilot called.

"Fantastic," she shouted into the wind, letting it carry her words.

His laughter reached her, and she couldn't have wiped the grin off her face if she'd tried.

Next, the biplane shot west toward Hancock and flew over the shipping canal between the two cities. Nancy watched with fascination the ongoings of the towns below her. Miniature buildings, roads, horses, people—the scenery straight from a fairy-tale book.

"This is what we call a buzz," the pilot called out, taking the biplane lower until they flew directly over the brick buildings of Shelden

Avenue. People on the sidewalk looked up and froze. Some ran to cross the street, as if to get out of the way.

Nancy wondered if her mother was among any of them, shopping. Wouldn't she be surprised to learn it had been Nancy in the biplane that day? Below, the Houghton National Bank came into view, followed by the Masonic Temple. Soon, they neared her neighborhood on College Avenue.

The biplane rose higher into the sky, and the pilot rocked the wings right, then left.

Nancy's heart rate climbed with the elevation, and she felt separated from her body for a moment. Despite the roar of the engine, it was peaceful in the sky. A quiet stillness in an odd way. As if she were viewing her life from another person's perspective.

The Victorian house her family lived in was the size of a Model T Ford. It was amazing to think that she'd lived all her life there but now she was seeing it from a different perspective. Her life and everything else below seemed so . . . small and insignificant. Up here in the sky, endless possibilities opened like a scroll unraveling right before her.

All too soon, the biplane turned around and headed back to the field. Nancy had lost track of time, as if she'd been in a dream—but the best kind of dream. Not until after the biplane descended did her heart rate finally slow. The wheels touched the dirt, bouncing once, twice, and the engine slowed. Finally, the engine cut, but Nancy didn't want to move.

"Need help, miss?" the pilot asked, peering at her, his hand extended. He'd climbed out onto the wing without her realizing it.

She took his hand but only because she knew she was supposed to get out. As she climbed onto the wing, she scanned the crowd for her brother.

Robert's head rose above most, and she waved at him. "I need five more dollars, Bobbin," she said, calling him by the nickname her family had given him in his youth. She ignored the pilot's laughter and focused on her brother. "Please, Robert." She reached him and grasped his hand, still wearing the helmet and goggles. "I'll do your chores for a week and pay you back."

Robert grinned. "How can I turn down that offer?" He leaned down. "It's your lucky day, Sis. I brought extra just in case."

Nancy snatched the money and ran back to the biplane and the pilot, who was talking to another gentleman. It turned out that she had to hand over her gear and wait her turn after the next passenger, but that only made her look forward to it more.

The second ride was even better than the first. They took a different route, and the pilot indulged her with more rolls of the biplane. Nancy's stomach pitched but in a thrilling way.

She couldn't wait to tell her friends about this. And her parents. Surely they'd want her to do something special with her life—something like flying airplanes. It wouldn't be too hard to learn. She could get a license, then work as a barnstormer pilot, giving people rides.

School was great and all, but flying was much better. Anyone could go to school, but probably not everyone could fly.

Unfortunately, when she landed, Robert said he was out of money.

"Are you coming back anytime soon?" she asked the pilot.

His grin was easy. "I can't rightly say. I go where the people are willing to pay, and I might have dried up this town for a while."

Nancy had a better plan, though, and as she and Robert drove back home, she plotted ways to get her parents to approve her plan.

"Don't be hyper about it when you talk to Mom and Dad," Robert cautioned her.

Dinner was humdrum, or should have been humdrum, save for the burning spot of anticipation in Nancy's chest. She waited until her parents were nearly finished with their meals so they'd have full bellies and positive thoughts.

"Robert and I went up in a biplane with a barnstormer pilot today," Nancy said. "Five dollars each ride."

Mother's carefully tweezed brows arched. "Were other ladies there too?"

"Oh, yes, but they chose to circle the field only. I went on two stunt rides."

The edges of Mother's mouth turned down. "Nancy, that was very presumptuous of you. What if you became sick? Or what if the pilot lost control?"

"He was an excellent pilot," Nancy said. "Ask Robert."

He nodded around a mouthful of meatloaf.

"And I didn't get sick, Mother," Nancy continued. "I felt like a flying bird."

Robert snickered, and she shot him a glare.

Father wiped his mouth with a cloth napkin and set it down. "Two stunt rides, huh? That's brave of you." But there was no censure in his eyes, only the twinkle of amusement.

Mother sipped the wine in her glass, then her mouth pressed into that tight line that told Nancy she wasn't saying everything she wanted to.

"I could fly for a job, you know," Nancy said. In for a penny, in for a pound, just like paying for the biplane ride. "Like the barnstormer pilot does. All I need is a license. You know that school isn't my passion, plus it's expensive—"

"*Nancy Harkness*, that is not a decent trade-off." Mother's voice went up a notch, her rouged cheeks pinking further. "Nice girls don't take strangers up on planes, or anywhere, for that matter. It would be like selling yourself—"

Father put a hand on Mother's, stopping her tangent, using his mild tone that was so effective in his profession as the Public Health Officer for Houghton County. "A lot has happened today, it seems. We can all sleep on this. Nothing has to be decided right now, Nance. But whatever happens, dropping out of school isn't an option."

Nancy chewed on her lip, feeling deflated. At least Father hadn't said no. And the only person in the family who could counter their mother was Father. "I could do both," she declared softer. "You want me to stay in school, and I want to fly. Summer's not over yet, so maybe I could take some lessons. See if I still like it after that."

Her parents exchanged glances, which could be good or bad.

When Nancy looked at Robert, he widened his eyes, and she tilted her head, encouraging him to join in the conversation. Supporting her side, of course.

"You let me take flying lessons," Robert said.

Both parents snapped their gazes to Robert.

"But you weren't sixteen years old," Father said in a dry tone.

Nancy knew her parents wanted to add the "girl" part, but neither did.

"The Fuller brothers fly, and they're not much older than Nancy," Robert continued. "I think Nancy would be good at it. She might hate school, but she's still smart."

Nancy wanted to beam, but she kept her expression painfully neutral. Leave it to her brother to be the voice of reason with their parents.

"Well, Bobbin, you make some good points . . ." Mother hedged. "We'll think about it." But she rubbed at her temple, which usually meant she either had an oncoming headache or didn't want to deal with the subject at hand.

Later that night, when Nancy was settled into bed with her favorite French novel, *Le Comte de Monte-Cristo* by Alexandre Dumas, her father came into her room.

"Did you decide yet?" she asked right away.

His smile was gentle as he sat on the corner of her bed, his long frame dwarfing her room. "It's a big decision, Nance. Not something to be made in a few hours."

Nancy pushed up to a sitting position and folded her arms. "I won't know until I try. Maybe I'll hate it after all."

Her father laughed. "I doubt that."

She let a smile sneak through. "Probably not."

"Tell you what, my dear. I'll make phone calls tomorrow. Ask around about flight instructors. See what the cost is and all that."

Nancy couldn't hold back her joy, and she moved to her knees and threw her arms about her father's neck. "Thank you, Daddy."

He pulled her close, chuckling. "Don't thank me too early. Mother is not thrilled. She doesn't think it's proper for a lady to fly machines."

Nancy drew away. "It's 1930, Daddy. Women can do all sorts of stuff. I mean, you're sending me away to a boarding school, and who knows what trouble I can get into there? Flying will keep me focused. Keep me making goals. A way for you to bribe good behavior out of me."

Father chuckled again and squeezed her shoulder. "If anything, you're a negotiator."

Nancy couldn't stop smiling after her father left the bedroom. Tonight, her dreams would be wonderful because she intended for them to be filled with soaring above the earth, sitting between a pair of silver wings, the wind tangling her hair.

# CHAPTER THREE

"The nation will hope that Ruth Elder and other girls will stay on the ground. . . . It is folly in anybody but a lion tamer to enter the lion's cage."

—*ANNISTON STAR* NEWSPAPER

*August 1930—Houghton, Michigan*

*Do it well or not at all.* Father's words echoed through Nancy's mind while she listened to Jimmy Hansen rattle off details about the Kinner Fleet biplane as they walked around it.

Father had driven her to the Upper Peninsula Airways, and although the day was a gray overcast, there wasn't much wind.

"This is what we call the preflight check," Jimmy said, eagerness in his expression. His black hair stuck out from beneath his leather flight helmet, and his goggles dangled at his neck. "We do this before every flight. The first thing you check is the wings and the pitot tube."

Nancy followed along on the checklist he'd given her.

"The wind is your master, or mistress." Jimmy was sure smiling at her a lot, as if he couldn't believe his luck at being an instructor.

He was only two years older than she and probably as green as any instructor could be. But Nancy didn't care. The tall, gangly boy could fly. And she wanted to learn everything he knew.

"Can we fly now?" Nancy asked. "I won't learn until I'm actually doing it."

Jimmy's face flushed—he'd been doing a lot of that the past hour. "Not until you can tell me all about this plane."

Nancy took a steady breath and tucked a lock of her honey-brown hair behind her ear. "This here is a tandem two-seater, single-engine Kinner Fleet biplane." She flashed him a smile. "Now can we get in?"

"Sure, but first, here's your logbook. The most important possession a pilot can have, with the exception of her parachute." He handed over a leather-bound book as if it were a glass egg. The logbook was smaller than Nancy had expected.

Jimmy tapped the black leather cover. "You record each of your flying hours in here, and it becomes your pass to train on bigger planes and get jobs flying. Or instructing."

The tips of his ears pinked.

"Swell," Nancy said. She pulled on the helmet and grabbed the goggles Jimmy had brought out for her.

"Now let's go over the instrument panel." Jimmy handed her onto the wing, and she climbed into the pilot seat. He crouched on the wing and pointed out the different gauges, explaining each one. "There's a lot of names to remember, so don't worry if we have to go over everything several times."

Nancy focused hard as Jimmy talked, committing everything to memory. "Can we fly today?" she cut in after he seemed to run out of explanations.

"I don't see why not," he hedged, resting an arm on her door. "If it's all right with your father."

"*You're* the instructor, Jimmy," she said. "Which means you're the boss."

He rubbed a hand over the rash of freckles on his face. "Oh, well, all right . . . let's fly."

Nancy stopped herself from squealing and pulled on her goggles. She was really going to do this.

"Hang on." Jimmy leaped down from the wing, started the prop rotating, then hurried back to the cockpit and climbed into the rear seat. He fired up the engine. "Now, ease up on the toe brakes, and increase the throttle. Right there. Now start taxiing."

Nancy followed his direction, and the plane moved forward. They taxied from the hangar to the beginning of the runway.

"That's it," Jimmy said. "Now toes off the brakes and heels on the floor so that only your feet are on the rudder pedals. Slowly increase the throttle to full power and maintain center line." He explained what to look for in the airspeed indicator.

"Now pull back on the control stick, toward you," he continued.

Nancy did and followed his next directions for the climb.

Once they reached 2,600 feet, Jimmy said, "Level off and point the nose to the horizon."

Nancy's arms pimpled with gooseflesh. She was flying, *really* flying.

"Now lean the mixture just a half swipe to the left," Jimmy said.

She focused once again on his words, trying to tamp down the exhilaration pouring through her.

"Adjust the mixture to the new altitude we're flying at. Next, decrease the mixture until we see an RPM drop." Jimmy's voice was clear and concise. He might be young, but he was a thorough instructor. "Once it drops, increase the mixture to where it was before it dropped. This gives the best engine performance while conserving fuel."

"Got it, boss," Nancy said.

His instruction continued as he talked about the compass and the pitch/bank indicator. She followed his lead until they entered the downwind. He talked her through setting the flaps, then turning toward the air base, and decreasing speed.

"Point the nose at the numbers on the runway," Jimmy said, "and hold the airspeed. We're fifty feet above the runway. Keep your eyes at the end of the runway."

Nancy held steady until Jimmy said, "Now we're fifteen feet above the runway. Pitch the plane up five to eight degrees. Here we go . . ."

Her breath caught as the wheels touched the ground, her pulse mimicking the bouncing of the plane.

"You did it," Jimmy said in triumph.

"Of course I did." Nancy grinned, her hands sweaty but the rest of her body still soaring. "Now what?"

"Let's go again, and keep up the flying speed."

"I can do that." She listened as Jimmy called out instructions, repeating what he'd said before. Her smile was surely permanent now. She'd never felt so exhilarated, not while riding Daisy or her bike or a sailboat with her family.

The air was colder now, but she didn't mind.

"How far can we go?" she called out once they were up over 2,000 feet again.

"You're not ready for cross-country yet, Harkness."

"How many hours do I need to have before I can solo?"

"Five."

That was fine with Nancy. As long as Jimmy wasn't busy, she could have that done by the end of the day. But by the time she had nearly five hours in, the sun had set, throwing wild colors across the sky. She'd crammed so much into her brain that her head was starting to hurt.

When she finally removed her helmet and goggles, her hair was smashed flat, her eyes looked like she'd morphed into a raccoon, and her clothing smelled of grease, but she'd never felt more beautiful, more alive.

"How was it, my dear?" Father asked on the drive home.

He might be smiling as much as she was.

"Positively the best day of my life," she gushed. "I'm going to try to solo tomorrow."

Father snapped a glance at her, and a line appeared between his brows. "So soon?"

"School's starting in a few weeks, Daddy, so there's no time to waste."

The next day, Nancy wore one of Jimmy's flight coveralls over her clothing to minimize the grease stains. She soloed after only four hours and thirty minutes of total flying time. Her logbook confirmed it, along with the personal note from Jimmy that he scrawled at the front of the book: *To Nancy, With best wishes for Happy Landings, Jimmy.*

When Nancy's father picked her up at the airfield later that afternoon, she couldn't wait to tell him. She hurried to his car, where he was leaning against the frame. "I soloed, and in a few days, we're doing a cross-country trip."

Two lines appeared on her father's forehead as he scrutinized the airfield. "Where?"

"Escanaba." It was a city in upper Michigan, and Nancy couldn't wait.

Father's breath released slowly as he set his hands on his hips, surveying her. "Well, Nance, you'd better inform your mother."

Nancy grinned. "Thank you, Daddy." She flung her arms about his neck, and he hugged her briefly.

"Your mother's going to be complaining all night about the grease stains in our clothing."

Nancy pulled away, sheepish. Her father's nice suit wasn't as disposable as her flying coveralls. "I'll tell her it's my fault."

Her father winked. "Jump in the car. Let's head home."

As they drove, Nancy thought of how her mother had grown used to the idea of her daughter flying planes—well, at least training to fly planes. She'd be surprised at how quickly Nancy had soloed. In the air, things like parental tension didn't bother Nancy much because she knew one thing: flying was her destiny.

She hated the thought of going back to boarding school and sitting at a desk with solid flooring beneath her feet and nothing to look at but a chalkboard. But she'd made a deal with her father. She had to stay in school to keep flying, and she never wanted to stop flying, so she'd be a diligent student even when it irked her.

When their car pulled up to the house, Mother was standing on the porch, hands on her hips.

"What's going on?" Nancy asked, cutting a glance to her father. "Is Mother upset?"

"I have no idea," Father said, but she heard the trepidation in his voice.

Nancy's stomach plummeted, and not like the dizzy feeling in the biplane. Mother had that expression on her face—the one where you had to listen to her or pay the consequences.

Nancy walked slowly to the wide porch. "I soloed today," she said just to get it out and in the hope that it would ease the knotting of her stomach.

Mother's gaze was steady on hers. "I want you to see something."

Nancy and Father followed her into the house. Mother showed them the newspaper, pointing at an article about a small plane crash. The headline seemed to leap off the page.

"How do I know this won't happen to you, Nancy?" Mother's question came out stern, almost angry, but Nancy knew it was masking her mother's fear.

Nancy had felt her own rush of fear when she'd soloed today, knowing that there had been no backup instructor if she'd made an error and also knowing that planes did have mechanical errors—some of them unrecoverable. But she'd also paid attention to every word Jimmy had spoken, had spent extra time in precheck, and hadn't been about to hotdog while flying.

"I'm being careful, Mother," she said. "If I didn't think the plane was safe, I wouldn't go up in it. I don't have a death wish."

Mother released a thready breath as she studied her closely. "Teenagers can be impulsive and not understand the value of life until it's too late."

"I promise I'll be safe—always—no matter what. Even if I have to turn down a flight."

Mother's sculpted brows were still pulled together, but the lines about her mouth eased. "Can you promise me that, Nancy? Promise to never take a flight where you have any doubts."

It wasn't hard to promise. "I promise."

Mother's eyes filled with tears, but she nodded. Turning, she headed down the hallway and quietly shut the door to her bedroom.

Nancy remained in the middle of the kitchen, a knot pressing into her chest. She felt unsure of what to do, as the scent of bubbling stew from the stove and fresh-baked rolls surrounded her. Her mother hadn't asked her to stop flying, but Mother's emotions were, nonetheless, like a vice on Nancy's heart.

Father's hand settled on her shoulder, his grip steady. "Your mother's concerns are valid, my dear. We both want you to be safe. Jimmy told me you're very thorough and an excellent student."

"Yes," she said, her eyes burning.

"Flying is fun and exhilarating, but it also carries many risks," he continued in a low tone.

"I know, Daddy," she whispered, swallowing painfully.

He moved in front of her and met her watery gaze. "Your parents worry about you, as any parents might about their little girl, but mostly, we're proud of you."

She saw it then. The light in his eyes that was much stronger than the worry. He was supporting her wholeheartedly. "Thanks, Daddy." She stepped into her father's embrace, and he pulled her close. Inhaling his clean scent of Ivory soap, she closed her eyes.

"What did I miss?" Robert's voice cut in as he walked into the kitchen.

Nancy released her father and wiped her eyes. "Mom just gave me the what-for about flying."

Robert paused in his step, his eyes widening as he took in the whole of Nancy—from her rat's-nest hair to her grease-stained knuckles. "She's making you quit?"

"No. She's worried about my safety, that's all."

Her brother's eyebrows popped. He opened the bread box and pulled out a loaf of bread. "No one's worried about my safety?" he teased as he deftly sliced a piece of bread. "I don't see anyone crying about me flying."

Nancy scoffed. The tears were gone now. "I guess you're not their precious angel daughter."

Robert found the jam jar in the refrigerator, his mouth pulled into a comical frown, but his eyes were laughing. "Good to know my place in the family."

Her brother's teasing had eased the pang in her heart, and she was suddenly very glad he came home on the weekends.

Over the next days, thoughts of flying consumed her night and day, and when she reported to the airfield for her cross-country flight with Jimmy, Mother was the one to drive her.

She didn't say much on the drive, but her stoic stillness was palpable between them. Her mother's careful coif and elegant makeup wouldn't last more than a handful of minutes at an airfield.

Which contributed to the rightness of Nancy flying—she didn't care much for fashion and all the fancy stuff her mother and some of her friends cared about.

When Mother stopped the car, she didn't get out but simply said, "I'll wait here for your return. Be safe."

"I will." Nancy leaned over and kissed her mother's cheek. She snatched the laundered coveralls from the back seat and climbed out of the car.

Her heart soared at the sight of Jimmy already at the side of the biplane, checking things out.

"Your mother?" he asked as she neared.

"Yes, she's going to wait for us to return."

Jimmy nodded, his eyes silently saying he understood. "Now, I did a precheck, but I want you to demonstrate for me. Make sure everything looks good."

She'd done prechecks before, of course, but knowing they'd be flying much farther than Houghton and landing at an unfamiliar airfield, she found herself double-checking everything.

"Ready," she said after a good thirty minutes.

Jimmy pulled on his helmet. "Let's go check out Escanaba, then."

Nancy grinned and turned to wave at her mother. She'd climbed out of the car after all, the breeze tugging at the pin curls beneath her hat as she leaned against the car.

Mother waved back. Nancy climbed into the plane and took off, leaving the place where she'd grown up—by air. This day might be even better than the day she'd flown stunts with the barnstormer.

# CHAPTER FOUR

"The women, well aware of the odds against them, met late
that year in New York to organize. 'For our own protection,
we must learn to think for ourselves, rely on ourselves,
and do as much work as possible on our planes.'"

—OPAL KUNZ, ORIGINAL NINETY-NINER

*November 1930—Milton Academy, Massachusetts*

"Come on, it will be fun," Nancy said. "And perfectly safe."

Three of her friends at Milton Academy—the girls' prep school in
Milton, Massachusetts—stared back at her. Rachel was always up for
something fun, her red hair and snappy personality a testament to that.
Beth was quieter but smarter than anyone in the group. Her green eyes
were calculating. Pauly's face had paled, two bright spots on her cheeks.

"I have a private pilot's license now—my own *mother* took me to
take the test, if that tells you anything." That early day in November
had been a red-banner day in Nancy's mind. Mother had driven her to
Chicago, where she'd taken the exam, then to Milwaukee for the flight
test. Nancy had been as nervous as a rabbit during hunting season, but
she'd felt exhilarated. No one could discredit her qualifications now. She
had a letter from the Department of Commerce, Aeronautics Branch,
out of Washington, DC, to prove her certification.

"We could *drive* to Vassar College," Pauly suggested, smoothing her
blonde hair.

"Where's the fun in that?" Nancy countered immediately. "Flying to
the Poughkeepsie airfield in New York will be much more exciting, and
we'll be the coolest girls of the school."

Rachel released a light laugh, absently braiding her red locks. "Don't
need a plane to do that, sis."

But Beth rose to her feet, her green eyes flashing. "I'll go, even though I don't care about *cool* points. I need to borrow a pair of breeches though."

Everyone looked at her in surprise.

Rachel stood, too, hands on hips. "Well, I can't let quiet Beth one-up me."

Pauly's pert nose scrunched. "You're acting like a *boy*. I'm not going to get into any plane with a sixteen-year-old girl pilot."

Nancy didn't take offense, exactly, although annoyance stirred in her belly. "I think *you're* the one acting like a boy, Pauly. I might be young, but female pilots are just as good as males. We all have to pass the same tests." Her face might be getting hot, but she kept her voice level. Pauly wasn't her best friend, but they were in the same friend circle.

Pauly tossed her long blonde hair over her shoulder. "What's the point of even learning to fly? It's not like you can ever work as a pilot, not if you want to get married."

Everyone fell silent.

Nancy swallowed down the steam rising in her throat and said in a steady voice, "I want to get married like all of you. But why should I sit around waiting for some boy to notice me? Why can't I have my own life? Besides, I've already decided that my husband is going to be very happy he married a pilot."

Rachel covered her mouth to stifle a laugh.

"Go have your fun, then," Pauly shot out and strode out of the room.

"I guess that's her answer," Rachel said with a sly grin. "Let's go. What kind of plane did you rent?"

"It's a surprise," Nancy said, letting Pauly's comments slide off her shoulders. Not every girl in the school had to like flying or be happy with Nancy's accomplishment. And not every girl could imagine or hope for a future other than marriage and children. Besides, she'd soloed fifteen hours now, and she was just getting started.

The three of them headed out of the residence hall together. The sky was clear, pale blue, the wind not even brisk enough to blow a seeded dandelion. Perfect weather, in Nancy's opinion.

They took off from the East Boston airport, and although the plane was a bigger model than Nancy was used to, she didn't want to change her mind. She'd flown more than one type of plane, and besides, the precheck didn't show any issues. Keeping her promise to her mother was always on the forefront of her mind.

Behind her, Rachel and Beth exclaimed over the scenery below. The copilot seat next to Nancy was piled with their luggage.

The bravado that Nancy had been feeling while putting this excursion together started to fade as she scrutinized the earth below. She'd mapped out the route from Boston to Poughkeepsie, but there were plenty of landmarks she didn't recognize.

And the compass, which was supposed to direct her—she didn't know how to read this particular aircraft's. A sinking feeling started low in her stomach, rising and rising until her throat felt uncomfortably tight. When flying cross-country with Jimmy, he'd already known the route, had already flown it.

Alarm flooded through Nancy. She tightened her hold on the control stick, and she inched up in her seat. She knew the general direction, and as long as she held steady, it would be fine, right?

Rachel and Beth were still chatting behind her, oblivious that their pilot was one green sixteen-year-old and that this plane was bigger and more complicated and that Nancy's confidence of only an hour before was fleeing like sand in an hourglass.

Taking slow, measured breaths, she focused on what she *did* know how to do: flying steady and keeping her eyes peeled.

That was when she noticed clouds coming in from the west. They weren't wispy or a friendly white either. The slate gray, bubbling concoction was moving fast. Another knot tightened in her chest. Jimmy had never let her fly in a storm. And smaller planes stayed grounded in bad weather.

Could she beat the clouds? Would they fizzle out?

Even as she wished it, they seemed to be increasing and boiling over by the second.

Still, Rachel and Beth seemed oblivious to the impending danger, and Nancy wasn't about to tell them she'd broken into a full-body sweat.

It wasn't like she could turn around now since, according to the time on her watch, they were more than halfway to their destination. But she had to make some sort of decision. The sky had grown murky all around her, and Nancy blinked rapidly, trying to focus to see better.

In her mind, she sorted through the emergency procedures Jimmy had reviewed with her. The dark cumulonimbus clouds in the distance were still heading her way. Still rapidly.

"Reduce the throttle and continue maintaining altitude," she imagined Jimmy instructing. She didn't want to fly too low, or she'd literally be in danger of buzzing the tops of roofs. But thankfully, for now, there was a patchwork of fields below.

"Oh, are those rain clouds?" Rachel said.

Before Nancy could answer, the plane began to bump with turbulence. Something black sprayed across the windscreen. "Oh no!" Nancy blurted.

A bird had struck. No . . . it was oil. *Black*, not red.

"What's happened?" one of her friends cried out.

"The oil gauge broke, I think," Nancy called back to them. What else could it be? She'd checked the oil level preflight, of course, but she hadn't noticed a crack in the gauge. There was no other option but to do a forced landing.

The plane bumped more, like they were driving over a bed of boulders in the sky. Nancy was pretty sure she'd flown straight into a cloud, but the oil smearing the windscreen made visibility nil. She opened the side window and stuck out her head. Her breath swept away with the fierce, cold wind, yet it was her only option to see where they were going.

Her friends squealed as the air rushed in, and they threw out panicked words, but Nancy couldn't distinguish them over the whoosh of the wind.

Frantically, she scanned the terrain below. There was a farm . . . a field between a couple of farmhouses . . . Was it big enough? Should she keep flying to find a larger field? She couldn't keep this up for long. If the oil gauge was leaking, would the engine cut out completely? Would they stall in the air, then plummet to the earth? Would her mother's deepest fears come true?

"We're landing," she called out, although she was pretty sure her friends couldn't hear anything she said. She was past the first field now. Desperately, she searched the ground below for another place to land. Houses, buildings, roads, fields . . . Yes, there was a field that appeared flat enough. Thankfully it was winter, and she wouldn't be bulldozing some farmer's new crops.

"Steady, easy," Nancy told herself. The engine sounded fine—right now—but that could change at any moment. She had to get the plane down. She had to get her friends out.

Nancy pulled back on the throttle, slowing the engine even more, and the plane descended. Within moments, the wheels touched the frozen dirt. They bumped hard, then bounced along the deep ruts. She pressed her feet on the brakes until the plane came to a jolting stop. They were safe, but Nancy's heart had climbed into her throat.

She took a breath and another. "Here we are, girls," she said with calm that she didn't feel. "I guess we're taking a bus the rest of the way?"

She turned around to see Rachel and Beth clutching at each other, expressions rigid.

"Things like this happen sometimes," Nancy continued as her heart rate slowed, her voice growing more steady. "Good news is that we're all fine and the plane just needs a minor repair."

Rachel's and Beth's features slowly relaxed.

"Right." Rachel released her death grip on Beth. "Maybe we should head back to Milton. We'll be too late if we take a bus both ways."

"Whatever you say." Nancy took another thready breath, forcing the trembling to stop. "Let's find a phone, call the airport to come get their plane, then we'll see about a bus back to Milton."

Three hours later, Nancy and her friends were safely back at the school. She called home to talk to her dad, but Robert answered, his words booming through the phone. "Hey, Sis, what's up? Staying out of trouble?"

The emotions she'd held at bay with her friends suddenly surfaced, and her voice cracked. "Robert?"

"Did something happen?" His question was filled with concern. "Where are you?"

"School," she said in a small voice. "I rented a plane today, and . . ." Closing her eyes, she rushed through the story of not being able to read the air compass, the fast-moving clouds, the broken oil gauge, and the forced landing.

"My golly, Nancy, you all right?"

Tears flooded her eyes, but she managed to speak through her tightened throat. "I'm all right. Just rattled my nerves a bit."

"I won't tell Mom if you don't want me to, but you should tell Dad."

"That's why I'm calling."

Robert released a half laugh. "Oh, right. I'm here for a few hours, then heading back to my job."

Robert had secured a position at the DuPont organization, but he was also talking about doing postgraduate work.

"You should fly with me for a bit, Sis," he continued. "Or take more lessons."

"I'm *in* lessons," Nancy protested. "I . . . hadn't flown that plane before."

"Too big for you to chew on right now, that's all," he mused. "You'll get it though. Wanna fly together next weekend?"

"Sure." Nancy's chest warmed. Her brother wasn't telling her to quit or blaming her for the forced landing and aborted trip.

"That'd be swell," he said gently. "Never thought I'd miss my little sister and want to spend weekends together. Seems like you're growing up way too fast."

"Oh yeah?"

"Yeah. Call the airfield and reserve one of the single-engine Kinner Kitty Hawks. Next Sunday. We'll take things easy, and I'll show you a few things."

"We're not hotdogging."

When Robert didn't answer, Nancy said, "I'm serious, Bobbin."

She heard the smile in his voice when he replied, "We may or may not hotdog a little because we gotta have some fun."

# CHAPTER FIVE

"[Ruth] Nichols set a transcontinental speed record [in December 1930], flying from New York to Los Angeles with four overnight stops but a total elapsed flying time of just sixteen hours and fifty-nine and a half minutes. . . . Unsatisfied, [Ruth] Nichols turned around, flew back east, and set another record going that direction—thirteen hours and twenty-two minutes, almost an hour and a half shorter than Lindbergh's fastest continental trip."

—*FLY GIRLS* BY KEITH O'BRIEN

*February 1931—Milton Academy, Massachusetts*

Nancy loved flying with her brother, but Robert took risks she'd never do solo flying. Since spring had finally arrived in Boston, she was taking more lessons and piling on more flight hours in her logbook.

"Ready?" Robert asked as she strode out of her residence hall. He was clean-shaven and wore his hat at a jaunty angle, his grin wide.

Nancy was nearly skipping. She hurried to the passenger side of his convertible and climbed in, enjoying the envious looks of other classmates. None of the students were allowed to drive cars, so seeing a young man pick up Nancy in a car . . . well, they didn't know it was her brother.

She laughed to herself.

"New boots?" Robert asked as she shut the car door.

"Yes." Nancy glanced down at her attire. Flying was the one excuse she had to wear breeches and boots. Flying in a skirt was not practical.

"Looking swell, Sis." Robert threw her a smile as he pulled out onto the main road. "Which is important since I have a surprise for you."

Nancy's pulse thrummed. "What?"

"You'll have to wait and see."

"Did Alison send cookies or something?" She twisted in the seat, but there wasn't a package of goodies behind her. Robert was engaged to be married to Alison Hardy Dempsey. When Nancy faced her brother again, she said, "Is it at the airport? Just tell me. You know I hate surprises."

Robert grinned and twisted the radio knob as Gene Austin started singing "Carolina Moon."

Nancy settled back into her seat, folding her arms. The airfield wasn't far, but it seemed Robert wasn't going to give her any clues. "All right, fine . . . This better be good. I need the break from certain girls."

Her brother looked over at her. "Who? What's going on?"

"Oh, you don't know them. They're gossipy and talk about me flying only for attention—to get the boys interested." Now that Nancy was talking about it, the heat rose in her neck. She'd tried to ignore the mean-spirited comments, but they bothered her deep down.

Robert chuckled. "You don't need to do anything extreme to get a boy's attention. I think every boy you've ever met falls half in love with you on the spot."

Nancy's cheeks warmed. "That's not true."

"You don't have to believe me, but I'm telling you what I see." He nudged her shoulder. "You're pretty—for a girl—and you're smart in many things. Maybe school isn't your first love, but you're also the type who draws people to you."

Nancy stared at her brother, but there was no laughter in his eyes or cocky grin on his face. She couldn't remember him giving her these sorts of compliments before.

"Don't act so dumbfounded," he said in a smooth tone. "You've got a way about you, Sis, and I'm proud to be your brother."

She blinked against the tears forming in her eyes.

"Ah, don't go soft on me. Those girls are jealous, that's all I'm saying."

Nancy wiped at her eyes, then drew in a breath. "You're really sappy today, Bobbin."

He threw his head back and laughed, and Nancy grinned. Her heart felt like it was soaring on a plane.

Her brother sobered. "Don't let other people make you feel bad, all right? And don't ever stop flying, Sis. Promise me. I've seen how much you love it. No one can take that away from you unless you let them."

"Thanks, favorite brother. I don't plan on stopping. Ever."

He winked at her, and she leaned over and kissed his cheek. She settled back in her seat and let the spring breeze and "Carolina Moon" wash over her.

By the time they pulled up to East Boston, clouds had gathered above, but that didn't dampen her excitement. She was ready to jump out of the car from anticipation.

Robert shut off the car engine, then threw her a grin. "Come on, Sis."

She followed his long strides to one of the hangars, where a broad-shouldered man came out to shake Robert's hand. The man's hooded eyes were alert beneath heavy, black eyebrows, and his mustached smile was friendly.

"Mr. Snow, this is my sister, Nancy Harkness. Nancy, this is Crocker Snow."

Nancy stood rooted to the ground, her mouth agape as the man extended his hand. Everyone knew who Crocker Snow was. He'd founded Skyways, one of the first commercial flying operations in the area. He also knew Amelia Earhart.

When Nancy found her voice, she said, "Very nice to meet you, sir." She gave his hand a hearty shake. Surely her cheeks were as red as apples.

"Nice to meet you, too, Miss Harkness," he said in a warm voice. "Want to take a spin?"

She blinked. "Really? Right now?"

Mr. Snow's thick brows lifted. "Do you have the time?"

Nancy looked at her brother, who nodded. Her gaze returned to Mr. Snow's. "Yes, sir. I'd love to."

He chuckled. "Right this way."

She wasn't sure if she was absorbing every word he said because little jolts of happiness kept buzzing through her, but she listened as closely as she could. "We'll take things easy, and I'll show you a few things."

They climbed into the plane, with Snow giving instructions, asking her to fly lower than she ever had in the past. She obeyed, although it was hard to keep such steady control while flying so low.

Once they were back on the ground, Nancy having landed with precision, Snow's compliments only added to her exhilaration.

"Your sister has a real sense of air," Snow told her brother as she took off her helmet and goggles. "She's well on her way to becoming a skilled pilot."

Robert extended his hand once again to the man. "Thanks for taking her up. I was curious to see what you thought."

Nancy wanted to hug her brother, but she waited until she'd thanked Mr. Snow—quite profusely.

"Have a great day, you two," Mr. Snow said. "Heard you're taking up the Kinner next."

"We sure are," Robert said.

As Nancy and her brother headed to another hangar, she gushed, "You really are my favorite brother."

He set an arm about her shoulders. "I'm your *only* brother, Sis."

"Still. You're the best."

He chuckled, and she wrapped her arms about his waist and squeezed.

"All right, now let's go have some real fun."

Nancy scoffed. "Nothing's going to top meeting Crocker Snow."

Robert cast her a wink, and they arrived at the hangar that contained their rented plane, the single-engine Kinner Kitty Hawk. Once they climbed inside, Nancy truly felt she was on top of the world. She sat in the pilot seat, with Robert in the front. Flying the Kitty Hawk felt exhilarating, so when her brother dared her to buzz the boys' prep school that neighbored Milton Academy, she took the dare.

"Just let them know you're keeping watch over them," Robert said, clearly amused.

Nancy laughed. "I think they'll know. I'm heading straight for the quadrangle."

"Super. That'll get their attention." The campus probably would have been busier on a weekday, but Nancy took the dive anyway. Her stomach pitching, she flew low over the quadrangle.

Boys in their prep school blazers, ties, shorts, and long socks, along with a few teachers, scrambled out of the way, gawking at the plane.

"Pull up," Robert said in a mild tone.

Nancy began to pull up, but the plane wasn't rising as fast as she thought it would.

"Pull up!" Robert yelled, his words hitting her like stones. "Now! Pull up!"

She tightened her hold on the control stick and pulled it back with all her strength. The weight of the plane was more than Nancy had estimated.

"You're going to hit the chapel!" Robert's voice was background noise though.

Nancy's heart bounced in her chest as perspiration heated her face. The stones of the building in front of her were strangely detailed, and she could only hope and pray that she wasn't about to destroy whatever skilled labor it had taken to construct the chapel.

"The bell tower! Watch the bell tower!" Robert shouted.

The plane was lifting at last, but Nancy knew it would take a miracle to clear the bell tower. Every muscle in her body tensed as she waited for impact.

But no crash came. No bump. No jostling.

"Woo-ee!" Robert craned his neck to look behind them. "You did it, Sis! Boy, oh, boy. You sure got their attention."

Nancy blinked away the sweat stinging her eyes. Her heart was hammering so hard that it pulsed in her ears.

"Well, I think you might have dislodged a few slates from the roof," Robert said with genuine amazement, "but otherwise, no harm done." He turned back around, facing the windscreen. "I think that's the closest buzzing I've ever seen in my life."

Nancy didn't know whether to laugh with pride, cry with relief, or berate Robert for his bad influence.

"Gee whiz . . . Feels like I ran in the Olympics." Robert's gaze finally landed on hers. "You all right?"

"I don't know," Nancy said on an exhale. "I think I've sweat through everything I'm wearing."

He smiled and let his head drop back. "This is one for the record books—well, just ours. Mom and Dad probably shouldn't hear about this."

"I agree."

By the time they landed, Nancy felt calm again. She'd be more careful next time. Well, there wouldn't be a next time, but at least she'd learned that the Kitty Hawk's reaction time was slower than expected. So, she could consider it a learning experience.

"Let's get you back to your school," Robert said. "No one will be the wiser unless you tell someone."

"Well, I'm certainly not telling a soul," she declared.

Robert laughed.

She was feeling almost normal when Robert pulled up to her residence hall. He climbed out and opened the door for her, acting the part of a gallant escort. They both froze.

"Uh, Nancy, are those . . . ?"

"Um-hm."

Clustered together outside the entrance stood the headmistress, housemistress, and two members of the board of trustees. None of them appeared happy, and all eyes were focused on her.

"Gotta go, Sis." Robert shut her passenger door, then hurried around the car and jumped back in. Seconds later, he pulled away from the residence hall, leaving her to face the adults alone.

Nancy didn't know if she should be mad at him for taking off or paranoid that she was about to be kicked out of school. There were no two ways about it. Somehow, her stunt had been found out, and she was in deep trouble.

"Hello," she said tentatively.

The headmistress spoke first. "Come inside, young lady."

Nancy followed the group into the residence hall. Strangely, the lobby was completely empty of any other students, and it smelled of floor wax, which only made her stomach rock.

The headmistress stopped and turned to face her. "We'd like an explanation, Miss Harkness."

Nancy swallowed over the dryness of her throat. "I, uh . . . An explanation about what?" Her mind raced with the possibility that maybe they *didn't* know. Maybe she was *assuming* because guilt kept stabbing her in the chest like a branding iron meant for an innocent cow.

"We received a call from the headmaster of the boys' prep school," the headmistress continued, her voice steely and her eyes even more so. "He called in the tail number of a biplane that nearly crashed into their bell tower. He asked the airport manager who the pilot was."

All right, so this *was* about her flying stunt. Nancy's legs felt like pudding, and she wasn't sure how much longer she could stand.

"The headmaster thought it might be one of the Fuller brothers," the headmistress continued. Had her voice always been so nasal? Or was the woman coming down with a cold?

*A logical deduction*, Nancy thought.

"Imagine his surprise"—the headmistress paused and folded her arms—"and then *our* surprise, when the airport manager reported that the pilot this afternoon was our very own Miss Nancy Harkness."

Although the lobby was empty of students, Nancy guessed that right now, they all had their doors cracked open and were listening to every single word.

She kept her posture erect and her eyes locked with the headmistress's. Surely they couldn't expel her, could they? They wouldn't want to lose her tuition—it was the Depression, after all—and not everyone could afford Milton. Why hadn't her brother stayed? He might have shouldered some of the blame and made things less precarious for her.

"We realize there aren't any specific rules against flying by Milton students." The headmistress tilted her head. "But that's because we didn't think it needed to be specified. Some things are *common sense*, Miss Harkness, and it seems you've lost yours."

Nancy released a stuttered breath. She wanted to move past all this lecturing and get to the consequences part. Would she be suspended? Worse?

"We have a new rule for you and for every young lady who attends Milton Academy."

She blinked, waiting for the pronouncement.

"You're to stay out of airplanes for the remainder of the semester." The headmistress glanced at the others with her, and they gave firm nods of unanimous agreement. "What do you have to say for yourself?"

"I'll stay out of airplanes for the rest of the semester," Nancy echoed. "Of course I will. And I apologize for the stunt." As she spoke, she wondered if this was all. No suspension? Surely her parents would be notified, but being banned from flying for the next couple of months was minor compared to what she'd feared.

The headmistress continued speaking, but Nancy's mind raced ahead. She'd miss flying, but that meant she'd anticipate summer even more. And if she had her way, she could start hopping passengers from place to place and earn some money. She'd be graduating from Milton soon, anyway, and if all went well with her college board exams, she'd be attending Vassar College in the fall. What were *their* rules about students flying?

When the lecture and admonitions ended, she headed to her room. Several girls poked their heads out of their doorways, eyes wide, smiles wider.

By the time Nancy reached her door, her heart had returned to its normal rhythm, and she decided it wasn't so bad to have gotten into trouble. She walked into her room to find Rachel and Beth perched on her bed.

"Oh, hello," Nancy said. "What a nice surprise."

Rachel laughed, her red curls bouncing at her shoulders. "How's your day going?"

Nancy smirked and sat between her two friends before she drew in a shaky breath. "Not bad."

The girls laughed again.

"What will your parents say?" Beth asked, her green eyes wide.

"Mother will be mortified," Nancy predicted as the exhilaration of the flight, then the mortification of the reprimand morphed into something new—determination. "Father will probably laugh, but I'll get a lecture from him too. I think Robert deserves a lecture as well. But no one can complain too much. My grades are up, and well, I pulled it off. Didn't hit the bell tower after all."

Her friends snorted, and they lay back on the mattress, staring at the ceiling where Nancy had hung two model airplanes.

"I'm not giving it up, girls," she said in a quiet voice. "It's in my blood now."

# CHAPTER SIX

"When the motor of her plane failed several hundred feet above Squantum Airport, Miss Nancy Harkness was sent to earth in a forced landing. Neither she nor her companion, Joseph H. Choate, 3rd, Harvard freshman, was injured. The pair had taken off from East Boston airport with Miss Harkness as pilot. Young Choate learned to fly last summer."

—APRIL 16, 1931 (NEWSPAPER)

*April 1932—Vassar College, Boston*

"What if *you're* bad luck?" Nancy asked, leaning against the smooth body of the plane she was about to take up. It was a two-seater, single-engine, Great Lakes-303Y biplane.

Joseph Choate's dark hair blew in the breeze as he propped his hand alongside the plane, facing Nancy. "We had one bad flight, a year ago."

"Yes, that's true," she said, "and then I was banned from flying."

"Because of the stunt you did with your *brother*, not because of flying with *me*." Joseph winked and stepped closer. "Our motor failed, and that only earned a little notice."

"That's because a newspaper literally reported on our forced landing."

"Right," he said. "Those darn journalists. How's your bother, by the way?"

"Completely respectable now. Married, with a baby on the way."

Joseph flashed that smile that got all the girls talking. He was a Harvard student, studying law, and Nancy had been flattered by his attention last year. But now she realized she'd only really gravitated toward him because he liked to fly too.

"You're still a legend, you know, at Milton," he said.

Nancy lifted a shoulder. "Maybe we can fly another time. I've got a lesson coming up with Johnny."

"Miller?" Joseph's brows shot up.

"That's the one. You know, Jack's boss."

Joseph lifted his hands, his easy grin appearing. "How is it that you're connected with all the great flyers? You casually drop John Miller's and Jack Ray's names as if they come to your house for Sunday dinner."

"Well, they don't do that. My mother probably wouldn't like those men at her table." Nancy wrinkled her nose. Jack Ray was the assistant manager of the Poughkeepsie Airport. He was also her main instructor as she worked on her limited commercial license now that she was attending Vassar College. John Miller ran the airport as well as Giro Flyers Ltd. that operated out of the hangar. "They're just pilots, Joe. More seasoned, sure, but men are men."

His laugh was warm. "You're different, you know that, Harkness? No other girl I know would be out here wearing breeches, goggles hanging off her neck, strapped up in a parachute, waiting for her flying instructor."

Nancy shrugged. "Don't forget I ferry passengers to pay for those lessons."

"That too." Joseph pushed off from the plane; his angular frame towered over her. "If you won't go flying with me, maybe we can go to dinner?"

"Can't." Nancy smiled up at him. He really was handsome, but nothing inside her twirled at the sight of him. "Don't have time for a boyfriend, Joe."

The edge of his mouth lifted. "So you've told me. Just wondered if you'd changed your mind."

"I haven't."

His gaze held hers for a couple of heartbeats. Joseph was a swell guy, but she wasn't interested in the intensity she saw in his eyes—those of a young man who knew where he was going and what he wanted—right now. She liked her life as it was, and she was focused on her own goals, ones she didn't want to get approval for.

"Be careful with those eyes, Joseph."

He studied her for another handful of seconds. "Safe travels, Nancy," he murmured, then turned and strode across the airfield.

Nancy watched him walk away—that confident walk of his masking her rejection. He'd find someone else to moon over him one day.

Joe paused when John Miller came out of the hangar. The two men greeted each other, but she had no idea what they said. Miller headed toward her.

"All checked out?" he asked with a friendly grin on his clean-shaven face.

"All checked out."

"Plane's a beauty, isn't she?" Miller strapped on his helmet. He handed her up to the front seat of the Great Lakes, then took the rear pilot seat. "Come on, Harkness, let me show you how we fly in the Marine Corps."

Yes, Miller was a former Marine, and Nancy wanted to learn from the best, but he was also a former barnstormer and the first person to make a US transcontinental flight in a rotorcraft, beating Amelia Earhart's effort to become the first. Nancy liked his easy-going nature and friendly laugh. Nothing really seemed to faze him, and that was a good quality in a pilot, she decided.

From the first few minutes, Nancy knew she was in the hands of an expert pilot. He handled the plane effortlessly. She listened to every word of his instructions, committing them all to memory.

Right before it was time to land, he said, "Let's try a stall, then we'll land her."

Miller cut the engine, pulled the nose up, and watched the airspeed drop. When the stall horn started to blare, the aircraft stalled, making the right wing fall. He pushed forward on the stick, pointing the nose down, then stepped on the left rudder and applied full power.

Nancy's heart flipped so hard she was sure it had switched places with her stomach. But the grin on her face wasn't leaving anytime soon. She was no daredevil, but flying with Miller was spectacular.

"Once you see the airspeed come back up, you can level with the horizon," Miller said. "Let's get 'er down, and we'll switch places."

A thrill ran all the way to Nancy's toes as she thought about checking out on the Great Lakes machine.

But the sound of the engine restarting didn't happen.

Miller cussed.

"What's wrong?" Nancy twisted to look back at him.

"The engine won't fire up," Miller muttered, an edge to his voice. He swore again.

This wasn't good, not good at all. "Parachute?" Nancy suggested, her throat turning sour.

"We're too close to the ground for that," Miller replied tightly. "Prepare yourself for a crash landing."

But there was nothing to do to prepare herself. The cockpit was open, so there wasn't any latch to release the hatch.

Should they jump? Before she could ask that, the plane tipped backward and plunged straight toward the ground.

Time seemed to slow as her stomach turned inside out. The sky above was robin-egg blue, the sun a golden sphere, and the wind had reversed, blowing bits of hair against her neck and cheek.

The churning in her stomach turned into a roil, and her head felt like she'd stuck it into a pond of cold water.

She heard the crash of the plane slamming into the ground almost before she felt it. Her body buzzed, her head buzzed, and her limbs felt like they were weighted down.

Someone asked if she was all right. Miller? Had he spoken? She couldn't tell.

Her fingers, of their own accord, worked at the seat belt. All she knew was that she was upside down, and she had to get out. What if the plane caught on fire? What if Miller was seriously injured?

"I'm fine, I'm fine," she whispered to herself as she released the seat belt.

Then she was falling . . . out of the plane she'd been strapped into. She flailed her arms, trying to break her fall, but her head did that for her, against a stone wall. The same wall that the plane had apparently crashed into.

Pain reverberated through every single bone.

Why had she done that? She should have waited for help . . . Was it coming?

She tasted the rusty tang of blood in her mouth—she must have bitten her tongue. She groaned as she moved to right herself, grasping the wall to keep herself from falling off it.

"Miller?" she rasped, trying to search for him even though her eyes weren't completely focused. "Where are you?"

She spotted his body not far from where she sat.

"Miller?" she whispered.

The man's face was bleeding, but he was moving, breathing.

"Miller?" she said again. "Are you all right?"

Slowly, his gaze swung to hers. "Yes."

But he didn't look all right. Blood streamed down his face, the livid red pooling at the collar of his shirt, and his complexion reflecting the gray in the stone wall.

"I think we . . . hit . . . a tree," he mumbled, but it was hard to understand him.

They had hit a tree, and maybe the branches had helped cushion the crash before the wall? Nancy wasn't sure, and her head was throbbing too much to think about it. Motion caught her attention. A car was heading toward them—was Jack Ray driving it?

Yes, that was him.

Another car followed, and soon, people were helping them both off the wall. Asking questions. Nancy didn't have any answers except to say the engine didn't restart after their fall. Miller would have to fill in the rest, but he was already being loaded into one of the cars to be taken to the hospital.

Nancy appeared to be fine. Nothing broken, nothing bleeding, just a searing headache. She'd been lucky, she knew, although she didn't feel lucky. This had been her third forced landing. Maybe three times would be her limit.

Jack broke away from where he was speaking to a couple of mechanics looking over the plane.

"How are you doing, Harkness?"

"Just take me back to Vassar," she told him.

Concern in his features, he scanned her face. "Are you sure? We can have a doctor check you out at the—"

"No," Nancy cut in, even as the pain in her head throbbed out a crescendo. "I want to rest."

On the return drive to Vassar, Jack talked about the plane and how the engine was found in the field east of Vassar Road. "You were both lucky, that's what. And Miller will be fine. Banged up is all. The mechanic thinks the plane can be repaired and made as good as new."

Nancy comprehended the words through her head pain, and she supposed it was good news that the plane could be repaired—she'd decide for sure after she'd had some rest.

Jack delivered her back to her residence hall, and after assuring him she'd be fine, she headed inside.

Her plan was to take a nap and sleep off the accident. But first, she'd phone her parents and then the airfield to ask after Miller.

Cradling her head, she dialed her parents' number from the phone in the lobby of the residence hall. "Mother?" she said when her mother answered.

"Nancy? Is everything all right?"

Her voice must have given something away. "I'm fine." She paused. Sucked in a breath. "But my instructor crashed our plane today."

"*What?*"

Nancy gave her mother a quick rundown, and while they were talking, her father came onto the phone. The minute she heard her father's voice, tears sprang to her eyes, and her next words came out choked.

"We'll come pick you up, my dear," Father said in his gentle way.

"I'll be fine," she said. "I'm tired, that's all. I don't want to miss classes."

Father chuckled. "You must have hit your head pretty hard to want to stay in school instead of coming home for a bit."

Nancy would have smiled, but the pain was slicing like a hot knife finding its mark over and over. "I'll let you know how I'm feeling tomorrow."

"Nancy, we're on our way," Mother said, determined. "You don't have to return with us, but we want to make sure everything is fine."

Mother's tone wasn't one to argue with.

"I might be asleep."

"That's okay. We'll see you when we get there."

Nancy took a steadying breath after hanging up with her parents, then she called the nearest hospital, guessing that was where John Miller had ended up. When she was connected to the room, Jack answered instead.

"Calling to check on John," Nancy said. "Is it bad?"

"He'll survive," Jack said. "They stitched up the cuts on his face. Lost a tooth. The doctors are worried about the sight in one of his eyes, but his bruises will all heal. How are you feeling?"

Nancy frowned, hoping that John's eye would be fine. "I can't complain. Sounds like John got the brunt of it. But we survived, and the plane can be repaired, right?"

"Correct."

They talked for another few seconds, but Nancy was having trouble focusing with the constant throbbing in her head. When they finished the call, she headed to her bedroom. She lay on her bed, but before closing her eyes, she wrote in her logbook, *John cracked Great Lakes-303Y.*

He'd been so proud to fly the plane and eager to show it off. His words echoed through her mind: "Come on, Harkness, let me show you how we fly in the Marine Corps."

Nancy closed her eyes. She didn't know how much faith she had in Marine pilots at the moment.

She fell asleep, her dreams invaded by different scenarios of flying with John Miller. Sometimes he was the pilot, other times she sat in the pilot seat. But they kept going through the same crash. Over and over. She woke with a start, her head aching anew. Her mind wouldn't shut off, and she found herself staring at the changing colors of the window, from slate gray to pale violet. Finally, she climbed out of bed and crossed to her desk as the dawn lightened her room to a rosy glow.

The mechanics would figure out whatever had happened to the plane, but she'd not trust anyone's precheck again. Even if he were a Marine. Taking out one of her notebooks, she began writing down her own precheck list in the stillness of the predawn. The list was more extensive than she'd been taught. One that would cover more than the usual issues.

Her parents would be arriving soon, and she guessed one or both of them would try to talk her into taking a few days off school. Or even giving up flying. She might be only eighteen, but she was determined not to let this be a setback. Her headache would fade, Miller would recover, and she had only a couple of weeks left of training before earning her commercial license.

# CHAPTER SEVEN

"My flying was done entirely in the cockpit. That is I depended on instruments alone to tell me the position of my plane in space. I could not see even to the wingtips and I could only know that I was flying right side up by what my instrument told me. I flew sometimes high and sometimes low. I flew near the water to escape the clouds and rain but found that the fog lay close to the surface, and I had to rise above it. As I went several 1000 feet higher I found the cold was severe enough to form ice on my wings. I knew that there was ice being formed because a slush pile up in front of me on the pane through which I er could see a few inches. Ice is a very serious er difficulty for fliers because it makes a ship er so inefficient that, at times, it er can't fly on. Thus I had to keep out of the altitude in which ice formed and yet be above er any danger of falling into the sea, as it were."

—AMELIA EARHART, INTERVIEW AFTER FIRST FEMALE
SOLO FLIGHT ACROSS THE ATLANTIC, MAY 21, 1932

*April–August 1932, Vassar College, Boston*

"Your brother's here," Rachel said, appearing in the doorway of Nancy's room. Rachel's red hair was still in curlers, and she wore a blue robe with matching blue slippers. "Pulling up now. Do you want me to tell him to wait?"

"I'm ready." Nancy gave herself a once-over in the mirror. She'd dolled up her makeup and hair and was wearing her flight gear— breeches and flight jacket—ready to be photographed and interviewed at the airfield. She grabbed her helmet and goggles and blew a kiss to Rachel.

"Go get 'em, fly girl," Rachel called after her.

Nancy hurried down the hallway. A couple of girls poked their heads out of their rooms as she passed by.

"Good luck!" one hollered.

Without turning around, Nancy waved a hand. "Thank you!"

Truth was, she felt as nervous as a mouse in a house full of cats, so she was very glad Robert was driving her to the airfield. Yesterday, on April 25, she'd passed her limited commercial license test at the New York Roosevelt Field, making her the fifty-sixth woman to hold a commercial license in the United States.

"Looking pretty, Sis," Robert said with a grin as she climbed into his car. "Like a real pilot."

She slugged his arm. "I've been a *real pilot* for ages. I don't think the reporters really need my picture, do they? I mean, an article would be fine—just to document things."

He smirked and pulled onto the road, cutting off a slower driver, who honked. Robert ignored it. "Everyone wants to see who this little Nancy Harkness is. You'll probably get lots of fan letters now. Make sure you don't tell them about saving me—don't want your head to get too big."

"That'll cost you."

Robert nodded as if he were very serious. "I'll pay whatever it takes." He flashed her a grin.

Nancy shook her head, smiling. "If they ask about it, I'll have to answer."

He released a good-natured groan.

Recently, he'd taken five of his friends on a Travel Air plane, but they'd had to make an emergency landing. Nancy had flown to where they'd landed, then had escorted them back in her own plane to the Poughkeepsie airport.

Right now, though, she wasn't too thrilled about the interview and photo shoot, and she had no idea what reporters would ask her . . . but she was downright pleased to have her commercial locked down. Next up was her transport license.

"How's Alison?" she asked her brother, who was tapping out the tune on the steering wheel of "You Can't Stop Me from Lovin' You" by Cab Calloway coming through the radio.

"Dreading the upcoming summer weather," Robert said. "She's heard all the old wives' tales about being pregnant during the summer."

"August will come soon enough, and you'll be a daddy. Funny to think about."

Robert grinned. "You're telling me. I need to get my act together whether I want to or not."

They both laughed.

As they pulled up to the airfield, Robert released a long whistle. "Would you look at that."

Up ahead, a gaggle of cars and reporters had gathered, wielding cameras and notebooks. Beyond them stood a stately Great Lakes plane, gleaming in the sunlight.

As they stepped out of the car, one of the reporters called out, "There's the Flying Freshman."

Robert chuckled.

"Hush." Nancy strode forward and shook the hand of each reporter. Nerves tumbled in her stomach, but she forced them away and pasted on a smile for the men in their suits and fedoras and polished shoes.

One of the cameramen stubbed his cigarette, then directed her to stand in front of the Great Lakes plane, where she posed for several photographs. "That's it, sweetheart," the cameraman said. "Smile like you stole something and got away with it."

Nancy laughed.

"Perfect," the cameraman drawled.

The questions set in.

"Did you always want to be a pilot?"

"What are your future plans?"

"How does it feel to be one of only fifty-six women to hold a commercial pilot's license?"

"Tell us about the plane crash with John Miller only three weeks ago."

"Did your brother's flying inspire you? And what did he think about you rescuing him?"

"Only forty-two women hold a transport license; are you trying to be number forty-three?"

"What does Vassar think about flying students?"

Nancy had to laugh—surely someone had heard about her stunt at Milton. "They require your parents' permission."

The reporters laughed.

"But once they have it, they're very good about it," she added.

The reporters continued with a few more questions, while Robert paced in the background, his expression amused.

Nancy was relieved when the interview was over and she was back in the car with Robert. "I'm starving."

Robert grinned as he fiddled with the radio. "Is that all my famous sister can say?"

"I'm not famous," she said, checking her lipstick that she'd so carefully applied in the car door mirror. "Flying shouldn't be such an anomaly for women. One of the reporters said that having a woman demonstrate flying shows that anyone can do it."

"Woo-ee, that's presumptuous."

"Right. I didn't know if that was an insult or a compliment."

As the scenery rushed by, she slid down in her seat and closed her eyes.

Robert turned down the radio. "You all right?"

"Headache, that's all."

Robert's response changed to one of concern. "You've been getting those a lot, Sis."

She shrugged, keeping her eyes closed.

"Maybe you should take some time off—you know, from school and flying. You're using up electricity at both ends."

"Semester's almost over, then I'll be home for the summer."

Robert went silent.

She knew he wanted her to leave now, but she was determined to finish the semester at least. She'd find a way to endure. When her parents drove down to visit, she told them the same thing. She was fine, and she'd last the semester. She told herself that when summer came, she'd focus on her health and hope that her frequent headaches would go away. Strangely enough, over the next weeks, a small section of her hair changed color as it grew, creating a gray streak right at her temple.

But when summer came, the headaches continued. Some of them were crippling enough that she couldn't fly on those days. Her biggest highlight was befriending Alice Hirschman. Alice was from Detroit and had graduated from the University of Michigan in 1927. Then she'd attended the Curtis-Wright School of Aviation and earned her private pilot's license last year.

It was refreshing to have a friend who was as obsessed with flying as Nancy. Her friends at Vassar were focused completely on boys, dating, and classes, but mostly boys. They spent late nights talking about dream wedding gowns and how many babies they wanted. Nancy wasn't opposed to marriage and children, but there was a lot she wanted to accomplish before then because most married women weren't allowed to hold jobs, and Nancy couldn't imagine a future without flying. And in order to afford her own plane, she'd have to earn money.

Alice was full of stories about Amelia Earhart—because they were personal friends. Nancy was enamored by the stories, but mostly, Alice made Nancy laugh. More than once, Alice tried to talk Nancy into entering air races. But Nancy knew she wasn't ready yet. Would she ever be ready? Maybe once her headaches stopped pestering her.

# CHAPTER EIGHT

"That airplane had no airspeed indicator—your own ears and the singing of the wind in the wires told you how fast you were going. There was an oil gauge and an altimeter on what passed for an instrument panel. The fuel gauge was a wire on a bobber. The Travel Air had no brakes—I found that out when he had me land it. And no tail wheel, just a skid, which was fine because we were landing on grass. You had to learn how to taxi."

—TERESA JAMES

*February–December 1933, Vassar College, Boston*

"Fly to Detroit this weekend; it will be great fun," Alice Hirschman said over the phone.

Nancy flipped through her logbook, half listening.

"Think of the hours."

"Are you spying on me?" Nancy asked with a laugh. She and Alice had spent a lot of time together over the past several months, but with classes at Vassar, Nancy's time was severely limited now. Alice also had her commercial license and used it mostly to socialize, but she'd entered the closed-course race for women in Michigan.

Nancy was happy to have a good time, too, but she wasn't interested in racing. At her father's insistence, she'd taken off the fall semester at Vassar to recover from her frequent headaches that hadn't eased after her crash with John Miller. Yes, the time off school had helped, but her headaches were still present. So now she was a semester behind in school, and she wanted to use her spare time to log more flight hours. It would take 200 to qualify for a transport license, and she'd achieved only eighty-seven when she'd received her commercial license the year before.

Over the past couple of months, other students at Vassar had started taking flying lessons from Jack Ray.

"It will be for your *birthday*," Alice continued into the phone. "Come to Detroit, and we'll take a couple Kinner Birds into Macomb County for lunch."

"Just like that?" Nancy asked.

"Just like that," Alice said, a smile in her voice.

"I feel like there's more, Alice. Am I right?"

Alice released a small sigh. "Of course there's more. Johnny Hammond will be in town with some of his buddies. They're all nice boys."

"Oh, that's what this is about. Not my birthday after all," Nancy teased. "You're sweet on Johnny and want me to date one of his friends."

Alice laughed. "Well, you know me—I don't want my friend Nancy to be a lone woman."

Nancy scrunched up her face and turned away from a student passing through the residence hall lobby. She lowered her voice. "I'm not lonely. I've gone on plenty of dates, you know."

"Plenty? Is that what you call two dates in two months?"

"Hush, I've been busy," Nancy said. "All right, I'm coming. Hanging up and booking a plane now."

"See you tomorrow," Alice said, her voice giddy. "Oh, and happy birthday."

Nancy hung up with a smile. She'd be turning nineteen, and well, going on a flying excursion could be the fun she needed right now. She wouldn't see her family until the semester break, so she was on her own.

It turned out that the flight to Detroit was perfect and spending time with Alice even better. Except Nancy felt like the third wheel with Alice and Johnny making lovey-dovey eyes at each other. She pinned her hopes on enjoying the rest of the group, but that didn't work out as she'd hoped.

The other boys in the group were nice, but they were just that . . . *boys*. Not that Nancy was any older, but her more serious outlook on life, with a set of concrete goals, with aviation as her career, made her feel a lot older.

Alice had an easy manner with the boys, almost as if she were one of them. Her short wavy hair had managed to stay perfect, even after wearing a flight helmet. And her smile was quick, her laugh quicker. It wasn't that Nancy was shy around boys—she had plenty of male friends, and she was always around them at the airfield—but today had started out with one of her doggone headaches, and she would have preferred to spend alone time with Alice.

"You've been quiet," Thad, one of the boys in the group, said when they were about halfway through their lunch meal at a café in Macomb County. His blond hair was cropped so short that she could see his pink scalp beneath. Nothing else stood out about him. Nothing sparked her interest.

"I'm enjoying the atmosphere," she said as popular swing music played at the jukebox.

Tom's chin tilted. "Alice tells us you started flying when you were sixteen."

"That's right."

Tom's blue eyes flickered with interest. "And your hair—the gray streak right there? Alice said it's from when you were in a famous plane crash."

"I don't know about it being *famous*," Nancy said, sipping at her iced lemonade, though most of the ice had melted, weakening the flavor. Her premature gray patch of hair had grown out over the past year, becoming more prominent. At first, she'd tried to figure out ways to dye it but had eventually given up and decided it was distinguished.

But she didn't feel like talking about herself. "Do you like flying?"

"Oh, sure." Thad tapped his fingers on the table. "You've got it all going on though. Flying. College. What are you majoring in?"

"French and French history."

The dark center of his eyes flared. "Well, that's pretty much perfect."

"Perfect for what?"

Thad nudged her knee with his. "You know."

Nancy drew her leg about as far away from Thad as possible, and she turned to Alice. "Gotta go."

Alice's thin brows rose. "You sure?"

Nancy flicked her gaze to Thad, then back to Alice.

Johnny caught it. "Everything all right?"

"Sure, but I'm headed out. Thanks for this." She motioned to the table. Standing, she pulled out some coins to add to the collection in the middle of the table, but Alice waved her away.

"It's your birthday—my treat."

"Well, thank you." Nancy offered a smile she didn't feel.

Everyone said goodbye, and as she left, she felt some regret making the trip. She loved spending time with Alice, and she was happy to get more flight hours, but she knew things were getting tighter financially at home. Oh, her parents hadn't said anything directly, but she had heard more than one conversation through closed doors. Taking off the fall semester had been a financial relief to her father.

Like most of America, her father had lost money in the stock market crash a few years back, and extras were getting harder to justify. At least Nancy was paying for her own flight lessons now by giving others rides.

Sort of like the original barnstormer she'd flown with . . . She didn't do any stunts, of course, but it seemed that life had moved full circle. Once she had her transport license, she could find a real flying job. And maybe she could pay back some of her tuition to her parents.

Later that afternoon, when she returned to the Poughkeepsie airfield and taxied the plane toward the hangar and parked, she went in search of Jack Ray.

Finding him in his office, sleeves rolled up, pencil behind his ear as he read the newspaper, she walked in and braced her palms on his desk. "I have a plan to make us both some money."

His brows popped up as he set down the newspaper and folded his arms.

"What if I bring you more students? You pay me a commission or something."

Jack gave a thoughtful nod. "I like the idea, but you know times are tough for a lot of people nowadays."

"Yes, but a lot of the students at Vassar are still well-off, and their parents are the ones who can afford flying lessons."

"You make a good point, Harkness, but not many girls are like you."

She smiled. "They might not be like me, but they might still be interested. I've decided to start a flying club. Everyone wants to join a club, right?"

Jack chuckled. "You might be onto something."

"Get ready to schedule some students." She walked out of the office, and as soon as she reached Vassar, she went straight to Rachel's room to tell her of her plans.

"I'll come to the meetings," Rachel said, leaning back on her desk chair. "I don't know if I want to sign up for lessons though."

"Not required," Nancy said. "But if the most popular girl in the school is part of the club, then maybe others will follow."

"And other clubs might partner with yours," Rachel predicted, her smile appearing. "You're already a trendsetter. How did it go with Alice?"

"Swell," Nancy said, biting off telling her about Thad. There was really nothing to tell, and Nancy didn't want to waste time thinking about him anyway.

As she turned to go, Rachel said, "Happy birthday!"

"Thank you."

In her own room, Nancy drew up a flier to post at the residence hall, coming up with the most enticing and energetic language possible.

"There's a phone call for you," a woman said, knocking on Nancy's partly open door. It was the housemistress, who Nancy was sure eavesdropped at doors. She always seemed to know everything going on.

Nancy hurried to the phone to answer the call from her parents.

"Happy birthday, my dear," Father said.

"Happy birthday," her mother added.

So she told them about her plans to start a flying club and how she could earn extra money once she got her transport license.

"You should be focusing most of your time on school," Mother said. "Flying jobs are scarce right now—for men. Women would be the last pick."

Before Nancy could answer, her father cut in. "What gives you the idea that you need to be spending so much time coming up with ways to earn money?"

Nancy paused, then decided to confess. "I've heard a few of your conversations. I didn't mean to overhear, but we all know a lot of people are struggling. I wanted to help out with whatever I can."

Their pause was so long that Nancy wondered if they were covering the phone to have a whispered conversation.

Finally, Nancy added, "If Vassar is too expensive, I can drop out."

"No, Nance, that won't be necessary," her father said quickly, maybe too quickly.

"You don't need to worry about tuition," Mother said more firmly.

But Nancy had heard the doubt in her father's voice. Their pride might not allow them to admit that tuition was too steep right now, but she would prepare if that became the case. She'd be ready. Right now, her opinions were a mile or two apart from her parents', but that could change.

A few weeks later, Jack Ray thanked her before one of their lessons started. "I've had three new students so far."

"That's great."

And it was great, but it wouldn't be enough. Nancy knew this. Things at home had changed too. The types of meals her mother served. Father had sold one of their cars. Robert and Alice's second baby would be born in July, and he was busy with his job at the Marrimax Chemical Company of Cambridge. As it was, he had pretty much given up flying, though he had found a new and cheaper sport this past winter: skiing.

Nancy wasn't too interested in skiing, so she'd turned down his invitations. Besides, traveling would cost her more money.

And when she passed the test for her transport license in August, she wasn't interested in celebrating much. There was too much to do. Fall semester was busier than ever, with her packing in the schoolwork and balancing her time to fly as she continued building her flying club and earning commission.

"Come with us," Robert said over the phone one winter day in December while Nancy perched on the corner of the hall table down the corridor from her dorm room. "I'm taking a short skiing break before my house fills with in-laws and Christmas activities."

"Ah, baby Charles keeping you awake?"

"It's more like the toddler is keeping us on our toes, but my mother-in-law is coming in town early to help, and Alice told me it was my one chance for a day of skiing."

Nancy loved spending time with her brother, but the fall semester would end shortly after the Christmas break, and she wanted all her free time reserved for flying. So she was making sure every assignment was caught up. "Can't."

"Sis . . ."

"Have fun. I'll see you at Christmas."

"All right, all right." Robert's words came out as an amused rumble. "With the rate you're going, you'll be the top pilot in the US."

"Hardly. I'm no daredevil, record-setting Amelia Earhart."

"Well, except her." His voice went quiet. "But you're a lady flyer in your own right. I'm proud of you—even though I've told you that many times."

Nancy's chest swelled. It was still good to hear.

"Don't quit flying," he said. "Not even when you meet the numb-skull man you'll fall in love with."

She laughed. "First of all, I'm not going to fall in love with a numb-skull, and if I *do* end up with some man—he won't be the type to cross me."

"No," Robert agreed with a hearty laugh. "He'll be your biggest supporter. Well, second only to your brother."

Nancy grinned. She felt a small twinge of regret for turning Robert down. She'd see him plenty in a few days, and she couldn't always be his sidekick.

The next couple of nights, she stayed up late to work on assignments, so she was awake when the housemistress found her three nights after she talked to her brother.

"Phone call for you, Nancy," the housemistress said.

Nancy turned in surprise. "What?" Late-night phone calls were rare, and the housemistress would usually be very upset about having to get up to answer.

"Phone call," the woman repeated. "It sounds urgent."

Something in her voice told Nancy this phone call wasn't a prank or from a boy breaking curfew rules. Was there an emergency, and if so, who'd be calling to tell her about it?

Her heart rate went up a few notches, and she didn't bother pulling on a robe or putting on slippers. Hurrying down the hallway, her padded footsteps were the only sound in the darkened residence hall.

"Hello?" she answered, out of breath even though she hadn't gone very far.

"Nance," her father said in a rasp. "We've had some bad news."

Nancy blinked in the dimness of the corridor. "What's happened?"

"Are you sitting down?"

She wasn't yet, but she moved to the nearby bench, the wood solid beneath her quaking legs. "Yes."

"It's Robert. He's been in a terrible accident. Skiing. He—" Father's voice broke.

If she hadn't been sitting down, her knees would have given out. A dull roar began in her ears, and her chest hitched as if manipulated by a puppet. "What . . . happened?"

"Robert didn't make it."

# CHAPTER NINE

"The US Department of Air Commerce is trying to develop a cheap popular type of plane. They should have women flyers as well as men to work in the Department and on the road to make the idea and the plane, when developed, popular. I should like to meet Mr. Eugene Vidal, through Secretary Roper, to talk this over with him. Mr. Vidal is in charge of this work in the Department. I must be in a position to make my own way as soon as possible and to do this I must have a job."

—NANCY LOVE'S LETTER TO HER UNCLE THOMAS L. CHADBOURNE

*January 1934—Vassar College, Boston*

Somehow, Nancy had returned at Vassar—after Christmas, after her brother's funeral, and after her heart had broken into dozens of pieces.

"Finish the semester," both of her parents had told her. "Robert would want you to."

Maybe Robert would have wanted that, but he was no longer here to tell them anything.

She sat in her room alone now because she'd sent every friend away for the evening. Nancy *wanted* to feel the loneliness because it let her focus her thoughts and feel rooted to her brother, as if he were within reach. And if she was by herself, their connection was stronger.

*What would Robert do if I died instead and left him behind?*

Nancy grabbed another box of tissues. She'd gone through several. After wiping her eyes and blowing her nose, she closed her eyes. Thinking beyond the grief and missing her brother—what would Robert do if he had been the one left behind? She drew in a shaky breath. Her brother would follow his dreams, his passions, citing that life was short and he'd want to make his baby sister proud.

Could she return to life as normal? Live when her brother wasn't? Laugh when he was in a grave? Or would her future morph into something cold, stiff, inert?

"Bobbin," she whispered. "Why did you have to go on that skiing trip? Why did you have to be taken so soon?" The questions only bounced off silent walls in a place she no longer wanted to be. She wouldn't continue at Vassar. She'd told her parents she wanted to leave at the end of the semester. They'd protested, sure. But there was also relief in their eyes.

They wouldn't have to pay her tuition.

Mostly, though, Nancy didn't want to be around so many people all the time. She didn't want to watch them laugh, tease, and talk about inconsequential things. She wanted to leave Vassar behind and find a way to live for her brother. Follow her dreams, live out her passions—in honor of Robert.

At the funeral, she'd talked to Uncle Thomas Chadbourne. She'd told him, before she'd told her parents, that she couldn't stay at Vassar. But that meant she needed to find employment. Uncle Thomas had offered to pay for her to attend the Katharine Gibbs Secretarial School on Park Avenue in New York City.

"So that's what I'll do," Nancy whispered to herself. If her brother were still alive, he'd get a kick out of that—leaving a prestigious women's college to attend a secretary school. She'd already written to the school about the curriculum.

She returned her attention to her desk, wiped at her eyes, and read through the courses. She'd focus on only the shorthand, typing, and filing. It was all she needed. She didn't have use for the economics, business English, or spelling. The sooner she was finished, the sooner she could get a job.

*Don't ever stop flying, Sis. Promise me.*

Her brother's words. Could she still do both? She grabbed another tissue and wiped at her eyes. She blinked back the ever-falling tears, and again, she studied the course schedule. If she left school early a couple of days a week and added on weekends, she could continue flying lessons. But she also needed a job in the meantime. Uncle Thomas might be paying for school, and he'd offered to sublease an apartment he owned in New York to her rent-free, but she needed living wages.

Tonight, she decided, she'd find a way to keep her promise to her brother. She wrote two letters to other women aviators to see if they wanted to be her roommate in New York—Suzanne Humphreys and Margaret Thomas. Susie already worked there, in a dress shop. So maybe Nancy could invite Susie to be her roommate, and she'd collect some rent.

She wrote to Margaret Thomas as well—whom everyone called Tommy.

Nancy pulled out another piece of paper and wrote a letter of application to the Ninety-Nines organization that was made up of solely female aviators. Started in 1929 with Amelia Earhart as the first president, it was named after the original number of women who were the first to join.

Nancy added to her letter of application that she'd logged 225 hours and she'd flown different types of airplanes, including the Fleet, Stearman, Waco, Great Lakes, Bird, Kitty Hawk, and Aeronca. She'd include the initiation fee of one dollar and agree to pay the two-dollar-and-fifty-cent annual subscription. In return, she'd be a member with resources and support and also receive the monthly newsletter.

"That's for you, Bobbin," she whispered as she sealed the application in an envelope. "And for me." She grabbed a tissue and blew her nose. She didn't know how long it would take to not cry over her brother every day, but focusing on ways to honor his memory would keep her moving forward.

Her next letter was to her uncle Thomas, updating him on her plans and telling him she was happy to take a flying job for the US Department of Commerce, should there be an opening—something he'd said he had connections to.

Someone tapped on her door.

"Come in," Nancy said.

"Hey." Rachel stood in the doorway, wearing her robe over her pajamas, her eyes bright despite the hour. "You're up late."

Nancy shrugged. "Rearranging my future, it seems."

Rachel walked into the room and sat across from her, cross-legged on the bed. "You're really leaving Vassar?"

Nancy could only nod because her throat had tightened.

Rachel's mouth turned down. "I'll miss you like crazy."

"I'll miss you too."

The two girls stood and hugged fiercely. When they broke apart, Nancy said, "You'd better come visit me in New York. I'll have my own place, you know, like a real grown-up."

Rachel wiped her cheeks with the sleeve of her robe. "I can't say I'm not jealous. I mean, I want to finish at Vassar, but it sounds dreamy to be out on my own. Away from the headmistress and housemistress."

"Sorry you won't have anyone to get in trouble with."

Rachel smirked. "I'll have to talk Beth into some pranks."

"Good luck with that." Nancy settled on the edge of the bed, and Rachel sat next to her. "Remember when she refused to help us with the prank on the white-glove tea party?"

"Yeah." While at Milton, Nancy and Rachel had come up with a prank to play on the seniors who'd been invited to a white-glove tea at the headmistress's house. After the tea had started, she and Rachel had moved the street signs on campus so that traffic was rerouted through the circle to pass in front of the headmistress's house.

"I'm definitely coming to visit you," Rachel said, cutting into the fond memory, "but only because you'll be in Mark Twain's former house."

Nancy threw up her hands. "Whatever it takes to get you there." It was true that her uncle's place had been Mark Twain's residence more than thirty years before. The house on 21 Fifth Avenue on the corner of Ninth Street had been subdivided into apartments.

"Call me when you arrive and give me the layout."

"Of course, and you'd better tell me how things are going with William."

Rachel's smile appeared now. "Certainly. And the invitation is always open if you want to double-date."

"I'll have to get back to you on that," Nancy said. "I'm going to be very busy."

"You always say that." Rachel bumped Nancy's shoulder. "One of these days, a man will catch your eye, and you won't be able to ignore him."

"As long as he's not a pilot," Nancy quipped. "They're all poor."

Rachel grinned, then stifled a yawn. "I'm not a night owl like you."

Nancy hugged her friend again and said goodnight.

The next few days were filled with end-of-semester tests and packing her things from her time at Vassar.

Father showed up to drive her into New York City, and when Nancy let him into the residence hall to help carry her things, he looked like a changed man. His face had thinned, his shoulders seemed to have shrunk, and there were new lines about his eyes. Was it possible to age ten years in less than a month? Had she aged just as much?

"Mother will come visit soon," Father said. "She, uh, was too upset to make this trip."

Nancy understood, she really did. Perhaps her mother wanted some quiet grieving time to herself. Nancy had been going back and forth on that herself. Sometimes she wanted to talk to her friends about her brother, and sometimes she wanted to be alone.

She decided that the bustle of New York City would be the perfect distraction from sad things. The drive passed quickly, and soon, they pulled alongside the curb past the Brevoort Hotel.

Her father turned off the engine in front of a three-story brick building. "This is it," he said.

Just then, both Margaret Thomas and Suzanne Humphreys came out of the building.

Something inside Nancy swelled. She was really doing this. She was really starting a new chapter of her life. She hopped out of the car.

"You made it!" Tommy gushed in her Texan drawl. Her red hair reminded Nancy of Rachel's, but Margaret's eyes were summer-lake blue. "We've been waiting for ages."

Susie laughed, the dimple in her chin appearing, and her blue eyes filling with amusement. She patted at her blonde curls as if to make sure they were still in place. "Ignore Tommy. She's been here maybe five minutes."

Nancy hugged both of her friends. "So, what do you think?"

"Truly perfect," Tommy said. "I can't believe I'm living in the same place as one of my favorite authors."

Susie looked past Nancy to her father. "Hello, Dr. Harkness."

Nancy's father came around the car and greeted the others. They all helped unload Nancy's things.

"This way," Tommy said, sounding all-knowing. "We're on the ground floor, which is truly perfect."

"Truly perfect," Susie mimicked.

Tommy linked arms with Nancy. "Ignore her. Come check out the living room."

"Do you folks need help with carrying?" A voice came from above them.

Nancy looked up to see a young man with lively brown eyes and a smile to match leaning over the balcony of a higher apartment.

"Oh, hi, Henry," Susie said, then turned to Nancy. "He's harmless, and he has a car."

"I can hear you," Henry said in an amiable voice, his brown, wavy hair falling over his forehead.

"Come on down," Susie said with a laugh.

In minutes, Henry had introduced himself as Henry Wilder. "I'm a pilot too. An instructor," he told Nancy. "Heard all about you from your friends."

She smiled and let him and her father bring in the heavier things.

They entered the apartment, and Nancy surveyed the place, landing on the french doors that opened onto a balcony above the sidewalk. The iron railing divided them from the sidewalk café of the Brevoort Hotel.

"See?" Tommy waved expansively. "It's like we're living in Paris. A quaint café right outside our windows."

"I love it," Nancy declared. She needed to make sure Uncle Thomas knew how grateful she was for his generosity.

"It's been nice meeting you, Miss Harkness," Henry said, then nodded to her father. "Dr. Harkness."

Everyone chorused their thanks for Henry's help, and after he left the apartment, Nancy's father walked through the small spaces. The furniture was sparse, but it looked like Susie had put some effort into making things pretty, with doilies, framed pictures, and a vase of white daisies on the kitchen table. She followed her father into her bedroom.

"It's a decent place," he said. "Don't you think? Your mother will be pleased."

"It's great, Daddy," Nancy told him. "Tell Mother not to worry."

He settled his hands on her shoulders. "I'm so proud of you, Nance. Call us if you need anything at all."

She blinked back a round of tears. "I will, Daddy. Love you."

He embraced her, and when he drew back, his eyes were wet. "Stay safe, my dear."

She'd heard the same words from her father many times, but this time, they carried much more weight. "I will."

Both Susie and Tommy helped her unpack. The next few days would be routine for all of them, so Susie came up with a plan to celebrate their first night of their shared adventure.

"Well, girls, gather around." Susie handed everyone a small glass of orange juice. "Let's toast to our future of making our way in the world and conquering the skies."

Tommy grinned. "We may be penniless, but at least we're good-looking."

"We'll certainly go far in life, then," Nancy said.

Susie clinked glasses with everyone and took a sip of her juice. "Who wants to go dancing at one of the nightclubs?"

Nancy knew she'd be dead on her feet before a real crowd could gather, so she said, "I'd rather check out the Roosevelt airfield."

"I'm in," Tommy said.

Susie sighed. "All right. Let me change my shoes."

The phone jangled, and Tommy crossed to answer it. Whoever the speaker was on the other end of the line made Tommy's eyes widen.

"Yes, ma'am. I can do that. No, I don't have any conflicts that can't be worked around. Sure thing. Bye." Tommy moved to the tiny kitchen table and sank onto a chair. "Hey, did I tell you gals that I met Jacqueline Cochran last week?"

"No," Susie said.

Nancy had heard bits and pieces about the woman and her eclectic life. Jacqueline Cochran, or Jackie, was a member of the Ninety-Nines. As a teen, she'd married Robert Cochran, and they'd lost a child. After that, she'd divorced her husband and begun working at the Saks Fifth Avenue salon.

Her next husband, Floyd Odlum, built a successful venture capital firm. Jackie had kept her Cochran last name, preferring Miss Cochran, and had taken flying lessons in order to travel quicker to sell her own cosmetic business, which she eventually called Wings to Beauty. She'd fallen in love with flying and had begun competing in air races across the country.

"Well, I did, and apparently . . . she likes me?" Tommy gave a little shake of her head.

Susie set her hands on her hips. "Spill the beans, Tommy."

Tommy blinked as if she were in a daze. "Cochran asked me to fly co-pilot in her Waco. She's heading to Florida for the All American Races."

"Whoa," Nancy said. "You're going to *race*?" She knew her friends were good pilots, but racing was a whole other level. Something her friend Alice Hirschman did.

Tommy absently smoothed a hand over her hair, her eyes full of stars. "I guess I am."

# CHAPTER TEN

"We all got in about the same time, very late, from our dates and nightclub visits. We talked awhile then decided to go to Roosevelt Field and fly as soon as the sun was up. Flying made women comrades in the same way that men can be comrades, but women seldom are. There are many ties women share, woman-to-woman, to men's exclusion, but we are rarely the companions in the 'Three Musketeers' sense."

—MARGARET "TOMMY" THOMAS

*April 1934—New York City*

"I can't believe how tedious secretarial school is," Nancy told Henry Wilder as they drove to the East Boston airport. He hung around her apartment a lot, but not because there was a romantic interest between him and any of her friends. At least Nancy didn't think so. He'd become one of the group. "Besides, I don't know if I can eat another bowl of tomato soup and stay sane. I used to like that stuff, but now, it's how I literally survive."

"You need to stick it out." Henry took a drag on his cigarette and tapped it out the open car window. "Times are tough for most people."

They both sobered. The founder of the secretarial school, Katharine Gibbs, had recently lost her oldest son, Howard, to suicide. Stories like that were becoming too common.

"Times are tough," Nancy agreed, but she knew she was still blessed. "Which is why I need to find a job much sooner than later."

Henry slowed the car to turn into the airport. "My friend Bob Love might have a job available, or if he doesn't, he might know of something. Did I tell you he's a college dropout too?" Henry's mood had turned lighter, which Nancy was grateful for.

She nudged his arm. "Oh, so that's how you view me too? A drop-out?"

He nudged her back.

Truth was, Nancy would rather be working in aviation than staying in school. She had her transport license, so surely there was something she could do with it that paid the same as secretarial work. She'd been accepted into the Ninety-Nines earlier that year, and she'd written a few of the ladies, inquiring about possible jobs, but had come up empty. So, she'd talked Henry into taking her job hunting in Boston. She and her roommates only had their apartment until summer, then Susie would go live with her parents in Far Hills, New Jersey. Tommy was now tied at the hip with Jacqueline Cochran and had been invited to work for her in Springfield, Massachusetts.

"Here we are." Henry tossed his cigarette out the window. "I have a good feeling that Bob will come through for us."

Nancy didn't know Henry's friend, Bob Love. She usually flew out of Newark, and Mr. Love owned Inter City Aviation, which served flights out of the East Boston airport.

"Crossing my fingers," she said, doing just that. She didn't mention that she'd once met Crocker Snow at this very airport years ago.

"Bob has his hands in a little bit of everything," Henry continued. "He offers flight instruction and charters flights."

"I could be the pilot for that."

"He also does aerial surveying and brokers airplanes."

Nancy spread her hands wide. "Again, I can do that."

Henry threw her a wry grin as he parked the car. "Come on. We'll go to his office and see what's what."

Nancy followed Henry into one of the hangars, and the familiar scent of fuel, exhaust, paint, and glue made her feel nostalgic.

"Hello there," Henry said to a mechanic hunched over a plane. "Is Bob Love around?"

The man lifted his head and caught sight of Nancy. He straightened and wiped his hands on a grease-stained towel. "He's picking up a plane right now but shouldn't be too long."

Henry glanced at Nancy, then back at the mechanic. "Are we talking 'too long' being twenty minutes or more like a couple of hours?"

"Closer to twenty minutes."

"Excellent." Henry slipped his hands into his pockets and rocked back on his heels. "When Bob shows up, let him know he has a visitor waiting in his office. I told him I'd be around sometime this week but didn't know it would be this early."

"I'll let him know." The mechanic flashed Nancy a smile.

She returned it with her own polite smile, then followed Henry across the hangar to a side door.

"This way," Henry said in a cheerful tone.

Nancy scoped the place out. The hangar held a couple of planes in different stages of repair, but everything seemed organized and tidy. Henry opened a door, and they stepped into a narrow corridor. At the end, he opened another door to a rather small room that served as an office.

The place needed some cleanup. Stacks of papers and various boxes were scattered about, illuminated by the blinds that cut the sunlight coming from the lone window. Truthfully, the office was junky in contrast to the hangar. The couple of chairs were clear, at least, and Henry took the one behind the desk and propped his feet up.

Instead of moving papers and sitting on the other chair, Nancy perched on the edge of the desk, which was ironically about the cleanest spot in the room. She crossed her legs and looked over at Henry. "Exactly how big is this operation, and how many planes does Mr. Love own?"

"I'm not sure." Henry lit up another cigarette. "He's always buying something and selling something else."

Nancy held out her hand, and Henry handed over the cigarette. She took a puff, then handed it back.

"Love the lipstick mark," Henry said with a smirk.

Nancy shrugged. "And how old is Bob?"

"My age."

"So, twenty-five?" At his nod, she continued. "He's accomplished a lot for his age."

Henry coughed, and not from the cigarette. "As opposed to *me*? Not accomplishing much?"

"Oh, you're a successful man in your own right." She waved a hand as she smirked. "Not comparing here, Wilder."

He shook his head, a smile on his face.

Nancy swept her gaze about the office. Several framed pictures decorated the wall—one of a man who must be Bob and someone else she recognized—Crocker Snow. Interesting. The aviation world really was very small. Memories of her brother surged through her—of how he'd surprised her with an introduction to Crocker Snow at this same airport. Her brother had been her favorite person in the world, and now he was gone.

She blinked against the stinging in her eyes and straightened her posture.

The office door suddenly opened, and the doorknob smacked against the side of the wall. A man strode in, obviously straight from flying. His flight coveralls were grease-stained, and his reddish hair was part plastered to his scalp, part sticking up, a testament of recently pulling off his flight helmet. Goggles dangled in his hand, and his blue eyes were as cold as an icy windstorm.

"No smoking in my office, Henry," he snapped.

His icy gaze shifted to Nancy. "Off my desk, lady."

*Well.* Nancy's nostalgia over her brother took a sharp turn, and annoyance burned in her chest. She slid off the desk and smoothed down her skirt.

Henry seemed unfazed as he lowered his feet and stubbed out his cigarette. "Sorry, Bob, won't happen again."

Bob Love's eyes moved from Nancy to Henry, giving her a bit of a reprieve from his glower. "I told you I was swamped, and I don't need some two-bit secretary. I'm up to my eyeballs in transactions and scheduling. I'm not playing host to whatever . . ." His attention snapped to Nancy again. "*Whomever* you've decided to take on a drive through Boston."

Nancy was quite stunned. She'd been around dozens of male pilots, but she'd never met one so dismissive. The annoyance in her chest simmered into anger.

"Glad you got my message." Henry pushed away from the desk and stood. "Let's start again. Bob, this is Nancy Harkness, and she's—"

"Don't bother, Wilder," Nancy cut in, her voice quaking with indignation. "I don't want to be anyone's waste of time." She moved past Mr. Love and stepped through the doorway, then pulled the door shut behind her. Well, maybe she slammed it—if the echoing bang off the corridor walls was any indication. The sound made her feel better, though, and she strode to the exit.

She'd wait at the car for Henry to finish his conversation with Mr. Love. She wasn't interested in working for a man who was clearly arrogant and rude and unfairly presumptuous. Maybe this was his acumen to stay afloat as an aviator during the Depression, but his people skills were horrendous. And Nancy didn't need a bad-mannered employer.

Perhaps she could beg something at the Newark or Roosevelt airfields. She knew there weren't any openings, but maybe she could help bring in student pilots like she had at Vassar.

She entered the hangar, and the same mechanic spotted her. He gave her a friendly wave. "Finished already, miss?"

Nancy gave him a tight smile. "Yes, thank you. Have a nice day." There. She could be polite and courteous when she was as mad as a trapped bee. Her adrenaline didn't slow down when she reached Henry's car, so she walked to one of the open-cockpit planes, letting the spring breeze cool off her heated skin. The plane was likely the very one Mr. Love had recently flown.

Just looking at it made her heart both soar and ache. How would it be to own an aviation business? Fly whenever you wanted to, without paying rental fees or working around booking times? She could wake up in the morning, and instead of heading to a classroom filled with typewriters, she'd suit up and climb into a cockpit.

Her heart rate eventually slowed, and her pulse calmed.

"Nancy!" Henry hurried out of the hangar. "Nancy? Oh, there you are. Please, I'm so sorry about all this. I think the messages got mixed up when I reached out to Bob."

Nancy watched her friend approach. He really did sound apologetic. She folded her arms and waited for him to reach her. Might as well hear him out.

"I mentioned that you were in secretarial school," he said in a rush, "but I guess wires were crossed. Bob thought that meant you were a secretary and you're after a typist position."

Nancy snorted.

"So, I messed up." Henry scrubbed a hand through his wavy hair. "I told Bob all about you, and he really does want to meet you."

"We've met," Nancy deadpanned.

Henry released a choked laugh and glanced over at the hangar. "Yes, that's true. But he's calmed down now. Had some issues with the customer he was selling a plane to, so that's why he was all blustery."

Nancy lifted a brow. "And rude?"

"And rude. Yes, very rude." Henry smiled, but Nancy didn't return it. "Please, will you give it another chance? Bob needs help, and he knows it."

"Did he *say* that?"

"Not in those, uh, exact words." Henry set his hands on his hips, releasing a sigh.

"What were his words *exactly*, Wilder?"

Henry answered in a hesitant voice. "Bob said he could always use a good pilot but that he'd be very picky."

Nancy looked up at the sky, then toward the hangar. "Perfect. He just got his second chance."

"Really?" Henry asked. "That's swell. Let's go, Harkness."

But Nancy had already strode past him. If this had the potential for a real job in aviation, she'd give the cranky Mr. Love another chance. Flying she could do. And if that didn't impress the man, he could keep his airfield and greasy coveralls and messy office.

When she reentered the office, Bob Love was standing at the small window, his back to her, his gaze pinned to something outside.

She didn't speak, didn't need to. Obviously, he'd heard her enter because he swung around to face her.

He'd taken off his flight suit, and beneath it, he wore a button-down shirt and slacks. His shirt sleeves were rolled up, but otherwise, he looked like he could fit into any university campus. He'd tamed his hair, although it was still disheveled, and his blue eyes were much less . . . icy.

In fact, they were calm. Not exactly welcoming, but Nancy didn't need his immediate approval. She'd demonstrate her skills in an airplane.

Instead of walking all the way into the office, she remained in the doorway, as if giving him a warning.

"Miss Harkness," Bob said with a head tilt. "Nice to meet you."

She stared at him. *Just like that?* He wasn't going to address the two-ton elephant in the room? "I'm not sure what to say."

"Nice to meet *me*?"

"I'm still deciding."

He nodded; his gaze locked on her. "Fair enough. And I apologize for mistaking you for a . . ." He waved his hand toward her.

Nancy waited. "For a *what*, Mr. Love?"

"A secretary." He rubbed the back of his neck. "You look like a secretary, and I guess I misunderstood Henry's message from the get-go."

"I *look* like a secretary?" Nancy folded her arms. "How's that?"

She felt rather gratified when the man's neck flushed. Maybe it had to do with being a redhead, or maybe he had *some* remorse in those cranky bones of his.

"You're, you know—" He cut himself off.

"I don't *know*, in fact. Can you be more clear, sir?"

He paused, and it was as if she could literally see his mind working—choosing his words carefully. "You're dressed nicely, and you're, uh, pretty, and, you know, proper."

She wasn't sure if he was complimenting her or insulting her. "And other women aviators you've met wear dirty rags, have bulbous noses, and cuss like navy men?"

His eyes popped wide, and his mouth twitched. Then he smiled.

Bob Love might have a very nice smile, but she wasn't ready to forgive him yet. Not until he offered her a job.

"That's not what I meant, Miss Harkness," he said with a shade of amusement.

"So, you're mixing your words? Henry led me to believe you're an educated man, even though you did drop out of both Princeton and MIT . . ."

He was still smiling, not offended or shocked in the least. Nancy wanted to laugh. She could feel it bubbling up inside of her, but she kept it tamped down.

"You're quite direct for—" He stopped.

"For a *woman*?"

"I wasn't going to say that."

She pierced him with her best glare. "Maybe not. But you're *thinking* it. Look, Mr. Love, I earned my private pilot's license at sixteen, so I've been around male pilots for a good four years. There's not much you could say that will get the hairs on my neck to rise, but don't ever discredit my worth as a pilot *or* as a woman. Besides, secretaries make the business world go around. I just happen to want to fly. Either you need help at your airfield, or you don't. If you're hiring, I'm interested. If you're not, let's stop wasting each other's time."

Bob swallowed but kept his gaze steady, possibly to his credit. His next words sounded carefully chosen. "Can I see your pilot's logbook, Miss Harkness?"

Now, this made Nancy feel like they were finally coming to a meeting of the minds. She pulled out her logbook from her bag and handed it over.

Bob leafed through it, stopping at a few places. His eyebrows didn't rise, and he didn't seem particularly surprised or even pleased. Maybe that was to his credit again.

When he handed the logbook back, he said, "Want to take something up right now? Test out one of the new Wacos? I'm trying to move them as fast as I can, and it would be nice to have someone on hand to demonstrate the line."

"I'd love to fly a Waco."

Bob nodded, then glanced at her person. "I don't have an extra flight suit, but you're welcome to borrow mine."

"No need. I brought a change of clothing."

"Somehow I'm not surprised." His blue eyes were decidedly warmer. He motioned toward the office door to lead the way out.

She stepped into the corridor first, her steps so much lighter now. And she found she was smiling after all.

# CHAPTER ELEVEN

"Miss Harkness is a transport pilot and in the future will demonstrate the Waco line of airplanes to prospective customers. She has been flying for four years.... She is quite reserved but like all pilots warms up to the topic of flying so eventually some of her past experiences come to light.... It is anticipated that when this latest employee of the ICA becomes a little better acquainted she is going to be more than busy with her gray demonstrator which by the way is the only ambulance plane in New England."

—ROBERT C. CODMAN, *N.E. AVIATION*

*April 1934—Boston, Massachusetts*

Nancy climbed out of the passenger plane after escorting a chatty couple from the East Boston airport to New York. "Here we are, folks." She guided them out of the plane and made sure they hadn't left anything behind.

"Thank you, miss, for delivering us safely." Mr. Johnson tipped his gray fedora.

His wife, a curly haired blonde with bright-pink lipstick and a dress to match, gushed a little more. "You're a super pilot. I've never felt such a smooth landing. I feel like I should give you a bouquet of daffodils."

Nancy only smiled. Daffodils wouldn't mix with her breeches and flight jacket. "You're welcome for the flight, and I hope you'll charter us again."

"Of course we will, right, Harold?"

"That we will," her husband agreed. "You can tell Mr. Love that we're pleased."

Nancy held back a laugh. She wouldn't have been hired for this job if she couldn't do it well. She'd started this weekend, working for Inter City. Bob Love had been in a much better mood and had surprisingly given her the job of transporting this couple right away. She didn't miss the surprise in *their* eyes, though, when they realized their pilot would be a woman. No matter, Nancy was used to it.

"Where did you train in flying?" Mrs. Johnson continued, smoothing back a curl from her face that kept tugging loose in the breeze. "You seem so young."

Nancy shrugged and gave her a quick rundown. It was time to fuel up the plane, then do the next preflight check. She was about to say goodbye to the Johnsons so she could climb back into the plane to drive it to the fueling pump when a man came out of the hangar, walking toward them.

"Ma'am?" He wore a bowler hat, and his button-down shirt was rolled up at the sleeves. He also carried a camera and a notebook. "Mind if I take a picture of you and your passengers? I'm Robert Codman, and I'm a reporter for the *N.E. Aviation*. I'd like to write an article about ICA's newest hire."

Nancy hid her surprise. Why was a journalist suddenly here? And why was being hired at the ICA newsworthy?

"Oh, that would be super," Mrs. Johnson exclaimed. "Don't you think so, Harold?"

He rocked back on his heels as if he had all day to dilly dally. "Sure thing."

So, Nancy climbed into the cockpit, and the journalist staged the photo with her leaning out of the window, chatting with the couple.

After the photo, and when the Johnsons finally headed out after more gushing by the missus, the journalist asked Nancy a few questions, ones she'd heard a dozen times.

"This is part of my job, Mr. Codman," she clarified, staying upbeat as the breeze swirled about them. "Nothing to write an article about."

Mr. Codman looked up from his notebook, the corner of the pages ruffling. "Oh, it's newsworthy, ma'am. The aviation publication is always seeking special-interest stories, and you're special, Miss Harkness."

Nancy wasn't sure if the man was being sincere or flirtatious. "Did Bob Love send you?"

"Not particularly." Codman wrote something else in his notebook. "Word gets around though."

"I suppose it does. Now, I need to get back to East Boston if you don't mind."

"Be my guest." Codman took a few steps back, but he hung around, watching as Nancy fueled the plane and completed the precheck.

It was a fine April day for flying, no weather issues, the wind mellow. When she landed at East Boston, she headed through the hangar, lifting a hand in greeting to the smiling mechanic. She continued along the stale-coffee-scented corridor to Bob's office. The door was shut, but she heard his voice coming through the door. Was he on the phone or in a meeting?

"She's a good pilot, and she's available right now." Bob paused.

Nancy hesitated outside the office door. She hadn't planned on eavesdropping, but she didn't want to interrupt either. So she waited.

"You said you couldn't commit until midsummer, and that wasn't a sure thing either."

Another pause.

"If things change, I'll let you know. But she says she can go full time, and from what I've seen, I won't be regretting anything."

Nancy wondered if she was being complimented? Bob Love didn't even have the report from her first charter job. Maybe this fellow wasn't so bad after all.

The click of the receiver told her he was off the phone. She opened the door without knocking.

Bob sat at his desk, his head lowered, propped against his hand. His shirt sleeves were dingy with engine smoke, and although he wasn't in a flight suit, his knuckles were stained with grease. It was a connection that all pilots had.

"Are you sure you don't regret hiring me?" Nancy ventured. "You don't look too pleased."

His chin snapped up, and he straightened, dropping his hands to the desk. "Miss Harkness."

She tilted her head. "Mr. Love."

"You heard."

She leaned against the doorframe. "I didn't intend to, but your voice carries. Look, I didn't mean to oust anyone, but I'm happy to have this job. So, thank you. And sorry to the other person?"

Bob's blue gaze was steady. "He's an old friend. Thinks I owe him a favor, but I've paid that tenfold." He rose from his desk and walked around it. "Not the most reliable fellow, and it's easier to run a business with someone who's reliable."

"Understood."

Bob stopped near the edge of the desk, leaned against it, not far from a half-filled coffee mug and scattered crumpled papers, and crossed his arms. "How did the flight go?"

"No problems. Although, it seems that I'm being stalked by a journalist."

Bob's neck had the grace to flush. "Ah, Codman found you?"

She smirked. "He did. Who do I thank for that?"

"Publicity is good for business." He exhaled. "Do you mind?"

She had minded, but now that Bob was being polite about it, that all faded. "It's fine." She straightened from the doorframe. "I've done interviews before."

"So I've read."

This surprised her. And his eyes were dancing. "You've read my interviews?" she asked.

His nod was short. "Had to do some homework to make sure you were a good hire."

"My *flying* didn't impress you, Mr. Love?"

The edge of his mouth lifted, but his eyes didn't change their focus. "Oh, it impressed me, Miss Harkness."

The office was warmer than Nancy remembered. Maybe the place needed a fan, or at least the window could be cracked open?

The phone jangled to life behind Bob, but he didn't seem to notice or care.

"I should let you get that." She took a step back. "I've got another charter coming up."

"Right." Bob's gaze held hers through another ring.

"I'll report in after the next flight." She moved into the hallway, not sure why her pulse was suddenly jittery.

"Miss Harkness," he said, not moving from his position on the corner of the desk, "how are you getting home tomorrow?"

Apparently, he was ignoring the ringing phone.

"Train."

"I'll fly you back." He paused. "If you want."

She blinked.

The phone rang again. Still, Bob ignored it.

"All right," she said on an exhale. "That would be fine—if it's not too much trouble. You have a lot going on."

"It's no trouble," he said without hesitation.

The phone stopped ringing, and the silence seemed to breathe between them. As far as Nancy knew, the man really didn't have time to fly her back to New York, but she wasn't the mistress of his schedule. What was the harm in accepting? It would save her a lot of time . . . "I'll accept. Flying is always preferable to any land transportation."

The edge of his mouth lifted. "Agreed."

The ringing phone started up again; the caller was sure persistent.

Nancy waved a hand toward the desk. "Get back to work, Bob. You've got customers."

He smiled that smile she decided she liked very much, and this time, she smiled back. Then she forced herself to turn and walk away. The phone was still ringing when she exited the hallway. Was Bob going to keep staring after her and ignore his job?

She couldn't worry about his work ethic right now because she, at least, would be doing *her* job—and doing it well. She planned on going full time as soon as she completed the secretarial course. She'd have to break the news to her parents and Uncle Thomas. She'd find a place in Boston to live. And that all seemed even more appealing since, evidently, Mr. Love wasn't that cranky after all.

Nancy enjoyed the surprise on the next customers' faces when she introduced herself as their charter pilot. Their excitement was contagious, but best of all, she was getting paid to fly. The rest of the day and the next morning went by quickly, and before she knew it, she found Bob waiting for her upon her return to East Boston after her final charter of the afternoon. He stood at the side of the hangar, leaning against the outer wall, the auburn of his hair glinting gold in the sunlight.

He wasn't wearing a flight suit, which made her wonder which plane they were taking. In fact, he looked rather nice, in a button-down shirt and dark tie, even handsome, if she were to admit it to herself.

She should probably change out of her breeches, but she didn't know if there'd be time. Bob might have to fly back to Boston in the dark as it was.

"How'd it go?" he asked as she approached.

"Great." Why did she suddenly feel breathless? "Talked up the Waco the entire time, and they're calling you tomorrow."

The two customers she'd ferried were railroad executives. Kind of ironic that they'd buy a plane.

"Excellent," Bob acknowledged. He hadn't moved from his position. So maybe there wasn't any hurry?

Beyond him, all was silent in the hangar. Not surprising. Bob had told her the mechanics usually had Sundays off unless there was an emergency. But it was still surreal to have the airfield and the hangar so empty. It was just the pair of them, standing in the middle of the deserted airfield.

"Which plane are we taking?" Nancy asked.

"The cabin."

Nancy looked toward the Waco cabin plane. She'd just flown it, and it was the nicest one they owned. She was surprised Bob didn't want to take something smaller to save on fuel. "If you're sure?"

"I'm sure. How soon can you be ready?"

Oh, that. "I don't have to change. I'll grab my bag from your office." Bob had told her to keep her things in the office after she'd packed this morning at her rented motel room and arrived by bus. He'd insisted on paying for the motel and the bus, and she hadn't turned him down.

Which told her that Bob Love wasn't roughing many things in this nationwide Depression. Yes, he was a hard worker, yet . . .

"That reminds me." He straightened from the wall. "I want to run something past you in my office."

"All right." Nancy walked with him through the hangar and into the corridor. For some reason, her pulse jumped, knowing she and Bob were alone. Together.

She had no idea what he wanted to run past her, but she hadn't expected to see several sheets of a sketched diagram of a plane.

"What's all this?" Nancy asked.

Bob rotated the pages to face them. "We're calling it a Staggerwing."

"We?"

"I'm working with Beechcraft on a new design."

She rested her palms on the desk and scanned the design. "You're designing a plane?"

He gave a short laugh. "Trying to. There's a ways to go, but Walter and his wife, Olive Ann, have agreed to add the Jacobs 225-horsepower engine."

"My golly." Nancy stared at the design. "Beechcraft is a major aviation company. How did you connect with them?"

"The general sales manager, Bill Ong, and I go back a ways. I might be a university dropout, but I did learn a few things."

She lifted her gaze to meet his. "Like how to design a plane?"

"Like how to not give up on my vision."

His answer was so serious, his gaze so intense, that Nancy felt something in her heart shift. This man was following his dreams. He was making it happen. Yes, he had to cobble multiple ventures together, but it was all connected. She admired him for that—truly admired him.

"I guess MIT wasn't a complete waste," she mused. "You're kind of remarkable, Mr. Love."

His eyes searched hers for a long moment, then finally, he said quietly, "I think that's the nicest thing you've ever said to me, Miss Harkness."

She straightened from the desk and moved back a step. "Well, don't get used to it. My brother says I'm bossy."

Bob's smile appeared. "I don't mind bossy."

Nancy ignored how his smile was becoming more and more charming each time she saw it. She picked up her bag, but Bob reached around her to grasp the handle. "I've got it."

So, she let him carry her bag to the Waco.

# CHAPTER TWELVE

"The [Bendix] race was, at best, a hard one, even when the skies were clear and smooth. More often than not, the weather was not so good and then it became an exceedingly grueling contest. Always, there were keen disappointments for pilots like me. Oftentimes they were heartbreaking."

—JACQUELINE COCHRAN, 1934

*May 1934—New York City*

"What's Bob Love like?" Susie asked as she pinned up her blonde curls, facing the mirror in the boxlike bathroom of their apartment.

Susie, Tommy, and Nancy were all getting ready to go out on the town. Their time together was winding down with the approaching summer. Nancy was grateful they'd decided to get out of their apartment and hopefully shake the gloom she'd felt. The founder of the Katharine Gibbs Secretarial School had died on May 9, and the program would continue under the direction of her youngest son, Gordon, and his wife.

"Are you going to tell us about this man?" Susie pressed.

"He's a bit hard to figure out, to be honest." Nancy leaned forward to peer into the corner of the mirror and apply her lipstick. Raspberry red.

Tommy materialized in the doorway, wearing a yellow dress with a white collar, belted at the waist, and sporting short, cuffed sleeves. The yellow of the dress brightened the red tones of her hair. "If you're trying to figure out a man, that means you're interested." She turned. "Can you zip me up?"

Nancy obliged and zipped up the back of Tommy's dress.

"Bob's my *employer*, ladies. Nothing more." Nancy met both of her roommates' gazes in the mirror but couldn't keep her smile hidden from them.

Tommy leaned against the doorframe and grinned. "And he's single, midtwenties, has a fledgling career, comes from wealth—"

Nancy swatted Tommy with a pair of white gloves. "All my friends at Vassar came from wealth. It doesn't impress me. In fact, it *un*-impresses me."

Tommy wrinkled her nose. "Is that a word?"

"Do you want to be impressed?" Susie cut in, tying her bow at the neckline of her red-and-white print dress.

"I think she does," Tommy said in a singsong voice as her eyebrows bounced.

"No comment." Nancy moved out of the now-too-crowded bathroom. "I'll wait for you gossips outside. Need to clear my head."

Her roommates laughed as she made good on her word and headed to the front door. It was a warm spring night in New York, and at the adjacent apartment, there seemed to be quite the party going on. The french doors to the patio stood wide open, and people either lounged at a couple of small tables or milled about, beers in hand. Henry Wilder's father owned a brewery, and even though their pilot friends could barely afford dinner, there was always plenty of free beer. With the prohibition laws finally lifted, parties didn't have to be sequestered to underground speakeasies anymore.

Speaking of Henry—he sat at the table with three other girls. He was certainly a flirt with everyone, which meant Nancy didn't take any of his compliments to heart.

"Nancy, is that you? Come on over."

She waved him off. "Not tonight. Plans with the roommates."

Henry's easy smile appeared, and his brown eyes sparked. He stood and hopped over the low wall separating them.

"You're all gussied up," he said with appreciation. "Where're you headed?"

"Not sure yet," Nancy said. "We'll know when we get there."

Henry was leaning a bit closer than she cared for, and she wondered how many beers he'd had.

"You're always so composed, Harkness," he drawled. "In the cockpit and out of it. Nothing ruffles you. A woman who can set a man like Bob Love to straights is a wonder indeed."

She had no idea what he was talking about. "Trying to butter me up for something, Wilder?"

He laughed, then swayed.

"You should sit down, Henry," she said, pressing a finger against his chest. "Wouldn't want to trip on something."

Henry obeyed and perched on the short wall. "See? You're always so wise. You say it like it is. Bob says you're smarter than any of the male pilots he's worked with."

Nancy shouldn't let herself take the compliment personally, but she couldn't help the warmth that simmered. "He did? When did he say that?"

"He called me up the other day."

Well, this was news to Nancy. Although it wasn't like she was having daily conversations with Henry Wilder anyway. Between cramming in her classes and working in Boston the last few weekends, tonight was the first time she'd been social in a while.

"What else did he say?" Nancy couldn't help but ask. Maybe Henry would forget this conversation by morning anyhow.

"Oh, he didn't *say* much . . . No, it was more like he was asking *me* questions about you, and I was doing all the talking."

Nancy didn't know if she should be pleased or nervous. What could Bob Love possibly be asking questions about? He knew the basics about her qualifications. He'd made it a habit of picking her up in New York, then flying her to Boston to work for the weekend, and later returning her by plane. Sometimes he piloted; sometimes she did.

"Well, he asked if you were going steady with anyone," Henry continued casually, though it rocked through her. "I said I wouldn't call any of your beaux *steady*—but you're always surrounded by men who want to pay for your dinner."

"That's an exaggeration, Henry." Nancy set her hands on her hips, her mind reeling at such a question from Bob Love. He could have asked her himself. So why hadn't he? And why did he want to know in the first place? She tamped down the fluttering in her chest. "I'm with my room-mates most of the time, and our male friends insist on paying, that's all. You're making it sound like I'm dating hordes of men." Dinner paid for was better than tomato soup, of course.

She wanted to ask Henry more questions, but Tommy and Susie came out of the apartment.

"Oh, maybe we should stay here with Henry." Susie flashed him a smile.

Henry held out his hand. "You can sit by me, doll."

"No, we're leaving. And you need to sober up." Nancy didn't want Henry to pick up the conversation they'd been having. If he had more to tell her about Bob Love, she wanted to hear it in private, not surrounded by her nosy friends.

She linked arms with Tommy and Susie, propelling them toward the street bathed in twilight. They headed along the sidewalk together, waving when Henry called after them.

"He's smitten with you, Nancy," Tommy said.

"Hardly." She cut a glance toward Susie, who was biting her lip. If Nancy were to guess, Susie had a small crush on Henry Wilder herself. "Susie's the one he invited to stay."

"True. What about it, Susie?"

Susie waved her hand in a flourish. "He'll have to follow me to New Jersey. I hate New York in the summer. My parents will be staying at Martha's Vineyard, and not even a man could tempt me to remain here."

Both Nancy and Tommy laughed.

"No one can ever hate New York City," Tommy gushed. "It's the city of speakeasies, skyscrapers, and the Yankees."

Susie only smiled, and after they grabbed dinner at a cozy diner none of them could really afford, Tommy said, "Let's go to the airfield and watch the sun rise."

Sunrise was still a whole night away, but it was one of Nancy's favor-ite things to do, sitting on the grassy knoll at the edge of Roosevelt Field.

They'd watch the final planes coming in, then wait for the sun to rise as the sky shifted from black to gray to violet.

The evening had yet to cool off, holding on to the afternoon heat in a tight-fisted grip, so they spread out their sweaters on the short, spiky grass and lay back, gazing up at the hopeful moon and the litter of stars.

"Anyone bring cigarettes?" Susie asked when their conversation slowed.

"Me." Tommy lit one up and passed it down the line.

After taking a drag, Nancy said, "If I fall asleep, make sure you wake me at dawn."

"No one's falling asleep," Susie insisted. "We're going to discuss our hopes and dreams and futures."

They all laughed.

"And how someday we'll purchase our own airplanes and fly whenever and wherever we please." Tommy puffed out another plume of smoke, and it lazily floated upward before dissipating into the black of night.

"Hear, hear," Nancy said, thinking of Bob and how he already had that privilege.

Susie had been right. They stayed awake all night talking about everything and nothing.

But when the rosy hues of dawn cracked the sky, Nancy felt reluctant to move and break up the magic of the timeless atmosphere. "I need to get home, clean up, then get to class," she mumbled. "I don't know about you girls, but I'll be taking a nap this afternoon, so keep things quiet."

"I'm calling in sick to the dress shop." Susie stood, stifled a yawn, and attempted to brush the wrinkles out of her skirt. "They can survive a day without me."

Nancy honestly wasn't sure why Susie worked in a dress shop. She loved clothing, sure, but her family was well-to-do. Nancy guessed it to be a power play between Susie and her parents. They'd said they wouldn't pay for flying if she wasn't holding a job. Nancy had offered to talk to Bob about Susie needing a job in flying, but she'd waved off the suggestion.

"I fly for fun," Susie had declared, "not work."

So, Nancy had left it at that.

When they made it back to their apartment, the next-door party was long over. Nancy headed to class, and by the time she was home in the early afternoon, she felt dead on her feet.

Still, she wouldn't trade the night out with her friends for extra sleep. When she climbed onto her bed and closed her eyes, she let her mind drift. Moments later, the ringing of a phone awakened her. She ignored the sound and tried to fall asleep again when the phone started up a second round.

"Someone answer the phone," she called, but no one answered back.

She cracked her eyes open. The setting sun had filled her room with a burnished glow. She'd fallen asleep and had slept much longer than she'd planned. Moving off the bed, she headed into the kitchen, half in a daze. The phone started ringing a third time.

"This better be important," she said into the receiver.

The person on the other end of the line must have been stunned into silence because no one said a word.

"Hello?" she asked, about a half second from hanging up, then leaving the phone off the hook.

"Miss Harkness?" a man's voice rumbled across the line.

Her back stiffened. It was *him*. "Mr. Love?"

"Yes. How are you?"

*How am I?* What employer calls to ask that? And why was Bob Love calling her in the first place? Was there bad news about his airport? Was he firing her? "Why are you calling? I'm fine, by the way."

She heard his chuckle all the way from Boston. He wouldn't be laughing if he were calling with bad news, right?

"Always direct."

"Bob, I mean, Mr. Love, I just woke up from a nap, and I'm a bit foggy-brained. It would be best if you got right to the point."

He didn't laugh a second time, but she swore she heard the smile in his voice when he asked, "Why were you asleep? It's not even dinnertime."

She looked toward the windows. Dinnertime wasn't the same for everyone. "Maybe I had my dinner, and I'm going to bed early."

"You said it was nap."

"I did."

He was still smiling—she'd bet on it. "You haven't answered my question. Now you're making me worried that you're going to fire me."

"No, I'm not going to fire you." He was definitely amused.

Relief shot through her, but she was only more curious now. Or maybe it was nerves. Why was he calling her? He hadn't called before, even though he'd written all her contact information.

"I wondered if you have dinner plans tomorrow night," Bob asked. "I'm coming to New York."

This was a surprise. Nancy leaned against the kitchen counter. "But tomorrow is Thursday."

"Yes, it *is* a Thursday."

Nancy's cheeks felt hot. "You're flying in a day early?"

"Correct, and I wondered if you'd like to go to dinner."

At his airport, they'd shared some random meals together, but this felt more . . . more like an official date. Was he asking her on a date, or did he just need someone to have dinner with before he . . . what? "I don't understand. Do you want me to meet some of your aviation friends?"

She heard his sigh on the phone.

"Not unless we happen to run into someone. You pick the restaurant. I'll pick you up. We'll have dinner and talk. You know, like men and women frequently do on a night out?"

Nancy's pulse was skipping all over the place, as if it couldn't decide whether to speed up or slow down or give her a heart attack right there. "Is this a date, Mr. Love?"

"I believe it is. Well, it would be if you agree."

She drew in a breath, then released it. Was there really any harm in saying yes? "Will my reply affect my employment status?"

"No, Nancy. I'd never . . ." He cleared his throat, and she imagined a flush creeping up his neck. "I'm a man of integrity, or at least, I try to be. I'd like to take you out for dinner tomorrow night. On a date." He paused. "I must admit that I've never had this much pushback before from a woman over a dinner invitation."

Did she really need to overanalyze this? It was dinner. Plain and simple. "Okay."

"Okay?" His voice sounded incredulous. "Okay, you'll go?"

"Yes." By the time Nancy hung up, she was the one with a flushed neck. She knew one thing—she wouldn't be going back to sleep anytime soon. She had a date to plan for.

# CHAPTER THIRTEEN

"The aeronautics branch of the US Department of Commerce had strict physical standards that every pilot needed to meet to be licensed. An aviator had to have strong eyes, functioning eardrums, good balance, and a healthy heart. Unrepaired harelips and stuttering speech could be cause for disqualification, as could a history of asthma or pneumonia."

—*FLY GIRLS* BY KEITH O'BRIEN

*May 1934—New York City*

When a wax-shined car slowed in front of the apartment complex, Nancy guessed it was Bob. There weren't any other cars slowing and stopping in front of her place. She'd been ready for a while, but that didn't mean she'd rush out to greet him.

No, she watched Bob climb out of the car and walk around it. From her place at the edge of the window, she observed him as an outsider might. Her first impression had been of a pompous and irritating man covered in grease stains, blustering rudely, his red hair at odds.

But the man walking up to her place wore a light-gray suit, dark-colored tie, polished shoes, hair combed neatly. His keys in his hand, he looked like a man on a mission. With intentions for something . . . or someone.

"Is that him?" Susie whispered right next to Nancy's ear.

Nancy nearly jumped a foot. "You startled me."

"Spying on your man?" Tommy joined in.

Three grown women crowded at the window, watching Bob walk toward their apartment, was quite ridiculous. Nancy huffed and moved away as a knock sounded at the door.

"You're not going to hide and make him wait ten minutes?" Susie asked, her eyes comically wide.

"Why should I?" Nancy ignored her roommates' chortles and opened the door.

Yes, her pulse might be doing acrobatics, but this was just Bob Love. Her employer. A man she'd been around plenty. So what if he was slicked up for a dinner date? She was wearing an emerald-green dress with short puff sleeves and a pleated bodice. Maybe she'd paid some extra careful attention to putting on makeup. It was more for her than for him. He'd seen her with raccoon eyes from goggles and plastered hair from helmets.

"You made it." Did her voice sound breathy?

Bob Love at her doorstep was a new experience. His eyes were bluer, and he seemed taller somehow, more than his usual five-inch advantage. Maybe because he wasn't hunched over a plane's engine or sitting at his desk, surrounded by crumpled papers. "Good afternoon, Miss Harkness."

"It's evening."

"So it is." Then he smiled.

Before she could let herself bask in that smile, she turned toward her roommates, who were conspicuously hovering a few feet away. "Uh, Mr. Love, this is Susie and Tommy. My roommates."

"Great to meet you." He stepped forward and shook each of their hands as if it were the most natural thing in the world to politely greet them.

Why was *their* first meeting with him so cordial?

She'd give him a hard time about that later . . .

Susie was all friendliness, and Tommy wore a calculated smirk on her face.

"Nancy told us all about Inter City, Mr. Love," Susie said in a leading tone. "Very impressive. I might take lessons from you if Boston were more conveniently located."

"To New York City?"

"Yes, well . . ." Susie giggled. "I guess Boston wouldn't be Boston if it were New York City."

To Bob's credit, his eyebrows only rose a tad, although Nancy could only imagine what he was thinking. And why was Susie being so . . . ridiculous?

"Tell us about the planes you have available," Tommy cut in, her maddening singsong voice making an appearance. "Did Nancy tell you I've worked on a plane with Jacqueline Cochran? Do you know her?"

"I know of Miss Cochran," Bob said. "As for the planes we have at Inter City, they include Waco cabin planes, Monocoupes, Fairchilds, and Kinner-powered Fleets."

"Very nice." Tommy tilted her head, looking a little too speculative for Nancy's taste. "Very impressive. I'll bet you don't have trouble getting flight students—"

"I'm ready to go," Nancy cut in.

Bob looked at her. Maybe with a bit of relief? "Great." He stepped aside and motioned for her to walk out. "Nice to meet you, ladies."

"Nice to meet you as well," Susie said sweetly, echoed by Tommy.

Nancy narrowed her gaze at her roommates before heading outside. As she walked ahead of Bob to the car, she knew her friends were watching every move from the window.

"Here we are." Bob reached around her and opened the passenger door of the Cadillac.

"Here we are." Nancy glanced at him before sliding inside. Not surprisingly, his eyes were filled with amusement. She might have paid a dollar or two to know his thoughts. "This your car?"

"Yes, one of them."

She tried not to act surprised. Or be impressed. Because she *wasn't* impressed. Just because his family was wealthy didn't mean that extended to the whole family. But it sure had given Bob a leg up in life, at least from her perspective. Although, it was clear the man was his own entrepreneur.

As she watched him walk around the car, she realized she knew little of his family. Everything she'd heard had come from Henry, or she'd put two and two together. She didn't know what Bob's intentions were for this "date," but *her* intentions were to find out more about his background. Who he really was beneath all his shifting moods, intense gazes, and hard-nosed decisions.

When he climbed in, he didn't start the car right away. Instead, he let the moment stretch between them. "How are you?"

"Fine."

He nodded, his eyes searching her face. Was he looking for something? "That's good news."

"Are you going to start the car?" she asked, not liking the fluster building inside of her. "You know we're being spied on."

His smile was slow, and she had to glance away because her stomach was doing flips off a high dive.

Finally, he started the motor. "Where to, Miss Harkness?"

"You can call me Nancy, you know."

"Does that mean you'll call me Bob?" He pulled out onto the street after a quick check for traffic.

She cut a glance at him. His smile was still in place. "You're my employer, so that's entirely up to you."

"I think it's appropriate since we are going out to dinner." He wasn't a hesitant driver, of course, and easily steered them through traffic.

"On a date?"

"On a date," he confirmed.

Nancy couldn't stop herself, and she laughed.

Bob grinned, and she felt inordinately pleased for some reason. But she shouldn't be noticing how his left hand guided the steering wheel and his right hand rested loosely on the seat, not far from her. "Do I need to apologize for my roommates?"

He looked over at her as he approached the next corner. "You should never apologize for someone else's behavior."

"Only one's own?"

His mouth turned up in a smirk. "Correct. You've told me a few things about your roommates, so it was nice to finally meet them."

Nancy had chatted about her roommates, she supposed, but only because they were also pilots. "You know, Henry told me you asked him questions about *me*. What was that all about?"

Bob sped up and pulled around a car going much slower than they were. She didn't say anything, but she'd commented plenty on his flying when she thought he was going too fast or not decelerating enough before landing. Apparently, his driving was similar to his flying.

"Ah. Good old Henry," Bob mused, unfazed by his daring traffic move. "Not too great about keeping things confidential. I didn't want to put you on the spot, so I asked Henry about your dating life to make sure I wasn't stepping on another fellow's toes."

Speaking of toes, Nancy was warming up from head to toe. That was when she noticed they were approaching the next corner a little fast. When was he going to brake? "Slow down, and turn up there," she said. "We're going to that diner."

"A diner?" He was clearly surprised, and for a moment, she thought he might argue. He was dressed to walk into a top-scale New York restaurant, but he slowed and pulled into the parking lot.

They headed into the diner, and the waitress led them to one of the booths.

"This is cozy," Bob commented, glancing around at the white walls full of framed photos of Yankee baseball players.

"We come here a lot—well, after our paydays. Usually, we're eating cans of soup in between."

"Not the actual cans, though, right?" he teased. "Just the contents inside . . ."

"Depends on how hungry we are."

He laughed. "Tell you what, tomorrow I'll pick the place we eat."

"Tomorrow? That's a bit presumptuous, Mr. Love."

A heartbeat passed. "Is it?"

They locked gazes for a moment, then she shrugged. "I won't turn down a free meal."

His smile was quick. He'd clearly taken no offense to her glib comment. "Good thing I'm paying."

Nancy's cheeks were going to flush red at any moment, so she picked up the menu and pretended to browse, even though she knew what she was going to order.

"Tell me about your family," Bob said casually after the waitress had taken their orders and delivered drinks.

"You know the basics." She took a sip of water from her glass. "Henry said he filled you in."

"Touché." Bob reached for his own glass. "I want to hear from you. Henry is a very poor substitute."

"It's all rather boring," she hedged. "At least, until I started flying— that's when I started waking up in the morning eager for the day to begin. And only if the day included a lesson somewhere, of course."

"Of course."

Nancy decided that Bob was easy to talk to. He listened closely and asked plenty of questions. Their meal came and went, and they ordered more drinks. By the time Nancy was telling him about when she and her brother had buzzed the boys' prep school, they had desserts in front of them.

She couldn't remember the last time she'd ordered dessert with a restaurant meal.

"So, your brother left you to face the angry headmistress by yourself?"

"Yes, that was Robert Harkness for you. Always stirring up a storm, then slipping away."

Bob turned his dessert spoon back and forth. He had yet to try the ice cream. "Henry told me a little bit about your brother. I'm sorry he died."

Talking about her brother tonight had made her miss him all the more fiercely. She looked down with a hard blink. "He left a wife and two little boys," she said in a quiet voice. "He was only twenty-five but was always a daredevil. Couldn't resist a race or challenge."

"It sounds like he lived a full life, on his terms, even though it was cut short." Bob set his spoon down, ice cream still untouched. "Some people never achieve their dreams. They wake up one day and discover they've lived decades without finding joy."

"Yes." She hadn't thought of it like that before, and it was strangely comforting. Her brother had always gone after his passions, taking them to the extreme sometimes but finding joy in every corner of his life. "My parents also lost two little girls at birth—born before either of us—Gertrude and Hanna."

"Sorry to hear that," Bob said, subdued. "When I was ten years old, my older brother, John, died."

Nancy blinked. "Oh, I didn't know that."

"He was born an invalid," Bob continued, his voice dropping low. "Had a lot of health problems, so I guess it wasn't a big shock, like your brother's unexpected death. John was in his early twenties."

She tried to imagine how it would be to have a sibling who was an invalid. The constant worry. The never-ending medical care. "Still, I'm sure it devastated everyone."

"Yes."

Nancy reached over and grasped his hand. "I'm really sorry, Bob. I know how big that hole can be."

He looked at her hand on his, then he turned his hand over and linked their fingers.

She didn't see it as romantic though—they were sharing their similar grief—so, then, why was her heart banging about? After a moment, she pulled her hand away, and he released it easily.

"What about other siblings?" she asked.

Bob's face shifted into something lighter. "Ah, my older sister, Margaret. She's eight years older than me, but she acts like my mother most of the time."

"She sounds delightfully bossy."

"Yes, she was, and still is." Bob finally took a bite of his half-melted ice cream. "She was pretty much my full-time nurse when I was about seven and contracted polio soon after my brother's death."

Nancy brought a hand to her mouth, staring at Bob. His life had not been easy. Her preconceived judgments of a privileged childhood took a hard right turn. Could wealth really soften the blow of a lost brother and a dire case of polio? This man had many more layers than she'd first thought. "Oh no, that must have been terrible."

He gave a small nod of acknowledgment. "It was compounded because the day before I found out I had polio, our chauffeur's son died from it."

She shook her head, trying to imagine so many tragedies at the same time. "But you recovered?"

"Due to Margaret's constant care. That, and my dad convincing a doctor to experiment and use me as a lab rat."

"What? How?"

Bob's shrug was nonchalant. "I guess there were experiments that were comprised of taking blood from polio survivors and injecting that serum into someone currently suffering polio."

"And . . . they injected serum into you?"

"Correct. Right into my spine. Paralyzed me for a while."

"Bob . . . I can't imagine."

The corners of his mouth curved upward, but the smile didn't reach his eyes. "Rough time all the way around. But . . . I recovered fully. I only limp when I've had an exhausting day. Modern medicine is a miracle, isn't it?"

Nancy exhaled slowly. "It is, yet that's still a lot to take in."

He leaned back in his chair, arms folded. "Sorry about the heavy stuff. My sister likes to remind me from time to time that I owe her my life—all that babying she did."

The things he'd confessed were remarkable, truly remarkable. "She sounds like the best sister, even if she wants all the accolades. I think she deserves them." Nancy smiled. "I always wished I had a sister, but I guess nosy roommates will have to do."

Bob released a chuckle, and Nancy was grateful the seriousness of the conversation had eased.

"Well, Margaret would be happy to meet you anytime."

Nancy didn't know what she thought of that comment. Had he told his sister about her—or told his *parents*?

"Henry told me a little about that accident you were in with John Miller—and how you got the gray streak in your hair."

Nancy absently touched the part of her hair that persistently stayed gray. "Yes, it's quite the thing. I've stumped all doctors." Bob smiled. She quite liked his smile. "Poor John, he ended up with pretty good scars. So, I guess we both have reminders."

"Well, I'm glad you both pulled through."

She nodded, then took a sip of the new glass of water the waitress had brought. How long had they been at the diner anyway? Darkness had fallen, and many customers had come and gone.

It seemed that Bob noticed the same thing at the same moment. His gaze moved to the dark windows, then back to her. "Do you have to get home right away, or are you interested in a walk about town?"

She didn't have to get home right away, but he'd given her the perfect out. She didn't want an out though. Bob had intrigued her tonight, more than she'd thought possible. She realized she wasn't quite ready for their date to end. "I'd love to take a walk."

# CHAPTER FOURTEEN

"The attraction of women to aviation was a strong one, for no activity better symbolized the freedom and power which was lacking in their daily lives. As pilots women experienced feelings of strength, mastery, and confidence which, particularly at a time when Victorian norms still rendered all strenuous effort and most public activity by women suspect, seemed delicious indeed."

—JOSEPH J. CORN, *THE WINGED GOSPEL*

*May 1934—New York City*

Nancy awakened much earlier than the singing sparrows that loved their apartment building, which gave her uninterrupted silence to go over the many conversations she'd had with Bob the night before. His childhood had been so different from hers. His family had followed the old British tradition of sending their son away to boarding school. At the age of eight.

She imagined a small, redheaded boy clinging to his mother's hand as she'd walked him into the St. Paul's boarding school in New York City.

"I cried myself to sleep for a year and half," Bob had told her.

Nancy's eyes had budded with tears, but she didn't think Bob had noticed. They'd been walking along one of the avenues, with only the benevolent moon and glittering stars to light the way. Nancy had quickly blinked back the tears and listened as he'd told her about his next school—Lawrenceville Prep, in New Jersey. That was followed by entering Princeton in 1927.

Nancy turned over in her bed and gazed out the window. She'd left the drapes open, and the pale gray of the sky had changed to lavender.

She'd asked Bob when he'd first flown, and he'd known the exact date. "April 10, 1929. My first flight was only twenty minutes, but I was hooked."

Nancy had laughed because she could relate. She'd told him about the barnstormer and borrowing money from her brother.

"Stunts might have scared me off," Bob had commented.

"Probably not."

"Probably not," he'd agreed. "I'm impressed you soloed so fast. Took me a couple of weeks. It was April 29, and I had seven hours of dual instruction in a 1928 OX-5 American Eagle."

As the sky lightened beyond her window and the sparrows began their song, Nancy imagined a young, gangly Bob Love earning his pilot's license out of Roosevelt Field. The same airfield she'd spent most of her time at in New York before he'd hired her. And the same airfield from which Charles Lindbergh had begun his famous transatlantic flight.

Aviation had taken over Bob's heart and mind, just like hers, and he'd said, "It was almost four years to the day when I flew for the first time that I opened Inter City."

"In April 1933?" she'd clarified, impressed. "You don't waste much time, Mr. Love."

He'd replied with a wink. "I don't like wasting time, Miss Harkness."

She'd certainly learned that upon her very first meeting with him. Bob Love wasn't late, and he didn't waste time, so she assumed that meant their date last night had been time well-spent?

She wouldn't ask him, of course. But that also reminded her that he'd be at her place in an hour. He was picking her up, and they'd fly back to Boston together to work the rest of the weekend. Nancy climbed out of bed. She planned to be gone before her roommates awakened. They'd surely pester her with questions, and she kind of relished having her date and all the things they'd said kept between the two of them for now.

Her plan was thwarted, though, because when she was cutting up a banana to put on toast for breakfast, Susie came into the kitchen, yawning.

"Oh, you were out late," Susie said, her voice raspy with sleep.

"Not that late," Nancy said. "Bob got me home before midnight."

"Of course he did," Susie teased. "Gentleman and all."

Nancy smashed the banana onto her toast.

"I don't know how you can stand that stuff." Susie pulled a jar of orange juice from the icebox and filled two glasses.

Nancy shrugged and swallowed down some orange juice Susie had handed her.

Susie carried her juice to the window, where she paused, the cup poised in her hand. "Well, blow my wig. There's a limousine in front of our building."

"What?" Nancy crossed to the window. Sure enough, parked at the curb sat a limo, and climbing out of the rear door was Bob Love.

He wasn't wearing a suit this time, but he had on khaki pants and a flight jacket. And he'd arrived early.

"Tommy, get in here," Susie called. "You've got to see this."

"Hush," Nancy said. "Bob doesn't need to be gawked at by you girls again. And don't say a word about the limo."

Nancy might be ordering her roommate around, but she was curious herself. Did Bob take limos frequently? She remembered him talking about a chauffeur's son in his childhood.

She'd reached the door by the time he knocked, so she opened it a crack. The sun had peeked over the horizon behind him, making everything a burnished gold. Bob's collar stood open, which meant he had no plans for a tie. He might not be as dressed up as last night, but his casualness was deceptive. She knew enough about him now to know that his button-down shirt and pants were top quality.

"Can you give me a minute and also wait outside?" she asked.

"I'm early, I guess."

"One minute." She shut the door and was met by a grinning Susie.

Tommy appeared from the hallway, her eyes half open. "What's going on?"

"There's a limo outside," Susie said. "That's what's going on."

"Don't open the door," Nancy told Tommy as she rushed to the front window.

"Why can't I open the door?" Tommy asked.

Nancy ignored her roommates as she gathered her bag and did a double-check of her appearance in the bathroom mirror. She already wore her breeches and flight jacket, and her bag contained extra clothing to change into later, after work at Inter City.

When she reached the front room again, her roommates were making no secret of openly gazing out the window at the limousine.

"Must have been a great date last night," Tommy commented dryly.

"It was fine."

Susie and Tommy both raised their brows, waiting for more.

Nancy gave an evasive shrug. "See you in a few days. I'll fill you in then."

"Holding you to it," Tommy said with a wry smile.

Nancy tugged the front door open and stepped out into the growing morning light. "Sorry about that."

Bob stood by the low wall, his arms folded as he surveyed the meager attempts of Susie's flowering plants. "Nothing to worry about," he said easily, lifting his blue gaze. "I was early. I hope I didn't rush you."

"No, I was ready, mostly. Just didn't expect my roommates to be awake and peppering me with questions."

Bob's mouth lifted into a half-smile, and he reached for her bag. His hand brushed hers, and she relinquished the bag.

"Questions about what?" he asked.

Was he a morning person or something? He must be, because his morning voice was normal, cheerful, even. No tired lines about his eyes— his baby blues as clear as the morning sky.

"About our date."

"Ah." He chuckled, a warm sound that seemed to brush against her skin.

As they approached the limousine, the driver opened his door and stepped out.

"I've got it, Richard," Bob called to him. "Nancy, this is Richard."

"Hello," she told the wiry man with a mustache and a black chauffeur cap. She guessed him to be in his fifties.

"Good morning, Miss Harkness. Nice to meet you."

Bob popped the trunk of the limo and set her bag inside, then closed it. Next, he opened the rear door for her.

She slid inside, immediately enveloped in the scent of leather and cigars. She knew Bob didn't smoke, but maybe the chauffeur did, or Bob's father?

Bob climbed in on the other side, and Richard pulled away from the curb.

"How are you?" Bob asked, turning to look at her.

She should be used to his questions, but this morning, it felt different. He wasn't being formal or polite. The sincerity of his words reached across the space between them.

"I'm a little surprised you showed up in a limo, but maybe I shouldn't be? I don't know what I expected, but it wasn't this."

His eyes glimmered with amusement. "Should I have warned you?"

"I made a good recovery."

"It's the family car, and I didn't want to leave my car at the airport for someone else to have to pick up."

"Makes sense." Nancy smirked.

"What?"

"It's just . . . you know, a limousine. And I'm a two-bit pilot trying to earn a few bucks because I can't hack it in secretarial school. Which is nothing compared to Princeton or MIT or—"

Bob's hand settled over hers, and she stopped all talk then.

"You're not a two-bit anything, Nancy. You have the potential to be one of the finest pilots I've ever known. We all have to work our way up the chain—you're just figuring out which chain that is."

Nancy's heart had lodged itself in her throat. And her pulse zoomed about like a trapped hummingbird. She studied his hand over hers—the light freckles and small tufts of pale-gold hair, but mostly, she noticed the strength and capability of his fingers. "Potential?"

"You're a fine pilot now, but there's a lot of aircraft out there to progress on. Women are making great strides in the industry."

"I'm no Amelia Earhart."

He barked a laugh. "I think she's one of a kind. But believe me, Nancy, you're swell just the way you are."

"Are you always this complimentary in the morning?" she asked.

Bob pretended to think about it for a moment, and laughter stirred inside Nancy. His hand remained on hers, too, and she didn't mind in the least.

"I think I am, actually," he said, as if this were the first time he'd ever considered it. "It's too early for something to go wrong, so I'm not in a sour mood . . . yet."

Nancy did laugh then, and Bob smiled, watching her. Which only made her heart do somersaults.

"Is this okay?" he asked in a quiet voice, his hand gently squeezing hers.

She knew he referred to his hand on hers, and surprisingly, it was okay. Yet she wasn't sure what it all meant—to him. Or what it should mean—to her. For a second, her words wouldn't come, then she finally said, "I think so."

His brows rose. "That's a start, I suppose."

She gave him a half-smile now. "Do you take all your employees out to dinner, followed by limo rides at dawn?"

His gaze was more sincere than she'd ever seen it. "No, never."

His words tugged the breath from her chest, but she played down the emotions rocking through her. "Oh, that's good, I guess."

"Nancy . . . I like you. I'm sure you've concluded that by now."

Well, she couldn't help blushing now. "There have been signs, but I don't always pay attention to signs since I'm too busy trying to figure out when I can fly next."

His expression relaxed. "I think that's a good quality when it comes to other men . . . but with me, I'm hoping you understand that I want to get to know you more."

Nancy smirked. "Is that why you asked me so many questions last night? I thought you were a journalist on the side, trying to write an exposé."

"Not quite." His thumb moved over her fingers.

She shouldn't react with goose bumps, but she did. "I like you, too, Bob, most of the time. But I'm only twenty. Not interested in being tied down to anyone or anything."

He didn't seem taken aback. "*Most* of the time?"

Nancy shrugged. "You can be a pest, but in a good way, I suppose."

Bob shook his head, but he was smiling. "How about this, Miss Harkness . . . You come work for Inter City full time. We'll be around each other plenty. You can decide how tied down you want to be."

Inside, her heart drummed. "I think I can support that plan."

He tugged her hand toward him and rested both of their hands on his leg. "And by the way, I'm twenty-five."

"Henry told me."

"Good chap."

They were nearly to the airfield, and Nancy wondered what would happen when the chauffeur stopped the car. Would he see them holding hands? Or should she let go first?

"By the way, I'm in no hurry for anything," Bob said in a quieter voice. "I wouldn't ever want you to feel tied down."

That statement only elevated Bob's status in her eyes. She didn't know what her parents would think of a man like Bob Love, but the fact that it had even crossed her mind to introduce them told her something. She already knew if her brother were still around, the two men would get along.

# CHAPTER FIFTEEN

"Flying jobs for women pilots have always been scarce, and 1935 was no exception to the rule. . . . Phoebe Omlie and Amelia Earhart had been working on the Bureau of Air Commerce for two years or more endeavoring to talk them into hiring a few women pilots."

—LOUISE THADEN, *HIGH, WIDE, AND FRIGHTENED*

*September 1934—Houghton, Michigan*

Nancy shouldn't be nervous, but she was. Extremely. She was about to introduce Bob Love to her parents. She and Bob had been going steady all summer, yet she hadn't told her parents he was more than her employer. They might suspect things were more advanced since she'd asked them if she could bring him home to meet them.

"So, you've told your parents about me, right?" Bob asked as they taxied the runway in Houghton. They'd just flown in from Boston in one of the Waco cabin planes.

Nancy slugged his arm. "Of course they know about you. My mother's having you to dinner."

"But as your *boss* or as your *man*?"

Nancy made a move to slug his arm again, but he caught her hand. And grinned. He'd worn a suit, although he'd traded out the suit jacket for his flight jacket temporarily.

"If you don't want me giving them a rundown of our dinner dates," he said, "you should tell me what I'm allowed to say."

"As if you'd listen to me anyway."

"I always listen to you."

"That's pretty much a lie, Mr. Love."

Bob chuckled. "I've never lied to you, Miss Harkness. To clarify, I always *listen* to you, even if I don't always do as you say." He steered the plane toward the hangar. He'd piloted today because, in truth, Nancy's nerves were a jumbled mess. Whatever she did or did not say to her parents about Bob Love didn't matter; she knew her father would see through any pretense. Not only that, but she and Bob were also staying overnight, so there would be plenty of time for disaster to happen.

What that disaster might be, Nancy didn't know. "Fine. I'm going to tell them we're good friends, you're my employer, and we've gone on a few dates. All things that are true. You may or may not have to win them over. My father is the easygoing one. He'll even take payments in eggs and vegetables from the community for his job. My mother's a bit more fearsome. On a random evening, she can be found knitting argyle socks, reading a novel, or beating everyone in a Scrabble game. If they have questions, then they have questions, but if they hate you, I guess I'm searching for a job in Houghton."

Bob parked the plane next to the hangar. "You wouldn't dare."

She looked over at him. In the shade of the hangar, his eyes were a darker blue. "I would dare."

Fire leaped into his gaze. "You'd quit on me?"

She shrugged, tamping down a smile. "My parents' opinions are very important to me."

Bob powered down the plane but made no move to open the door. "You've told me enough stories that we both very well know you're more likely to ask for forgiveness than for permission."

Nancy let her smile escape.

"So . . ." Bob said slowly. "I think we should get it over with."

"Meeting my parents?"

"Kissing."

She stared at him, but his eyes were dead serious. The heat in her chest began to rise into her throat. "Kissing has nothing to do with any of this."

"It has everything to do with this," Bob countered. "To even say the word *quit* tells me that I haven't made things very clear between us. You don't know how I feel about you."

Nancy was definitely blushing if the heat climbing into her cheeks was any indication. "And kissing will clear that up?"

"I believe so."

Nancy didn't know if she should laugh or argue or jump out of the plane. She'd kissed boys a time or two, but never . . . a man. "I don't think that's a good idea."

He didn't argue. "Let me know if you change your mind."

He popped open his door, and Nancy grabbed his arm, her heart practically jumping out of her chest. "I've changed my mind."

His gaze cut to hers. "Already?"

She nodded.

The plane door had swung open, but he turned toward her. Leaning close, he slid a thumb along her jaw. "Are you sure?" he whispered.

"I'm sure. Let's not debate it anymore." They'd had more than one discussion about kissing, which was kind of ridiculous. Did it really need to be analyzed? But that was how Bob was: technical, analytical, and making sure she was with him every step of the way.

"I couldn't agree more." He closed the distance.

Her eyes slid shut as his lips touched hers. His mouth was soft yet firm, as if he already knew what he wanted. Or *who* he wanted. Goose bumps raced across her skin, and she let her mind push away all other questions, to focus completely on this man as she kissed him back.

Of course her first kiss with Bob Love would be on a plane. At least they weren't flying—well, her *heart* was flying. Before she could internally debate anything further, she grasped his shoulders and tugged him closer. Bob smiled against her mouth and didn't complain. For once.

When they drew apart, he said, "That was an excellent plan."

"I need to find a powder room." Nancy tried to catch her breath. "I think you messed up my hair."

"I can help," he said, reaching for her again.

She put a hand on his chest to stop him. "Don't you dare try."

Bob laughed, then raised both hands. "Fine." He climbed out of the plane and extended his hand to help her out.

She kept her gaze averted as she climbed out, because he was looking at her like he might kiss her again. Now that they were outside the plane, someone might see them.

After she corrected her appearance in the ladies' room, she exited to find Bob in conversation with one of the airport mechanics. She recognized him—Jimmy Hansen—with his black hair and dozens of freckles.

"Nancy, you're back." Jimmy turned his wide grin on her. "You're looking swell."

She guessed he would have hugged her, but his coveralls were stained with grease. He always did like to do a lot of mechanical work.

"Thanks, Jimmy. Great to see you. I'm here for a quick visit to see my parents."

Jimmy wiped his hands on an equally stained cloth. "I told Mr. Love here that I was your first flight instructor."

"That's right—and you were excellent."

"Ah, I don't know about that." Jimmy rubbed the back of his neck, smudging his skin. "We were two kids trying to figure it all out."

Nancy wouldn't have put it quite that way.

Jimmy appraised her, quite openly, in fact. He was a good guy but had always liked her more than she'd liked him.

She reached for Bob's hand. Maybe to send a statement, not only to Jimmy but to Bob as well. After all, the man had just thoroughly kissed her.

Bob's fingers linked with hers.

Jimmy's face flushed. The silent message had been received. "Tell the folks hello."

"Will do. Thanks, Jimmy. Nice to see you again."

"You too," Jimmy said, and she turned with Bob and walked out of the hangar.

"Old flame?" Bob asked when they'd walked several yards and then stopped near the parking lot.

Nancy scoffed. "Not even close. He's a nice kid. He let me bulldoze my way into getting the private pilot's license as fast as humanly possible."

"I can see how—he was pretty enamored."

She looked up at Bob to find his eyes on her. She couldn't read the emotion on his face. "You don't have to worry about Jimmy."

"Oh, I wasn't worried." He smiled. "I kind of like how you claimed me." He brought their linked hands up.

Just then, Nancy spied her father's car pulling up. "Our ride is here."

"Should I let go of your hand?" Bob asked, still clasping it to his chest.

"No." She kept a firm hold on his hand as her father parked and climbed out of the car. If he was surprised, he didn't show it. "Daddy, I'd like you to meet Bob Love."

Only at that point did she release Bob's hand so that he could shake her father's.

"Dr. Harkness. A pleasure to meet you."

Nancy looked at the pair, trying to gauge the reaction of both men to each other. Both smiled easily, and she decided that was a good sign. She gave her father a hug.

On the drive to the house, her father asked Bob all sorts of questions about Inter City. Things that he already knew because Nancy had told him. But she understood that her father was vetting the man anyway. She'd made a pretty strong statement after all. From the men's conversation, Nancy knew her father respected Bob. She could hear the warmth in both of their voices.

Mother might be a different story.

And Nancy was right.

Oh, the dinner went well. But her mother was quiet, letting Nancy and the men carry the conversation.

Bob complimented her mother on the meal more than once, but she barely murmured a thank-you. Nancy could tell her father noticed, and he was trying to make up for her mother's lack of enthusiasm by being extra jovial. If only her brother were here. He could always sweet-talk Mother out of any of her moods.

And how would it be to have her brother meet Bob? A pang of nostalgia for her brother swept through her, and she thought of Alison, his widow. Nancy traded letters with Alison and loved getting cards and artwork from her nephews. Their visits, though, were relegated to holidays, and Nancy had learned not to talk about her sister-in-law or nephews around her mother unless her mother instigated the conversation. Nancy never knew if it would send her mother into tears.

Nancy had to quickly redirect her thoughts, so she stood to clear the plates after the meal. Bob rose as well to help.

"You're our guest," Mother pointedly told Bob. "Why don't you men visit in the living room, then we'll join you later." She looked at Nancy, including her in the *we* comment.

Nancy could see that Bob was about to protest, so she said, "Yes, why don't you and Dad go relax. I'll help my mother, and we'll be in soon."

A line between Bob's eyebrows appeared, but he agreed. "All right. If you change your mind—"

Nancy waved him off, then picked up two of the plates and followed her mother into the kitchen. Mother turned on the faucet and began to fill the sink with hot water.

Nancy set the plates down on the counter. She fetched the rest of the dishes and utensils. By the time she'd finished, her mother had started washing the dishes. So Nancy rinsed and dried.

Her mother worked silently, her lips pursed so that her mouth almost disappeared.

"What do you think of Bob?" Nancy finally asked because she was tired of waiting for her mother to speak.

"He seems to be a fine man," Mother said stiffly.

"But . . . ?"

Her mother handed over a sudsy serving bowl, and Nancy rinsed it off.

"I thought you were going back to secretarial school after your summer job."

Nancy had told both of her parents her plans, so this was an old argument. "You know aviation is what I want to do. I'm making close to what I might as a secretary."

Her mother's lips pursed again as she handed over a set of utensils.

Nancy took them and rinsed them off. Setting them in the drying rack, she turned to face her mother. "Is that all?"

Her mother met her gaze, and to Nancy's surprise, Mother's eyes filled with tears. "You're only twenty, Nancy. Are you going to marry that man and leave me too?"

Nancy's eyes widened. "What are you talking about?"

Mother reached into the soapy water and pulled out the drain stopper. She snatched the drying cloth and began to wipe down the sink area. "You said you were *friends*, although your father thought there might be more to it. But this is *much* more, Nancy."

Nancy had no words. Had Father told Mother about the hand holding when he'd picked them up? No, there hadn't been a private moment between them. She might as well fully confess. "We're going steady."

Her mother gave a soft laugh, but it wasn't in amusement. "It's more than that, Nancy. The way he watches you makes that obvious. And the way you look to him for every comment only seals the deal."

Nancy opened her mouth, then shut it. She hadn't known her mother would react so strongly to her having a boyfriend. She was twenty now, and that was plenty in age to make this sort of decision. "Father seems to like him."

Mother paused in her brisk work. "It's not about *liking* the man. It's about . . . well, he's very serious about you, Nancy. Is that what you want to be? Married to a man who has to depend on airplane sales when the country is in the middle of a depression? Normal people can't afford airplanes, and rich people are no longer rich!"

Had Mother's voice carried into the living room? Nancy's throat had soured. Her mother's complaints were only partially valid. People were buying planes, maybe not in droves, but Inter City was still in business, wasn't it? Truthfully, she'd never had a detailed conversation about finances with Bob. There hadn't been a need to.

Besides, this conversation was much too premature. She didn't want to be tied down to a husband because babies would follow, and then how would she keep rising in her aviation career? Bob was supportive of her dreams, yet she also knew that things could change if there were children involved.

"You don't have to worry, Mother," she said firmly. "I'm nowhere near getting married. Someday, I might marry and have children. But not today, and not for a long time."

Pink spots appeared on Mother's cheeks, but she looked only slightly mollified.

"I miss Bobbin too," Nancy said quietly.

And then they were hugging. She knew her mother must spend a lot of time alone when her father was working. Maybe she'd hoped Nancy would get a secretary job in Houghton and move back home, or at least be nearby. Nancy couldn't imagine a worse job for her. The most steady job for a pilot would be working for the government, but that would be a long shot.

When she drew away, she handed her mother a tissue.

"Thank you," Mother whispered. "I'll finish up in here. You can join the men."

"I have a better idea," Nancy said. "I'll show Bob around the property, and you can talk to Daddy about all this."

Mother released a breath. "All right."

Nancy gave her mother another squeeze, then headed to the front room. Both Bob and her father were playing a game of cards while debating some politics happening overseas in Europe.

"Want to play?" Bob asked, seeing her immediately.

"Yes, join us," Father said.

"Maybe later. I thought I'd take you on the grand tour before it gets too dark," Nancy said to Bob. She looked at her father. "Mother's in the kitchen."

Father's brows rose. "All right." He seemed to clue into the fact that maybe he should go into the kitchen as well.

Bob rose to his feet. "A tour sounds excellent."

Nancy headed toward the front door. Bob joined her, and they stepped out onto the porch together.

She folded her arms and walked down the steps. Bob kept pace with her as they moved around the side of the house. Memories of her childhood seemed to bombard her as she entered the backyard. Learning to ride a bicycle. Sleepovers with her friends as they'd tried to count all the stars. Picking apples with Robert.

"Everything all right?" Bob asked quietly when she finally stopped near the swell of apple trees.

"I feel like I brought you to a house of grieving."

"There's no timeline on grief." He moved closer and set his hands on her shoulders. "Is my name a problem, you know, the same as your brother's?"

Nancy wrinkled her nose. "No. Mother called him Bobbin anyway." Her gaze fell. "I think it's more . . ."

"More what?"

His hands on her shoulders were warm, steady, and comforting somehow. If she couldn't tell him about the conversation with her mother, then she couldn't claim to have an honest relationship with him. And she definitely wanted that. More than she'd realized.

"My mother thinks we're very serious, and she's worried that I'm too young to . . . you know, be serious."

He didn't seem too surprised. "Well, I am serious about you, Nancy. But I'll wait for you. As long as you need."

She stepped into his arms, holding him close and breathing in his leather-and-washed-cotton scent.

He pulled her in tight and rested his chin on top of her head.

Closing her eyes, she decided that when she was ready to commit to a man, she hoped Bob would still be waiting.

# CHAPTER SIXTEEN

"As long as our planes flew overhead, the skies of America were
free and that's what all of us everywhere are fighting for. And
that we, in a very small way, are being allowed to help keep
that sky free is the most beautiful thing I've ever known."

—CORNELIA FORT, 1943

*April 1935—Inter City, Boston*

"Write to him," Bob told Nancy.

"But his mother is Eleanor Roosevelt, and you know, his father, the
president of the United States."

Bob's smile appeared as he sat behind his small office desk, leaning
back in his chair. "And . . . ?"

"And . . . I can't write to J.R. Roosevelt just because Mr. Vidal told
me to. I don't *know* the Roosevelts."

"It's called networking, sweetie."

Nancy huffed out a breath. "I know that, Mr. Love. I wasn't born
yesterday."

Bob shot up from his chair and stalked around the desk. She knew
that teasing glint in his eyes, and she moved around the desk the opposite way.

"I don't want to be a beggar," she protested.

"That didn't stop you from buttering up Eugene Vidal at the Boston
Aero Club dinner last December. As the director of the Bureau of Air
Commerce, if Mr. Vidal takes your conversation seriously, then you
should too."

Nancy bit her lip. That night at the Hotel Lennox *had* been surreal.
She'd been included in a photo with Mr. Vidal, and aviator Mrs. Teddy
Kenyon, which had appeared in the *Boston Herald* the next day. In 1933,
Mrs. Kenyon had won the National Sportsman Flying Championship

at Roosevelt Field, New York, besting twenty-eight men and eleven women. Nancy had also dared to tell Mr. Vidal of her desire to work at a government aviation job. It wasn't that she wanted to leave Inter City. It was far from that. She'd spent her time over the past several months demonstrating and selling airplanes and being the all-around girl Friday. But airplane sales were slow.

She took another step around the desk. The most recent letter from Mr. Vidal had informed her that he'd spoken with Amelia Earhart and her husband, G.P. Putnam, about Nancy working with them on a project. Imagine! In January, Earhart had set a record by becoming the first pilot ever to fly solo from Hawaii to the mainland.

Earhart had also announced other plans to fly solo from Burbank to Mexico City, which would set another record. To be involved with anything Earhart had her hands in was breathtaking to think about. Vidal had also mentioned that Earhart was thinking about accepting a position at Purdue University as an aviation adviser.

Nancy could get on board with any or all of that.

"Write to J.R. Roosevelt," Bob said again, stepping nearer. "Make the connection. You never know what might come of it."

She'd let her mind wander too much, and now he'd caught her around the waist. She set her hands on his chest. "What if they offer me a job outside of Boston and I have to leave Inter City?"

His eyes didn't waver. "You might leave Inter City, but as long as it's not leaving *me*, I'm supportive."

She tilted her head. "That's magnanimous of you. Should I be offended?"

He grinned. "From the moment you first stormed out of my office and slammed the door, I knew there was no holding you back from what you wanted."

Nancy patted his chest, enjoying the solid warmth there. "You're a smart man, Mr. Love."

"So I've been told." He kissed her then, as she'd suspected he might.

She wrapped her arms around his neck and melted into him, telling herself to only indulge for a moment. She had a letter to write. It would be at least a week before she'd hear back, she knew, but when it turned into more than that, she was positively jumping out of her skin.

Fourteen long days passed before she received a reply from J.R. Roosevelt. "He wrote back," Nancy said, bursting into Bob's office.

He stood immediately, pushing back his chair. "What did he say?"

"Here, read it for yourself."

Bob did, then looked up at her. "This is excellent. Sounds like J.R. will get the wheels turning and see what he can do."

"Right, and here's a letter from Vidal." Nancy held out the next letter.

Bob perched on the edge of the desk as he read the longer letter aloud. "I had a wire from James Roosevelt—his father is very well known in Washington—about you wanting a job." Bob smirked. "Stating the obvious, I see."

She moved to sit next to him at the edge of the desk, shoulder to shoulder. He didn't seem to mind her doing so.

Bob continued reading. "There's nothing for you to do but wait until P.W.A. funds are allotted to us for some interesting projects. For instance, we have an Airmarking Program with which we might send out a few girls in Hammond planes, touring the country." Bob's brows wagged. "That might be interesting. Airmarking?"

"Keep reading. It gets better."

Bob finished reading, silently this time. "So, Phoebe Omlie and Amelia Earhart are at the helm of this."

"They're the ones trying to get John Wynne on board." Phoebe Omlie was a veteran aviator—the first woman in the United States to earn her transport license. She also had an airplane engine mechanical accreditation. And John Wynne was the chief of the Airport Marking and Mapping Section of the Bureau of Air Commerce. "I could do it," Nancy continued. "Traveling to various towns and getting them to approve the program."

"What exactly would you be getting them to approve?"

"The government wants to make towns identifiable from the air. By painting the name of the town on the top of a barn roof or other building, small plane pilots would be able to identify where they are by reading the air markers below. If prominent buildings aren't available, towns will construct ground markers out of rocks and paint them white, some with arrow formations pointing to the airports."

"That would be a huge endeavor."

Nancy only smiled. Since most small planes didn't have navigational instruments, air markers would be useful. How hard would it be to convince others? "I could fly from town to town and meet with the government officials."

"Alone?"

She elbowed him. "Don't tell me you'd miss me."

He set his hand over hers, his calluses familiar. "Of course I'd miss you."

"I'll make every minute away useful. I don't think it will be too hard to convince mayors and town councils."

He squeezed her hand and nodded. "Right. This program will create jobs to paint the markers, plus this will help private pilots and, really, all airways."

Nancy slipped off the desk, turned toward him, then looped her arms about his neck. "Does this mean you approve, Mr. Love?" she asked.

"You don't need my approval, Miss Harkness."

She kissed him. Breaking her own rule of not kissing him at work, but this was an exception. When she drew away, she said, "I have letters to write."

"Good." He leaned his forehead against hers. "When you're finished, come out and meet with Mr. Rogerson. He wants a Beechcraft demonstration. He should be here in about an hour."

After Bob left the office, she settled into the chair and wrote a return letter to J.R. Roosevelt as a thank-you. She wrote a more lengthy letter to Mr. Vidal, in which she also requested the address of Phoebe Omlie. Nancy planned to take the chance and write the woman. In for a penny, in for a pound.

Over the next few days, Nancy felt like she was stepping on pins and needles as she waited for Mr. Vidal's reply. Bob convinced her to take a half day off, and they went for a drive to appreciate the spring flowers, then to dinner at a place she'd never be able to pay for on her own.

"You need to stop spoiling me," she told him as they sat together at the Boston restaurant in the North End that was filled with fine Italian restaurants. "I'm pretty sure this one meal will cost more than my commission on last week's sale."

"We're celebrating your success," he replied smoothly, setting the linen napkin on his lap.

"Sales are down," she said. "I don't need to see your ledger to know that."

Bob picked up the glass of wine the waiter had poured. "Forget all that for now. We're celebrating the progress of the Airmarking Program."

They'd both read about it in the papers. It had been approved, and any day now, any moment, Nancy hoped to receive a letter to invite her to be one of the pilots. The program that Phoebe Omlie had constructed had recommended the use of female pilots, specifically. With Earhart off setting world records, Omlie had recruited Louise Thaden to help with the push.

"Okay, we can celebrate, then," she said.

"And you'll not comment on the menu prices?"

Nancy smiled. "I'll try to hold back."

Bob moved his glass toward hers, and she tapped it with her own. He winked, then sipped. Nancy did as well, feeling lucky that the man across from her didn't seem fazed with her ambitions. They'd known each other a year now, and although their relationship continued to progress, he hadn't pressured her into marriage. Oh, he'd brought it up once in a while, but only to say he was content to wait for her.

She loved that about him. And yes, she did love him. It had taken a while for her to realize it. They hadn't spoken the words to each other, although more than once, Nancy had thought he'd been about to tell her. He'd get that intense look in his eyes, as if he were trying to read her thoughts, but then the conversation would shift.

Once dinner was finished, Nancy was anxious to get back to her living quarters—if only to check her mail, which she did every day in case Mr. Vidal wrote back. Or even Phoebe Omlie.

So, when Bob pulled up in front of her place, she said, "Come check the mail with me. The suspense is making me regret that expensive Italian food."

He didn't laugh or complain—probably because he was used to her quirks.

When she stepped into the hallway leading to her rented room, she paused at the row of postal boxes. Unlocking hers, she pulled out two letters. She held them to her chest before looking at them.

"What are you doing?" Bob asked, amused.

"Wishing."

"They're already written and in your hand. Just read them."

Nancy puffed out a breath. "All right." She turned over the letters. One was from Mr. Vidal. The other was from Ms. Omlie. "My golly. I can't believe it. Which do I open first?"

"*Now* you can't decide?"

Looking between the two, she finally made a choice. Hands shaking, she carefully opened Mr. Vidal's letter first. She scanned the words, and her eyes filled with tears.

"The Bureau of Commerce has invited me to join the Airmarking Program," she whispered. "The WPA funds have been approved through the New Deal Program. And with the approval, they're hiring two more pilots. Me and a woman named Helen MacCloskey." She blinked rapidly and looked up at Bob.

He pulled her close and kissed the top of her head. "Congratulations, Miss Harkness."

She laughed shakily and wiped at her cheeks. "Mr. Vidal really came through. That's the only reason I got the job."

Bob chuckled, his chest vibrating against hers. "That's far from the only reason. They needed a talented pilot, and you happened to be standing in their path."

Nancy held on for a few moments. She would miss him when she was gone, whether it was for weeks or months, she wasn't quite sure. She had another letter to read.

Again, nerves zinged through her as she opened Phoebe Omlie's letter. Bob leaned close and read with her, and Nancy couldn't help but grin at the contents. "We'll have a plane assigned to us. Imagine! And we're getting paid twice a month." She looked up at Bob. "No commissions for me."

He smiled. "That's a cushy government job for you."

Nancy only smirked. She finished reading the letter, folded it, then tucked both letters into her handbag. "Will you miss me?" she asked Bob, meeting his blue eyes.

"You know I will." His voice was low, soft in the empty hallway.

"How much?" she teased, although her heart had begun a slow pound. She'd come to rely on this man for many things, and she was rarely apart from him—only when she was in the sky or sleeping.

Bob's hand slid around her. "I probably shouldn't tell you. I don't want you to change your mind because of it."

Setting her hands on his shoulders, she lifted up on her toes and kissed him. Drawing away a half inch, she whispered, "I won't change my mind. You can tell me your secrets."

"Which secrets are you talking about?"

"Well, if they're secrets, then how would I know?"

Bob laughed. "I think you're a vixen. Should we call you the flying vixen?"

"I like *sweetie* better. Coming from you, of course."

"Of course. And it should be only from me."

"It should?"

His gaze took on that intensity again. "You know I'm waiting for you."

"So you've said."

His brows shifted together. "Why else would I be following you around like a puppy?"

Nancy snorted. "You're the farthest thing from a cuddly puppy, Mr. Love. But you do bark."

"I'm not perfect."

She smiled. "No, you're not."

"But perfect enough?"

She moved her hands behind his neck, grateful they were still alone in the hallway. "I can overlook your flaws, and I expect you to overlook mine."

"Done." He smiled before he leaned down to kiss her, but she drew away.

"Wait. I have flaws?" she asked. "What are they?"

He paused, his eyes alight. "I can't remember right now."

"Oh, that's a good save, sir."

"One of my strengths." He did kiss her then, and she allowed herself to relish the moment. "I'm proud of you, Nancy," he whispered when they drew apart to breathe. "You've gone after what you wanted, and now you'll be part of a landmark program."

"Thanks for telling me to write J.R. Roosevelt." She smoothed a hand over Bob's shoulder. "And for not telling me it was a fool's errand. I'm grateful for your support—even though you're going to lose an employee."

"I'll always support you, sweetie." Bob moved his fingers along her jawline and slipped them behind her neck.

"I think I love you," Nancy whispered. "Well, maybe I know I do."

Bob's gaze searched hers, his eyes turning a blue-gray in the dimness. "I definitely love you, Miss Harkness, and I hope that someday you'll agree to add my name to yours."

She moved fully into his arms, holding him close and pressing her face against his neck as his hand moved slowly down her back.

"I'm only twenty-one," she murmured after a moment.

"And next year, you'll be twenty-two, then twenty-three the year after—"

"I know my age."

"Me, too, so why do you keep pointing it out?" His voice rumbled through her.

She lifted her head. "Maybe so you don't get too many ideas in your head?"

His eyes crinkled at the corners. "Too late for that."

# CHAPTER SEVENTEEN

"Miss Harkness has secured approval of a programme to place airmarkers in 290 cities and towns [in Massachusetts]. The other 65 have already been so marked. Since her appointment a little over a month ago, Miss Harkness has also got the airmarking programme signed up in New Jersey and now she is working in Maryland."

*BOSTON POST,* OCTOBER 21, 1935

*September–October 1935—Washington, DC*

"We don't have a plane," Louise Thaden said, walking into the aircraft hangar just outside of Washington, DC, where Nancy had been told to meet up with her team, which included Louise and Helen MacCloskey. Phoebe Omlie had bowed out of the hands-on flying for the Airmarking Program, returning instead to her NACA job.

Louise Thaden's deep-blue eyes set off her high cheekbones and brown hair. Her height was a touch over five foot eight, one of the taller female aviators Nancy had met. "This letter explains it all," Louise continued, holding up an envelope she carried.

It was September, and Nancy had been assigned to the East Coast as her territory.

"Why not?" Helen demanded with a shake of her wavy brunette bob.

"WPA funds won't cover it." Louise stopped by the desk in the corner of the hangar, where Helen and Nancy pored over maps of their divided territories.

"Are we expensing our own travel?" Nancy had planned for this job to be a boon to her finances, not a drain.

Louise handed over the official-looking letter, and Nancy scanned through it, then said, "We're to travel on regularly scheduled airlines as long as the cost doesn't exceed rail plus Pullman."

Pointing to the next paragraph, Louise added, "But we're to use government aircraft and automobiles whenever they're available."

Helen frowned, peering at the letter. "It also says that we can use our own automobiles if we can do it more economically. We'll be reimbursed five cents a mile."

"Don't," Louise said with a laugh. "It won't be more economical since you'll be paying for your own car repairs."

"The five cents a mile won't cover that?" Nancy asked.

Louise smirked. "It sounds good in theory, but I recommend using public or government transportation."

"It will take ages to drive to all these locations," Nancy mused. "I'm going to book the next flight to New Jersey." She pointed to the map. "Tomorrow."

Louise clapped a hand on her shoulder. "That's the way. Now, we have funds to hire two more women—so you'll be crossing paths with them from time to time. Blanche Noyes and Helen Richey."

Nancy hadn't met either woman yet. She'd been part of these planning meetings for only a couple of days, and it was all wonderful so far—well, except for this change in transportation method. And she was already missing Bob. It was a strange thing to miss someone who wasn't related to her this much. She supposed she missed her parents, but she didn't yearn to call them every few hours or to write them lengthy letters. Which, of course, she wasn't doing with Bob, even though she wanted to.

The sooner she started working in her territory, the better. Letters had gone out to all the towns and cities in advance of her arrival, but she knew it wouldn't be easy. She'd packed as light as possible, adding her flight jacket, helmet, and goggles, just in case she had any chances to fly.

Throughout the first week, Nancy stuck to wearing her print dresses, heels, hat, and white gloves. No one seemed resistant to a program in which the government was hiring workers and paying them. In fact, there were meetings she attended to explain the program in which men and women lined up outside buildings, thinking she was part of the actual hiring committee.

A couple of farmers didn't want their barns painted, but Nancy would let the city officials deal with those kinds of details.

She met in offices, in coffee shops, in front of barns, before town councils, and, once, in a barber shop. It wasn't difficult to secure approval after approval. She also got to fly more than once. A perfect job if she didn't count her aching heart.

"You're a lady flyer?" one town mayor asked after his council had approved the program. They'd be painting the roof of a factory near the airfield, along with constructing arrow markers.

"Yes, sir."

The man, with a rather large nose and bushy mustache, eyed her. "How long have you been flying?"

The afternoon sun had nearly reached the horizon, splashing gold streaks everywhere, and Nancy would be spending the night in this town's bed-and-breakfast. As she walked with the mayor into the parking lot, she filled him in on her aviation experience, wondering if he'd be nosy enough to ask for her pilot logbook.

He didn't ask but informed her, "I own a Waco. Comes in handy."

Nancy stopped near a parked car. She'd be heading the other direction, and she wasn't about to accept a ride from this man. "I'll bet it does. If the government had the budget, I'd rent it from you and finish New Jersey."

The mayor eyed her. "I could give you a deal if you return me a favor."

Nancy's heart skipped a couple of beats. She didn't exactly like the gleam in this man's eyes. "What sort of favor, sir?"

"My son is about your age," the mayor said. "He'd be pleased to meet a fine girl like you. One with so much ambition and a good job. What do you say?"

"I'm . . ." Nancy couldn't say she was engaged because it wasn't true. "I have a sweetheart back in Boston."

The mayor didn't seem put off. "I don't see a ring on your finger, miss. Or are you feeding me a line?"

Her neck heated. "I'm not feeding you a line, sir. Bob and I have come to an agreement, even if things aren't official yet." She might be stretching the truth, but this man would never know.

The mayor rocked back on his heels. "If it's not official, there's no harm in meeting someone for dinner. My son lives down the road. Works part-time at the bank as a clerk, but he'll move up quickly."

Nancy drew in a breath. "I'm sure he's a nice fellow, but I should get going. I wish you and your family all the best." She turned away from him, almost expecting him to call her back to ask her more questions or to continue to insist that she meet his son.

But the mayor didn't call out to her, so Nancy continued to the sidewalk, moving as briskly as her heels allowed.

By the time she reached the bed-and-breakfast, she'd perspired through her checkered dress, and it wasn't even a hot day. She didn't take time to change before sitting at the desk in her small boarding room, then she picked up the phone receiver and dialed the number she'd memorized.

"Inter City Aviation," Bob answered.

Relief at the sound of his voice swept through her. She usually called him when he was home for the evening. "Bob, it's me."

"Nancy, how are you?" He paused, probably realizing the early hour. "Is everything all right?"

"Yes, everything's all right," she said. "Mostly."

"What is it? Are you still in New Jersey?"

"Yes. I'm almost finished. In two days, I'll be heading to Massachusetts." Her voice sounded raw, scratchy, and she wished she weren't having to talk to Bob over the phone. She wanted to see him in person.

"Great, we can meet up for dinner." At her silence, he continued. "Any problems? Are people signing up for the program?"

"Yes, that's all fine."

"What's going on, Nancy?"

"Nothing really. I just miss you, I guess . . ." Her voice hitched.

"I miss you, too, sweetie."

Tears stung her eyes, and she twisted the telephone cord around her fingers. She was enjoying this job, most of the time. So why did she feel like crying when she heard Bob's voice? She didn't feel that way talking to her parents. There was so much she wanted to say to Bob, but it was too stilted over the phone, not to mention expensive. She'd have to keep herself busier until she saw him again. The other pilots who were working other states hadn't made as fast progress as she had, but she could do even more. She knew it.

"When will you be back in Boston?" His voice cut through her thoughts.

She reviewed her schedule and told him.

"That will be here before we know it," he said. "I'm already counting the days."

She heard the smile in his voice, but her heart only felt heavier. "Me too."

"Look, sweetie, you sound melancholy. If this job isn't all it's cracked up to be, come back to Inter City. I'd never turn down the help. You gave it your best shot with airmarking and already made significant progress."

"No, I need to stick this out." Nancy moved to her feet and stood before the window that overlooked an unfamiliar street. "I told the mayor of this town that I was almost engaged."

Bob chuckled. "What? I hope you were referring to *me* . . . unless you've met someone?"

"I was referring to you, but the mayor didn't believe me. Said I was trying to get out of being set up on a date with his son."

Bob laughed, then went silent. "Really? He really said that? Which town are you in? I'll call him myself."

Nancy leaned her head against the window. It was cool with the approaching twilight. She didn't want Bob to call the mayor, and it was probably an empty threat anyway, but now she was curious. "What would you tell him?"

"I'd tell him to stay out of your way," Bob said, his voice rising. "Maybe I'll fly in. I could be there first thing in the morning. What's the nearest airfield?"

At this, Nancy did smile. "You can't do that for every city I visit."

"This has happened more than once?"

"You know how charming I can be."

Bob released a groan. "You're lucky you're hundreds of miles away. I hope you're not out there being a flirt."

She knew he was teasing, but she didn't like it anyway. "I'm not a flirt, Bob." She straightened from the window. "You know that better than anyone. I'm more likely to slam a door in a man's face."

"Well, that's true. I guess I'd better do something about all of this."

Nancy scoffed. "You're not calling the mayor or anyone else. I'll try to be less charming."

"Nancy, be yourself. Charming and all. That's not what I meant."

"What *do* you mean?"

His pause seemed significant, and she wondered if he was changing his mind about what he almost said.

"Keep your chin up, sweetie, and I'll see you in Boston next week."

It was a few more minutes before Nancy hung up with Bob, and she was no closer to finding out what he was referring to, yet she felt better, and that was significant. It wasn't like she could talk to him for hours on end each night because that would deplete her paycheck on long-distance phone calls.

Over the next week, she hardly took a break and even pushed up some of her appointments so she could head to Boston a full day early. When she called Bob to tell him the news, he seemed surprised, and distracted. But he told her to fly into Inter City, ferrying a plane that he had at another airfield.

When Nancy flew into Inter City just as she said she would, he was there, waiting for her.

She'd been thrilled to fly again, but she realized she was more happy to see Bob Love standing at the entrance of the hangar.

As she taxied toward the hangar, her heart leaped. Talking to him at night had only slightly eased the ache in her chest. Now the ache was back full force with her knowing she had to be back on the road again soon.

Bob wasn't wearing a flight jacket but a tailored suit, complete with a tie. He stood with his hands in his pockets, hair stirring in the wind.

She stopped the plane and turned off the engine.

Before she could climb out, Bob scrambled onto the wing. "Welcome home," he said the second the door was open.

"Is that where I am?"

He grinned, then leaned over and kissed her, and when he pulled away, it was much too soon. Still grinning, he grasped her hand and helped her climb out. Once they were on level ground, she hugged him, and he tugged her close.

Chuckling, he said, "So, you did miss me."

Nancy only held on tighter. "Maybe a little."

It was a long moment before she finally released him. "You're dressed up. Are you going somewhere?"

"*We're* going somewhere."

She wrinkled her nose. "I'm dead on my feet, Bob, and I smell like airplane fuel."

"I have reservations."

Nancy's pulse skipped a beat; he'd put in some planning. "I'd need a shower and a change of clothing and—"

"I can wait." He linked their fingers and led her toward his car.

Once settled inside, Nancy let her body relax, but her mind continued jumping ahead. She felt like she'd been gone months instead of weeks, and it was surreal to be back in Bob's car. It wasn't like she'd forgotten anything about him, but the small things were so endearingly familiar, and her heart felt like it had swollen two times inside her chest.

The way he fiddled with the radio only to land back on the original station that overplayed Bing Crosby. The way he studied her at every stoplight. The way his thumb brushed over her knuckles as they held hands while he drove, even while shifting gears. The roughness of his calluses that came from helping the mechanics.

Once they reached her place, she tried to hurry through getting ready for dinner, but it was a full hour before she emerged.

Bob was still waiting and didn't even seem put out.

"Did we miss the reservation?" she asked.

A smile lit his eyes. "I called ahead."

"Must be your favorite place?"

"My parents like it."

"Wait, are they going to be there?" She'd met his parents a few times, but she wanted Bob all to herself right now.

"It's only us." He held the door open for her, and they headed out of the building.

As they drove, he told her about a couple of new airplane clients.

"Things are looking up?" she asked. "Maybe I should have left earlier."

"No, that's not any sort of reason. The economy is getting better, that's all. I'm sure when my number-one salesgirl returns, it will be even better."

"I'm your only salesgirl."

Bob laughed.

The sound warmed her through—if only time could race forward, and she could be finished with the Airmarking Program.

They pulled into a parking lot of a restaurant, and she caught a glimpse of candles and crystal goblets through the large front windows. "This place looks very posh. I don't think we need to be spending all this money on food."

Bob simply opened his car door, climbed out, and walked around to open hers.

When she stood, she said, "Really, Bob. A simple meal is fine. Or maybe we can order an appetizer at the bar so we don't brush off the reservation."

"Nancy, you're making this really hard."

"What's so hard? I think it would be much easier and quicker to eat at a diner. We can talk without being interrupted by a tuxedoed waiter every two minutes."

"I'd have to cancel the reservation," Bob said on a sigh.

She didn't know why she was protesting so much, but she couldn't back down now. "Is that so hard?"

The edge of his mouth lifted. "No, but I did wait an hour for you to get ready."

"You said you didn't mind waiting."

He rubbed a spot on his forehead. "I don't think I'll ever win an argument with you."

Nancy simply folded her arms.

"Fine. I'll be right back."

She watched with amusement as he strode into the restaurant and spoke with the maître d'. She should feel guilty that he had gone to some trouble tonight, but she didn't want all the fuss, all the people. She just wanted him.

When he returned, she said, "Thank you," and gave him a quick hug.

He squeezed her back, then opened the car door for her again.

Once they were resettled in the car, he said with what had to be purposeful patience, "Where to, Miss Harkness?"

"We passed a diner a couple of streets back. Let's try it out."

The place was almost empty, and Nancy didn't know if that boded well. But the waitress was welcoming and, most importantly, left them alone to talk.

"Much better," Nancy said, taking a bite of the chicken dish she'd ordered. It was good, and she took a few more bites because she suddenly felt ravenous. "How's your steak?"

"Fine." Bob had taken only a single bite though. He was studying her.

She took a sip of her drink. "If you don't like the steak, I can trade you. The chicken's good."

"Look, Nancy," Bob said, low and serious. "I spoke with your father earlier today."

Her brows popped up. "You did? Is everything all right?"

"Yes, he's fine," he continued. "I asked him for permission to marry you."

Just like that? Bob had . . . Nancy set her fork down. She wasn't sure she was breathing right. "Bob . . ."

"He gave me, gave *us*, his blessing."

Nancy had no words. Literally.

Bob's gaze scanned the quiet diner. "I hadn't really planned to do this in a place like this, but maybe it's fitting. Our first date was in a diner in New York City."

"Do *what?*" Nancy's heart had lodged into her throat.

He reached into his suit jacket pocket and pulled out a small object—a black box—then moved off the red leather bench and knelt on one knee.

"Bob, what are you doing . . . ?" she whispered.

"I'm proposing, Nancy," he said matter-of-factly.

She felt a strange urge to laugh, but nothing about Bob's expression held amusement. That meant in the black velvet box could be only one thing. "Did you buy me a ring? How did you know my size? I hope you didn't spend a fortune."

"Nancy, may I proceed here?"

She clamped her mouth shut and nodded.

He waited a heartbeat, as if to make sure she was finished. "You know I love you and that I was willing to wait for you. I still am, but I think we can be engaged while I'm doing all this waiting."

He opened the black box. The diamond ring glittered against the black velvet, and she didn't know much about sizes and carats, but Bob had gone way overboard.

"You did spend a fortune," Nancy burst out.

His voice scratched out, sounding amused. "I love you, Nancy, and I want the world to know it. Especially small-town mayors."

But she couldn't take her eyes off the ring. She'd always imagined that she and Bob would one day visit a jewelry store and argue over the selections. But he'd gone ahead and bought the ring himself. She didn't know how she felt about that.

"It's really big, Bob," she blurted, "and I don't know if it would be prudent to wear something so fancy."

"Prudent?"

"You know, *prudent* means 'sensible'—"

"I know what *prudent* means, Nancy," Bob cut in, shifting a little on his knee. "Can we focus on something else besides the size of the ring? I'm trying to ask you to marry me."

She met his gaze. "So, then, ask."

Lines appeared between his eyebrows, and she didn't know if he was amused or fed up with their debate. "Nancy Harkness, will you marry me? You can pick the wedding date, but don't torture me for too long."

She gave him a sweet smile. "I'm torturing you?"

"Immensely."

Nancy laughed. "I kind of like that idea."

He released a soft groan. "I probably shouldn't have brought it up."

"I have one question, Bob: Why did you buy a ring without my input?"

"See? There's a perfect example of your torturing. Do you like the ring or not? We could take it back if you prefer—"

"Oh, don't take it back. I love it."

He stared at her. "You could have said that from the beginning."

"Can I try it on?"

"Are you going to say yes?"

Nancy covered her mouth. "I haven't even answered."

"No, you haven't," Bob said in a dry tone.

She lowered her hand and leaned forward. "Yes, Mr. Love, I'll marry you."

"Thank the heavens above, she finally answered." He looked toward the ceiling as if someone were actually listening.

Nancy laughed, then rose from the bench and tugged him to his feet. She wrapped her arms about his neck. "I love you, Bob."

"I love you, too, sweetie." He kissed her, and Nancy had no idea where the waitress had gone, but she wouldn't have cared if they'd had a restaurant full of people watching.

"Oh." Nancy drew away. "This is why you wanted to do a fancy dinner and everything."

Bob's mouth quirked. "Yes."

"I'm sorry if I ruined that."

"I think the outcome is the important part," he mused, looking down at her.

"Right. Now can I try on the ring?"

Bob kissed her again, harder and fiercer, then he pulled the ring out of its little box.

It turned out that the ring fit perfectly. Nancy drew in her breath at the sight of the sparkling diamond on her finger. It looked so official, so permanent. And she decided she loved it even more because Bob had done this on his own.

"It's almost too beautiful to wear," she said.

"It's where it belongs."

She smiled up at him, her heart knocking against her chest. "Are you crying?"

"No." But he wiped at his eyes.

She hugged him again. "I'm not going to make you wait that long, Bob," she whispered against his ear. She felt his smile against her neck as he tightened his hold.

# CHAPTER EIGHTEEN

"What's more, while performing this unique job, she's flying
a unique plane. It's a tricycle affair that reverses the order
of things. . . . You do everything wrong and it comes out
right. In a plane of this sort, it's impossible to nose over. It
simplifies landing no end. You just land, it takes no skill."

—*BOSTON EVENING AMERICAN*

*January 1936—Hastings, Michigan*

Nancy didn't mind the blustery winter day in the town of Hastings,
Michigan, where her parents' new home was. After all, she'd picked
the date of January 11 to marry Robert MacLure Love. The First
Presbyterian Church of Hastings was decked out in evergreen boughs
and a variety of white roses and calla lilies. All the *who's who* were here—
mostly because of her parents and Bob's parents. As the day approached,
Nancy had thought more and more of her brother. How she would have
loved for him to meet Bob. How her brother would have been so excited
about his sister getting married, and how his enthusiasm would have
brightened all the wedding preparations.

"Let me fix your veil," Alice Hirschman said, standing next to
Nancy, where she surveyed her appearance in the mirror in the bridal
changing room at the back of the church.

Nancy dipped her head as Alice adjusted the short tulle veil attached
to her small white cap.

"There." Alice stepped back. "Now tell me what you think."

"Perfect," Nancy said.

Alice had arrived a couple of days before the wedding to help with
preparations. Somewhere out in the wedding audience was her now-
fiancé, John Hammond. Other guests had already arrived and were
seated, including her cousin Georgina; Robert's widow, Alison, who was

serving as her matron-of-honor; and Bob's sister, Margaret, who'd come all the way from Tucson, Arizona.

"Great. Here's your bouquet." Alice ceremoniously produced the bouquet of white orchids and lilies of the valley.

Nancy took it and held it against her waist. Her dress was a princess cut, made of satin, with a high cowl neck. The long sleeves were fitted, and a train extended behind her. She'd never felt so regal and stuffed into a dress at the same time.

"What's wrong?" Alice said. "You're dead quiet."

Nancy dragged in a breath. "Nothing's wrong. I think I'm overwhelmed."

Alice's brows slanted. "In a good way or a bad way? Are you having doubts about marrying Bob?"

"No, nothing like that. You know I don't like all the fanfare around this. I mean, this dress cost my parents an arm and a leg."

"I thought you paid for half of it."

"I did." Nancy bit her lip, then quickly remembered not to mess up her lipstick. "So, a half arm and half leg."

Alice tilted her head. "Today's *your* day, Nancy, and it's all right to wear beautiful things. Everyone wants to celebrate this once-in-a-lifetime event, or, at least, it had better be once. You and Bob have been dating forever, and we were all getting tired of waiting."

Nancy smirked. "You've been dating Hammond for even longer."

"Yes, but that's different."

"How?"

"Okay, it's not different, but Nancy, just enjoy the day. Enjoy being spoiled. Enjoy some frippery."

Nancy understood Alice's point, but the weight of her brother's absence remained. "I miss him."

Alice squeezed her hand, not having to be told that Nancy was referring to her brother. "I know you do. He's watching from wherever he is."

Nancy nodded, blinking back the tears gathering in her eyes as she looked down at the diamond ring she'd worn for over three months. The sparkle and size still dazzled her, but Bob would not let her complain about it. Neither would Alice. "My ring really does look pretty with this dress."

"See? It was all meant to be." Alice met her gaze in the mirror and winked.

*Was* it all meant to be? Nancy had quit the Airmarking Program at the end of November. Three months of straight traveling and not being around Bob had been harder than she'd ever imagined. Even when she was wearing her engagement ring. Yes, it cut down on the men outright asking her to dinner, but it hadn't cut down on her aching heart. And now she was about to pledge a lifetime of loyalty to Bob Love.

She should be happy, ecstatic, but she could only think of all the things that were missing. Like her brother. And Bob's brother.

A tap sounded at the door, and her mother opened it, poking her head inside. "Ready, Nancy?"

Beyond the door, organ music played softly.

"She's ready, Mrs. Harkness," Alice announced, then grinned at Nancy.

Her mother stepped into the room, her eyes wide. "You look lovely, dear. I can't quite believe the day has arrived. You are still so young."

Nancy was nearly twenty-two, and although her mother had married at age twenty-six, not everyone waited that long.

Nancy drew in a breath. "I'm ready. Where's Daddy?"

"I'm here." Her father stepped into the doorway.

Her sister-in-law, Alison, joined him in the doorway. She looked beautiful in her ankle-length, gray, crepe dress, accented by an aquamarine sash, and topped with a gray velvet hat.

Now it was starting to feel very real—seeing Alison ready to precede her down the aisle, and seeing her father dressed up and waiting to take her arm to escort her.

Father smiled at her and held out his hand. Nancy walked forward and slipped her hand over the crook of his elbow. Father bent to kiss her cheek. "Ready?"

"Ready," she whispered.

Alison and Mother disappeared into the chapel. Mother must have signaled to the organist because the music switched to Lohengrin's "Wedding March."

This was really happening . . . They entered the back of the chapel and began to walk up the aisle as the music and scent of roses and lilies floated around them. People on both sides in their finery blurred together, because Nancy could see only the man standing up at the front of the church, a few steps ahead of the minister.

Bob Love was all smiles.

Her heart lifted and felt lighter already. Bob had waited for her as he'd promised, and she'd also kept her promise of not keeping him waiting for too much longer. The year of 1936 was starting off with flowers, music, family, and promises. And would be followed by a cross-country plane trip. Bob's idea. But Nancy wouldn't mind seeing other parts of the country, especially since she planned on flying at least half of it. Bob had flown up in a Staggerwing, which was currently waiting for them in Chicago.

Her father delivered her to Bob, who grasped her hand. She found that holding on to Bob's hand was one of her favorite things, and right now, it made her feel anchored.

The minister welcomed the congregation somberly, then quoted scripture about the institution of marriage. His words seemed to both last forever and be over faster than she'd expected. No one objected, and after the final prayer, they exchanged vows and rings. Bob kissed her, but she barely felt his touch before they were swept into everyone's congratulations.

Exiting the church, Nancy and Bob waved at all their family and friends. He pulled her close as they moved through the people lined up outside, then he paused and tugged her into a searing kiss as everyone cheered. She definitely felt that one.

She hugged her parents again, then Alison and her boys, and Bob's parents. His mother's eyes were rimmed in red, and looking at her only made Nancy feel like crying too. Finally, Nancy hugged Alice before she turned to Margaret, whose dark-auburn hair set off the pale blue of her dress.

"You're an angel for marrying my brother, Nancy."

Nancy grinned. "I'll keep him on his toes."

All the other goodbyes and well-wishes blended together, and Nancy doubted she'd be able to remember half of them.

They climbed into a limo he'd hired, and blessed silence fell as the doors shut and they pulled away from the church.

Nancy leaned back on the cool leather, her pulse skipping. She was finally married—they'd truly tied the knot.

"Which hotel are we going to, Mr. Love?" she asked. Bob had refused to tell anyone where he was taking her. He'd said he didn't want any pranks.

"It's a surprise, Mrs. Love," he murmured, settling an arm about her shoulders.

"Still?"

"Still."

She nestled against him. He linked their fingers and brought her hand up to his mouth and pressed a kiss there.

"I can't believe we really did it," she said.

"I can't either," Bob said, his other hand tightening around her. "I wondered if I'd be in my thirties before you walked down that aisle."

She elbowed him, and he chuckled.

"Well, you have me now, Bob. What are you going to do with me?"

"I have many, many plans, sweetie."

"Starting with Cheyenne?"

"No, we're not leaving for two days."

She straightened. "What? I thought you were in a hurry to get in the first leg today."

Bob moved his arm and cradled her face with both his hands. "I'm not rushing anything. We'll spend two nights in the hotel. After, we'll fly out of Chicago."

"Oh. That's a surprise."

He kissed her softly, and her eyes slid shut. "I have a few more on the way," he murmured.

Bob remained true to his word, and two days later, they arrived at the Chicago airport and boarded the Staggerwing. They'd already decided that Bob would fly the first leg to Omaha, then Nancy would fly from Omaha to North Platt.

It was thrilling to fly a route she'd never been on, and she was pleased to see Bob writing her married name in his pilot logbook.

When they landed in North Platt to refuel, Nancy said, "It will be dark if we continue to Cheyenne." She'd never flown in the dark before, but Bob had no such reservations.

"It's only two hours to Cheyenne, and I know you're not afraid of the dark."

Nancy scoffed. "No, but flying in the dark is another matter."

"Trust me." Bob grasped her hand and kissed her cheek.

"I trust you—you know that. I just don't have experience in this."

"Better to learn now with a brilliant pilot next to you."

Nancy smirked.

On their way to Cheyenne, she stared out the windscreen, marveling at the moon and the stars and the tiny pricks of light on the earth below. The exhilaration coursing through her reminded her of her first few times flying. When her soul had felt like it was flying too.

"What do you think of night flying?" Bob asked her after they landed in Cheyenne.

"I love it." She smiled up at him, and he pulled her close.

"You might be the only woman at the Sportsmen's Association dinner."

They were heading to Frontier Park as guests of the Wyoming Sportsmen's Association.

"Is that where we're eating tonight?" Nancy asked.

"Yes. I hope you like elk meat."

She shrugged. She didn't care much, as long as she was with her new husband. "I guess I'll find out. Lead the way, Mr. Love."

Nancy was, indeed, the only woman at the dinner, but she felt secure knowing that she was a married woman in the crowd of men. Bob introduced her over and over as his wife, and that felt surreal in and of itself. The evening dragged but mostly because she was tired. Flying all day had taken more out of her than she'd expected, so she was only too happy to retire for the night.

They spent the following day touring Frontier Park. Bob got it into his head that they could fly from Cheyenne to Albuquerque, New Mexico, without stopping.

"The fuel tank isn't big enough," Nancy said as they both worked on the precheck—Bob looking things over and she double-checking everything.

"We'll be coasting with the tail wind," Bob said as he examined the rudder's trim tab.

"It's over four hours to Albuquerque," she said.

"And?"

"And we'll have to stop to refuel, so we need to plan that out. Call the airport in advance to let them know we're coming."

"We'll make it, sweetie."

Nancy straightened and folded her arms. "Bob, this is foolish. We need a plan. You're not a cowboy, and this plane isn't a horse."

He straightened as well and fully faced her. "I've flown planes all over the country, so I think I know what this Staggerwing can do."

He might have more flying experience, but she still knew they couldn't make it that far on one tank of fuel. She grabbed one of the maps and snapped it open, scanning for the airfields along their route. She began to circle the ones that had fuel stations.

"I thought you trusted me," Bob said, an edge to his voice.

She looked up to find his blue eyes stormy. "It's not about trust. It's about reality."

His jaw flexed, but instead of arguing again, he finished the rest of the precheck in silence.

Nancy climbed into the cockpit ahead of him, keeping the map prominently on her lap. Maybe it annoyed him, and if he was right, she could apologize. Maybe . . . But she'd bet her diamond ring that they wouldn't make it.

About thirty minutes into the flight, Bob broke the thick silence between them. "You don't have to use your finger to follow the route."

Nancy didn't know she could feel even more irritated, but it happened. "How about you focus on flying, and when that fuel gauge is on fumes, I'll point you to the nearest airfield."

He snapped his attention back to the windscreen.

Nancy felt only more annoyed when Bob took a few detours, as if tempting fate. He buzzed over a long, twisting river. He tipped the wings back and forth when there was a wild horse herd below.

If she hadn't been feeling so anxious about the decreasing fuel gauge, she might have enjoyed the scenery.

As it was, the fuel gauge continued to drop slowly but surely until it dropped lower than any fuel point she'd ever had on a plane.

"Bob, we need to land," she said above the rumble of the engine.

He opened his mouth, likely to argue, then he noticed the gauge. He had the good sense to look surprised. A moment passed, then two, both in silence. "Let me see the map."

She handed it over, and he scanned the markings she'd circled.

Nancy pointed to a small town. "Otto has an airstrip."

Bob handed the map back. "Guide me in."

So, she did. She might be highly annoyed with the pilot next to her, but they set emotions aside to make the forced landing a safe one. Fortunately, the minuscule airport had fuel they could buy, and after taking off again, thirty minutes later, they were in Albuquerque.

As they carried their bits of luggage into the motel room that Bob had rented, Nancy wondered how long her new husband's pride would last.

He set the bags down and scrubbed a hand through his helmet-matted hair. "Do you hate me?"

She turned to face him. His height seemed to dwarf the small room. "Only a little bit."

Relief flooded his eyes, and he smiled.

She smiled back.

"Sometimes, I'm a knucklehead."

"That's an understatement."

He shut the door and walked toward her, his eyes holding her gaze. "Am I sleeping on the couch?"

"I thought about it, but there isn't actually a couch in this room. What did you pay for it?"

He chuckled. "Not much, and now I'm glad." He moved closer, and she slipped her arms about his neck. Peace with her husband was much better than what they'd experienced today.

"You were right, sweetie, as usual." His hands moved around her waist and along her back.

She lifted up on her toes and kissed the edge of his mouth. "You really shouldn't ever forget that. I already have a souvenir from one plane wreck."

His gaze shifted to the gray streak in her hair. "It's distinctive, but I agree, one souvenir is more than enough."

# CHAPTER NINETEEN

"Now I'm going South and then West to survey the marking that's been done. What's next? I suppose I'll keep doing what I'm doing now. It's such fun. And safer than automobiles, really. You can make a mistake of 1,000 feet in the air and correct the mistake, but make a mistake of a single foot on the highway and you'll smash into a telephone pole.... It's quite easy to fly this plane."

—NANCY LOVE, *BOSTON TRAVELER*

*August–September 1936—Inter City, Boston*

"No, Mother, we're not pregnant yet." Nancy hid her exasperated sigh as they chatted on the phone during their regular Sunday night call. Nancy had been married eight months, and yes, many new brides became pregnant in the first year of marriage, but she wasn't going to fret over her situation; her mother was doing that for her.

Bob hadn't seemed too worried either. He'd only said they had plenty of time and would be married for many years to come, so what was the rush?

Just because her mother had pointed out that all other young, married couples were starting their families.

Her mother's next statement was no surprise either. "Maybe you should slow down. You're always up in the air someplace, and Bob works all hours."

Yes, they were busy. Nancy was flying demos, hopping passengers, and staying useful at Inter City. Bob was constantly either on business calls or ferrying planes around.

"We're together most of the time, day and night, Mother. You don't have to worry so much. Children will come when they come." Privately, she'd wondered if something were medically wrong with her, but if she and Bob got antsy, she could consult with a doctor. Right now, though, her mother was the only one pushing for it.

"But you aren't opposed to them?" Hope laced her mother's voice. "You aren't trying to prevent them?"

Nancy should be used to this, but tonight, she was tired from a busy week, and her mother's questions were feeling more intrusive than usual. "Like you've pointed out many times, I'm still very young. I think we have time."

Her mother's silence stretched, and a prickle of guilt moved through Nancy. Time was a crux for all of them. No one had had enough time with her brother. Her parents were getting older. Besides, Nancy wasn't opposed to getting pregnant. It simply hadn't happened.

Bob walked into the kitchen, where she sat at the table. He'd probably overheard her end of the conversation and the stress in her voice. He paused behind her and set his hands on her shoulders, then rubbed gently.

The tension began to ease. "Mother, I'm sorry to be so short with you. It's been a long week."

"Well, I understand that sometimes these things take time," Mother conceded, but her voice had stiffened again. "I hope you have a good week."

"You too. I'll call next Sunday."

After they hung up, Nancy put her hand on Bob's. "Don't stop."

He continued rubbing her shoulders, then leaned down and kissed the top of her head. "Your mother's talking about babies again?"

"Yes, but I think it's more . . ." She paused.

"What could be more than babies?" he asked, sounding amused.

Nancy rose from her chair and turned to face him. "I think she's becoming a recluse. Father said she's not going to her regular activities."

"Ah, so she's focusing on your life instead."

"Yes, I mean, I am an only child now."

Bob drew her close. "We could go visit in the next couple of weeks."

"That would be great." They'd settled down outside of Boston at Trapelo Farm in Waltham, so visits home weren't as often as her parents would like them to be. "You're kind of a great husband."

He raised his eyebrows. "You're just figuring that out?"

"I've known it for a while, but I didn't want your ego to get too inflated."

With a laugh, Bob slid his arms behind her. "A little ego inflation never hurt any man."

"Ha." She kissed him. "Maybe not *you* since you're one of the good ones."

Bob's smile was brief. "Which is why we need to talk about Pappy's telegram from earlier today. Have you thought more about it?"

Nancy stepped out of his arms and picked up the telegram sitting in the middle of the kitchen table. William A. Ong had written to her—they called him *Pappy*—about the Bendix Race. Louise Thaden was searching for a copilot.

SUGGEST YOU CONTACT LOUISE THADEN BY TELEGRAPH—
SHE WILL BE AT THE FACTORY TOMORROW—AND ASK TO
GO AS COPILOT IN BENDIX RACE FLYING FOUR TWENTY
BEECHCRAFT. I THINK YOU WOULD BE OF GREAT ASSISTANCE
AND IT WOULD BE A FINE EXPERIENCE FOR YOU. HOPE TO
SEE YOU IN LOS ANGELES.

    BILL ONG

She set the telegram down again. "I don't know."

"Why don't you know?" Bob asked with genuine curiosity. "Because of the racing aspect? You're as good a flyer as any of the other women."

Nancy lifted her gaze to meet his direct one. "I don't know if racing is my thing, even if I would win money. If anyone is going to race, it should be you, cowboy."

Bob touched her chin. "Well, I'm not the one who was invited. If you want to join Louise, then do it, but only do it because you want to. Not for anyone else."

"Well, I am tempted."

He nodded. "Thought so."

She slipped her hand into his. "Like I said, you're a great husband. Not many men would want their wives racing across the skies in a small plane."

"I'm not going to hold you back on anything you want to do."

She grinned at him. "Just don't tell Mother until after the fact."

"Deal."

The very next day, Nancy telegraphed Louise at the Beechcraft factory. Louise's reply came back within the hour, and Nancy went to find Bob out in the hangar at Inter City.

"It's off." She held out the telegraph.

Bob turned from where he was speaking to a mechanic. "The race?"

"No. Louise has a copilot already. She asked Blanche Noyes."

Bob took the telegraph and scanned through it. After a moment, his gaze connected with hers. "There are more races."

*He knew.* How he knew, she wasn't sure. She hadn't even known herself until she'd received the reply from Louise. Nancy did want to race. At least once. Try it out. Maybe it was for her; maybe it wasn't. But money could be made, and she was very curious to see how her skills might match up to other women pilots'.

"You're right, there are more races," Nancy said slowly. "Pappy wrote again."

Bob's eyes sparked as he read the next telegram from Bill Ong.

SORRY ABOUT BENDIX BUT WILL ENTER YOU IN THE AMELIA EARHART RACE FLYING JACOBS BEECHCRAFT IF YOU WILL ACCEPT. THIS EVENT IS HANDICAPPED CLOSE-COURSE RACE, AND I THINK YOU WILL HAVE EXCELLENT CHANCE. WIRE ME IMMEDIATELY . . . HAVE BEAUTIFUL SHIP HERE NOW WHICH I COULD DELIVER TO YOU FOLKS AT ONCE AND YOU COULD RACE THIS SHIP IF YOU DESIRE. DON'T LET US DOWN AND TELL BOB WE WON'T KIDNAP YOU EVEN THOUGH WE MIGHT LIKE TO.

BILL ONG

"No one's going to kidnap you," Bob said, looking up from the telegram. "I'm coming too."

Nancy's brows shot up. "You think I should do it?"

He didn't answer, just waited.

"All right. I want to do it." She threw her arms about his neck. "I can't believe I'm doing this."

Bob's laugh warmed her through. "Go write back to Pappy. Let him know we've got room for that new Beechcraft."

Plans came together quickly, and a few days later, she and Bob took turns between pilot and copilot as they flew across the country to make it to the National Air Races in Los Angeles. Pappy had entered her into the Amelia Earhart Trophy Race, which was a handicap pylon race of flying a triangular course against other planes.

Nancy had expected to be nervous, but it was also thrilling. On the day of the race, her pulse thrummed as she waited for the starter's flag to go up. She'd kept the throttle on her plane wide open while at the same time pressing her heels on the brakes.

The instant the flag went down, her adrenaline spiked, and she tried to keep her focus on a steady takeoff. It was almost impossible not to pay attention to the other planes around her as she took the first turn, tipping her left wing to make the maneuver smooth. Another plane was already ahead of her, but she didn't expect first place. She didn't want to be last either. Lap after lap, she repeated the turns, trying not to ease up on speed too much. She passed a plane, then another passed her, like they were playing cat and mouse, although she wasn't sure who the cat was and who the mouse was.

Another plane edged ahead of her, and she had to move to take the outside of the next turn. Her eyes stung with sweat, and her wrist ached from working the throttle. Finally, she crossed the final marker, and she pulled the plane up to coast in the sky for a few moments before finally landing.

She hadn't won, but she hadn't been last either.

The first person she searched for was Bob.

He reached her within minutes of her landing. "Fifth place," Bob said, sweeping her into his arms. She was dizzy, not from flying but from the race. "Hot dog, sweetheart! You even won seventy-five dollars."

She was still breathless and needed to wash off all the perspiration, but she laughed. "I guess I'm paying for dinner?"

"Definitely," Bob said, then kissed her soundly.

Others came to congratulate her, and while it was exhilarating to have placed fifth in her very first race, her mind was already on the next race she'd entered. The Women's Air Race in Detroit on September 20. She'd be flying a Monocoupe, and she wanted to get more practice on that plane.

A couple of days after she and Bob returned to Inter City, Louise Thaden and Blanche Noyes won the Bendix—a 2,500-mile race from Bennett Field in New York to Mines Field in Los Angeles.

Nancy and Bob both pored over the newspaper articles about the victory of the female pilots. "Four hours and fifty-five minutes of flying time. Imagine!" Nancy mused.

"They'll be going down in the history and record books," Bob said. "The first women pilot team to win the Bendix, beating out everyone."

"Impressive." Nancy regretted not being the copilot of the race, but nothing could be changed now. Maybe someday . . . ?

"Ready to get more flying hours on the Monocoupe?" Bob asked.

"Sure, but there's no way to really train for speed unless we want to set up pylons."

"You can use landmarks as pinpoints."

That was Nancy's only real option. She reached for the helmet she'd set on the edge of the desk and pulled it on. Then she tugged on her goggles, keeping them on her forehead for now. Bob walked with her out of the hangar and to the plane. He inspected a few things while she did her precheck. She knew she spent more time than most, but she never regretted it.

"Ready?" Bob asked when she finally came back around the plane.

"Ready."

He kissed her softly. "Go get 'em."

"Be back soon." She climbed into the cockpit. Closed the door. Pulled on her goggles. Started the engine. The propeller gained speed. She was off, down the runway. As she lifted into the air, her stomach tightened in its familiar way. She flew her training route, increasing her speed with each pass of her designated landmarks.

The race was coming up quickly, and she wanted to be ready, but she also didn't want to waste time and fuel, not at Inter City's expense, which was also her expense now. So, she did the route only a few times before she ended for the day.

She practiced every day until September 20 arrived, and Nancy hoped she was ready. She got to the Wayne County Airport an hour before most of the other racers. She wanted to oversee the fuel being put into her plane to make sure it was the best quality offered. It wasn't that she didn't trust the mechanics, but a woman could never be too careful.

At the start of the race, her heart began its familiar pound. She might have raced before, but her pulse seemed to have forgotten. She felt better, though, stronger and more confident. Mostly, it was thrilling, but once the race got underway, it was basically a free-for-all. No one had to prove qualifications to fly in the race, and at least two of the pilots had mechanical issues and were forced to land early.

"Second place!" Bob called out the moment she opened the plane door.

She already knew that, but it was nice to hear it confirmed. Photographers rushed to her plane and snapped photos as she climbed out. She lifted up her goggles and did a quick pose before hugging Bob.

"That was incredible," he said with a laugh. "I'll admit, my heart rate was going crazy."

"My heart almost stopped a few times," Nancy teased, but there was also truth behind those words. She hadn't liked feeling pressured to keep going fast even when she hadn't been sure that she was in full control of her plane.

Congratulations came from race officials, other pilots, and onlookers. They stuck around the rest of the day, watching other races. It was like a minireunion with pilots she'd known for a long time as well as ones she'd met more recently at the Amelia Earhart Trophy Race.

When they made it back to their hotel room, Bob asked, "What do you need? Wine? A bath? Sleep?"

"All of it." Nancy was dog-tired, so she decided to let Bob spoil her tonight. Well, he always did that. "I guess I'd better call my folks first. Let them know the results."

After the phone call in which Nancy spoke only to her father, she turned to Bob. "As fun as that was, I don't think racing is my thing."

"You placed second, Nancy. That's nothing to sniff at."

"That's not what I mean." She sat on the corner of the bed. "It's so chaotic. Not that I think racing should be smooth sailing, but once we all took off, it felt like a dogfight. The tension wasn't enjoyable for me. I mean, I love flying, and flying fast is fun, but I'm not flying to prove anything to anyone. I fly because I love it."

Bob crossed to sit by her, taking her hand. "Did your father say something to you?"

"No, he was excited about the results." She leaned her head against his shoulder. "You know me. I have to arrive an hour early to do my long precheck. I don't like racing against others who haven't been as thorough and only care about pushing their aircraft to the absolute limits. Even if it's dangerous. I'm not a cowboy pilot like you."

Bob tightened his hold on her hand. "You've got flying skills that all those women and men envy, Nancy."

"Maybe." She lifted her chin. "But that was my last race."

# CHAPTER TWENTY

"If her last flight was into eternity, one can mourn her loss but not regret her effort. Amelia did not lose, for her last flight was endless. Like in a relay race of progress she had merely placed the torch in the hands of others to carry on to the next goal and from there on and on forever."

—JACQUELINE COCHRAN, QUOTED IN *THOSE WONDERFUL WOMEN IN THEIR FLYING MACHINES* BY SALLY VAN WAGENEN KEIL

*March–September 1937—Boston*

"It cruises at about ninety-five miles an hour," Nancy told the group of scribbling reporters, their hats pushed back, collars open, ties dangling as the unseasonably hot day grew hotter. "Her limit is 112, and she stops within 100 feet after touching the ground."

Nancy leaned against the wing of the Stearman-Hammond Y plane, the star aircraft of the day. The Hammond Y was a tricycle-gear aircraft and had won the design competition at the Department of Commerce, and Nancy had been hired to fly and demonstrate the plane to show off how safe it was to fly. The only downside was that Bob had to remain behind to run Inter City.

"How safe is the Hammond compared to other planes?" one of the reporters asked, cigarette dangling.

"Safer than an automobile, and that's all that matters," Nancy said with a coy smile. "You can make a mistake a thousand feet in the air and correct the mistake, but make a mistake of a single foot on the highway and you'll smash into a telephone pole."

The reporters chuckled.

She surveyed the men in front of her. "Anyone want a demo ride? I'll let you take over the controls for a bit."

The reporters glanced at each other, some with surprised looks on their faces, others with doubtful expressions. Finally, one man, sporting a scant blond mustache, lifted a hand. "I'll go up with you, Mrs. Love."

"Excellent." She reached into the plane and handed over an extra helmet and goggles.

"Right now?" the man asked.

"Is there a better time?"

Everyone laughed, and the reporter's face flushed. He took the helmet and goggles, and soon, they were taking off. Circling the airport, Nancy explained the basic controls of the aircraft, then said, "All right, you're on the controls. Just follow what I say."

The man's face had paled, but he gamely took over. Nancy gave him a few more instructions and corrections, but he was flying the plane. As they prepared to land, she took over again, but he was beaming with his accomplishment.

"Did I dream all of that?" he asked, his voice one pitch higher.

Nancy smiled, knowing exactly how he felt. "It can be surreal, but I assure you, sir, that you did, indeed, fly this plane."

When her father called the next day, they both exclaimed over the article printed in the *Christian Science Monitor*. "The reporter was really bowled over by the experience," he said.

"He was pretty nervous, but he loved it," Nancy mused, remembering the fair-haired reporter's astonishment.

"What's next? Continuing the demos?"

"No. Tomorrow I'm back in my own plane and heading to meet with officials throughout Maine to continue pitching the Airmarking Program." Nancy had recently signed on with the Airmarking Program again. "This time, though, I'll get reimbursed for flying my own private plane."

"A Stinson, right?"

"Yes, the new 1937 five-passenger Stinson."

"Room enough for me and Mother?"

"Both of you are welcome anytime." Nancy could almost hear his smile through the phone.

After she hung up with her father, she called Bob. It was good to hear his voice, as usual. She was happy to do this new job for the government, but she was working harder and faster in order to finish sooner.

"We miss you around here," Bob said into the phone. "Lots going on."

"Ah, and what about you? Do *you* miss me?"

"You know I do."

"Not unless you say it."

Bob chuckled quietly. "I miss you, sweetie. Now, is that good enough?"

She was smiling. "How much?"

He groaned. "A lot, all right? When do we see each other again?"

She'd already told him the night before, but she repeated her plans again, then they chatted about the comings and goings at Inter City. Things were looking up all the way around.

"We're going to be taking passengers to the yacht races near Marblehead the last week of August," Bob said. "Will you be done by then?"

"I plan to be done. If not, I'll take the week off."

But in July, the world seemed to stop for Nancy, and everyone else in the country. The radios and newspapers had been following the news of Amelia Earhart's 29,000-mile, around-the-world flight that had started from Miami on June 1. There'd been stopovers in South America, Africa, Southeast Asia, and, most recently, a landing in Lae, New Guinea, on June 29. Earhart had taken off the morning of July 2 from Lae Airfield with her only crew member, Fred Noonan. The remaining 7,000 miles would be over the Pacific Ocean, where their next destination would be Howland Island.

They never made it.

The United States Navy and Coast Guard spent the next days and weeks in a massive air and sea hunt for Earhart's Electra plane. But the long days and nights passed, and by July 19, they had found nothing and had called off the official search. Amelia's husband, George P. Putnam, financed his own private search, hiring local authorities from nearby islands, but still no trace of the Electra.

It was all everyone talked about as Nancy worked her airmarking job. She pushed through the days, feeling slow, sluggish, surrounded by a sense of surrealness—much like after she'd lost her brother. Although she hadn't known Amelia Earhart personally, the woman was an icon to all pilots, especially women pilots. Her loss was unbelievable and tragic and numbing. It also gave Nancy a stronger sense of purpose. If Amelia could reach for her dreams at all cost, even risking her life, Nancy could excel in something as homegrown as the Airmarking Program and push aside the long hours and how much she missed Bob.

By the time August rolled around, she was ahead of schedule. Upon Nancy's return to Boston, Bob took the day off so they could spend time together without work getting in the way for either of them. They'd spent many late nights on the phone discussing all the theories surrounding Amelia Earhart's disappearance. Now Nancy just wanted to be with Bob, and she needed to catch up on home matters.

"Tomorrow, we're catering to a Paramount News film crew," Bob said as they sat on their porch, watching the sun set as the air finally cooled. Nancy had made tomato soup, which had made them both laugh, and Bob had put together sandwiches and a salad.

"Paramount? That's exciting." She reached for his hand, happy to just be with him again. "They're going to the races and filming?"

"Apparently so. They're staying in Boston, and they've booked two trips out there over the next few days."

"I'll fly them."

Bob looked at her. "I thought you were running errands tomorrow."

"You'll be at Inter City, so I want to be there too."

He grinned and leaned over to kiss her. "I won't complain about that." He tugged her onto his lap.

She nestled against him. "It will be fun, so it's only a benefit to me."

Sure enough, flying the film crew turned out to be an adventure. First, the crew's faces were completely comical when Bob introduced them to Nancy—their pilot.

With her new passengers, she buzzed the plane low over the yachting events, going as slowly as possible so they got great aerial shots. The crew was more than pleased by the time they landed back at Inter City. They were all sunburned and windblown but were thrilled with the filming and photography they did.

"She's a top-notch pilot," one of the crewmen told Bob. "I don't know if I've ever flown with a better one."

Bob only nodded.

"And she's your wife to boot."

Bob nodded again, a smile edging his mouth.

"Hollywood could always use a good stunt pilot," the photographer continued.

"I'm more of an East Coast gal," Nancy cut in, throwing Bob a wink. She moved to his side. "Now, tomorrow, we need to get an earlier start so we can see more of the races."

"Yes, ma'am," the men chorused.

As they headed to their hired car, Nancy turned to Bob. "They'd better tip well when you settle the bill tomorrow."

His eyes gleamed. "I have no doubt they will, sweetie. Now, do you have a minute? There's something you need to see in my office."

They walked through the hangar and into his office. When he handed her the telegram, she read through it quickly. Then a second time, more slowly. Joseph Marr Gwinn Jr. was inviting her to New York to be the test pilot for his newly designed Gwinn Aircar. The plane was built around the tricycle-landing-gear design that Nancy was already experienced with.

"Why is he asking me?"

Bob raised his brows. "You have sixty hours on the Hammond and tons of experience demonstrating planes, not to mention over 500 flight hours total. You're a natural fit."

"You mean a poster girl."

His head tilted. "That too."

Nancy set the letter down and sighed. "Is this too gimmicky?"

"Maybe?" Bob said. "But Gwinn is no dreamer. He flew in the Great War, and he's a brilliant aeronautical engineer. Been designing trainer airplanes for the past decade, at least."

"But it's in Buffalo, and I feel like we've been apart too much this year."

Bob moved toward her and set his hands on her hips. "I'll come with you to Buffalo."

"You can't—we have an airfield to run. Well, you've been doing all the work lately."

He kissed her forehead, his lips warm from the sunny day. "This is innovation, Nancy. We're witnesses to the future of flying evolving around us. You can be my demo girl or Gwinn's, but he pays more. Whatever you decide, I'll support you. But I don't have a new invention that might set off a storm of other improvements in aviation."

"Oh, I see. You're kind of excited about this," she teased.

"It sounds fascinating."

"It does . . ." Nancy gnawed her lip. "I guess I could try it out, and if Joe Gwinn is too much of a pest, I'll tell him to find another person." She tapped Bob's chest. "But you're coming out regularly. Buffalo isn't far, and I'm tired of having to tell you everything through a phone receiver."

"That does get old." He tilted his head to fully look into her eyes. "Are you sure? Should we sleep on it?"

"No, I'm going to reply right now. Just in case he has others in mind."

Nancy took the job and soon learned that as intelligent and dynamic as Joe Gwinn was, he was also a cowboy pilot—more so than her husband. At the end of August, they met at the Consolidated Field, where the Gwinn Aircar Company was headquartered. After introductions to some of Joe's employees, they headed out to the aircraft for an inspection. The Aircar had two seats, side by side, and the front wheel was steerable.

"I want to demonstrate this in the National Air Races," Joe said as they walked around the plane.

Nancy stopped cold. "This year? That's only a few days away."

Joe nodded and pushed up his glasses. He was a shorter man, with a dark receding hairline and close-set eyes that didn't miss a thing. "That's why we can't waste a minute."

Nancy weighed her options. She wouldn't be able to make an assessment until she flew the thing. "Show me everything about this plane so I can create an accurate precheck."

Joe smiled, and they climbed into the plane.

"All right, you're going to accelerate fast on takeoff," Joe said. "Then you step on the foot pedal that lets down the flaps, and we'll lift from the ground."

Nancy listened, committing everything to memory.

"Once we're fifty or so feet in the air, let off the pedal, but keep climbing. There's no rudder, so use the steering wheel to operate the ailerons. Ready?"

Nancy was ready. They took off, and she followed Joe's instructions.

Once they were in the air, he said, "Now, keep the fore and aft control within seventeen degrees, either up or down."

Flying with Joe Gwinn amounted to Nancy doing all the flying as Joe told her what to do—or *experiment* might be a better description. He wanted to make sure that another pilot, other than himself, could manage his contraption. In all of Nancy's previous experiences in demonstrating planes, she'd flown them how they'd been meant to be flown. Safely, and within the parameters of the machinery.

But Joe wanted her to test things she'd never tried before—things opposite of how she'd been taught and trained.

"On this landing, keep the control column full back," Joe said when they were 2,000 feet in the air. "Keep the flaps down and the engine throttled."

"But we're going over 900 feet per minute," Nancy protested.

"It will be fine," Joe said. "Just hold the wheel back."

She shot him a glance, but he was perfectly serious, perfectly intent.

Clenching her jaw, she did as asked, even though every instinct in her was telling her to slow down, to pull up. She just hoped he was getting the data he needed.

After the maneuver, she was finally allowed to slow down, and Joe said, "Now, to land, push on the flaps with the foot pedal. Lose the fore and aft control, then you'll move into a level position."

After the first landing and a short break, he was on to their next experiment. "Let's find out the minimum speed this beauty can fly while still maintaining altitude."

Nancy began to climb the plane, but Joe said, "Keep it at twenty feet above ground."

She hadn't even done that with the Paramount News crew. She bit back her protest and descended.

"Keep the nose higher," Joe said once they were cruising at twenty feet altitude. "Open the engine and fully extend the flaps."

The plane dipped.

"Faster," Joe demanded.

Nancy watched the airspeed; they'd nearly reached fifty miles per hour.

"Slow it down."

She did, and they finally found the minimum at forty-two miles per hour.

"That's with two pilots inside," Joe mused. "We need to find out what the minimum is with one pilot."

Over the next few days, she flew at all hours, until somehow, some way, Nancy was ready to fly the Aircar for the National Air Races as well as in the parade that went through Cleveland. She demonstrated takeoffs and landings. Later in September, she piloted her first solo long-distance flight in the Aircar from Buffalo to Washington, DC.

Nancy was officially enamored by the family-friendly aircraft.

# PART TWO

## 1939–1944

# CHAPTER TWENTY-ONE

"On Thursday, twenty planes will take off from various points on the Atlantic seaboard for New Hampshire's Lake Winnipesaukee. There the pilots and their guests will lunch before their joint departure for Moosehead Lake in Maine for a weekend of fishing, swimming and aviation gossip.... These inveterate fliers, and Robert M. Loves, will fly from Boston to the New Hampshire starting point."

—DOROTHY G. WALKER, SOCIETY REPORTER

*July 1939–May 1940—Lake Winnipesaukee, New Hampshire*

Nancy lifted her hand to shade her eyes as she stood with Bob, watching the incoming seaplane. The annual pilot's cruise had started, and everyone was meeting in Lake Winnipesaukee. She'd earned her seaplane rating the summer before, and they'd joined an elite social group of pilots for a weekend holiday.

The seaplanes were like flying pontoons, able to land in the harbors all along the eastern seaboard. Their group of flyers had even made the *New York World Telegram* newspaper headlines as "Society Fliers Are Getting Ready for Annual Cruise."

"Is that the Gillieses?" Bob asked, also shading his eyes to watch the incoming seaplane.

"Must be," Nancy said. She'd met Betty through the Ninety-Nines, and Betty had come with her husband, Bud Gillies, the year before on the annual cruise. They were from Syosset, New York, and they'd all become fast friends. Betty worked for an aircraft company on Long Island, and she was currently the president of the Ninety-Nines. Bud served as one of the executives of Grumman Aircraft and worked as a test pilot for military planes.

The seaplane made an effortless landing, then taxied to the dock. The wings caught the midday sunlight and made a pretty picture on a summer day as the plane motored on the crystal-blue water. Above, the royal-blue sky was dotted with scattered clouds of innocent white.

Nancy's chest expanded, and she linked her hand with Bob's. This could be, quite possibly, the most perfect summer day.

When the seaplane reached the dock, Betty Gillies climbed out of the cockpit, followed by her husband. When Betty spotted Nancy and Bob walking toward them, she waved vigorously. She was in her early thirties, petite at only five foot one and couldn't weigh more than a hundred pounds. Her ready smile was accented by her high cheekbones and pert nose.

The two women embraced, then Nancy stepped back. "How was the flight?"

"Beautiful," Betty said. "Are you both ready for a fantastic weekend?"

"Brought the fishing rods," Bob said, but he'd been eyeing the sailboats for the past hour, and Nancy wouldn't be surprised if he rented one when they reached their final destination at Moosehead Lake in Maine.

"Are we the last to arrive?" Bud glanced about the harbor for more of their aviator friends.

"You are," Nancy said. "We wanted to watch for you. Everyone's at the harbor restaurant."

The two couples continued along the dock and walked into the restaurant, where the pilots had all gathered for a luncheon. Some of them had brought along guests, but most of the crowd were aviators.

They found seats at one of the tables.

"I love the ambiance here," Betty said, settling next to Nancy.

Across from them sat Mrs. Teddy Kenyon, whom Nancy remembered meeting several years before at the Hotel Lennox. They'd shared a photo with Mr. Vidal—and from that one meeting, so much of Nancy's last few years of her aviation career had formed.

"Wonderful to see you again, Mrs. Kenyon." Nancy extended her hand across the table.

Mrs. Kenyon's smile was quick, displaying her dimples. Her dark hair waved to her shoulders, longer than most women's in the room.

"You're looking well, Mrs. Love. Marriage suits you. But I think we can be more informal here. Call me Cecil, or Teddy; everyone does."

"Of course. And call me Nancy."

"Will do," Teddy said. "You've been busy with Gwinn, haven't you? Demonstrated at the National Air Races, then made long-distance flights in the Aircar."

"That's right," Nancy said.

"What do you think about the aircraft?"

"Very friendly and safe to fly in good weather conditions."

"I read an article about what you said," Betty cut in. "That a grandma could take an Aircar to a ladies' aid meeting without nervous tension."

Everyone around the table laughed.

Nancy smiled. "That sounds familiar."

"And now you're a member of the Gwinn's company board of directors?" Teddy continued. "Impressive."

"That was Harry Bruno's idea, but not everyone on the board agreed." Nancy drank from her glass, then added, "I was the wrong sex. Too pretty. Too young."

Teddy scoffed and waved her hand. "That makes your input even more important."

"That's what I said," Bob said, bemused.

"And that's what Harry argued for," Nancy said. "Told the board that he didn't want me to attend board meetings, exactly, but the title and representing the face of Aircar would open doors for the company."

Teddy's smile was broad. "You certainly did that. Well done, Nancy."

She shrugged and took a sip of water. Bob and Bud fell into their own conversation, something about fishing lures.

Nancy looked over at Teddy. "In the end, I became an assistant manager, and they paired me up with Frank Hawks."

Teddy's expression sobered. "Sorry to hear about Frank's death. I didn't know him, but it's a huge loss to the aviation industry."

"Yes," Nancy agreed. It had been a blow when the news had come, and she still couldn't believe the vibrant, charismatic daredevil of a man was gone.

Betty squeezed her shoulder. "You weren't flying the Aircar any longer at the time of Frank's crash, right?"

"Right." Nancy traced a finger along the outside of her glass of water, absorbing the condensation. "My last flight was June of last year. Frank's crash was in August."

The three fell silent for a moment as conversation droned from the other tables.

"What exactly happened?" Teddy asked in a subdued voice. "If you don't mind my asking?"

"Nothing was covered up, if that's what you mean." Nancy didn't mind clarifying. "The newspaper reports were accurate. Frank took off with a client, and the wind gusts weren't accounted for. They struck telephone wires, and when they crashed, the plane caught fire. Neither of them had a chance."

The women about the table shook their heads.

"The irony of it," Nancy said thoughtfully, "is that through all the flying Frank did before—his daredevil stuff: setting speed records in racing—he was fine. He earned over 200 flying records."

Teddy folded her hands atop the table. "He was certainly a legend. Loved the Hollywood scene too. Have you ever thought of working for Hollywood?"

Nancy reached for Bob's hand, and he glanced at her, breaking from his conversation with Bud.

"Not for me." Nancy shrugged. "And you?"

"Oh, heavens no." Teddy flashed a wry smile. "I don't do dives and snap rolls for entertainment. Flying is serious business for me. I've long thought female pilots shouldn't be relegated to demo girls. No offense, Nancy."

"None taken," Nancy said.

Teddy leaned forward, her dark brows arched, her tone conspiratorial. "There's no reason there can't be women pilots in the military. We've proven time and time again that we can beat them in air races."

The men's conversation about them quieted as Teddy spoke.

"Racing isn't for everyone though," Nancy countered as a waiter set salads in front of everyone around the table. She reached for her fork. "Two were good enough for me. It's not that I don't like speed; I don't like the idea of competing for it."

Teddy's nod was thoughtful as she picked up her own fork and speared a slice of tomato. "That's my point exactly. Racing isn't for everyone, and demonstrating private planes to potential buyers isn't for everyone either. I think we need more options and variety. It's like an entire population of skilled pilots is continually looked over. Last year when Roosevelt opened the Civilian Pilot Training Program on college campuses, it gave me hope." She ate the tomato, then reached for the salt and pepper, liberally dousing the rest of her salad.

Nancy had heard of the CPT Program that provided pilot training for college students, although only one woman per ten men was allowed to enroll.

Bob took a couple of bites of his salad. He set his arm around the back of Nancy's chair, his focus shifting to Teddy. "If women flew for the military, next thing you'd know is they'd be flying combat. No one wants that."

Teddy sipped at her drink, then cocked her head. "Perhaps. Perhaps not." She lifted a nonchalant shoulder. "But women can do many things for their country in the air forces, just like they do in England, France, Germany, and the Soviet Union, where women are trained and ready to help with any war efforts."

"Ah," Betty cut in. "You're talking about the German-Soviet Non-aggression Pact that Hitler and Stalin signed."

Nancy felt cold prickles along her arms, as if she'd rubbed pieces of ice on her skin. Newspapers had been screaming about Hitler's planned invasion of Poland, and the Soviets weren't protesting. In fact, Stalin had promised to help conquer and divide the nation. But Great Britain and France had promised Poland military support if the invasion should happen. It all had the makings of another world war.

Teddy looked at Bob. "You're in the Air Corps Reserve, right, Bob?"

"Yes. I signed up in '37 and accepted the commission as a second lieutenant."

"What's the commitment like?" Teddy pressed.

Nancy was surprised at Teddy's persistence at all of this, but the more the woman talked, the more Nancy agreed.

"Two weeks of active duty each January." Bob added more dressing to his salad, then took another bite.

"He's mostly doing experimental flying and weather observation flights for the government," Nancy added.

"No combat missions, and yet"—Teddy tapped her fingers on the table—"your work is helping to further the Air Corps Programs, correct?"

"Sure." Bob moved his arm from the back of Nancy's chair and pushed his salad plate aside to lean forward too. "What are you suggesting?"

Teddy's sharp gaze pinned Bob. "Why shouldn't the Army Air Corps employ female pilots? Do you think, say, your wife could do the same experimental flying that you do?"

"Of course," Bob said without hesitation. "Might even be better. She's very thorough."

"That's what I mean," Teddy said. "Women can handle the noncombat jobs for the Army Air Corps. Things like ferrying planes and other duties that pertain to jobs on American soil."

The conversation with Teddy Kenyon stayed with Nancy throughout the rest of the weekend. And continued to resonate for weeks after. On September 1, Hitler made good on his promises and invaded Poland from the west. Two days later, France and Britain declared war on Germany. Finally, on September 17, Soviet troops invaded Poland from the east.

Nancy and Bob watched it all unfold through the newspapers and listening to radio broadcasts.

"It's unbelievable," Betty said one night on the phone when Nancy called her. "Poland is pretty much in the hands of the Germans and Soviets. One of the Air Corps captains, William H. Tunner, is actively recruiting local pilots for the reserve. But my husband is talking about going to England and flying for the Royal Air Force."

Nancy drew in a breath and sat at the scrubbed kitchen table. Bob knew Tunner too. But thankfully Bob hadn't brought up flying with the RAFs, though she'd heard plenty of buzz from other pilots.

"Jacqueline Cochran told me she wrote a letter to Eleanor Roosevelt," Betty continued.

"Personal friends now, huh?" Nancy said with a laugh. She knew Jackie Cochran only through Margaret Thomas's association with her, and the Ninety-Nines group. Cochran was ambitiously pursuing any air races where women were allowed.

"Not exactly. You've heard how Cochran makes everything her business."

"For better or for worse." Nancy rose from the kitchen table and crossed to the window. She gazed out at the peaceful landscape that spread before their farmhouse. Peace and quiet was easily come by here—not so much in Poland.

"Cochran suggested that women pilots be utilized by the Army Air Corps during this time of unrest," Betty said. "Flying ambulance planes, couriers, as well as commercial and transport planes."

"Sounds like what Teddy's been suggesting for a while," Nancy mused.

"But Cochran went straight to the top because she's pushing for militarizing women pilots."

This made Nancy pause. "What was Mrs. Roosevelt's reply?"

"She's favorable," Betty said, "although there's a lot of organizing to do if something were to actually be implemented. But until then, as you and Teddy discussed, we can't wait for an emergency to enact a plan if a plan isn't already in place, and pilots aren't already trained."

"Exactly." Nancy looked over at the kitchen counter, where she'd left the most recent newsletter of the Ninety-Nines. She thoroughly read it each month and knew the stats. "We have about 650 licensed female pilots in the nation."

"That's what Cochran pointed out too," Betty said. "Proper training should begin well in advance."

As Betty continued to talk, Nancy wondered what approach might truly be effective in training women pilots to qualify to work for the Army Air Corps. Maybe someone like Captain Tunner might have an idea? From everything Bob had told her about him, he was very active in the recruitment side of things.

Throughout the next weeks and months, the news coming from Europe became more grim. Nancy and Bob were in constant conversation about the happenings, as were all the other pilots they saw. Several of their male pilot friends headed over to England to join the RAFs.

Poland fell quickly, and Stalin's forces were moving in on the Baltic States, the Russo-Finnish War in full swing. The British and German navies faced off as German U-boat submarines destroyed merchant ships heading for Britain. Over 100 vessels had been sunk.

In January 1940, the British ATA, organized at the beginning of the war, invited eight female pilots to join their Civilian Ferry Pilots Program. The ATA oversaw the transporting of all military aircraft from factories to maintenance units. They also delivered planes to transatlantic locations and active service squadrons. So far, the women pilots were allowed to fly only the Tiger Moth biplanes, but rumors were coming in that some of the women were training on bigger aircraft.

Betty was the first person Nancy called when she read the headlines while sitting in the cramped office of Inter City.

"It's a new age," Betty declared over the phone.

"Exactly." Nancy stood to pace about the room, the phone cord dragging along with her. "The Attagirls are part of the war effort. Imagine. Female pilots aiding in the war effort for their country—using their hard-earned skills." She paused. "We can do more. *I* can do more."

"I agree—we can all do more," Betty said. "Between you and Bob, you pretty much know everyone. More people than Jackie Cochran, I'm guessing."

"Cochran's primary focus is on militarizing female pilots, which is a long shot at this point, but I think we have a more immediate need that civilian pilots can help with."

"What's your plan, then, Love?" Betty asked, both amusement and excitement in her voice.

"Making phone calls, of course."

Betty laughed. "Count me in. Whatever you do, I want to be a part of it."

After hanging up with Betty, Nancy found Bob out in the hangar. He was wearing his grease-stained coveralls, working on one of the planes.

"Look at this." She handed over the newspaper.

Bob straightened, his eyes flicking to her before he took the newspaper to read the headlines. "You're not going over to England, are you?" She'd been married to this man for three and a half years, and sometimes, she swore he knew her better than she knew herself. The genuine concern in his voice warmed her all the way through. He was supportive of her aviation dreams, but going to another continent might put some friction in that support.

Nancy tilted her head. "I have a better idea."

"What's that?"

"We should be on the front lines, getting those planes out to our Allies."

Bob's nod was slow. Through Tunner, they'd learned that the United States was planning on sending planes over to Europe for war service. "There's already talk of reserve pilots going into full combat training."

"Which means the Army Air Corps needs the women to ferry," she said. "What if I call your friend Lt. Colonel Robert Olds?" Not only was Lt. Colonel Olds one of Bob's friends, but he also currently served as assistant to the chief of the Plans Division of the Air Corps. Olds had recently commanded a flight of seven B-17s to Brazil for the fiftieth anniversary of the Republic of Brazil. "He can only tell me no."

"I think Lt. Colonel Olds is your best bet," Bob said with a thoughtful expression. "Do you want me on the call too?"

"No, I've got this." She leaned over and kissed his cheek, about the only spot where there wasn't grease. "I'll let you know what he says though."

Heading back into the office, it took only a few minutes of waiting until Lt. Colonel Olds came on the line.

"Mrs. Love, great to hear from you," Olds said into the phone. "How are you and Bob?"

"Swell—considering all that's going on in Europe." She paused. "Thank you for taking my call, sir. I don't want to waste your time, so I'll get straight to my proposal." She ran through her ideas about women pilots ferrying planes into Canada that were bound for Europe. "The more female aviators helping out, the more men can be freed up for other training, such as combat."

Olds listened to her speak without interruption, then finally asked, "How many women have commercial ratings?"

"About a hundred."

"That many?" Olds sounded surprised. "How many of those are instrument rated?"

Nancy didn't know the exact number. She herself wasn't instrument rated, although she'd logged 825 flying hours. She told Olds this, and he simply said, "You'll need to get rated too. Not that I can guarantee you'll be ferrying sports planes or bombers anytime soon. This sort of thing is unprecedented in the United States, and there will be opposition. Warning you in advance."

Nancy blew out a breath. "I understand, which is why we need to get started right away."

Olds chuckled. "Send me a list of the women with commercial ratings, Mrs. Love, and any other qualifications you can think of. That list will be our starting point."

Nancy was beaming when she hung up. She debated between starting her list right away or telling Bob the good news. Finally, Bob won out.

She would have hugged him fiercely, but she didn't want to spend all night working out grease stains from her blouse.

As it was, she came up with 105 names after verifying with a few phone calls.

Betty Gillies was on that list, of course.

# CHAPTER TWENTY-TWO

"With a Boston girl and three men pilots participating, 33 American sport planes destined for French war service yesterday were flown to the Canadian border in one of the first mass flights of its kind under US Neutrality Laws. The planes, piloted to the border town of Houlton, Maine, by a group of private pilots, were hauled across the international boundary by trucks—because the neutrality law prohibits their flying over—and then with the same pilots took off for Moncton, New Brunswick, and Halifax, Nova Scotia."

—*BOSTON RECORD*

*June 1940–July 1941—Boston*

Nancy closed her eyes when Lt. Colonel Olds shared the bad news over the phone.

"General Hap Arnold turned down our proposal."

The dread that had been churning her stomach all day had turned out to be a premonition. She'd been expecting Olds's call, but she'd hoped it would be with good news. The man Olds had sent their proposal to was General Henry "Hap" Arnold, a highly decorated military general who had been named chief of staff of the Air Corps in 1938. Arnold was also in discussion with President Roosevelt about the weakness of US air power versus German air power.

"General Arnold did suggest that women could be used as copilots on commercial airliners," Olds continued, his words filled with irony.

The same irony burned hot in Nancy's chest because General Arnold's words had become another barrier set up between women and male aviators. "That's all well and good, but we want to help in the *war* effort. Does he not understand that? We're ready and willing."

"I agree. No one's giving up here."

"Thank you, sir."

When she told Bob the news, he didn't seem surprised. "There's no reason to let this be swept out of sight though. You're coming with me on a ferry mission. We'll show that women are perfectly capable of completing such a mission."

"To Canada?"

"Yes, we're ferrying thirty-three sports planes to Maine, then we'll have to truck them over the border because of the no-fly neutrality zone. Finally, we'll fly the planes to the different ports."

Nancy was 100 percent on board. "How are we getting back?"

"Steamer from Halifax to New York."

She couldn't stop her smile from escaping. "I'll be ready."

Bob grinned. "I've no doubt. Now, when are you going to get instrument rated?"

"Soon."

The ferrying job ended up going nearly perfectly, although Nancy would have loved to be one of the pilots. They flew the sports planes to the border town of Houlton, Maine. The planes were loaded onto trucks and hauled across the international boundary. The Royal Canadian Mounted Police and Woodstock N.H. militiamen supervised the towing operation.

Once the entire operation was over, Bob and Nancy returned by steamer to New York.

But less than two weeks later, it seemed that their ferrying work was all for naught. France had just surrendered to the Germans, this on the heels of the mass evacuation of British soldiers from Dunkirk the week before.

Whatever concerns Nancy had about the war overseas, they were now elevated. "I can't believe France is occupied," she told Bob as they pored over the newspaper headlines together while sitting in their Inter City office. The sun had already set, and the hangar was deserted. "It's hard to imagine Paris now under German control."

Bob was on his third or fourth cup of coffee, his eyelids hooded, tired lines about his eyes. "This is going to send even more pilots over to England to join the RAFs."

Nancy swallowed, her throat sour with the increasingly bad news. "I don't blame them." She didn't ask Bob if he wanted to go because she was afraid of the answer. Right now, though, there was plenty to do at home to support the Allied war effort. It now felt that much more personal. Bob was currently on active duty with the Air Corps. Although his job was routine, that could change any day as the war progressed through the months of autumn.

When December rolled around, Nancy received a phone call from Betty. "Cochran's still pushing."

Nancy assumed this and added, "Colonel Olds is, too, but no luck yet. What did Cochran do?" That fall, Lieutenant Colonel Olds had been promoted to Colonel.

"She met with General Hap Arnold and Clayton Knight, who's running the recruiting for the British Ferry Command."

Nancy motioned to Bob, who was sitting in the living room, reading the newspaper as the fading winter light slipped from the windows. He walked into the kitchen and sat next to her at the table. Leaning close, he listened to both sides of the conversation.

"Bob's here," Nancy said. "Tell us both what's happening."

"England is hurting for pilots and airplanes," Betty said, "especially since the Blitz and the Battle of Britain."

Nancy nodded, her chest growing tight. "Don't tell me you and Cochran are heading over."

"I'm not." Betty paused. "But General Arnold suggested that Cochran ferry a bomber to England."

Nancy looked at Bob and saw agreement there. "General Arnold won't even let American female pilots create a Ferrying Program in our own country. Sounds like a publicity stunt."

"I agree," Betty said. "But Cochran won't turn it down."

"I don't blame her." Nancy glanced at Bob again. "I don't think I would either. I'd just need to check out on a twin-engine bomber."

Betty gave a soft laugh. "If that's what Cochran is planning on doing, then other pilots can't protest. What does Bob think?"

"He can tell you himself." Nancy handed him the phone.

They talked for a few minutes, and Bob predicted that Cochran would get plenty of pushback from other male pilots, but as long as General Arnold gave the all clear, the transatlantic trip would happen.

It turned out that Bob was right.

Over the next several months, Congress debated over Roosevelt's Lend-Lease Program, and it was finally approved in March 1941, which enabled the US government to sell military supplies to Britain and France without actually entering the war. In June, the Soviet Union broke its neutrality stance toward the war and allied with Britain against Nazi Germany. Changes around the world were coming fast, one of which happened on June 17 when Jackie Cochran took off from Gander, Newfoundland, ferrying a Lockheed Hudson.

Reports came back through Bob, and he informed Nancy. Cochran had flown the bomber for part of the transatlantic flight, but the male pilots, who weren't supportive of her having only twenty-five hours flight time in the bomber, didn't want her doing the takeoff or landing. They also didn't want to be blamed for her demise if the Germans shot down the bomber.

No one was shot down, and word came through that Cochran met with Pauline Gower, commander of the ATA women pilots.

"Gower asked Cochran if she knew of any American women who might want to ferry for ATA in England," Bob told Nancy, leaning against the office doorframe, dressed in his marine-blue military uniform. He wore his uniform most days, and while Nancy loved him in it, the sight also reminded her of how close the war seemed to be getting.

"What did Cochran say?"

"I don't know what she told Gower, but I wondered if she'll call you up."

Nancy had thought of this, but she kept pushing it to the back of her mind. "Time will tell, but I still think I can do more good setting up a program in the US. And I think Colonel Olds is getting closer to working out things here at home."

Three days later, the Army Air Corps was renamed the US Army Air Forces, and Olds was put in charge of setting up an official ferrying command.

"This is good news," Nancy said, looking up from the newspaper. She and Bob were taking a rare lunch break in his office, eating some ham and cheese sandwiches she'd packed that morning. "Colonel Olds is over the Ferrying Program. Now it's only a matter of time to implement female pilots."

"I wouldn't be surprised if he calls us today."

Just then the phone rang, and Nancy laughed, but it was more of a nervous laugh. Being closer to the phone, she answered, "Inter City. Nancy Love speaking."

"This is Harry Hopkins calling from the White House," a man said through the phone. "Might I speak with Bob Love?"

Nancy's throat went dry. "Yes, he's right here." She covered the receiver with her hand. "Harry Hopkins, calling from the White House."

Bob reached for the phone. "This is Bob Love. How can I help you?"

Nancy wished she could hear the other end of the conversation, but the expression on her husband's face told her all she needed to know. Their lives were changing.

When Bob hung up the phone, his eyes settled on Nancy. "I've been assigned as control officer at Houlton, Maine."

She stared at her husband. Houlton was a border town to Canada, where they'd flown the sports planes.

"The recommendation came through Colonel Robert Olds," Bob said, "and I'm to be part of the Lend-Lease airplane ferrying operation that will deliver planes across the Atlantic."

"Are you ferrying across the ocean too?" It wasn't lost on Nancy that her own husband might be flying combat if this war continued to escalate.

"I don't think so," he said. Their eyes held. "The conversation with Mr. Hopkins was rather short."

A knock sounded on the partially open office door.

Bob and Nancy both looked over at the door. Colonel Olds stood there dressed in full uniform.

Nancy couldn't have been more surprised. She straightened, and Bob crossed the room to shake his hand. Next, Olds vigorously shook Nancy's hand, his dynamic personality and frankness as clear in person as they were over the phone.

Once everyone was settled in chairs, Olds's gaze turned intense as he said to Nancy, "You've heard of Bob's assignment by now?"

"Yes, of course. He just finished speaking with Mr. Hopkins."

"Excellent." Olds rapped the desk between them. "I have news that applies to you and a request that I think you'll be happy with."

Nancy's heart was racing now, if it hadn't been already. "Go ahead."

"Jackie Cochran is drawing up an official proposal to have women pilots considered for ferrying planes, both basic and advanced trainers. These planes will be ferried from factories to the Air Corps stations, which will, as you know, free male pilots for combat duty."

Nancy released a slow breath. "What is different about this proposal versus ours over a year ago?"

"A lot of things have changed in the war, as you know, but mostly, it's because all the important players are now engaged."

"Who?"

"Cochran reported on her England trip to Eleanor Roosevelt and the president, who then sent Cochran to the secretary of war."

"Henry Stimson," Nancy murmured.

"Correct." Olds sat back and threaded his fingers together. "That instigated a meeting with Cochran, General Arnold, Robert Lovett, who is assistant secretary of war for air, and . . . myself."

This was all good, all moving forward, so why did Nancy feel trepidation building inside?

"Cochran is sending out a survey to 150 female pilots to gauge interest and possible commitments."

Nancy felt the pang of envy and glanced at Bob, who was intently listening to the exchange. Probably noticing the range of emotions moving across her face.

"That's much farther than I've been allowed to go," she said. "What's she basing the 150 on?" She could probably guess, but she wanted details.

"Cochran said that according to her research, 154 women currently hold commercial licenses."

She nodded. The numbers matched Nancy's findings too.

"Cochran also reported that fifty women have more than 500 flying hours," Olds continued, "and eighty-three have more than 200 hours."

Nancy was aware of this as well. "And out of those, who knows who might agree to join a Ferrying Program. There are a lot of things to take into consideration."

"Right." Olds leaned forward, elbows on his knees. "But that's why I'm here, in person, Nancy. Cochran is a dynamic woman, but I consider her only a tactical benefit to the program that you pitched earlier. Immediate action can be taken if we attach women pilots to *my* Ferrying Program. And I already know I can work with you since you're a natural leader and great with people."

Nancy's neck flushed. "Well, thank you, sir."

"It's more than that," Olds said. "Your personality is suited for gathering the right female pilots and getting them qualified for the program. You're level-headed and think smart."

"I don't know what to say." Nancy brushed past the compliments. It was no secret Olds was good with people. "Nothing's been approved from what we've already submitted. How far is this proposal of Jackie Cochran's going to go?"

"We'll find out," Olds said. "I want you to come to Washington, DC, to meet Cochran. She'll be at my office part of the month, working on all the specifics of her proposal. Her research and surveys will be useful, yes, but you're going to head up the women's program under my umbrella."

Nancy opened her mouth, then shut it. A glance at Bob told her he was supportive. "Does Jackie Cochran know this?" she asked.

"She will soon if she doesn't already." Olds paused, his eyes gleaming. "Nancy, will you come to Washington?"

Nancy didn't need to dither over her decision. It had been made more than a year ago. "Yes, I'll come."

# CHAPTER TWENTY-THREE

"One of the two most important ladies who have so far come in contact with the Army, one is named Love and the other is named Hobby. That will show you how respectable the Army is."

—HENRY L. STIMSON, US SECRETARY OF WAR

*July–August 1941—Washington, DC*

"You can come in with me," Nancy told Bob as they stopped in front of the building that housed Olds's Washington, DC, office. "I'm sure Colonel Olds won't mind."

Bob stepped close and kissed her cheek, his clean soap scent washing over her despite the sweltering heat of the summer day. "I'm going to walk around the city, then I'll come back and wait in the lobby."

A couple of cars rumbled by, and a newspaper boy on the corner called out the day's headlines of the Allied victory in the Battle of Palmyra in Syria.

Nancy set a hand on her hip. "You don't want to be in the line of fire?"

Bob's eyes filled with amusement. "Are you planning on there *being* a line of fire?"

She held back a smile. "I'm going in with an open mind."

His brows quirked.

Her smile escaped. "It's nothing but a brainstorming meeting," she clarified. "I want to see what Cochran's proposal is all about. I'm not too worried about there being surprises, though, since Colonel Olds assured me that our own plans will be moving forward soon. And neither of us has a problem with Cochran contributing."

Bob nodded along, but she knew she wasn't fooling her husband. She felt like a lasso had gathered every ounce of worry and cramped her stomach as she anticipated what Jackie Cochran wanted to say.

Nancy said goodbye to Bob, then headed to the elevator that would take her to Olds's office. As she walked, she reveled in the cooler interior of the building and steeled her mind and thoughts for what lay ahead.

The elevator doors opened, and as Nancy walked to the office, she tried to ignore the exhaustion pressing on the edges of her mind since she'd slept only a handful of hours the night before in anticipation of this meeting.

Voices came from the other side of the office door, and she knocked without pausing to decipher who might be talking.

Olds himself opened the door, and Nancy shook his hand, his grip firm, as always.

"Come in, Mrs. Love," Olds said. "You're right on time. Miss Cochran has arrived as well, and we're about to go over her relay map."

Nancy had no idea what a relay map was, but she turned toward the woman on the other side of the desk, who was also standing.

Jackie Cochran was a striking woman, with dark-blonde hair and brown eyes. Her makeup was flawless, as if it had been applied by an expert. And Nancy supposed Cochran was an expert; she owned her own cosmetics line after all. Cochran wore a tailored dress and jacket that screamed expensive and probably was.

Cochran thrust out her hand. "Great to meet you."

Although Cochran sounded friendly and upbeat, Nancy immediately felt that she was being scrutinized. She shook Cochran's cool, papery hand and caught a scent of perfume—likely expensive. "Great to meet you too. I've been fascinated by the reports coming back on the female pilots ferrying for the ATA in England."

Cochran's smile became more genuine. "We have a lot of work to do in our country. Granted, we aren't officially at war but close enough."

"Agreed." Nancy drew in a steadying breath. Her nervousness was beginning to fade, and that was a good thing. "Now, what's a relay map?"

Cochran's eyes glimmered. "It's the framework of how the female pilots will be transporting bombers from factories to air bases across the country."

Nancy scanned the routes as Cochran traced them with her finger.

"I've created a system of zones across the country," Cochran continued. "Each pilot will ferry the plane from one zone to the next. She returns to her original base that night."

Nancy frowned. "So the pilot will only travel a short distance in one day, then turn her plane over to another pilot to be flown to the next zone the next day?"

"Correct."

Nancy glanced at Olds. Did he not see how cumbersome and needless this would be? "Why can't the pilot take the plane all the way to the base where it should be delivered? She can deliver the plane, then return back to her base, or possibly ferry another plane on the way back. It would keep things more simple and straightforward instead of coordinating such an elaborate relay."

It was Cochran's turn to frown. "Not many women can fly long distances."

Nancy straightened. Why was this coming from a female pilot, one who'd completed a transatlantic flight, no less? "Plenty of women pilots can fly across the country, no problem. They just need to transition to the bigger planes."

Cochran laughed. Actually laughed.

"I know about *your* flight skills," Cochran conceded. "Which is why I agreed to go over this with you. But not everyone is *Nancy Harkness Love*. Most of the women we'll be recruiting have only flown small planes."

Nancy folded her arms, trying not to take offense, but it was too late. She was also becoming annoyed with Cochran's cloying perfume. They weren't at a ladies' luncheon. "It's not much of a leap to check out on larger planes."

"So, you're suggesting that women be trained on piloting bombers?" Cochran shot back.

"Why not?"

"General Hap Arnold will never go for it."

Nancy tensed her jaw. "*You've* flown a Lockheed Martin."

Cochran's shrug was dismissive. "There aren't many *Jackie Cochrans* out there either."

"Maybe not, but there's Betty Gillies, Barbara Towne, Byrd Granger, Gertrude Meserve, Evelyn Sharp, Cornelia Fort, Teresa James—to name a few."

Cochran's brows popped up. "Would Betty do this?"

"Of course. I receive phone calls and letters regularly from women asking when they'll be able to do some real work for the war effort. They want to use their skills and are willing to do even more training. They aren't intimidated, Miss Cochran."

Nancy didn't mention that Betty had just found out her youngest daughter, Barbara, had leukemia. They were trying every treatment possible, but the girl was only four years old. Nancy didn't know how Betty and Bud were making it through all this, but she could only hope and pray that the treatments would work for little Barbara.

Cochran drew in a breath, the brewing storm in her eyes evident. When she spoke again, her words were stiff. "You know how much red tape there is to get through. I'm looking toward the future in order to create a large women's pilot organization that will be militarized. It will take time though. But the goal is to find ways to support the Air Corps until then."

"Is one of those goals ferrying small sport planes between zones?" Nancy asked, her words spilling out. "We aren't going to win any wars with sport planes. Bigger bombers are being built in droves, and new ones are being developed as we speak. If America joins the war, they'll need all the male combat pilots they can get. The women need to be trained and ready to transport those planes, and the best way to do that is to start ferrying *now* and begin training on the bigger planes too." Nancy drew in a breath. She was probably red in the face, but she didn't care.

Cochran stared at her for a long moment, her artful makeup looking less lustrous and more comical now. "Are you against a women's division in the Air Corps?"

It was like Cochran hadn't heard a word she'd spoken. "Not at all," Nancy said. "But as you said, the red tape might take years. We need to put women to work *now* as civilian pilots under the direction of Ferry Command." She looked at Olds to verify that she wasn't reading this entire situation wrong.

Olds dipped his chin, then cleared his throat. "I agree that we could use women pilots right away. As you said, Mrs. Love, preparing now will only benefit the future. In the meantime, Cochran can keep pushing her agenda through for a permanent women's pilot organization."

Cochran seemed mollified at this, but Nancy's chest was still burning.

"What can we do to push through an action plan, Colonel Olds?" Nancy finally asked. "It won't matter whether or not we agree to this relay map idea until we get approval for women to join the Ferrying Program in the first place."

He braced his hands on the desk. "Right. What if we propose fifty women pilots on a ninety-day service test? We'd require that the pilots have at least 500 flying hours to be considered for the program."

There would be a lot of details and commitments to organize, but if that proposal could be accepted, Nancy would happily iron out the logistics. "I like it," she said. "Gets our foot in the door, slowly but surely."

"I agree," Cochran said, although her expression exposed that she was holding back many comments.

"Great," Olds said with a conciliatory grin toward both women. "I'll draft up a proposal to General Arnold by the end of the day. I'd like each of you to review it."

By the time Nancy left the office, she'd had enough of clashing personalities. Both she and Cochran wanted essentially the same thing— for women to be given a chance to fly in service for the country, in one way or another—but Cochran was trying to leap over hoops that still had to be walked through, which meant that everything was at a stall, and no women were ferrying in the first place.

When Nancy entered the lobby and saw Bob waiting for her, she crossed to him and gave him a tight hug.

His arms came around her, and he murmured, "That bad?"

She didn't answer for a moment, then finally, she drew away. "It ended well, I think. We'll find out when General Arnold approves our proposal. But I'm starving. Think you could feed me?"

Bob kissed the top of her head. "Come on, Mrs. Love, let's get you something to eat, and you can tell me all about your day."

As they walked to a nearby restaurant in the muggy heat, Nancy decided that whatever happened to the proposal, she'd be grateful for this moment, right now. Grateful for her husband. Grateful for her parents. Grateful that her country wasn't under threat of bombing. Grateful that she had talents she could hopefully one day use in better service.

The days of waiting turned into weeks of waiting, and it wasn't until August that she finally heard from Olds.

When she answered the phone at the Inter City office, she sighed with relief when Olds said, "Mrs. Love? It's Robert Olds."

He could only be calling about the outcome of the proposal. "If you're being this formal, I assume the news is bad?"

Olds's too-long pause made Nancy's stomach sink to her toes.

"General Arnold turned down our proposal," Olds said in a rush. "Although, he left the door open for women pilots in the future—if things change."

"Like what things?" she asked. "*After* America enters the war? Then it will be too late."

"I'm frustrated too," he said. "But General Arnold claims he has plenty of men, and they don't have use or room for female pilots."

Nancy closed her eyes and released a slow exhale. "What else?"

Olds seemed to hesitate. "He's questioning whether a woman could handle an Army plane."

Nancy's eyes popped open. "That's exactly why we proposed training *now*."

"Right."

"You don't agree with General Arnold, do you?" She had to ask, even though she hoped she knew the answer already.

"I wouldn't be working on this if I agreed with General Arnold," Olds said firmly. "I know there are a lot of factors at play here, but I'm not giving up."

"I'm not either." She moved to her feet and paced the office. "What did Cochran say?"

"She didn't seem too surprised, actually. In fact, she's putting together a group of women to take over to England to join the ATA women's ferrying group."

"How many?"

"She's estimating she'll have twenty-five women confirm."

If that many female pilots went over to England, it would deplete the American pool should Arnold find reasons to let them join Olds's Ferrying Program. "All right, sir. Thanks for the phone call. I'm going to let a few others know, and then we'll keep preparing and waiting."

"You're a good sport," Olds said. "Thank you for everything."

"Thank *you*."

Her first phone call was to Bob, who was on a business trip to meet with potential clients. He listened to the entire story, then said, "I know this feels like a setback, sweetie. But it's only a matter of time. I can feel it."

Nancy went quiet, mollified. It might seem strange, but she felt it too. "I believe that, too, Bob, but it's hard when the setbacks continue."

# CHAPTER TWENTY-FOUR

"With confidence in our armed forces with the unbounding determination
of our people we will gain the inevitable triumph so help us God. I
ask that the Congress declare that since the unprovoked and dastardly
attack by Japan on Sunday, December 7, 1941, a state of war has
existed between the United States and the Japanese Empire."

—PRESIDENT FRANKLIN D. ROOSEVELT, "A DATE WHICH WILL LIVE IN INFAMY"
SPEECH DELIVERED TO US CONGRESS ON DECEMBER 8, 1941

*December 1941–March 1942—Inter City, Boston*

Nancy's rare quiet Sunday at home was interrupted when her phone
rang.

"Nancy," Bob said in a rough tone. "Are you listening to the radio?"

"I've had it off for a couple of hours," Nancy said, crossing to the
radio and twisting the knob. "What's going on?"

If Bob answered, she didn't hear it because the radio host's voice
filled the small kitchen. "The White House has just announced that all
naval and military activities on the principal island of Oahu in Hawaii
have been attacked from the air by planes that bear the mark of the rising sun."

"Japan," Nancy whispered into the phone. "Is this real?"

"It's real," Bob said. "I'm coming home. This changes everything."

Nancy might have said goodbye and hung up, but she had no memory of it. At some point, Bob called again. Said that he was being sent
from Houlton to Washington, DC. He didn't know when yet. Nancy
felt numb at the news—she wanted her husband with her, but she also
understood that he was needed elsewhere.

Every minute, the news grew worse. Pearl Harbor was in flames.
Hundreds, maybe thousands, of people were dead. It was impossible
to fully comprehend. Even as the news flooded in, overwhelming with

details of mass destruction, Nancy couldn't help but think of the pilots who had died. And those they'd left behind. The military personnel and civilians running for cover. The explosions and flames and smoke.

Someone called, and the phone rang multiple times before it finally snapped her out of her numbness.

"Nance?" her father said when she picked up.

The tears started then. "I'm here," she said on a choked sob. "Bob's heading to Washington, DC, in the next day or two."

"Do you want to come home for a few days?"

That, Nancy knew, wasn't an option. "I need to watch over Inter City. I don't know what will happen, but it's better I'm here."

After speaking with both of her parents, she called a few friends.

It seemed that no one knew what to say. The heaviness of her heart was palpable, compressing, until that weight made her feel suffocated. Hours before, their entire nation had fallen to its knees.

Nancy knew that nothing would ever be the same again. The United States would no longer be playing a sidelined, supportive role in this war. No, their country was at war. And their boys would be going into combat as an American force.

In the late afternoon, Nancy arrived at Inter City. She stood just outside the hangar, beneath the gray winter sky. She watched and listened, as if she could see a Japanese bomber or hear a war plane. But time seemed to hover, neither moving forward nor backward, and all was quiet in the skies above her portion of the world.

She tried to imagine the beauty of the island of Oahu, the blue skies, the tropical foliage, the warm ocean breeze, and the turquoise sea . . . now shattered by death and terror. Burning ships, burning planes, craters of dug-out earth. Sirens . . .

She felt so far away. So helpless. Reading about the war in Europe had been surreal enough. But now . . . She and Bob knew pilots who were stationed at Pearl Harbor, including Cornelia Fort, who was a civilian flight instructor on Oahu. Cornelia was a woman Nancy hoped would join the Ferrying Division if women were ever allowed to become a part of it.

The war news came flooding in, dominating all radio channels.

From a distance, Nancy heard the office phone ringing. With hurried footsteps, she headed inside to answer.

"Inter City," her voice rasped.

"Mrs. Love, it's Robert Olds. I hate to call you on a day like today."

"No one could have predicted this."

"You know what it means for *you*, right?"

Nancy moved toward the office window and peered out at the airfield. "I do, and I'm ready."

"I thought you'd say that." His voice held no excitement though. Not after such a terrible event. He sounded exhausted, depleted. "Things are going to be happening very fast, and I need to know who my key people are. Decisions are being made every second."

"You can count on me," Nancy said, although her emotions were wrung out. "I never wanted this day to come—at least not like this."

"None of us did." Olds paused. "But we're going to put a stop to this war. Too much has been lost, and now, we're finally going to act. Canada has already declared war on Japan."

Nancy had listened to the broadcast of how the Japanese had bombed the British colony of Hong Kong only hours after leaving Hawaii in shambles.

"Is it true that Roosevelt is going to declare war on Japan tomorrow?"

"Yes, Roosevelt will get the declaration through the Senate and the House. Winston Churchill will be doing it almost immediately, so he'll beat us to it."

Nancy had read about Churchill saying he'd declare war on any nation who attacked the United States. Now that was all happening.

After hanging up with Olds, she called Bob, her mind reeling as she told him about the phone call.

"I'm leaving Houlton and coming home now," Bob said first thing. "I don't know where we'll end up or what will happen to Inter City, but I want to be with you while we figure all this out."

Nancy's eyes pricked with tears. "Thank you," she whispered.

As the sun set on one of the most horrific days in anyone's memory, Nancy waited for Bob's plane to taxi into the hangar. As he climbed out of the cockpit, she could see the violet circles beneath his eyes, likely matching her own. His uniform had a more significant meaning now, a sight that made her both proud and fearful.

He swept her into his arms, and she clung fiercely to him.

"What's going to happen to all of us, Bob?" she whispered.

"I don't know, sweetie," he said against her ear. "But we're going to end this war, one way or another. We'll give it everything we've got."

Nancy nodded against his neck, breathing in his clean soap scent, wishing she wouldn't have to release him. Wishing she could turn back time to when life had been routine and settled, before Hitler had invaded Poland . . .

"All airfields and airline companies within fifty miles of the coastline are being shut down," Bob said.

Nancy drew back and stared at her husband. "That includes Inter City."

"Yes." He grasped her hands. "Colonel Olds will be calling tomorrow to give us our orders."

Her breathing shortened. Everything was changing, in both of their lives, in all of America.

The following day, she and Bob held hands in the Inter City office as Olds informed them that Bob's new assignment would be in Washington, DC. He'd work for the Ferrying Command from there, so they'd have to move for the duration.

"We need you around, too, Nancy," Olds said, his tone determined. "We'll find you something, which means you'll be in place for the Women's Ferrying Program when it comes to fruition."

Nancy heard the optimism in his voice, and her heart mirrored that.

After hanging up with Olds, Bob looked at her. "Well? Are you ready to move?"

"I'll be ready," Nancy said. This was no time for taking things slow. "I just need to process all of this." They would be closing Inter City

Aviation for the time being. Bob was certainly putting on a brave face with all these changes.

He squeezed her hand, then kissed her temple.

Nancy called her parents to tell them the latest news. Then she turned on the radio.

Leaning against Bob's shoulder, they listened to the incoming news, the reports from around the world reverberating against one another like dominos.

Winston Churchill had declared war on Japan.

That day, at 12:30 p.m., President Roosevelt's declaration was presented to Congress and the nation. The declaration had been brought to a vote and had passed the Senate 82-0, then the House 388-1. Roosevelt signed the declaration of war at 4:10 p.m.

This had been followed by Japan's allies—Germany and Italy—declaring war on the United States.

The Netherlands had declared war on Japan.

Costa Rica had declared war on Japan.

The Dominican Republic had declared war on Japan.

The Union of South Africa, Panama, and Cuba had all declared war on Japan.

China had declared war on Japan.

Finally, Bob shut off the radio. "Let's go home and get some rest. Tomorrow, we'll start packing."

Nancy couldn't agree more. The news of the last twenty-four hours had been hard to stomach, and her heart felt wrung out. She walked with Bob to their car, and they both remained silent on the way home.

When Nancy walked into their house, it was to a ringing phone. She answered and found an emotional Betty on the other end. "Betty, what's wrong?"

She could hear the strain in her friend's voice. "It's little Barbara," Betty said. "The doctors said there aren't any more treatments. It's like they've given up, but I know they're right. We can't keep putting Barbara through more pain. Her body is so small and frail."

Nancy's heart squeezed. "I'm so sorry, Betty. She's such a sweet angel." As much as she felt like an anomaly among her friends, being childless, she didn't envy the pain that Betty was suffering.

Betty sniffled, her next words faint. "She really is. It hurts to see her suffer."

They talked for a few more minutes, and by the time they hung up, Nancy was reminded that whatever was happening with the world at large, there was still deep, personal pain in everyone's lives.

Within a few days, they'd settled in Washington, DC, in a small apartment, and two days after Christmas, Betty called with the terrible news that her daughter had finally succumbed to her cancer. Even though everyone had known the day was coming, Nancy didn't know her heart could hurt so much again. Losing her brother had been devastating. He'd had many more years than Barbara had though.

"Barbara's finally free of pain and sickness," Bob told Nancy as he held her in his arms that night while the moon cast a silvery glow across their bed.

"I know, and for that I'm glad," Nancy said. "It still hurts so much."

Bob tightened his hold as his throat bobbed up and down. They both understood the grief of losing a sibling, and now Betty's two older children knew it firsthand as well. Probably the only silver lining was that Bud Gillies was exempt from the draft because of how critical his work at Grumman was for the war effort, so at least Betty had her husband around to navigate this loss together.

"I don't know if I could ever survive losing a child—if we ever have children," Nancy said.

Bob kissed the top of her head. They'd discussed this worry more than once. "Have you thought more about going to a doctor?"

"I don't want bad news, if that's what you mean," she said on a sigh. "But I know I should go. After the war."

Bob's arms only tightened about her. She knew he hoped for children as much as she did, but they both kept their heads up by staying busy.

And Washington, DC, was no different. Work flew at them at a frantic pace, with so many changes and so many new orders and directives going out. The reunion with Olds was bittersweet. When Nancy had seen him in the summer during the meeting with Cochran, he'd seemed lighter, more hopeful. Now he was a brigadier general and the head of the Ferrying Command, and it was easy to see that he carried much of the weight of the world on his shoulders.

"Nancy, I want you to meet Major Robert H. Baker," Olds told her over a dinner appointment a few weeks after they'd arrived in Washington, DC.

It was a miracle they were all able to coordinate a time for dinner. Both Olds and Bob had been working nonstop, and Nancy had been unpacking and fielding phone calls from family and friends, who all had the same fears and unanswered questions. She couldn't remember when she'd last had a full night's sleep.

"Is Major Baker in Washington?" Bob asked as the waiter cleared their plates and handed over the dessert menu.

"No, we'd have to go to Baltimore," Olds said. "He's reported to Logan Field, Dundalk, since he's on orders to set up the Northeast Sector, Domestic Wing of the Ferrying Command."

"He's a great man," Bob answered, then said to Nancy, "Flew in World War I, and he's been with the 154th Observation Squad of the Arkansas National Guard, recently working for the Ferrying Command."

That was all very well and good, but Nancy was curious about one thing. "Why should *I* meet Major Baker all the way in Baltimore?"

Olds smiled, temporarily lifting the tired lines about his eyes. "He's going to need an assistant."

Nancy turned to her husband. "Did you know about this?"

The smile playing on his lips told her he'd had some advance knowledge.

"I'm not leaving Washington, DC," she declared. "And gas is getting scarcer for driving, you know."

"But not airplane fuel," Bob said. "You could fly our Fairchild back and forth."

Nancy set her linen napkin on the table and sat back in her chair, considering this. They'd brought along their high-winged, single-engine, four-seater Fairchild 24. "Where exactly would I be working?"

"You mean, *if* you get the job?" Olds asked.

Nancy smirked. Did she really need to answer that? "I think we're beyond that question. You introduce me, and if I like the major, I'll have the job."

Olds chuckled, and Bob raised his half-empty glass in a mock toast. "Hear, hear."

"I assume it will be the Martin Plant, where the offices are." Olds shrugged. "Want me to find out beforehand?"

"Don't you dare make the phone call," she rushed to say. "I'm happy to meet Major Baker though. See what happens from there."

"Excellent," Olds said.

She met Bob's earnest gaze. "Are you all right with all this?"

He reached over and linked their fingers. "You know I am."

Yes, she knew that. Bob had only been supportive and encouraging, opening doors whenever he could. She leaned over and kissed his cheek.

Olds grinned. "That's enough, lovebirds."

Both Nancy and Bob laughed. It felt good to laugh about something.

She looked over at Olds. "Thank you, sir, for offering yet another opportunity." Olds nodded, his smile genuine, but that didn't chase away the exhaustion in his eyes. "Now we'll order our dessert to go because our general here needs some shut-eye."

Olds yawned again as if to emphasize her sentence. "Sorry. Things have been nonstop since Pearl Harbor."

"And you recently put out more fires with General Arnold," Nancy commented. Soon after Pearl Harbor, Olds had made a big push again for the women pilots to join the Ferrying Program. Cochran had caught wind of it and confronted both Olds and Arnold, who promised that nothing would be done until her commitment to the British ATA was over.

Arnold's words to Olds had been, "You will make no plans or reopen negotiations for hiring women pilots until Miss Jacqueline Cochran has completed her present agreement with the British authorities and has returned to the United States."

Now they were at a standstill once again. "I'm sorry, sir," Nancy said, patting his arm.

"I'm the one who's sorry." His expression held genuine regret. "But the fight isn't over yet because General Arnold is now talking like it will happen—once Cochran returns from England, that is."

Nancy bit back her frustration. They didn't need to wait for Cochran's return.

The following day, Nancy made the trip to Baltimore with Olds and Bob to meet Major Baker. A brief smile appeared beneath the major's mustache, and in the first few minutes, Nancy decided she was honestly interested in the position.

Baker took her on a tour of the facilities, then led her to the operations office.

"This is where operations are run," Baker said, motioning to the office space containing a few desks, phones, file cabinets along one wall, and maps tacked to the opposite wall. "You'll need to learn military procedures, and your job would entail mapping the flights for ferrying. You'll also be the point person to help find resources for pilots as they are traveling across the country."

He walked farther into the room and tapped his fingers on one of the desks. "This is where you'll be working."

Nancy raised a brow. "Have you decided to hire me, sir?"

"I have." He leaned against the desk, folding his arms. "You were basically hired on paper already. Meeting was a formality."

Nancy surveyed the office, knowing she wouldn't have come to Baltimore in the first place if she hadn't been interested. She refocused on the major, wondering if being bold now rather than later would work in her favor. "Would you ever consider using female pilots to ferry your planes?"

Major Baker didn't seem taken aback at the question. "I'm not opposed, Mrs. Love, and I'm not surprised this is one of your first questions. I do need to say that making such a decision wouldn't be mine alone."

The tension in Nancy's shoulders relaxed. "Of course not. I understand the red tape. I just wanted to know what sort of attitude you have toward the idea."

"Fair enough."

"Well, Major Baker." She stuck out her hand. "You have a new employee."

He straightened and grasped her hand. "Welcome to the Northeast Sector, Mrs. Love."

# CHAPTER TWENTY-FIVE

"General Olds has informed me that he is planning on hiring women pilots for his Ferrying Command almost at once. His plan, as outlined to me, is not only bad in my opinion from the organizational standpoint, and contrary to what you told me yesterday but is in direct conflict, in fact, with the plans of a women's unit for England. In addition, it would wash me out of the supervision of the women flyers here rather than the contrary as we contemplated."

—LETTER FROM JACQUELINE COCHRAN TO HAP ARNOLD, JANUARY 18, 1942

*March–May 1942—Baltimore, Maryland*

Nancy had been surprised to receive a phone call from her husband during work hours on an overcast spring day in March, so her mind was already racing with worry before Bob could even share his reason for calling.

"You need to get to Washington, DC, as soon as possible," he said.

"What's happened?"

"General Olds collapsed at his desk, and he's been taken to the hospital." Concern marred Bob's words. "I'm here now, and the doctors are saying he's going to need several weeks of rest."

"Did he have a stroke? A heart attack?"

"Not that the doctors have said." Bob paused. "They're calling it exhaustion from overwork. We've contacted his fiancée and, of course, his sons and their mothers."

General Olds had been married three times and had four sons. Currently he was engaged to Nina Gore. Nancy had seen the signs of exhaustion—they all had—and frustration pulsed through her. Olds should have been able to take days off—or at least weekends.

"He's been working around the clock since December." Nancy rose from her desk. She was the only one in the office currently, and she'd need to find Baker to inform him. "Is there anything we can do?"

"I don't know yet," Bob said. "I have a phone call with General Arnold soon, and we'll discuss the options. General Olds will have to be replaced temporarily. That could affect my position here."

Nancy stiffened. She was accomplishing her job with Baker on her own merits. But if Bob had to relocate . . . that might change things up again. "All right. I'll see you when I land. Give General Olds my best wishes."

"I will. Bye, sweetie. I love you."

"I love you too."

Her limbs were heavy as she hung up and walked out of the office. General Olds was a lovely, charismatic man who'd put his heart and soul into the Ferrying Command. She hated to hear that he was suffering. Hopefully, he'd make a full recovery very soon. And when he did, she'd insist that he take things easier. Hard to do, she knew. It seemed the entire country was out of sorts.

She informed Major Baker of her plans to return to Washington, DC, and he ushered her on her way, asking her to keep him updated on Olds's condition. A man down in one part of the organization was a blow to everyone.

She grabbed her bag and tucked the daily newspaper she'd been reading that morning inside. The headlines were full of the Executive Order 9066 that Roosevelt had signed the previous month, on February 19, which enabled the War Department powers to create military exclusion areas. And now Americans of Japanese descent were being sent to "assembly centers"—to await relocation.

*To where?* Nancy wondered.

It was all so complicated—all so raw. Were these American citizens really being asked to abandon homes, families, careers?

By the time Nancy arrived home in Washington, DC, Bob was there to greet her at the airfield.

"You're limping," she said as she watched him approach. "You're working too hard if your bout with polio is showing."

"Just tired. And I missed you."

"We saw each other this morning." She stepped into his arms. The hug was brief because curiosity got the better of her. "Tell me everything."

Bob nodded, linking their hands and leading her to the car. "I'll tell you once we're driving." After pulling away from the airfield, he said, "General Olds is on the mend, but the doctors want him home for several weeks, at least. General Arnold assigned Colonel Harold L. George as a replacement."

"Do we know him?" Nancy asked.

"I've met him before. He's a strategic bombardment specialist."

"So not exactly the leader to be moving men and supplies across the country?" she asked.

"No, and that's exactly the conversation I had with General Arnold." It wasn't long before Bob pulled in front of their rented apartment and turned off the car. His shadowed gaze met hers. "General Arnold contacted General C.R. Smith today."

"The president of American Airlines?"

"One and the same. He's agreed to become Colonel George's chief of staff at Ferrying Command."

Nancy waited in the silence of the car, wondering if Bob had another announcement.

"Everything about us is the same, at least right now," he assured her, "but that could change too."

Of course. The moment Bob had called to tell her about Olds, she'd known change could be a real possibility.

"Come on, let's go inside," he said gently. "I'm starving, and I plan on making you an amazing sandwich."

Nancy had to be grateful for the small things in life since she had no control over the larger matters. "I'll eat anything at this point."

Bob opened the car door, then walked around the front of the car and opened Nancy's, offering his hand. She took it, and they walked into their small, rented apartment, where Bob set to work making sandwiches, and she perched on one of the two kitchen chairs.

For the time being, they left the radio off, and it was nice to feel like it was only the two of them inside these four walls—tucked away from the rest of the world.

But moments after they began eating, the phone rang.

Bob glanced at Nancy.

"You'd better answer it," she said calmly, although her pulse was skipping ahead.

When he answered, Bob's spine immediately straightened, and Nancy heard a lot of "yes, sirs."

"That was General Arnold," he told her after he hung up.

She nodded because she'd assumed as much.

"Colonel George is officially replacing General Olds, and when he recovers, Olds will head up the Second Air Force."

"What does that mean for you?"

Bob slipped his hands into his pockets. "Colonel George is reorganizing the command, and for starters, it will now be called Air Transport Command—or ATC. Colonel George wants me to be his deputy chief of staff for operations, over the domestic wing, which is now going to be called the Ferrying Division. We'll be over all ferrying operations, *both* domestic and international." He drew in a deep breath.

Nancy clapped her hand over her mouth.

"There's more."

She lowered her hand, her mind racing with a dozen questions.

"Major Baker is being promoted to colonel and will be put in command of New Castle Army Base in Delaware. And Colonel William H. Tunner will be the commanding officer with me in the Ferrying Division. He's moving out to join me at ATC."

"Well . . . I don't know what to think—it's a lot." She sorted through her thoughts. "I'm happy about Major Baker—for his promotion, although I'll miss working with him. And you're probably happy about Colonel Tunner since you're already friends."

Bob sat at the table again and reached for her hand. "It's a lot of changes. Are you all right with it?"

"Not that I have a choice, but I'm sure it will be for the best in the end."

Bob squeezed her hand. "Let's hope so. I know you enjoyed working in Baltimore."

"Yes, but I'm happy to do anything that would help."

His eyes smiled. "I know."

She breathed out a sigh, her heart rate tapping. "We need another champion for women pilots with General Olds out of the picture for now."

"No one's giving up, Nancy."

She leaned forward and kissed him on the cheek. "That's good to hear because we can help, and we need the Air Force to acknowledge that."

Over the next few weeks, Nancy spent most of her time in Baltimore, still working at Logan Field in Dundalk, even though Major Baker had been reassigned. She scanned the newspaper headlines as part of her morning routine. More and more Japanese Americans, those who were at least one-sixteenth Japanese, had been relocated to remote areas converted to serve as "Relocation Centers." Nancy wasn't sure how livable places like the livestock pavilion of the Pacific International Livestock Exposition Facilities could be for any human.

She moved to the next article, which was about the WAAC—Women's Army Auxiliary Corps—proposal before Congress. It had finally passed, even though it had been introduced a year earlier, in May 1941, by Congresswoman Edith Nourse Rogers. Rogers had proposed an official women's corps as an auxiliary to the Army so that women who worked for the military during wartime would receive benefits just as the men did. Rogers had been a nurse in a Great Britain hospital during World War I and had received no compensation or recognition as a patriot.

Now it appeared as though Congresswoman Rogers had a victory. Oveta Culp Hobby was named the director of the WAAC. Finally, some news to smile about. Nancy read the next article about how the Women

Accepted for Voluntary Emergency Service—WAVES—was being added to the agenda, pitched as the comparable Navy branch for women, which would make it easier for the Navy to fill clerical roles at home and allow men to return to sea duty. The WAVES would also aid in bombing calculations, parachute rigging, radio operations, and health care.

Nancy was sure that Jackie Cochran was also eating up this news. It only propelled Cochran closer to having women pilots as a branch of the Air Force.

For Nancy, it was changing the way the nation valued their women. Her skills were more specialized, but if the country wanted women pilots' aid now, they didn't have time to wait for approval of militarization. She didn't want to wait a year or two years or three. Who knew what would happen with the war by then?

She set down the newspaper and called Bob a second time, but no one answered his office phone. He'd told her to call and report on her safe arrival since she'd flown through a spring storm. The flight had been bumpy but nothing that would force an emergency landing. They'd discussed her looking for something else in Washington, DC, but for now, there was still work to be done in Baltimore.

When she arrived home late that afternoon, in much more moderate weather, Bob was waiting at the airport to pick her up, as usual. But he wasn't alone.

As Nancy approached the two men, she pushed her goggles to the top of her helmet, then undid the chin strap. Over one shoulder, she carried a bag with a few essentials, including some ferrying maps she planned to go over tonight.

"Nancy, I'd like you to meet Colonel Bill Tunner," Bob said with polite formality, though his eyes were bright.

Nancy had heard plenty about this man, so she was happy to finally meet him. She shook his hand. "Nice to meet you, Colonel."

His handshake was firm, and his mouth quirked into a half smile, his eyes warm. "Very nice to meet you, too, Mrs. Love. I had a conversation with Bob today outside our offices that made it imperative to meet you right away. Sorry to spring this on you."

"Spring what?" She looked from Tunner to her husband, but Bob wasn't giving anything away. Pulling off her flight helmet, she ran her fingers through her hair.

Bob motioned for Tunner to continue.

Tunner's gaze locked with Nancy's. "Over a water cooler break, your husband mentioned he was hoping you'd landed your plane safely in Baltimore for your job. And I don't know what I thought—or missed—but I didn't realize you were a pilot." He paused. "So, I told Bob I'd been combing the woods for pilots, and here you are. Right under my nose. I asked Bob if there were more women like his wife."

Bob smiled, and Nancy laughed.

"And what did Bob say?" she asked.

Tunner's smile appeared. "He said to ask you myself."

She wasn't surprised. "Of course he did. He knows better than to answer for me, even though he likely knows my answers like the back of his own hand."

"Well?"

"I know over a hundred commercially rated female pilots, Colonel."

Tunner folded his arms. "Really?" he deadpanned, but his eyes were dancing.

"Really," she confirmed. Tunner didn't say anything, but Nancy imagined his thoughts turning over possibilities. "I think I should fill you in on the previous proposals I'd put together with General Olds," she said, "which General Arnold turned down. And how Jacqueline Cochran has been making a push for a military organization of women pilots."

Tunner folded his arms. "Can I buy you both dinner? I need all the information I can get about what's been done, what's been rejected, and how many women could potentially qualify to ferry planes. It's time for the new guard to take over from the old guard."

Nancy couldn't agree more, but she also couldn't allow herself to get her hopes up too much. She'd been down this twisty path too many times.

They headed to the nearest diner, and over their meal, Tunner suggested they commission women as officers in the WAAC—Women's

Army Auxiliary Corps—that had been formed in May. But that would take an amendment before Congress. Which meant extra time and rolls of red tape.

"General Olds and I talked about having women serve as civilians instead of military employees," Nancy said after their meal had been cleared.

Tunner smacked a hand on the table, making their utensils jump. "That's it. If we hire women pilots as Civil Service employees, that keeps them civilians, and we don't need to go through the red-taped sludge of Congressional approval."

Nancy's heart jumped along with the utensils. Was this the breakthrough suggestion that would finally give the women their opportunity?

# CHAPTER TWENTY-SIX

"When I walked into General Arnold's office to keep my appointment
I had the press clipping in my hand and asked him what it was all about.
He was mad all over and when mad, General Arnold could make the
fur fly. He said that he had asked the Ferry Command to prepare plans
for activation of a women's group, but expected to have such plan
submitted to him and through him to me for study and approval."

—JACQUELINE COCHRAN, *THE STARS AT NOON*

*June–September 1942—Washington, DC*

"What are the qualifications?" Betty asked Nancy over the phone.

Nancy sat in front of a fan, lounging in her house dress, with all the
windows opened in the apartment. "Five hundred hours."

"Check," Betty said.

"Commercial license."

"Check again."

Nancy continued. "Between the ages of twenty-one and thirty-five.
And a high school diploma."

"I fit the age requirement, but why is the cap at thirty-five?" Betty
asked, dubious. "I mean, I understand the high school diploma requirement. A pilot who can stick with something and has more education is
probably better than one who can't."

"Well . . ."

"Nancy?"

"It's ridiculous, really, but I'm picking my battles. Some men, and I
won't name names, think that when a woman reaches menopause, she
can't make logical decisions."

Betty was silent for so long that Nancy wondered if their connection
had been lost. "Betty?"

Betty wheezed.

"Are you *laughing*?"

"I can't . . ." Betty gasped. "I can't believe someone said that. You must tell me who. I'm going to start sending them long letters and article clippings—"

Nancy laughed along with her friend. "Don't you dare."

"Besides, how many thirty-five-year-old women do you know who are going through menopause?"

"Can't think of any."

When Betty's laughter died down, she said, "This reminds me of during my term as the Ninety-Nines president, when I had to petition against the Civil Aeronautics Authority over their pregnancy regulations."

"I remember that," Nancy said. Jackie Cochran was the current Ninety-Nines president, having taken over from Betty in 1941. "A woman should be able to fly when pregnant, or she'll lose the ten required hours every six months that's needed to retain a commercial license."

"Exactly. I wouldn't be where I am today if I had to take time off for every pregnancy. It would have been expensive to take all of those tests again." Betty snickered. "And now they're bringing menopause into it. Well, I must say, despite all that, this is very good news. What else is on the list?"

So, Nancy told her about the requirements of the 200-horsepower rating, letters of recommendation, and US citizenship. "Salary is proposed at $250 a month plus a $6 per diem on ferrying trips."

"That's less than the men," Betty observed. "Fifty dollars less."

"Colonel Tunner says it's because the women will be ferrying lighter aircraft, and that will make it an easier foothold to be approved."

"Huh." Betty paused. "When will you hear back?"

"Soon, we hope." Nancy turned the kitchen fan more toward her face. The apartment had yet to cool off with the setting sun. "Colonel Tunner's already sent our plan to both General Harold Lee George and General C.R. Smith, and he's also visited Colonel Baker at the New Castle Army Air Base."

"Oh, is the NCAAB where the program will be centered?"

"That's the plan." Nancy felt the excitement build once again. "Colonel Baker is being very accommodating. The base is currently under construction, and he's going to figure out living quarters and a mess hall for the women. He also suggested that I be commissioned a first lieutenant and given the job of operations officer over the women."

"Sounds excellent, and I agree."

Nancy smirked and rose from her chair. "Although Colonel Baker is recommending that twenty-five women be part of the trial instead of fifty."

"Twenty-five is better than none," Betty said. "We can make a real dent. Prove that more women should be invited. Assuming I make the cut?"

"You'll make the cut," Nancy said with a laugh, then sobered as she walked to the open kitchen window. "Are you sure you want to do this? Will Bud be able to manage the children?"

"I'm not fooling myself that it will be easy—especially after losing little Barbara. But my mother-in-law has already told me she'd help with caring for them. I think she wants to see me doing what I love again."

"You're definitely on the list," Nancy said, gazing out at the quiet neighborhood, "but I'd totally understand if you couldn't come."

"I'd love to come, Nancy. Maybe my mother-in-law is right. I need to do something like this to move on from grief." Her voice quieted. "It comes in waves, you know, and sometimes I can hardly breathe. But speaking to you makes me feel like I'm on top of the wave instead of beneath it."

Nancy's heart lifted a little. Betty had been keeping busy as a utility pilot for Grumman Aircraft. Her husband, Bud, was still the vice president and engineering test pilot for Grumman Aircraft. Betty mostly flew the engineers and the Navy inspectors to their wartime meetings. She also went on errands to pick up parts from satellite manufacturers, flying them back to the factory on Long Island. Everyone was busy, but everyone wanted to help as much as possible.

"Well then," Nancy said, "I'll let you know that we're already talking about uniforms. Can you send me your measurements?"

The smile came through Betty's voice. "No problem."

"We still have to get this through General Arnold," Nancy said, more subdued. "Once that happens, we have a lot of work to do getting the pilots to commit, plus writing up the training syllabus."

"I can help wherever and however you need me to."

"Thanks, Betty," Nancy said. "That means a lot."

Memos and letters continued between departments the rest of June and into July. Nancy met with Tunner more than once, so she wasn't surprised when he called her one evening while both she and Bob were at home on another sweltering night.

When she answered the phone, Bob set down the newspaper and turned his attention to her.

Tunner's voice came through the phone clearly. "General Arnold is asking for an outline of the women pilots you expect to get."

Nancy exhaled. "Does this mean he's accepted the proposal?"

"Not technically," Tunner said, "but I'm taking this as good news."

She sat in a kitchen chair, next to Bob, feeling a weight slide off her shoulders. "Did he say anything about your suggestion regarding me leading the organization?"

"No, and he didn't mention Cochran either, although she's tied up in England still."

Nancy wasn't sure what Cochran's reaction would be to all that had been going on these past few weeks, but there would certainly be a lot more negotiating if she were in the picture right now. "Once I get that list, are we in the clear?"

Tunner chuckled. "Not quite, but we'll keep pushing forward as if we are. Colonel Baker wants you to work with one of his top flight instructors, Lt. Joe Tracy, on the training syllabus for the program. Outlining everything from base rules to physical conditioning to ground school and flight instruction policies. We also need you on our board—unofficially—to review the women's applications."

Hope zinged through Nancy. "No problem."

The weeks passed, and by August, there was still no further word from Arnold, but Nancy continued working with Tunner and Baker on their planning. She crafted a training syllabus with Lt. Joe Tracy's input, and when September rolled around, everyone became more antsy.

And then Mrs. Roosevelt unintentionally propelled the momentum with her "My Day" column.

"Read this," Nancy said, walking into Bob's ATC office. She'd been spending the week in the Washington, DC, offices to work with Tunner.

Bob took the newspaper from her and read aloud, "It seems to me that in the civil air patrol and in our own ferry command, women, if they can pass the tests imposed upon our men, should have an equal opportunity for noncombat service. . . . Women pilots are a weapon waiting to be used."

Bob looked up at Nancy and grinned. "Even the First Lady agrees. What could be better than that? Has Colonel Tunner seen this?"

"He showed me." She returned his smile.

"That's right," Tunner spoke behind them, coming through the doorway. "General George is going to reach out to General Arnold again. This article gives us more weight and an excuse to do so."

"Excellent," Bob said.

A few days later, on September 5, Nancy's more than two-year-long wait came to an end.

Several people were gathered on the Washington, DC, airfield as she landed the Fairchild after a day of working in Baltimore—Bob, Tunner, and even General George. Either they had very bad news or very good news. She hoped it was the latter. She taxied toward them, turned off the engine, then climbed out of the cockpit. All three men were striding toward her, and Nancy's heart felt like it was bouncing around in her chest as she removed her goggles and unfastened her helmet.

Bob was smiling, though, and her hope soared.

"Mrs. Love," Tunner said. "We've received word from General Arnold."

"Yes?" Nancy asked in a guarded tone.

"General Arnold has directed that the recruiting of women pilots should begin immediately, in the next twenty-four hours, and you are to be appointed the director of the Women's Auxiliary Ferrying Squadron—otherwise known as the WAFS."

Nancy clapped a hand over her mouth, the tears forming instantly. Then she shook Tunner's hand, followed by George's, followed by throwing her arms around her husband's neck. He chuckled and pulled her in tight.

"I can't believe it." She drew away, wiping at her eyes. "Can this be true?"

"It's true, Mrs. Love," General George said with a broad smile. "I suggest you begin sending out the telegrams right away."

"Yes, of course." She slid her hand into Bob's. "I already have the messages drawn up." Her head spun, but she'd send out all the telegrams today even if it took her until midnight. She already knew there were eighty-three.

Over the next few days, Nancy monitored the replies to the telegrams. Betty Gillies was in, of course, and Barbara Towne, Gertrude Meserve, Evelyn Sharp, Dorothy Fulton, Aline Rhonie, Teresa James, and Lenore McElroy had all confirmed. It was a decent start.

Bob accompanied Nancy to General George's office on September 10, where Arnold would make the official announcement to the press. Nancy wore one of her nicer dresses along with a hat and gloves for formality, but when she walked into the general's office, there was no Arnold and no press.

General George stepped forward to shake her hand, his dark brows pinched. "I'm glad you arrived early. General Arnold was called away unexpectedly, so we'll be making the announcement with Secretary of War Stimson."

Nancy exchanged glances with Bob but didn't want to say anything in front of the general. It was odd for Arnold to be conveniently gone when he'd been the one to give final approval for the WAFS.

The group of them headed to Secretary Stimson's office, where Stimson himself greeted them. He smiled beneath his carefully groomed mustache. "Welcome, Mrs. Love. I'm honored to be part of this banner day for women pilots."

Nancy thanked him.

Several journalists gathered to take notes on Stimson's announcement, ask questions, and take photographs.

"Today, I'd like to introduce to you Nancy Love," Stimson said with a regal nod of his head, "if you don't already know who she is."

The journalists chuckled. Nancy didn't recognize any of them, but that didn't mean she hadn't met them.

"If you don't know Mrs. Love, I'll tell you that she's one of the two most important ladies who have so far come in contact with the Army—one is named Love, and the other is named Hobby. That will show you how respectable the Army is." He paused as a few reporters scribbled notes. Stimson put on glasses to read the paper he held. "It's an honor today to introduce the Women's Auxiliary Ferrying Squadron, which will comprise a highly specialized all-women squadron. This group will consist of twenty-five women pilots and will be hired by the Ferrying Division and be attached to the 2nd Ferrying Group at NCAAB in Wilmington, Delaware. These women are not militarized but are considered Civil Service employees."

After Stimson's speech, and after he and Nancy fielded questions from the journalists, Nancy posed for a photo with Secretary Stimson and General George. Other than her wedding, she didn't think she'd smiled so much in one day.

"We should celebrate," Bob said as they walked back to his office, hand-in-hand.

"What did you have in mind?"

"Dinner at a diner?" he teased.

Nancy laughed. "That actually sounds heavenly. And what would be even better is taking tomorrow morning off and sleeping in a little."

"*You*, sleep in? I don't think I've ever been a witness to that."

She nudged him. "You're about to see history in the making, then."

# CHAPTER TWENTY-SEVEN

"There is just a chance that this is not a time when women should be patient. We are in a war and we need to fight it with all our ability and every weapon possible. Women pilots, in this particular case, are a weapon waiting to be used."

—FIRST LADY ELEANOR ROOSEVELT, "MY DAY" COLUMN, SEPTEMBER 1, 1942

*September 1942—Washington, DC*

Nancy might have slept in, but a ringing phone awakened her at the first glimpse of dawn. Late-night or early-morning phone calls never boded well, and her heart rate zoomed when she said, "Hello?" into the receiver.

"Nancy, sorry to call so early," Tunner said, "but I've received word that Jacqueline Cochran landed in New York the day we met with the press. Yesterday, she met with General Arnold. Let's just say she wasn't pleased about discovering that the WAFS had been set up without her involvement."

Nancy hadn't expected Cochran's return so soon; none of them had.

Bob padded into the kitchen, curiosity etched on his face. Nancy waved at him to sit down next to her as Tunner continued.

"Late yesterday, General Arnold called a meeting with General George and General C.R. Smith. Cochran was in that meeting, too, and Arnold demanded that the ferrying project be revised, with Cochran representing him on the revision."

Nancy met Bob's questioning gaze, then asked Tunner, "What's really going on?"

"General Arnold is playing dumb, and I don't know why." Tunner paused. "According to Cochran, he promised her the leadership role should a women pilots organization be established. And now he's told her that he gave instructions for the preparation of a plan to use women pilots but that the announcement had been made without his knowledge or approval."

Annoyance shot through Nancy. How many surprises would be lobbed at her? "That's ridiculous. Is Cochran buying that? I can understand why she's upset, but it should be with General Arnold, not *us*. We weren't the ones making promises to her."

"Agreed," Tunner said. "This should be General Arnold's mess to sort out with her, but he's bringing everyone into it now and making demands."

"So, what now?"

"That's what I needed to give you a heads-up about."

Nancy reached for Bob's hand and held on.

"General George is drafting up a two-part plan to send to General Arnold in order to satisfy Cochran," Tunner began.

Nancy wanted to protest, but instead, she bit her lip, listening carefully.

"General George will point out that the ATC's direction to employ qualified female ferry pilots will go forward, though ATC doesn't have the facilities to train additional women. But the Flight Training Command does have facilities and can be used for the training. The women pilots can go through the FTC Program, then be employed by ATC for flight duty."

Nancy let that absorb. "Granting that ATC is allowed to hire more female pilots after our original twenty-five or fifty?"

"Correct," Tunner confirmed. "And Miss Cochran would direct the Women's Pilot Training Program."

It made sense, and it was logical. But would Cochran go for it? If she did, this firestorm could be calmed quickly. "I understand the value of having a Women's Pilot Training Program, because if the Ferrying Program gets off the ground, I'd love to see it expanded beyond the initial squadron," Nancy said at last.

"I see that too."

"Maybe Cochran returning to the US this week and pushing her agenda is a blessing in disguise." Nancy released Bob's hand and rubbed the back of her neck. "At least I'm going to try to see it that way, although I'm sure none of this will be smooth sailing."

"I don't expect that it will be," Tunner said in a wry tone. "I'm sending Teague to the meeting since I can't get out of my commitments this week."

Captain James S. Teague was a lower-level captain, but if Tunner trusted him, Nancy would too. She wasn't about to get in the middle of whatever firestorm Cochran was going to stir up.

After hanging up with Tunner, she turned to Bob and filled him in on the conversation, although he'd ascertained most of it.

"Come to the office with me today so we can get Teague's report firsthand," Bob said.

"I'm planning on it." She folded her arms and leaned back in her chair. "I hope Cochran doesn't blow this all apart."

"She might squawk from her corner," Bob said, "but General George's proposal is very reasonable and logical."

"That's what I think too," she said. "But will Cochran agree?"

Bob gave Nancy a half smile. "The Army can't renege on the WAFS. It's a done deal. We'll focus on getting *your* squadron ready to ferry. Whatever happens in the Training Program will be Cochran's responsibility."

Nancy couldn't agree more, but new concerns were now popping up. "We can't hire everyone who goes through training—that's never a 100 percent guarantee," she said. "They'll still have to meet all of ATC's flight test and physical requirements."

"Yes, and you'll have to make that clear from the beginning."

She grimaced. "I see more debates coming up."

Bob grasped her hand and squeezed. "Like Secretary Stimson said, you're one of the most important women associated with the Army right now. This program is making history, and we'll just have to ride out all the bumps."

Nancy slipped her other hand over Bob's but couldn't hide her sigh. "You're right. We all want female pilots to be given this chance, so it's imperative to keep our egos out of the way. Which might not be possible for some, but *I'll* make every effort." At least, she'd try, even if she collapsed into bed every night from sheer exhaustion of keeping a level head.

Bob leaned close and kissed her cheek. "Want coffee?"

"I love you."

He grinned and rose from the table. As he busied himself about the kitchen, Nancy called Betty, needing her one-step-removed opinion.

"You have the support you need, Nancy. Focus on moving forward in your program," Betty said in a raspy voice. It was still early for all of them. "Let Cochran storm about and blame whoever she wants for being left out of the original planning. It was noble of her to go to England, but it was also noble of you to stay and work out utilizing female pilots in our homeland. In the end, the war is our priority—and winning this war should be everyone's priority. Not placating bruised egos."

"Exactly," Nancy said. "That's what I needed to hear. You and Bob are like parrots." She gratefully sipped at the coffee he'd set before her.

The next hours spent at Bob's ATC office were filled with phone calls as Nancy fielded questions and fine-tuned the ferrying training syllabus. In the next week, she'd be moving to Wilmington and working with Colonel Baker to make candidate selections. There wasn't any time to waste.

"Do you have a few minutes?" Tunner asked, walking into the office with Captain Teague.

Nancy looked up from where she'd commandeered one end of Bob's desk.

"Come in," Bob said immediately, then moved to shut the door behind them.

Tunner and Teague took two available seats. "Captain Teague has brought a report of the meeting with General Arnold, Miss Cochran, and other representatives of Air Staff and CAA."

Teague gave a brief smile of acknowledgment. He was a thin-faced, sharp-eyed man with a mellow voice. "The good news is that there are now two female pilot groups: the WAFS Ferrying Program, headed up by Mrs. Love, and a pilots training program, headed up by

Jacqueline Cochran, which will be called the Women's Flying Training Detachment, or the WFTD. The Training Program will be set up at the Houston Municipal Airport."

Nancy wasn't surprised, and frankly, she felt relieved that Cochran had accepted General George's suggestion.

"But . . ." Teague hesitated. "Cochran looked clearly agitated about the Ferrying Program being organized in her absence. I had the feeling she wants to be over *all* women pilots in the United States. She didn't say it outright, but Cochran made it no secret that she sees herself as fully qualified to do so."

Nancy exhaled, holding back her comments. She'd save them for later, for Bob.

"In addition, I was asked to pass on the message that Mrs. Love's program would not give flight checks to women who Miss Cochran has already passed off."

Nancy stiffened. She couldn't keep silent any longer. "Unless Miss Cochran is at Wilmington and part of the daily training, she won't know exactly what we're looking for or requiring. Our testing needs to be hands-on, not blindly accepted because of a graduation certificate."

"True, and I didn't agree with the demand or make any promises on Mrs. Love's behalf." Teague glanced at Tunner, then at Nancy. "We're putting the summary of the meeting in writing so that everyone will be on the same page."

"Excellent," Tunner cut in. "We'll say something to the effect that graduates of WFTD will only be employed by the 2nd Ferrying Group if they pass the flight test and physical examination and not because they are graduates."

Nancy breathed easier. Tunner had once again proven to be her full supporter.

"And surely, as more women become trained and qualified, more squadrons will be organized," Bob offered. "Nancy's leadership will be a natural fit for the expansion."

"We've considered that as well and agree," Tunner said. "We all need to keep our noses clean and focus on the purpose of the program of utilizing female pilots to free up the male pilots for combat missions."

It was a heavy thing to consider—women pilots being trained to ferry so men could risk their lives overseas.

Over the next few days, Nancy was caught up in packing and moving to Wilmington. She wasn't excited about leaving Bob, but everything else was going better than she could have planned.

"They've just pulled up," Bob said, coming into their bedroom one evening.

Nancy set down a folded blouse. Her parents had insisted on traveling in for an overnight visit before she embarked on her new adventure. Hurrying out of the room, she reached the front door and opened it. Her parents were coming up the steps. "Mother! Daddy!" She stepped forward into the early crispness of the September afternoon and hugged both of her parents.

Each time she saw them, her heart tugged because they'd aged a little more. She supposed she was aging, too, but time existed in a whirlwind for her. Seeing her parents brought everything to a standstill.

"Come in," she said, motioning them inside. "Dinner should be out of the oven soon."

Bob stepped onto the porch and took the two bags her father held.

"Smells wonderful," her mother said, although Nancy knew she wouldn't hold back her opinion of the actual dinner once it was served. But Nancy didn't mind. It was her mother's way of speaking whatever was on her mind. Which meant the subject of children would be brought up again.

The war had been Nancy's most recent excuse. Well, she didn't need an excuse because lately, she wondered if there was something wrong with her inner workings. She'd never tried to prevent babies, so why hadn't she become pregnant? She'd come to the conclusion that she needed to see a doctor who specialized in women's health, but she was almost afraid of the answer. What if she were told she was barren? Would it be better to know or better to hope she wasn't?

"This is cozy," her father said, his voice surprisingly loud in the small space.

She'd almost forgotten how quiet things were with only her and Bob in the apartment. She gave her parents a quick tour, and when they paused at the bedroom door where evidence of packing spread across the bed, her mother said, "Must you really leave your husband for this job?"

"It's a short flight away," Nancy said, not surprised by this question either. "We only see each other at night most of the time anyway."

"Because of that Baltimore job," her mother said none too cheerfully.

"Yes, but that's over now, although I'll still be working with Colonel Baker in Wilmington."

"It's a fine thing you're doing, Nance," her father cut in. "You've put your heart and soul into this, and it's finally coming to fruition."

Her mother gave a tight smile, then headed down the hallway, saying that she'd check the oven.

"Don't mind her," Father said quietly. "She's worried about you flying the larger bomber planes."

"Oh, that's a ways off." But Nancy was smiling, and her dad returned it. "Mother will have to get used to it."

"She's proud of you, though, but she's worried, too, if that makes sense."

"It makes perfect sense. I know she wants grandchildren. Win the war, stay safe, have babies . . . It's all rather straightforward."

Her father chuckled and set an arm around her shoulders. She leaned into him as they walked together to the kitchen, where Bob had pulled out the chicken casserole from the oven, and Mother was filling up glasses with lemonade, which Nancy had saved some rationed sugar for. Nancy suspected more food items would soon be rationed.

The dinner conversation was as Nancy had expected. Talk of the war and the Battle of Stalingrad that had begun in August, with Nazi Germany trying to gain control of the city of Stalingrad from the Soviet Union. Then, surprisingly, Father pulled out the day's copy of the *Washington Daily News.* "I snatched this on our last stop, and I was surprised at Miss Cochran's comments."

Nancy took the paper from him and read Cochran's printed comments aloud, "Yes, I've been called back by General Arnold to be head of the women's air corps in this country. Our goal is 1,500. I've had such success with my girls in England that I know this will work."

Nancy stared at the words, rereading them silently. She felt everyone around the table watching her, waiting for her reply. Finally, she looked up. "Well, the sky in Jackie Cochran's world is certainly a different color than mine."

"That's right." The lines about Bob's eyes had tightened. "Who wants dessert?" he asked with false cheerfulness.

"I do," Nancy said immediately. A cold chocolate pudding would be just the thing right now. She rose from the table and helped Bob serve. Irritation snaked through her, but mostly, she felt tired. Tired of the press following the story so closely. Tired of hearing things about Jackie Cochran second- or thirdhand—especially when she sensed some personal digs at herself. Nancy knew that wasn't the case, but her emotions jumbled whenever that woman was brought up.

She had to keep in mind what Bob and Betty had told her—there was room for both programs—and they should be interconnected. But it seemed Nancy had made all the concessions, staying quiet and conciliatory, whereas Cochran made brazen, public statements and actively alienated those she should be keeping as her closest allies.

# CHAPTER TWENTY-EIGHT

"I didn't get back to New Castle AAB until [September] tenth. I took the train down because the weather was lousy in the morning. But it cleared in time for me to get my check flight with Lt. Joe Tracy in a Fairchild trainer. Lieutenant Joe was a civilian pilot before they let him into the ATC, so his flight test didn't have any surprises. We were out about fifty minutes. Then after a bull session with Nancy Love, I caught the train for home.

"I guess I'm going to join the WAFS. Bud thinks it's very worthwhile trying out, and so do I. We have to sign up for three month stretches and duty begins on September 21."

—BETTY GILLIES'S DIARY

*September–October 1942—Wilmington, Delaware*

It was a brisk fall day as Nancy walked with Colonel Baker toward the sturdy BOQ 14 barracks in order to inspect them for the arriving women pilots. Twenty-seven women had been chosen and approved out of the telegrams Nancy had originally sent out.

The BOQ 14 sat in the center of the base and next to the officers' club. There were forty-four rooms, plenty in number to house the incoming WAFS. Nancy had already reserved a second-floor room for herself. She figured it was first come, first served.

The day that Betty's train arrived, Nancy could hardly contain her excitement. Betty was coming to inspect things before fully committing. Nancy would give her the grand tour and then hope for the best, whatever that might be.

Normally, Betty would have flown her Grumman Widgeon twin-engine airplane, but the weather had been stormy. As the train arrived in a bluster of black smoke from the diesel-electric engine, Nancy's pulse sped up in anticipation of seeing her friend again. She craned her neck to spot her familiar face. When a woman in a smart navy dress suit and matching beret stepped off the train, Nancy waved and hurried toward Betty.

"You made it," Nancy said, hugging her friend. "I can't believe you're really here."

Betty released her, grinning. "I can't either. Now, let's check out New Castle. Bud is eagerly waiting for a report."

The women linked arms, and Nancy led her to the car. "We'll tour the living quarters, then you can say hello to Colonel Baker. Later, Lieutenant Joe Tracy will give you a check flight if the weather clears up." She paused. "Is Bud good with all of this?"

Betty gave a soft laugh, peeling off her gloves once they settled in the car. "He practically pushed me out the door. He told me this is what I've been preparing for, and my mother-in-law even chimed in."

Nancy arched her brows before starting the engine. "Quite the formidable front."

Betty only smiled. "This feels good, Nancy. Really good."

Nancy squeezed her arm. "I'm glad. And I'm so happy you're here. You don't have to stay long in the program, you know. Just the first ninety days until we get things off the ground."

Once they reached the base, Nancy drove to the two-story barracks. "This is BOQ 14, and up until now, men were housed here. We had to make some adjustments for women to come in, such as putting up blinds over the windows."

Betty leaned forward to peer out the car window. "Interesting."

"We also added a few wooden planks over the muddy ditch so we wouldn't have to trudge through the mire when coming and going."

"I suppose the men hopped over the ditch?"

Nancy shrugged. "Who knows?" She parked the car, and she and Betty climbed out, picking their way around recent rain puddles while carrying luggage. The sky was beginning to clear now, and Nancy hoped that meant Betty would be able to do her flight check.

Inside, they walked past the square rooms, each containing a dresser, a cot, and an iron chair.

"No doors?"

"I guess that would be too presumptuous of us to expect?" Nancy motioned to a pipe held up by a pair of two-by-four planks. "This is your hanging closet."

"This is quite . . . primitive." Betty turned to face Nancy with a smile. "There really is no place like home."

"Right, but I've been staying at the guesthouse called Kent Manor—so this isn't as much a shock for me as it might be for you."

"Where's your room?"

"Second floor—quieter up there."

"Show me the way," Betty said. They headed up the stairs, lugging the bags, then she stopped at a room in the northwest corner. She walked into the small space. "I'll take this one. A little drafty, but it will do."

"If you're sure?"

"I'm sure. It will be an adventure." Betty spun slowly, hands on hips. "But I think it will be a lot of fun too."

Nancy could only hope so. Hearing the cheer and positivity in her friend's voice was gratifying.

"How are the numbers coming along?" Betty asked, setting one of her bags on the bed.

"Ah, it's a bit tricky." Nancy helped with the second bag. "We're getting responses, of course, but some of the women are tied up in contracts of flight instructing through WTS." The War Training Service Program had replaced the original CPT, and some of the women instructors would be a good fit for Nancy's WAFS. If not, they could join Cochran in Texas for training when it started up in November.

"How many will be in the first group?" She unzipped one of the bags and pulled out a framed picture of her little family.

Nancy eyed the photo—so timeless, especially now that little Barbara was gone. "Nine in the first group if you say yes."

Betty set the photo on the small table by the bed. "I'm saying yes." She turned to face Nancy, but instead of the expected sorrow Nancy guessed would be in Betty's eyes, they twinkled. "As long as I pass the flight test."

Nancy laughed, relief spiking through her. "Let's get it over with, then. No more dillydallying."

As they walked to the office to meet Baker and book the flight test, Betty asked, "Did Cornelia Fort agree to come?"

"Yes," Nancy said. "She shared a few things about her experience at Pearl Harbor, but I can see that it's still hard for her to talk about."

Betty went quiet for a moment. "I'm impressed she still wants to fly."

"Oh, she wants to fly more than ever," Nancy said. "She's very determined to make this program a success too." Cornelia had been the first woman in Tennessee to earn her instructor's license. She'd worked in Colorado, then had taken a job offer in Hawaii. She was flying as an instructor in Hawaii the morning of the Japanese attack on Pearl Harbor. She'd narrowly escaped an air collision with one of the Japanese bombers and had had to make a forced landing. She again escaped being shot at on the ground in a strafing attack.

"Good for her," Betty said. "She's a tough lady. I guess none of us get through life unscathed."

Nancy was about to respond when Colonel Baker and Lieutenant Joe Tracy came out of the office. She introduced everyone, then Tracy took Betty on her flight check.

Nancy headed into Baker's office with him to review any new correspondence they'd received. The first group of women was already set, with Cornelia Fort, Aline Rhonie, Helen Mary Clark, Catherine Slocum, Adela Scharr, Teresa James, and Esther Nelson. And more were on their way. Part of the program would also incorporate the thirty-day Army indoctrination.

Other women who'd committed to go through the pretesting included Barbara Poole, who was a flight instructor in Detroit. Her experience also included barnstorming, stunts such as jumping out of planes, and CPT training. She had 1,800 qualifying hours but still had to get her 200-horsepower rating. That shouldn't be a problem. Gertrude Meserve, Esther Manning, Nancy Batson, and Barbara Jane "B.J." Erickson were all incoming as well. B.J. had graduated from CPT out of the University of Washington, and she was an instructor who flew both land and sea planes.

When Betty walked into the office with Joe Tracy, she wore a big grin on her face. "I passed."

Nancy rose from where she was sitting across from Baker's desk. "That's great news because I need an executive officer to act as second-in-command."

Betty's eyes widened. "I know nothing."

"You know more than everyone else but me," Nancy said. "Besides, you're good at bossing people plus carrying out orders."

"Then, I accept." Betty laughed, a sound Nancy would never take for granted. "Or maybe I should call and tell my husband first, although I'm pretty sure he already knows the outcome of today."

"Great, you do that, and then I need my executive officer to give me an opinion on the uniforms."

A few minutes later, a beaming Betty joined Nancy, and they spent the next hour going over the rudimentary sketches of a WAFS uniform that Nancy had outlined.

"There will be several parts to the uniform," Nancy said, pointing to the sketch of a shirt. "We'll have shirts and ties made of tan broadcloth. The slacks will be narrow-cut slacks, for when we're flying, and these gored-style skirts are for street wear."

"I like it so far." Betty picked up the sketch with a jacket. "Jackets with four pockets?"

"Yes, they'll be tailored, made from gray-green wool gabardine, and trimmed with brass buttons."

To complete the uniform, Nancy had decided they'd wear low-heeled, brown-leather pumps, carry a leather shoulder bag, and don an overseas cap, overcoat, and gloves.

"I love all of it." Betty continued leafing through the sketches, marking a couple of places with a pencil. "The belt needs to be detachable, and the jacket a short cut so it doesn't interfere with wearing a parachute."

"Good ideas." Nancy jotted down the notes. "The women will be paying for their own uniforms since we're not militarized." She hoped that wouldn't be too much of a strain, but she planned to help out if it was.

Betty tapped her pencil on the desk. "Hopefully a budget can be put in place at some point."

Nancy hoped it would happen as well. The women would swear in as civilian pilots of the ATC, taking the same oath as the men who joined the Ferrying Division. The women wouldn't be receiving a commission at the end of the ninety-day commitment, even though they'd have officer privileges.

"Also, the WAFS will wear the command insignia over the left breast pocket here." Nancy pointed to her sketch.

"The civilian pilot wings of the ATC," Betty mused.

"Correct." Nancy straightened the sketches into a pile. "The flight suit won't be so pretty since we'll have to put up with what's already in distribution until new sizes can be made."

"Let me guess," Betty said, "we're wearing men's flight suits?"

Nancy crossed to the corner of the room where she'd stashed a few things. "Here's one of them."

Betty took the flight suit, holding it up by the shoulders. The suit draped to the floor, pooling there, clearly several sizes too big, especially against Betty's five-foot-one frame.

"We'll each have parachutes and goggles, of course, along with . . ." Nancy picked up the next item. "A white silk AAF flying scarf."

Betty smoothed her hand over the silk scarf.

"And finally," Nancy continued, "we'll have leather flying jackets that will sport the ATC patch."

"Very official, all of this."

Nancy smiled. "Very."

Within a few days, the women pilots had reported to base, sworn in as civilian pilots, and settled into their barracks. The second floor of the barracks soon filled up with Nancy, Betty, Cornelia Fort, Esther Nelson, Catherine Slocum, Adela "Del" Scharr, Teresa James, Aline "Pat" Rhonie, and Helen Mary Clark.

When October 19 rolled around, nine WAFS members officially graduated from training, with Barbara Towne and Helen Richards still working on their training.

Shortly after graduation, Catherine Slocum showed up in Nancy's office, hovering in the doorway. "Mrs. Love, I need to speak with you," she said, her blonde curls tamed into a tight bun at the nape of her neck.

Nancy went on alert at the gravity of her words and motioned for her to enter. "Of course. Have a seat."

Catherine shut the door before taking a seat, and this alerted Nancy even more. The woman's face was pale, and she clasped her hands tightly in front of her. "As you know, my husband is the general manager of the *Philadelphia Evening Bulletin*, and things are very busy in the newspaper world right now."

Nancy nodded. She'd heard Catherine talk about her husband and four children more than once.

"The thing is, the childcare for our children has fallen through, and it would be impossible for Richard to take a leave of absence from his job, you see. Even part-time." She drew in a shaky breath. "So, I must resign from the WAFS."

Nancy had also heard rumblings of Catherine's childcare problem but had hoped they'd found a solution. Catherine had graduated, after all, and was about to take on ferrying assignments. Nancy could see both determination and regret in Catherine's eyes. She was a fine pilot and would have been an excellent addition.

"I'm sorry to hear that, Catherine, but I know family is a priority."

"Thank you for this opportunity, Mrs. Love." She blinked back the tears gathering in her eyes. "This was a dream to participate in, and maybe if things change, I can ring you up?"

"Yes, I'd love that." Nancy smiled, although her eyes had teared too. "You'd be welcome back anytime. I'd never turn down an excellent pilot."

Catherine sniffled and stood.

Nancy walked around the desk and hugged the woman. "Safe journey, and tell those kids of yours that they're very lucky."

Catherine laughed and released Nancy. "It might take them a while to really appreciate things. But maybe with my absence so far, they'll be glad to see me."

"I have no doubt about that." After a second hug, Catherine left the office.

Nancy stood in the quiet space for a moment. She'd seen firsthand Catherine's dedication, and the other women's. They were all making great sacrifices. It wasn't easy, not on any of them. Nancy predicted that more hardships would come, and all she could do was deal with them one day at a time.

She herself missed Bob fiercely, and their nightly phone calls only eased that somewhat. But she wouldn't have it any other way at that moment.

By the time she joined the other women in the mess hall that evening for dinner, Catherine had already packed and left on a train. Conversation veered from missing Catherine to news about the war—the Battle of Stalingrad still raged in the Soviet Union. And the Japanese had conquered Guam, Hong Kong, the Philippines, the Dutch East Indies, Malaya, Singapore, and Burma. But the Allies were on the offensive—they'd won the Battle of Midway in June, and in August, American troops forced Japan to withdraw from the Solomon Islands.

With every bad news report, something else came through as victorious. The Battle of Milne Bay was over, and the Allies had defeated the Japanese in New Guinea in a land battle—the first major land battle Japan had lost.

# CHAPTER TWENTY-NINE

"This notion that women should be of high moral character and
technical competence while no such standards were used for men
set the tone for the double standards that were to characterize
the women's [military] programs for the next forty years."

—MAJOR GENERAL JEANNE HOLM

*October–December 1942—Wilmington, Delaware*

Nancy readily admitted she felt envious that Betty would lead the
inaugural WAFS ferrying assignment. Nancy would remain at New
Castle, running operations and overseeing the training of the next group
of women. She'd appointed Betty to lead the flight of six L-4B Cubs and
transport them from the Piper factory in Lockhaven, Pennsylvania, to
Mitchel Field on Long Island.

As Nancy and Betty planned out the flight route, she thought of the
run-in she'd had the year before with Jackie Cochran over setting up a
relay map. This first ferrying group wouldn't be stopping to switch pilots. On this assignment, pilots Fort, James, Clark, Rhonie, and Scharr
would make up the team, with Betty at the head. Of course, if there was
bad weather, they'd have to land for safety and wait it out, possibly remaining overnight—RON. November was around the corner, after all.

But Nancy would stay apprised of every incident. Success was not
optional when it came to the WAFS. They needed to succeed. And she'd
do everything in her power to make sure it happened.

So when the ferrying assignment Betty led turned out to be a success, Nancy had never been so happy to call Bob. "They made it to Long
Island. Everything and everyone is intact."

"Fantastic," Bob said in a warm voice. "Congratulations, sweetie."

Nancy couldn't stop the grin on her face. "It wasn't me. It was—"

"Oh, it was you," Bob cut in. *"Mostly* you, that is."

Nancy let out a breathy laugh. "I'm so happy everything went smoothly. I know that won't always be the case. We've nearly reached twenty graduated pilots, though, and we can now take on more assignments. We won't have to wait for someone to return before handling the next assignment. Once we have twenty-five, we'll be at the goal Colonel Baker and I set. We're getting so close."

Bob let her chatter on, most of which he'd already heard before, but he only encouraged her to tell him all the details. Then he dropped some news that shifted her mood.

"The ATC is sending me on an international trip."

Nancy's heart froze. Other men were being sent overseas to fly bombers, so there was no reason Bob would be an exception. "What kind of trip?" she asked, trepidation catching in her throat.

"It's not what you think," he said. "We're flying the Fireball route—checking out the course for any inaccuracies or issues in the supply chain into India and China."

Nancy released a slow breath. He wasn't flying bombers, going into combat. Yet the trip sounded extensive, with its own complications and risks. "How long will you be gone?"

"Six weeks, at least. I'll miss Thanksgiving and probably Christmas."

Nancy reached for the calendar and flipped to the month of December. "You can miss those holidays as long as you stay safe."

He gave a soft chuckle. "I'll stay safe."

"Where exactly are you traveling?"

He paused, and it sounded like he was shuffling papers. "The route takes us through Puerto Rico, British Guiana, and Brazil. Next, we'll head across the mid-Atlantic to Ascension Island. We'll hit Nigeria, Egypt, then Iraq."

Nancy stood from her desk and crossed to the large world map she'd tacked to the office wall. She traced her finger along the locations as Bob continued.

"From Iraq, we head into India. We're establishing the Hump airlift that will move supplies over the Himalayas and the Burmese jungle and into Kunming, China."

Nancy's finger paused. "That's quite a supply route."

"We hope to make it smooth sailing," he said. "We'll look for issues that might cause delays or be dangerous for other reasons. We'll find out what the lodging is like and how the pilots will be received at the different airfields."

"Is there already pushback?"

"Potential pushback, but we won't know with certainty until we visit each location. I'm not wearing military dress. I'll present myself as a civilian pilot ferrying supplies since I'll get more inside information that way."

"I think that's smart." She turned from the map and perched on the corner of her desk. "What type of planes?"

"There's a C-53 and a C-47 in India that I'll be flying."

She heard the smile in his voice. "You sound excited about that."

"I am, and one day, you'll be flying them too."

Nancy scoffed. "That's a ways off—we're ferrying Cubstuff, PT-17s and -19s now."

"It will come," Bob predicted with his usual confidence.

"Well, you'll know it when it happens."

His laugh was soft. "I'll miss you, sweetie. I don't know how phone calls are going to work."

"You're going to call me when you can—that's how it will work."

"As usual, you're right, Mrs. Love."

She'd miss their regular phone calls, but right now, she wanted to keep the conversation light and not think about how long he'd be gone. "Don't forget the little people at New Castle."

"Never. Now, are you coming home this weekend?"

She didn't need to check her schedule to answer. "No, you're coming here. Make it happen, Mr. Love."

"Will do, ma'am."

When she hung up with her husband, she was still smiling. And counting the hours until she got to hug him tightly.

In the meantime, she'd stay busy, as usual. As it turned out, Dorothy Scott arrived the week before Thanksgiving, making the twenty-fifth member of the WAFS. Dorothy was a twin, and she'd learned to fly at the University of Washington and then had taken on a flight instructor position at Pullman. She had the bare minimum of 504 hours in her pilot logbook when she arrived at Wilmington. She'd declared that she had lucky room number 13 in the barracks, and Nancy proudly added Dorothy's name to the WAFS roster once she graduated.

Each day, Nancy read through the names that she'd written in order of the women joining up, feeling personal pride in this growing group of WAFS. She'd removed Catherine Slocum's, but the rest remained: Nancy Love, Betty Gillies, Cornelia Fort, Aline "Pat" Rhonie, Helen Mary Clark, Adela "Del" Scharr, Esther Nelson, Teresa James, Barbara Poole, Helen Richards, Barbara Towne, Gertrude Meserve, Florene Miller, Barbara Jane "B.J." Erickson, Delphine Bohn, Barbara "Donnie" Donahue, Evelyn Sharp, Phyllis Burchfield, Esther Manning, Nancy Batson, Katherine "Kay" Rawls Thompson, Dorothy Fulton, Opal "Betsy" Ferguson, Bernice Batten, and Dorothy Scott.

Other women had accepted and were on their way to join the program: Helen "Little Mac" McGilvery and Kathryn "Sis" Bernheim.

The number of women in the program meant that Colonel Baker had deemed there was a sufficient number to practice a close-order drill each Saturday morning. Nancy was called to lead their formation for their march in review.

It should have been simple to call out the orders loud and clear, but for some reason, Nancy felt like the winter breeze stole her voice each time.

One such Saturday, Nancy peered out the barracks window as the women were in a flurry of getting dressed in their uniforms. The low, dark clouds promised rain, and the wind didn't seem too friendly for flying. But they could at least march.

Nancy was the third one out of the barracks and met up with Delphine Bohn and Pat Rhonie. Their full squad wasn't at the base—some were on a ferrying mission—but Nancy would still carry out her orders.

"Good morning, Mrs. Love," Pat said. "Hello, Delphine."

"Good morning," Nancy replied.

"Morning always comes too soon," Delphine said in a sleep-rough voice.

"Agreed," Nancy said. "Good reports have come in on your last mission."

Pat flashed a smile, her short, dark hair blowing in the wind beneath her cap. "Great news. I guess no one is flying today?"

"Not unless the clouds move along."

Aline Rhonie, or "Pat," was good friends with Betty Gillies, and one of the first American women to receive a US transport pilot license. In 1934, Pat had been the first woman to fly solo from New York to Mexico City. She was also an artist and had created a 126-foot-long mural depicting the history of aviation at Roosevelt Field. She'd earned her British pilot's license as well as an Irish commercial license.

More women came out of the barracks, and at precisely eight o'clock, Nancy ordered, "Line up, ladies."

Conversation ceased, and everyone moved into their lines.

Nancy waited a few beats, then called out, "Forward, march!"

Everyone stepped forward with their left foot in the precise action of putting their heel to the ground first. They were also supposed to swing their arms in coordination. Marching wasn't difficult in and of itself, but calling out commands at the same time felt awkward to Nancy. She'd already been teased about it, but today, she determined to execute perfectly.

"Mark time," she called next, but her voice sounded small, and she wondered if the women at the back of the line could hear. They were marching toward the inactive runway and would need to make a left turn. Nancy drew in a breath as the wind tugged at her hair and clothing, and she tried to remember why the opposite command had to be given to turn left. "Column right, march," she called out. The wind drowned out her command, so she said it louder. "Column right, march?"

Someone snickered behind her, and Nancy was pretty sure that snickering wasn't allowed in marching. She kept her attention forward, though, focusing on her next command as the runway loomed. "Change step. I mean, *column left*, march."

There was a rather awkward shifting as the women marched along the runway. She heard a couple of giggles but ignored them.

"Hup, two, three, four," Nancy continued, her palms sweating. The wind speed had increased, but it did nothing to cool her down. They could march straight for a while, right? "Hup, two, three, four."

As they neared the end of the runway, Nancy knew there was a drop-off about ten feet ahead, and she sorted through the commands. Should they halt, then turn and walk toward another location?

As the drop-off neared, she second-guessed herself more than once, panic freezing all reason inside her head, and she finally called out, "To the rear, march!"

But instead of halting like Nancy did, even though she hadn't actually commanded it, the women continued past her. Half-marching, half-sliding down the embankment to the field below.

Nancy stared as they continued marching into the field. Laughing. They were all laughing. Every last one of them.

Nancy set her hands on her hips as the wind made a rat's nest of her hair. She had no words.

Delphine Bohn laughed so hard, she'd bent over, bracing her hands on her knees.

Nancy's mouth quirked. All right, so maybe it was a little funny. Once her sheer panic had subsided, of course. It was quite ridiculous that she was on top of the precipice, and they'd all marched straight down it into no-man's land.

"Come back here, all of you," Nancy called.

"Is that an *order*, Commander?"

"It doesn't sound like an order," Pat said, grinning. "Shouldn't it have the word *march* in there somewhere?"

Nancy groaned. "March forward and come up the hill. We're starting over."

More laughter, but the women obliged.

They marched back to their barracks without any more precipices getting in their way. But Nancy knew she wasn't going to live the incident down anytime soon.

A few days later, Colonel Baker called her into his office, his expression grim. The tapping of his pen on the desk testified to his irritation. "Pat Rhonie is late."

This, Nancy knew. Pat was supposed to return to base the day before but had called Nancy with an excuse. Nancy had reported it to Baker.

"Has she asked for another day?"

"Another day we can't afford," Baker said. "I told her to report this morning."

Nancy didn't need to check the clock to know it was late afternoon. "Is something else going on?"

"If there is, she hasn't informed me," Baker clipped. "Emergencies happen, but Rhonie is being tight-lipped about this."

It was rather strange, but Nancy wasn't going to hold it against the woman on a personal level. Yet she realized that running an operation like this, they needed to be strictly accountable. The cogs of the wheel would go off-balance if one person didn't report when they were supposed to. Assignments would have to be reconfigured, which might mean missing ferrying deadlines.

Baker's brows remained furrowed, and Nancy didn't blame him for his frustration. She felt the same, but she also hated to see any negative repercussions.

Nancy stayed up later than usual that night, hoping Pat would turn up. But she didn't.

Nancy finally called Bob, and he told her, "Rhonie will have to be dealt with through the board now."

It turned out that Bob was right, as much as Nancy hadn't want to believe it. When Pat Rhonie did return to base the following day, she spent a long time in Baker's office, later coming out looking like she'd been crying.

But to her credit, she only told Nancy, "I'm meeting with the board, and I'll be discharged. Thank you for this opportunity, Mrs. Love. I think this program is necessary and important, and it's already making an impact."

"I'm sorry to hear about all this," Nancy said, otherwise at a loss for what to say. "Let's keep in touch. I'd love to hear about your next endeavor."

"That means a lot to me, Mrs. Love, thank you."

Nancy wondered if there was something personal going on that Pat wasn't telling anyone. Was she willing to endure discharge instead of opening up?

By the end of the day, Pat had packed her things, said goodbye to the women waiting for their next ferrying assignment, then flown out on her 125 hp Luscombe Phantom that she'd flown to New Castle.

The Original WAFS Squadron was now only twenty-seven women.

The entire court hearing had been kept quiet, and Nancy could only hope to keep it out of the press. Which was probably why, the following weekend, she had to use a little more backbone.

It was nearly time to march in the parade review when a knock sounded at her bedroom door. Nancy answered to find Nancy Batson standing there, not dressed in uniform yet. In fact, she wore her robe, as if she'd just rolled out of bed. Unusual for Batson since she was such a level-headed pilot from Alabama, who didn't let mechanical mishaps deter her from making smooth landings.

Now her Southern drawl sounded raspy. "Mrs. Love, I don't think I can march this morning." Batson sniffled, peering through bloodshot eyes. "I've got an awful cold, and I feel lousy."

The woman had been stuffy all week. And when Nancy had accompanied some of the women to the DuPont Hotel the night before for drinks, Batson had been among them—dancing the night away.

"Didn't I see you out dancing at the DuPont Hotel last night?"

Batson lowered her eyes and tugged her bathrobe a little tighter. "Yes, ma'am."

Nancy waited a heartbeat. "Well, I think you can manage to march this morning, Miss Batson."

Batson didn't answer for a moment, then she raised her bleary gaze. With another sniffle, she said, "Yes, ma'am."

Nancy watched her shuffle away. After Pat's discharge, Nancy didn't want any rumors to start if women were suddenly missing from the parade review. It wasn't that she didn't think Batson had a cold—she certainly did—but if she could rally to drink and dance the jitterbug at a hotel, she could march this morning.

It seemed that problems came in threes, and the next weekend, Nancy was called into a meeting with Baker.

"Close the door, please." He stood by the window, back to her.

Nancy did so, but instead of taking a seat, she asked, "What's happened?"

Baker turned, shadows beneath his eyes. "We've had a report on Teresa James."

Nancy frowned. "What type of report?"

"She was spotted dancing with another woman in Wilmington last night."

Nancy's mind raced, thinking through what she knew about Teresa. "Teresa requested and was granted the night off."

"Yes, that's all fine." Baker paused, folding his arms. "Yet we can't have gossip sully the WAFS."

Nancy understood perfectly what he meant, but she wouldn't have any answers until she spoke to Teresa directly. "I'll call her in as soon as she lands this afternoon."

Teresa was currently on a shorter ferrying trip that would take only the day, an easy case for a pilot who'd passed her flight tests with flying colors. She'd recently married George Martin, and she seemed to be mad about him. Word was he was heading overseas as a bomber pilot. Nancy couldn't picture Teresa carrying on a relationship with a woman, or else why would she have married Martin?

When Teresa finally reported to Nancy's office, still wearing her flight suit, Nancy had come up with various scenarios but none of them satisfactory. She knew this could be an uncomfortable conversation, but she dove right in and reported on what Baker had said.

Teresa didn't answer for a moment. Then she laughed. "Mrs. Love, I guess Wilmington sees things differently? My sister Betty was visiting, which is why I asked permission to take a few hours off base. Back home in Pittsburgh, women dance together all the time." She set her hands on her hips. "See, if the men aren't keen on dancing, the women aren't about to be left out. So, we dance with each other."

Nancy blinked. "Ah."

Teresa's smile remained in place, and Nancy felt as if a tremendous weight had been lifted off, which could have led to complications she didn't want to be in the middle of.

"I understand, and thank you for explaining." Nancy released her breath. "You're right about one thing, Teresa: things are different in Wilmington. We need to remain above gossip, no matter how innocent or how things are done back home."

Teresa nodded, but her cheeks had stained red.

"Custom or not, I'd like to ask you to not dance with your sister, or any other woman, for that matter. We have many eyes upon the WAFS." Nancy's throat burned, and she hated that she had to draw finicky lines like this. But someone had seen fit to report it to Colonel Baker.

"Yes, ma'am. I understand."

# CHAPTER THIRTY

"Contemplated expansion of the armed forces will tax the nation's manpower. Women must be used wherever it is practical to do so. It is desired that you take immediate and positive action to augment to the maximum possible extent the training of women pilots. The Air Forces objective is to provide at the earliest possible date a sufficient number of women pilots to replace men in every noncombatant flying duty in which it is feasible to employ women."

—GENERAL ARNOLD, DIRECTIVE TO TRAINING COMMAND, NOVEMBER 3, 1942

*December 1942–January 1943—Wilmington, Delaware*

"We need to increase our classifications and put the women to work transitioning into larger and more powerful aircraft," Nancy told Colonel Baker and Colonel Tunner as they sat together in Baker's office. As far as she could tell, both men agreed with her, but she knew they were battling red tape. "I've put together a database of our superiors and their flying qualifications. If we can't ferry the planes needed for their own transitions and training, then we'll hit a bottleneck."

"I'm not disagreeing, Nancy," Tunner said. "But I can't give the green light that easily."

Baker steepled his hands, his frown in place. Nancy had seen that frown more often lately.

"I've already sent in the proposal about removing the Cubs' wings and shipping them by rail," Baker said.

Nancy had discussed this with Baker already. The Cubs were so slow to fly and unsafe in winter weather; therefore, it would be faster and cheaper to send them by rail to the air bases in the South.

"Right," Nancy conceded, "and the other thing to consider is that Cochran is getting in AT-6s for advanced training for the two classes she's recruited. We can't have our current ferrying pilots eclipsed by incoming graduates."

Tunner nodded, but Colonel Baker's brows pinched. "We are doing well with the Fairchilds, and our WAFS are staying busy."

Nancy pursed her lips. She wasn't even checked out on the AT-6 herself, which she needed to change as soon as possible. She had an upcoming trip planned to visit various bases, and when she got to Texas, she planned to make flying an AT-6 her top priority.

She pressed on. "I want to make Teresa James the flight leader for the group heading to Montana." Seven WAFS were taking a train to Great Falls, Montana, then ferrying PT-17s from Great Falls to Jackson, Tennessee. There they'd join a group of male pilots to ferry thirty-three trainers coming in from the Canadian RAF and move them to the warmer-climate training fields.

"I thought *you* were going," Baker said.

"No, I have too much to do," Nancy said, motioning toward Tunner. "We need to start preparations for the first class of Cochran's group to report to New Castle in the spring. A second class is right on their heels. Our numbers are going to explode."

"Right." Tunner's gaze shifted to Baker. "We need Nancy and the representative ferrying officers to visit other air bases and pitch the idea of a women's squadron to operate among their ferrying divisions."

"Of course," Baker said. "I thought this would take place in January."

"We're pushing it up," Tunner said simply. "Starting with phone calls, then visits."

"I'll get to work and keep both of you apprised," Nancy said.

The following week, after dozens of phone calls to ferrying groups across the nation, Nancy found herself back in Washington, climbing aboard a Lockheed C-36 to copilot to Great Falls. The WAFS group had returned to Great Falls after their ferrying mission, and she was about to deliver big news to them. They were getting split up.

She needed the trained WAFS to divide and become the core of new squadrons at different air bases. When the newly graduated arrived from Cochran, the numbers at Wilmington would eventually be replaced and the new squadrons filled in.

Her goal was to get women's ferry squadrons established in Romulus, Michigan, then Memphis, and Love Field in Dallas as well as Long Beach.

With mixed feelings, Nancy left Great Falls. The last few months of camaraderie among the Originals at Wilmington would never be repeated. She was determined to continue pushing her agenda of the women transitioning to bigger planes, and she'd be setting the standard. Baker could no longer push back if she were transitioned herself.

To only add fuel to her determination, she was surprised to receive a phone call one evening from Camp Gordon Army Base in Georgia.

"Nancy, this is Barbara Poole," the woman said in a rush, clearly distressed. "I've just landed a PT-19 at Camp Gordon to avoid storm clouds. With no radio, I couldn't contact the control tower."

"Of course, I understand," Nancy said. "What's going on? Did you land in one piece?"

Barbara blew out a breath. "Yes, but I have the commanding officer here, and he's ordering me off their base. Says that he doesn't believe I'm the one who landed the trainer."

"Say what?"

"Here, he wants to talk to you," Barbara said shakily.

Seconds later, a man's voice barked, "Who is this?"

Nancy gave a quick introduction, then said, "What seems to be the problem, sir?"

"I'll tell you what the problem is," the commander ground out. "I don't know what kind of joke you girls are playing, but you're not going to play it on my base."

The man hung up before Nancy could get another word in. For several seconds she sat in stunned silence, then tried to call the base back. No one answered. It wasn't until the next day that Nancy found out that Barbara had been ordered off the base that night, but the following morning, she'd sneaked back into the base and had taken off in the PT-19 without any clearance at all. Setbacks like Barbara's had to stop. Nancy had to find a way to make the military recognize women's abilities to manage aircraft and serve their country.

Next stop for Nancy was Long Beach, where she met with the 6th Ferrying Command Group. There, she also checked out on the 450-horsepower BT-13, which had been built at the Vultee factory not far from Long Beach. Nancy thought of B.J. as the potential leader of the women's squadron here, who'd ferry BT-13s to start.

Next stop was Dallas, and she felt ecstatic when she piloted a C-36 from Phoenix to Dallas.

"This airport named after you, Nancy?" her copilot asked as they called into the radio tower for landing permission at Love Field.

It was a common misconception, and her husband often fielded this question. "Love Field is named after 1st Lieutenant Moss L. Love. He's from Wright County, South Carolina, and he was the tenth army officer to lose his life in an airplane accident. That was in 1913."

"Ah, I'm sure it's a common question you get."

"For my husband," Nancy said. "But you're the first person to ask me about it."

Her copilot chuckled.

She only smiled, her thoughts turning to smoothly landing the C-36, then checking out on the AT-6 as soon as she met with the 5th Ferrying Group.

By the time she'd met with the 4th Ferrying Group in Memphis, Tennessee, and the 3rd Ferrying Group in Romulus, Michigan, she'd checked out on the AT-6 and flown as copilot of the twin-engine B-25.

She asked Tunner to come to Wilmington for her meeting with Baker because she needed all the support she could get. She hadn't quite gotten over the fact that Baker wanted the women to keep ferrying single-engines, because, in her opinion, that could not remain the status quo if they wanted the Ferrying Program to be a true success.

"Thanks for joining us," she told Tunner as he met her in the hallway before they entered Baker's office. She'd kept both men apprised of her meetings and her transitions. But talking in person would be a different matter because decisions needed to be made. Today.

"My pleasure," Tunner said. "You have my full support."

Nancy let a small smile escape. Tunner's words meant a lot, no matter the outcome of this meeting.

They walked in together, and after some preamble, Nancy said, "We have agreement from the 3rd, 4th, 5th, and 6th Ferrying Groups for women's squadrons. I'm going to be heading to Dallas for a short time in order to oversee the program from a more central location, and I'd like Betty Gillies to be in command here at Wilmington, with Helen Mary Clark as her executive officer."

The announcement wasn't a surprise to Tunner, but this was the first Baker had heard of it.

"That's drastic, Mrs. Love," Baker said. "And quite unnecessary."

"It's necessary," Nancy said evenly. "Things are running like clockwork here, and I'm needed elsewhere. The Original WAFS are trained and ready to lead other squadrons. We all need to split up, and that includes me." Before Baker could protest more, she pushed on. "I'm recommending Del Scharr to command the Romulus group, B.J. Erickson the Long Beach group—"

"And you'll be heading up Dallas?" Baker cut in.

"I'm assigning Florene Miller," she said. "I need to be more flexible and not tied to an office chair."

The furrows between Baker's brows deepened. "But as the director of the program, you should be located where it all started."

Nancy took a careful breath. "I need to check out on as many war planes as possible, and I can't do that here." She handed over her prepared list of squadrons, leaders, and planes. "At Romulus, the WAFS will be flying L-2Bs, L-5s, PT-23s, PT-26s, AT-19s, and AT-6s. At Long Beach, the women will be ferrying BT-13s."

Baker studied the list for a long moment, the deep lines between his brows still present. "Safety is paramount. We're putting these women at risk when they fly planes they can't handle. One major mishap and everything could be reorganized."

Nancy glanced at Tunner. He was letting her take the lead, it seemed. "Safety is my priority too. The women will have to check out on each aircraft before copiloting or piloting a ferry mission. This is our standard procedure for any plane, no matter the size or the number of engines. Cochran's classes are training on PT-19s and ending with AT-6s. As you know, I checked out on an AT-6 in Dallas and also flew one in Romulus. After a patch of bad weather, I flight-tested Lenore McElroy on the AT-6."

Lenore was a former flight instructor, with 3,500 hours. Her husband was a ferry pilot at Romulus, and they were the parents of three teenagers, so having a women's ferrying squadron in Romulus allowed Lenore to join the WAFS.

Baker looked at Tunner, but he returned a bland expression. With a sigh, Baker said, "Things are moving faster than I thought they might. I assume General Arnold is on board?"

"Yes," Tunner said. "He's been kept apprised of everything."

That was the case, for the most part, although Nancy was staying out of anything coming from Jackie Cochran—letting Tunner handle that side of things. She'd heard plenty of secondhand information through the grapevine but didn't feel like she could share it with anyone—not even Betty. Nancy wanted to be viewed as a leader who didn't get mixed up in petty back-and-forth jabs. Bob was really the only one she could vent to, but their international phone calls were sporadic, and she didn't want to fill their precious time with political angst.

December finally arrived, and Bob made it home by Christmas after all. His six-week international trip had felt like six months, and Nancy was more than ready to talk to her husband in person. So much had happened, and her heart was heavy for another reason too. During the month, news reports had reached the US about the Nazi's mass extermination of Jewish people. The reports were horrifying, and like all war news, Nancy knew that only the bare basics were being shared with the general public.

"You're thinner," Nancy told Bob the moment she stepped off the train where she was meeting him for a too-short weekend at their Washington, DC, apartment. And he was thinner. His dark-red hair needed a good haircut, and the lines about his eyes let her know he hadn't slept much.

"You're more beautiful," he said, pulling her close.

She melted into him. "Your memory needs work."

"My memory is perfectly fine." He drew away, and she noted the somber depth to his eyes. When he kissed her, she was able to forget the tragedies happening all over the world for a few moments. She supposed that kissing on the train platform went unnoticed nowadays, with people moving about the country, saying their goodbyes to loved ones.

As they drove to their apartment, Nancy said, "The news about the Nazis killing the Jews makes me sick."

"It's despicable," Bob said. "I read the Declaration on Atrocities that the Allied nations put out."

Nancy had read it, too, in the newspapers. December 2 had been an international day of mourning, and then on December 17, the declaration had been released, condemning the cruelties and extermination of Europe's Jews. The Allies had vowed to punish war criminals as soon as the war was over. "Why can't we do something now about the war criminals? Jews are being exterminated right now—where are the rescue efforts?"

Bob reached for her hand. "War progress is being made."

"But not fast enough." Nancy blew out a breath to steel her emotions, but the tears came nonetheless. "Two million Jews have already been murdered, and we're just learning about it. All this time—I've been worrying about petty things while innocent people are being rounded up and killed. I can't even imagine . . . What's the purpose?"

Bob's hand tightened on hers. "America knows now, so we can do something about it. I don't know what, but this only fuels the war effort, makes our nation's sacrifices even more justified."

Nancy nodded, her throat too tight to speak. Over the next couple of days, she used Bob as her emotional sounding board. She needed to get it all out here, because once she returned to Wilmington, she'd have to again take on her leadership role and set an example of strength for everyone else. The nights in Bob's arms were comforting, and she knew all too well that once she was sleeping alone again, the nights would be filled with the darkness of knowing others were suffering so deeply.

Much too soon, Nancy's time with her husband was over, and she had to return to Wilmington. She was pleased, though, to welcome Lenore McElroy into the WAFS in January 1943.

"These are the women's barracks," Nancy said, giving Lenore the grand tour of the base.

"Not much to write home about," Lenore said, but her smile was broad. "Looks like everyone has made themselves comfortable."

"That's a good way to put it," Nancy said with a smirk. They were currently standing in the doorway of one of the bedrooms. A lavender-colored comforter covered one of the beds, and someone had used a rope strung across the room to hang up pairs of stockings to dry.

"I'm tickled pink to be here for training," Lenore said. "My kids are kind of in awe too. At least until they get tired of cooking their own meals."

"They'll be even more grateful when you return after training," Nancy said.

"No children for you and Bob?" Lenore asked. "Sorry if that's too personal. Tell me if I'm being too nosy."

Nancy didn't mind. Lenore was open, friendly, and very talented. "No children yet. We're not opposed. Things haven't happened like we thought they might."

Lenore's expression turned thoughtful. "Well, maybe it's a medical thing. Ever get checked by a doctor?"

"Not yet." It was still in the back of Nancy's mind though. "I haven't had time. Not really a priority right now, anyway, with a war going on and every day being an unknown. Don't know where a fussy baby will fit in."

Lenore rested a hand on Nancy's shoulder. "Well, we're all in flux right now. War can't last forever though."

"Right." Nancy hadn't realized that she kind of needed this talk. Having children was always bouncing somewhere in her mind, but she also wasn't trying to prevent getting pregnant. She hadn't ever voiced her private concern of whether she could have children to someone who wasn't her mother or Betty. "Another advantage of the war being over will be living in the same house as my husband."

Lenore nodded, her smile coy. "No one would disagree."

Two days later, on January 25, 1943, a letter came from General Arnold with a directive to Colonel Tunner. When Tunner called Nancy with the details, she immediately called Bob at his ATC office.

"It's set in stone, apparently," she told Bob. "General Arnold has mandated that we can't take on any more WAFS unless they're graduates of Cochran's Women's Flying Training school in Texas, now called the WFT."

Bob sounded as fed up as she felt. "Those graduates won't be arriving until May—and it's the end of January. What are you supposed to do until then? You're already operating on such a small squadron of women while the ferrying demand is increasing weekly."

"Believe me, that's only half of what I complained about to Tunner." Nancy rubbed the back of her neck. "The Original WAFS are putting in as many hours as humanly possible, and the demand for new bombers only continues to increase. The pilot shortage is a real concern, yet General Arnold is blocking perfectly qualified recruits."

"What's Colonel Tunner going to do about it?" Bob asked.

"He says his hands are tied. Ironically, I received a letter from Helen Richey—remember her from my airmarking days?"

"I remember her. There were two Helens."

"Right, Richey and MacCloskey," Nancy said. "Anyway, Helen Richey wants to join the WAFS. But under this new guideline, she'll have to attend Cochran's school. Which, by the way, the school is being moved to Avenger Airfield in Sweetwater, Texas."

"Oh boy. That's an arid place. The wind will rattle their bones, and they'll be constantly battling dust, not to mention boiling temperatures most days."

"It will be all women, apparently," Nancy said. "And at least they won't have to compete for flying hours with the male pilots there." The first few weeks in Houston had been really rough for the women. Since there weren't available barracks, the women had to find rented rooms or inexpensive hotels. In addition, they weren't allowed to use the airfield's dining room or the bathrooms. So, the women had to walk a half mile to the nearest toilet.

"Wait, I just remembered something about Helen Richey," Bob said. "Hasn't she been over in Europe with the ATA?"

"Yes, Cochran put her in charge of the ATA's American women flyers when Cochran returned here in September. Richey has more than 2,000 hours, and she's flown for major airlines."

Bob whistled. "That's some training Cochran has in Texas."

Nancy smirked. "Yes, well, we could use Richey." She sobered and added, "I've told Colonel Baker I'm leaving Wilmington. Dallas will be a nice change."

"Just a little farther of a plane trip away from me," Bob mused.

"That's definitely a downside." Her voice softened. "I can't wait until this war is over. I'll be able to live in the same house as my husband again."

"Amen."

Nancy's job in Dallas lasted only a month. She requested a transfer to Long Beach in order to help with the new squadron. B.J. Erickson was heading it up, with Cornelia Fort, Evelyn Sharp, Barbara Towne, and Bernice Batten under her.

Nancy looked forward to flying the bigger war planes—anything that would end this war quicker and put a stop to the overseas atrocities. She knew the smaller stature of a woman could be a complication, but she wouldn't let it be a barrier.

She herself was five foot six, which was about midrange for the WAFS. Fort, Scharr, Richards, and Nelson were all taller. But Gillies, Burchfield, and Batten were all about five foot or five one, at the max. Height would make a difference in flying the larger planes since they'd been designed for a man's larger stature, and the women had to be able to see through the windshield. They also needed enough strength to control the toe brakes as well as shoulder strength for the more powerful throttle.

Nancy knew that Cochran had added physical training to her school's program, such as running, push-ups, and pull-ups. The more endurance and upper-body training the women had, the better and the more easily they'd qualify on the bigger planes.

It was what Nancy thought of as she did her own workouts. Because at Long Beach, she planned to fly the P-51 Mustang.

# CHAPTER THIRTY-ONE

"The heavens have opened up and rained blessings on me. The army has decided to let women ferry ships and I'm going to be one of them."

—TELEGRAM FROM CORNELIA FORT TO HER MOTHER, 1942

*February–March 1943—Long Beach, California*

"Sweetie, there's no rush," Bob told Nancy over the phone.

"You're lucky you're not in the same room with me," Nancy said. "Someone would have to hold me back from clobbering my own husband. It's *all* about the rush, Bob, in more ways than one. You said so yourself—we need pilots. If we can't move bombers, how will they get ferried in time to make any sort of difference in the war? More people are dying every single day."

Bob's sigh came through the phone. "The P-51 Mustang is the fastest of all the pursuits in America."

"I know."

"I know you know, but I'm trying to say that you need to study the heck out of the machine. Know it from the inside out. You can't know too much about it."

"I can fly from the back seat of the AT-6 with someone sitting in front of me, so I'm ready." She paused. Flying the AT-6 from the back seat should be similar to flying the P-51 since visibility was limited with the shoulders of the person in the front seat adding to the size of the engine cowling. The pilot had to look to the sides of the runway to taxi and to land. Nancy had learned to guide the AT-6 into a series of S-turns in order to see where she was going.

"Or I *will* be ready, that is," she amended, "and I'm not going to fly until I'm ready."

"Good girl."

She smirked, although Bob couldn't see her. "I wish you were here to be a witness."

His chuckle was low. "It would be a beautiful thing to see. Won't Baker be surprised?"

Nancy sighed. "I don't know why he's taken such a hard stance lately. He was very supportive all the way through until I started pushing for the more powerful planes."

"He has a comfort zone, that's all."

Nancy thought about this, but the longer she was away from Wilmington, the more she knew she needed to have an honest conversation with Baker. She needed to tell him *why* she really left. "If I had a comfort zone, I'd be teaching French history to high schoolers."

"If you were teaching history to high schoolers, I don't think we would have met," Bob said. "That's not a happy thought."

"So come to Long Beach, and I can make all your thoughts happy."

His familiar laugh warmed her through. "Unfortunately, I don't think the ATC will assign me there anytime soon."

After hanging up with him, Nancy left the office. It was after hours anyway, and the sun had already set against the blue California sky, turning everything violet as she made her way to the women's barracks. She'd be up late tonight, continuing her reading of the P-51 manual and memorizing all the technical aspects.

"Are you really going to fly the Mustang?" A soft voice came from one of the doorways as Nancy walked down the hallway.

She turned to see Cornelia Fort leaning against the doorframe of her room. The lighting was dim, but Cornelia's wildly curly blonde hair was unmistakable. Even wearing a night robe with scalloped edging, she looked the proper Southern belle, which, of course, she'd left far behind when she'd become a flight instructor in Fort Collins.

Nancy smiled at Cornelia. "I am. Tomorrow maybe, or later in the week. Whenever Dunlap says I'm ready."

"You'll make it seem easy," Cornelia mused. "The men can't balk if the women are flying the pursuits."

Nancy tilted her head. "Exactly. What are you doing up so late?"

The door across the hallway opened, and B.J. appeared, wearing a robe and curlers in her hair. "We're all up late," she declared. "Too excited for tomorrow?"

Nancy laughed. "I don't even know if I'll be flying, girls. Dunlap says we need to review everything first." She held up the manual. "I've got to get through this tonight."

B.J. checked her wrist as if she were wearing a watch. "Well, get a move on, Mrs. Love."

They all laughed, and B.J. nodded, her grin still in place as her dark eyes sparkled. "Good night, everyone. I've got a letter to write." She shut the door with a click.

Cornelia didn't move, though, so Nancy said, "Writing letters too?"

"Writing in my diary."

"You're so diligent at that."

"Helps me get through things, I suppose, by dumping all my thoughts onto the page." She offered a small smile. "I always feel better after. Like I've shared something with a good friend."

"I should try it more, I guess," Nancy said. "I think I run out of words after talking on the phone to Bob or my parents, or bossing the WAFS around."

"I understand that," Cornelia said, tugging on one of her curls. "I guess I keep my thoughts to myself, and they need to go somewhere eventually."

Cornelia did keep to herself more than most. She was always a part of what everyone did, but she didn't usually start conversations.

Since it was only the two of them and Nancy was more than curious, she asked, "Did you write about Pearl Harbor too?"

"Sure did." Cornelia didn't even hesitate. "Not for days afterward, though, and I don't think I'll ever read through it. But I wrote down every detail that I could remember. From the feel of the morning air when we loaded up in the plane to the color of the pale-blue sky to the first moments I realized the plane coming at us was a Japanese bomber." Her voice cut off. "I guess I *am* talking about it."

Nancy stepped closer to Cornelia and leaned against the cool wall a couple of feet from her. "You told me a little when you first arrived at New Castle."

"The basics," Cornelia said.

Nancy nodded, hoping the woman would continue but not wanting to force anything. She could tell this subject was still an ache in Cornelia's heart—in all their hearts.

"The mind and body are an interesting pair," Cornelia said thoughtfully. "I'd flown a lot of hours, and I knew that plane like the back of my hand."

Nancy stayed quiet in case Cornelia wanted to share more.

"It was a regular Sunday morning lesson for my student," Cornelia continued. "He was close to qualifying to solo, so we were practicing takeoff and landing skills. On our last route, I told him to take the plane higher. It was then I spotted a military airplane headed in our direction."

She shrugged. "Not unusual since the civilian airport we'd flown out of was right next to the military base at Pearl Harbor. Except it wasn't usual for a Sunday morning. That's the first thing that crossed my mind. My stomach did a funny pinch, and I guess it was instinct or something, but I took over the controls from my student and jammed the throttle wide open to pull above the oncoming plane."

"I wondered if the other plane had seen us because it passed so close beneath us that our celluloid windows rattled—thought they'd bust." She drew in a breath. "I was furious and looked down to see which plane had buzzed us. That's when I saw the red painted circles on the tops of the wings. I couldn't believe it. I thought my mind was playing tricks on me."

Cornelia shifted her position against the doorframe, her voice quieter when she said, "I looked over at the harbor, and my spine tingled when I saw billowing black smoke." She folded her arms and rubbed them, as if she were cold. "I still wasn't comprehending it, thinking there had to be some sort of explanation."

Nancy pictured the sight in her mind—and the same emotions of disbelief from when she'd first heard the news on the radio swept through her.

"I saw the formations of silver bombers flying in," Cornelia continued. "A silver object detached from the planes and fell straight to earth. I watched one of those bombs explode in the middle of the harbor." She paused.

Nancy didn't move. She couldn't fathom what it would be like to have witnessed all this from the air.

"We sped toward the landing strip, and another civilian plane behind us was peppered with bullets. Once we landed, we ran to the hangar to report the Japanese planes." Cornelia shook her head. "Everyone laughed. Thought it was a joke—but who would joke about that? It wasn't until one of the mechanics ran in a few moments later and reported Bob Tyce's death that they got it. He was the airport manager. Everyone knew there was no joking going on."

She dragged in a heavy breath, and Nancy rested a hand on her shoulder. "Your instincts were incredible," Nancy said, "and you saved your life and your student's."

Cornelia gave a little shrug. "It's surreal to think about, even now. One misstep in either direction could have made the end result much different. Others weren't so lucky, of course, and it leaves me wondering why. Why me? Why them? Why anything?"

Nancy didn't have those answers and likely never would. "I don't know if we'll ever truly know. All we can do is move forward each day. One hour at a time."

"Yes, and sometimes one minute at a time."

Nancy squeezed her arm. "You're a remarkable woman, Cornelia. You've seen the worst of humanity firsthand, yet here you are, still serving because you want to."

"Because I want to, and because I can, and because I should." Cornelia placed her hand over Nancy's. "Thank you for your service, too, Nancy. None of this would have happened without your persistence."

Nancy gave her a half smile. "I don't know about that. There were others pushing too—Cochran wasn't about to relent."

"Most things would still be mired in red tape if Cochran had been at the helm," Cornelia said. "She wasn't about to relax her hold on her agenda. With you running the Ferrying Program, things fell into place much quicker. And now hearts and minds are already changing about women's ability to fly larger aircraft, and Cochran will have her militarized pilots eventually."

"You think so?"

Cornelia smiled. "You're about to check out on a P-51—so I'd say yes."

Nancy held up her manual. "Speaking of that, I have a long night ahead."

"You do, and good luck. I'm going to be adding your feat to my diary."

"I'm honored." And she was.

Moments later, Nancy settled into her room at her desk, manual opened. As she read, she wrote down notes, nearly copying the whole manual. It helped her process the information. She'd be meeting with her instructor Major Samuel C. Dunlap tomorrow to go over the specifications of flying the P-51, and she wanted to be prepared. If she was fully prepared, she'd learn more from Dunlap, who was currently serving as operations officer of the 6th Ferrying Group.

As Bob had told her, preparation was the key. This wouldn't be like her first solo flight when she was sixteen, when she'd flown the Fleet Biplane with her instructor Jimmy Hansen until he had declared her ready to solo.

That wouldn't happen with the P-51 Mustang because there was only one seat in the pursuit—for the pilot. Her first flight would be solo.

When the sun finally rose, Nancy wasn't sure if she'd slept much. The night had been spent in a state of semiwakefulness as her thoughts spun with the details from the tech orders. But now her thoughts were clear and the sky outside her small barracks window an endless blue.

Nancy dressed in her WAFS uniform, pulled on her flight jacket, grabbed her helmet and goggles, then tucked the manual under her arm. She was ready. For whatever the next step would be. And she hoped that would include flying today.

Dunlap waited for her in the early-morning light at the start of the taxiway, just as he'd said he would.

"Good morning, Mrs. Love."

"We go way back, Major Dunlap," she quipped. "You can call me Nancy."

"I'm your instructor, so we're being more formal."

"Yes, sir."

His eyes crinkled with a smile. "Let's begin."

As they talked their way through the details of the plane and the bones from the inside out, Dunlap quizzed her mercilessly.

The cockpit was three feet, three inches from panel to seat, and the width only two feet. Good thing she wasn't claustrophobic. She ran through the details of everything inside and outside the plane: the hydraulic-controlled landing gear, manual backup system, trim tabs on the ailerons and on the elevator, the gauges in the cockpit and what they monitored, the pressure of the engine coolant, fuel consumption, the gyroscopic vacuum, exhausted gases, just to start. Also, she went over the navigational radio equipment, then how to use the throat microphone.

Dunlap's questions became more complicated, but Nancy managed to stay a step ahead of him until he finally said, "Is there anything you don't know about the P-51, Mrs. Love?"

Nancy leaned against the plane and folded her arms. "I don't know what it feels like to fly one."

Dunlap chuckled. "Well, ma'am, how about you take her up?"

Nancy's eyes about popped out. "What? Now?"

The major motioned a hand toward the cockpit. "I don't see any reason to wait another day, unless you do."

"No, sir, I don't." She wanted to run to the office and phone her husband, but instead, she decided it would be more fun to tell him after she'd checked out on the plane.

Dunlap grinned and motioned for a crewman to join them.

Nancy walked around the plane, checking everything, including the tires, the landing gear, the tailwheel, and the level of fuel.

She stuffed the manual into the pocket of her flight jacket, then she strapped on the parachute pack, securing it over her shoulders, clipping the straps across her chest and around each thigh. She climbed up onto the wing and settled into the cockpit. The seat was tight, and she wondered how the larger men fit inside. They probably couldn't move more than an inch.

Dunlap followed her up and squatted next to her, perched on the wing. He ran over all the controls with her once again. Her next test was the rudders and the toe brakes. Once she verified that the control stick moved in all directions, she did her radio check.

"Don't forget, every touch is amplified in this beauty," Dunlap said. "Response time is faster, the engine is faster, and you'll have to account for all that. Especially on landing." He patted her shoulder. "Take your time up there. No harm will come to you in the air. Get a good practice in."

"Yes, sir," Nancy said, her pulse drumming, her mouth dry. "Thank you."

Dunlap hopped down from the wing and took several steps back. "Anticipate in advance," he called out. "Once you're in the throttle, you'll feel like you're in a rocket."

She fitted her goggles, then secured the hatch. Next, she moved the throttle to idle cutoff. The crewman whom Dunlap had called over turned the propeller several revolutions, then stuck the battery charger into the side of the engine. When the engine started, it sent goose bumps across her skin. She activated the microphone at her throat and called the tower to get clearance for takeoff.

As she made S-turns along the taxiway, she craned to look out both sides of the plane, her front vision obscured. She inhaled as she worked the rudders, keeping the toe brakes on and keeping the engine's power at bay until she was ready to push the throttle forward. At the end of the taxiway, she ran through her checklist again. She counted down, for no other reason but to try to calm her own thumping heart. Calling the tower once again, she was cleared for takeoff.

This was it.

She released the toe brakes and eased the throttle forward, though there was no easing with the Mustang. There was no resistance either.

The airplane surged forward, and Nancy's breath stopped in her chest. She continued pushing the throttle until it hit the firewall, and seconds later, the tail lifted. Smoothly. Even though she couldn't see the runway in front of her. Somehow, she managed to take a full breath. The tail lifted more, coming even with the nose, then the plane lifted, climbing. She was airborne.

And she could now see straight down the runway, but she was flying above it, and fast. She knew the maximum speed was over 400 mph. Which was why the Allies had great hopes for the British-developed P-51. Its performance rivaled Germany's premier fighters, the Me 109 and Fw 190. And now the United States had been given license to produce the Mustangs with the new Rolls-Royce Merlin engine. The Packard Motor company was currently building new engines, and there would be a plethora of new P-51 Cs and Ds by the summer. Another reason why the women needed to be ferrying them so the men could start training on them.

If Nancy could get checked out on this plane, which was the current model with the 1325-horsepower Allison engine, the transition to the Merlin engine wouldn't be a huge step. But it would be one more step in the chain of winning this war. The blue of the sky engulfed her as she rose the next few thousand feet, and all she could do was think about how fast, how smooth, how powerful this plane was. Operating it wasn't all that different from any other plane, although it was, as Dunlap had said, quicker at everything. More finely tuned.

Everything she did with the control stick and rudders brought an immediate response. It was fantastic. She spent over an hour in the sky, growing accustomed to the superior machine and reveling in the way she felt like she was truly soaring. Above the earth. Above civilization. It was just Nancy and the blue sky. A surreal, almost lonely feeling bloomed inside her chest, as if she were the only person in the world right now.

She was the first woman to fly the P-51 Mustang.

After her final maneuver, she headed toward the runway, slanting downward. The runway was coming fast, and as she pulled up to land, she lost her central view. But the plane was smooth, responding to the lightest pressure.

When the wheels touched the runway, her heart was thrumming with the engine. She pressed on the toe brakes, then put her weight into it. As the plane finally came to a stop, she realized a small crowd had gathered near the closest hangar.

Climbing out, her heart feeling two sizes too big, she grinned when she heard people clapping and cheering. She tugged up her goggles and wiped her eyes. The WAFS were all lined up. B.J. Erickson and Cornelia Fort were clapping along with Evelyn Sharp, Barbara Towne, and Bernice Batten.

"You ladies are next," Nancy called out, and they all cheered.

Major Dunlap reached her first, a wide grin on his face.

"Can I see your logbook, Mrs. Love?"

She handed it over, her hands perspiring.

He opened it right there and inscribed, "Qualified at Long Beach, California."

She'd just checked out on the P-51.

After congratulations all the way around, Nancy met with a couple of reporters who had been called in after Dunlap had sent her into the air. She posed for a photograph, then answered their questions as patiently as possible, but really, she wanted to call Bob to tell him the news.

"What was it like flying the Mustang?" one of the reporters asked.

"It reminded me of my first solo—not the speed or the engine, of course, but the feeling of being the only person in existence. It's a lonely but wonderful feeling."

The men madly scribbled her replies into their notebooks. After she'd chatted with them for a few more minutes, she headed toward her office. But Dunlap stopped her in the hallway before she could escape. "I need a copilot this afternoon if you don't have other plans."

Nancy stared at the man. "Which airplane?"

Dunlap's smile appeared. "The C-47."

Nancy's brows peaked. The C-47 was a twin-engine cargo plane with 1200 horsepower, one of the planes her husband had flown on his international trip to China. Copiloting with Dunlap would be the next step in transitioning as pilot. "I'm not busy."

He clapped her shoulder. "See you after lunch, Mrs. Love."

In a bit of a daze, she headed into her office. Taking a deep breath, she called Bob and told him about checking out on the P-51. "In addition, I'll be copiloting a C-47 with Dunlap this afternoon."

Bob hadn't said a word. "Bob? Are you there?" Had their line been severed, or was he speechless?

"Today? Just now?" he asked, his voice incredulous.

"Just now. You can read about it in the papers tomorrow."

Bob laughed. "I'll do that, sweetie. Congratulations. I'm so proud my wife is the first female to fly one of the fastest airplanes ever built."

"That's what I hear."

Bob laughed again. "And the C-47 too? You're going to be famous, Nancy dearest, you know that? I'm talking about worldwide. Boy, oh boy. Wait until Colonel Tunner and General Arnold hear about this. Are you going to let it go to your head?"

He was teasing, but she scoffed. "I don't think I could let any of this go to my head, knowing why Americans are racing to build the P-51 in the first place. War is never anything to inflate an ego over. Besides, sleeping in barracks at an army base keeps me humble."

"True, so very true."

Nancy sat back in her office chair, her legs stretched before her. Today had been a good day, a really good day. Made some of the frustrations of the past seem like such small things.

"Evelyn Sharp, Barbara Towne, and B.J. Erickson are going to transition next."

"Woo-ee, that's fantastic. Really. Incredible." Bob paused, his voice filling with emotion. "You're changing the lives of women pilots everywhere. And their contributions will lead to other lives saved. The sooner this war is over, the sooner we can start rebuilding."

Nancy blinked at the burning in her eyes. Accolades hadn't ever been her goal. She wanted only to prove to her superiors that she and the WAFS were all in with the war effort. Female pilots could do the hard work. They were qualified, trained, and ready to help.

"Are you going to call Colonel Baker?" Bob asked in a soft voice.

She knew what he was asking, what he was saying. "No, he can read about it in the papers. But can you call Colonel Tunner for me? I'm meeting the ladies in the mess hall for lunch, and I'm sure I'll be answering tons of questions. Then you can watch for me in the C-47."

He chuckled. "Sure thing, sweetie. I love you. Fly safe."

"I love you, too, Bob."

Two days later, on Monday, Nancy took another flight on the P-51, followed by a third flight the next day. She'd flown it enough now that she'd proven that a woman could fly pursuits. Besides, Sharp, Towne, and Erickson were now all in furious study to transition as well. Nancy didn't have a particular need to fly other single-engine pursuits, the P-39, P-40, or P-47. No, she'd leave that to the other girls.

Bob's letter that arrived that day made her laugh. He'd obviously written after that first phone call since he mentioned her becoming famous again. His letter included, "I'm so afraid you will be so famous and involved with things that you won't care for the things that we have longed for before."

Was he really that concerned? Did he really think she'd let things go to her head? She'd been talking to reporters and posing for photographs since her days at Vassar. None of this was going to interfere with her future with her husband, and their lives after the war. She'd just have to assure Bob of that.

But for now, her next aim was to transition on the twin-engine pursuits—the P-38 and A-20 attack bombers. The four-engine aircraft would be down the road, this she knew. She could wait, but not too long.

# CHAPTER THIRTY-TWO

"In the fog, rain, and mud of the Houston airfield, [Lieutenant Alfred Fleishman] taught the women how to survive the army. 'There is a simple directive about Army life. If the Army can dish it out, I can take it. If it should develop that women can't take it, it might affect the whole program. You will have to stick out your chin and show them.'"

—LIEUTENANT ALFRED FLEISHMAN, HOUSTON, FEBRUARY 1943

*March 1943—Long Beach, California*

A phone call from Jackie Cochran wasn't always bad news, but this time, Nancy had to sit down as Cochran told her about the tragedy that had taken place that day. Margaret Oldenburg had been killed in a training accident at the Houston Municipal Airport, where the WFTD were based.

"What happened?" Nancy asked while sitting in her office at Long Beach, the coffee she'd had with her breakfast souring in her stomach.

Cochran's voice was measured. "Margy was starting her second week of training with Class 43-4. She and her instructor Norris Morgan went up in their PT-19A. They failed to recover from a spin." Her tone turned tight. "There were witnesses since they were only six miles south of the Houston Texas Army Air Field. They only said that it looked like the pilot was practicing a forced landing."

Nancy rubbed her forehead with a trembling hand. "That's tragic. We don't know anything beyond that? No calls to the tower?"

"Nothing. Margy had three and a half hours overall in the PT-19, but her instructor had over twenty-one hours in the craft, and a total of 786 hours of flying time."

"Do you think it was mechanical?" Nancy ventured.

"It's hard to say," Cochran said. "But right now, we're considering it pilot error. Also, we're not reporting the accident beyond command, but Major Walter Framer is going to flight check all instructors."

"That's good," Nancy said. "And the funeral? What are the plans?"

Cochran's voice stiffened. "Well . . . I'm sending my executive officer Leni Deaton to escort the body home to Oakland, but I'll be paying the funeral expenses out of my own pocket."

They both knew that some families were in dire straits. After hanging up with Cochran, Nancy sat in the stillness of her office for a few moments. Beyond her window, planes were taking off and landing. The work was going forward. Margaret Oldenburg had just given her life for it.

Nancy was glad that they were putting in place more measures to qualify instructors. The women deserved the best instructors, the best training, and the most mechanically sound planes. It was with this resolve that she decided to call Colonel Baker at New Castle to have a difficult conversation.

She knew the conversation had to happen, but she needed to wait until after the emotions over Margaret Oldenburg's death had calmed, so it still took her a few days to do it.

The first person she called after hanging up with him was Betty. "I told him everything," Nancy said into the phone.

"Everything?" Betty asked, clearly surprised.

"I was frank." Nancy gazed out her office window. Beyond the midday blue sky, wispy clouds decorated the expanse like brushstrokes. "I told Colonel Baker I left Wilmington because of his reluctance to let women transition into high-powered aircraft."

"Well." Betty breathed out. "What was his response?"

"He blustered around for a bit, but then I asked him how you were doing."

"I'm sure he gave you an earful," Betty mused. "It's been like pulling toenails around here to transition to anything larger than a Fairchild."

"Be ready for that to change."

"Really? Your phone call was that effective?" Betty sounded incredulous.

Nancy scoffed. "I don't know about that, but he can't hold any of the WAFS back, not anymore. We're transitioning to fighter planes in the west, and he won't want to be left behind. B.J. and I have already checked out on the C-47."

The next day, Betty called Nancy to report that she'd been given permission by Baker to transition on the P-47. The plane, nicknamed the Thunderbolt or The Jug, was a 2300-horsepower single engine with a single pilot seat. To check out on the plane would be a solo flight, like the P-51.

"That's wonderful," Nancy said. "Is there one coming into New Castle?"

"No, I'm going to Farmingdale, New York," Betty said, joy evident in her voice. "The Republic Aviation factory on Long Island is building P-47s there, and I'm meeting with the control officer."

"Perfect." Nancy couldn't stop the grin on her face.

"My husband says I need to figure out a way to reach the rudder pedals, because if I slouch down to reach them, I won't be able to see out of the windshield."

Nancy nodded to herself. Betty was only five foot one, and that would pose a problem for the P-47. "What does Bud suggest?"

"I'm going to talk to one of the pilots at Grumman Aircraft who's flown them before. He's a shorter man, and Bud says he's been creative when flying larger planes."

A few days later, Nancy had her report from an ecstatic Betty. On March 8, she checked out on the P-47, using a custom-made set of blocks over the rudder pedals. This way, she was able to reach them with her feet and still see out of the windshield.

"That's brilliant," Nancy gushed. "How long did you fly?"

"Fourteen hours," Betty said with a contented sigh. "I didn't want to stop, but the sun was setting. I practiced landing and taking off so much, I could probably do it in the dark now. I mostly landed at New Castle, but I landed at two other airports as well to pass the qualifications."

"Nice job," Nancy said. "When do you ferry your first P-47?"

Betty's smile came through the phone. "I don't know, but I'm ready anytime. What's coming up on your docket next?"

"I'm flying every chance I get," Nancy said. "B.J. is now copiloting with me on the C-47. Cornelia is going to join six male pilots in a ferrying mission from Long Beach to Dallas, delivering BT-13s."

"Ah, good luck to them," Betty said.

Her words turned out to be needed because luck was nobody's friend on the ferry mission to Dallas.

On Sunday, March 21, Nancy received a call that she had hoped to never receive. At approximately 15:30 Central War Time, the landing gear of F/O Frank E. Stamme Jr.'s BT-13A struck the left wooden wing of Cornelia Fort's aircraft.

With the wing clipped, Cornelia's plane rolled, then plunged into an inverted dive.

Stamme was able to recover, but Cornelia did not, or she could not.

Nancy listened in disbelief as Dunlap shared the scant details he'd gathered from the initial call. Cornelia's plane had crashed into the earth below, instantly killing her. She hadn't even tried to bail out with her parachute.

After Nancy returned to her office, she sank onto a chair and cradled her head in her hands for a long time, absorbing the information. Whatever had happened, or not happened, Cornelia Fort was dead. She'd survived being targeted by a Japanese Zero in Pearl Harbor, yet now, she'd died as a civilian pilot on a routine assignment.

The numbness washed through Nancy, and she couldn't think, she couldn't move, and even breathing hurt—knowing that Cornelia would never draw in a breath again.

Earlier that day, she'd sat with Cornelia and B.J. at the mess hall for breakfast. Cornelia had been her usual quiet self, but she'd laughed at something B.J. had said—what had it been? Why couldn't Nancy remember now?

Other words came to her mind—the conversation she'd shared with Cornelia only a few short weeks ago in the hallway when she'd talked about Pearl Harbor. The pilot instincts she'd relied on at such a time—something that was innate and couldn't be taught except through years of experience. Which Cornelia had. She was one of the best and most talented pilots Nancy had ever known. Male or female.

Nothing about this made sense. Why hadn't Cornelia bailed with her parachute?

Nancy's eyes were red-raw, and her chest ached as if a plane engine were sitting right on top of her. The burning in her throat scorched all the way to her stomach as she tried to comprehend what had happened over Merkel, Texas. The image of seven BT-13s flying in formation took shape in her mind. Were they keeping in formation? Or were they racing? Hotdogging? Six men and one woman together. All professional, all trained and skilled. Why hadn't Cornelia bailed out? She was an expert pilot. Had the canopy latches been stuck?

The idea of Cornelia trapped and desperate brought new horrors to Nancy's mind . . . Cornelia fighting to control a damaged plane. Fighting to open a malfunctioning hatch. The worst-case scenario magnified as the plane plummeted. Her panic, then her realization that the end was approaching in seconds.

Nancy covered her mouth and stumbled to the waste basket, where she sank to her knees and threw up. She heaved until there was nothing left to expel. Then she sagged against the wall.

How was this real? What had made Stamme fly so close to Cornelia? Or was it the other way around?

Nancy lost track of time, not caring that her stomach rolled and her head pounded. Far away, she heard a ringing phone and another. Why did phones have to ring so much? Where was everybody? Why weren't the phones being answered?

"Nancy," someone said in a soft voice. A hand settled on her shoulder, the pressure light. "Nancy," he repeated. "Your husband has been trying to reach you."

She lifted her head and stared with bleary eyes at Major Dunlap. His face seemed etched with new lines, as if he'd aged ten years. And perhaps he had. Perhaps they all had.

"Does he know?" Nancy whispered, a hot tear sliding down her cheek. She'd thought she couldn't possibly have any tears left.

"Yes." Dunlap crouched before her, his hand still on her shoulder. "Do you want him to come out? He's getting leave, he says—"

"I don't know." She drew in a shaky breath. "I don't know anything anymore. Where is he?"

"On the phone. I said I'd find you."

She shifted away from the wall. Dunlap stood and extended his hand, and she grasped it. Her legs were like water, but somehow, she followed Dunlap into his office. He led her to his chair, and she settled into it, grateful that she hadn't fallen over. Her head felt stuffy with hollowness and grief and unanswered questions, but she took the receiver that Dunlap held out.

"Bob," she whispered. "Cornelia's gone."

"I know, sweetie," he said in a rasp. "I've been calling you for over an hour. Are you all right?"

She shook her head, then drew in a breath. "No. I don't know what to do. She was only twenty-four. She wrote in her diary every night. She survived bullets from a Japanese bomber, Bob. She survived *Pearl Harbor*."

Her voice was cracking and her pitch hysterical, but her soul hurt too much to care.

Bob's words became a murmur, adding to her already buzzing thoughts.

"I sent her on that mission, Bob," she whispered, her throat scraping raw. "I chose *her* to go on that mission. I inspected the plane with her. She smiled and thanked me. *Thanked* me. As if I weren't sending her to her death."

"Nancy," Bob said, his voice firm now. "This is not your fault. None of this is your fault. Cornelia Fort volunteered for the WAFS. She *wanted* to join. She knew the risks; *everyone* knows the risk. Every pilot knows the risk every time they step into a plane." He paused to draw in a breath. "We don't know the details yet, but even when we do, none of this will be your fault. It's a terrible accident and tragedy, Nancy. And now it's time to honor Cornelia's life. We'll do that and make sure she's never forgotten."

Nancy had no strength left. No energy to shed another tear. Her body felt like a sock puppet discarded on the floor. "We won't forget," she whispered.

"No, we won't forget," Bob echoed. "I'm getting on a plane in a few minutes, and I'll see you tonight. Okay?"

"No." Nancy swallowed at the painful pressure in her throat. "I don't want you in the air. I don't want—" Her voice broke off. Logic was telling her one thing, but pain and fear jagged through her, overtaking all that. "Stay where you are, Bob. I couldn't bear it if something happened."

Eventually, Bob agreed, and she hung up after telling him she'd call if she needed to talk more. She felt wrung out, boneless, but somehow better after talking to her husband.

When Dunlap returned to the office, he got Nancy to eat something. She insisted on walking to the barracks alone though. She needed to move, she needed to think, and she needed to be alone.

Curling on top of her bed, she tried to sleep, but it proved impossible. Even though her mind and body were way beyond exhaustion. The darkness of the night seemed to crowd around her, pressing into her skin until it was hard to breathe. Finally, she climbed out of bed and pulled on her robe. She left her room and moved along the dark hallway. Her hands trailed across the doors of the WAFS—likely all sleeping inside, with troubled thoughts of their own.

Nancy opened the door that led out of the barracks. The chilly night air met her skin, and she drew the robe tighter about her torso. She inhaled the clean, sharp air, lifting her chin and gazing at the moon—a pale, silvery sphere that hovered above the earth. So high up yet visible from every corner of the world.

Cornelia's body might have crashed to the earth, but her spirit had not.

Her spirit would never be buried. Her love of flying, her love of adventure and serving her country—all would live on.

Nancy took a shaky breath and stepped back into the hallway, then walked to the barracks phone.

Bob might be asleep, and if he was, would he sleep through a ringing phone? She didn't want to wake him, but she wanted to hear his voice. She needed to hear his voice.

He answered on the third ring in a sleep-edged voice.

"It's me," Nancy said. "Sorry to wake you."

"It's fine. How are you doing?"

Her eyes filled with tears, but her voice remained strong. "I can't sleep."

"I wish you'd let me come out there."

Nancy exhaled. "Dunlap said we're going to Washington, DC, after the funeral. There might be fires to put out once the official report is released."

"I hope there aren't any fires," Bob said. "But I want to see you—so that will be a good thing. I hate that it's because of these circumstances."

They both went silent for a while.

"What do you think went through her mind in her last moments?"

"Nancy," Bob gently chided. "Don't torture yourself like this."

She blotted her wet cheeks. "I know. I can't help but wonder."

"I think it was too fast for her to fully comprehend, and I think it was painless."

"You do?"

"Yes." His voice held conviction. "She's in a better place now."

"Everyone says that, but what does it really mean?"

Bob was soothing when he spoke. "She's free of mortal pain, physical and emotional turmoil. She's moved beyond the world's hardships and the atrocities of war. For whatever reason, her time was up, and she took her final solo flight. Her life will always be an example for the rest of us who remain on Earth."

Nancy let his words sink in. He was right, or at least, she had to believe he was right. Her body was finally starting to feel the weight of sleep. Would her mind follow? She stifled a yawn.

"You should sleep now," Bob said. "You'll be involved in the arrangements and need a clear mind."

"I know. I'm sure I'm breaking some sort of curfew rule, as it is, by calling you."

Bob released a soft chuckle. "I'll answer to Dunlap in the morning if anyone complains."

"No one will complain."

"Good," his voice rumbled. "Now, sleep, sweetie."

"Good night, Bob." She hung up and headed to her room. Once there, she climbed into her bed, pulling the covers over herself, wishing Bob were here, his arms around her. Secure and warm. She focused on his words, replaying them over and over in her mind until she finally tipped into the blessed nothingness of sleep.

The morning brought storm clouds and dreary rain, and with it, the weight of the dark memories of the day before. Nancy might have convinced herself it had all been a terrible nightmare, but when she opened her gritty eyelids, she remembered.

It had been real, all of it. Cornelia was truly gone.

Nancy rose and prepared for the morning, her eyes smarting, her nose running, but her hard day and her grief would be only a fraction of what Cornelia's family must be going through. She'd do as Bob had suggested: focus on the memory of Cornelia and honoring her life.

Nancy called Bob at home, but there was no answer, so she tried his office.

"Did you sleep?" she asked, her voice merely a scratch.

"A little," Bob said. "How are you?"

"Terrible."

"It will get better, eventually." He was somber, just how her heart felt. "Keep me posted on what you discover. Find out what the investigators are reporting. Cornelia's family deserves answers more than anyone."

And Nancy found herself very grateful for tasks. Action—she needed to take action. That was how she'd get through the clenching grief inside her.

She threw herself into her work, and three days later, she was on a C-47 with B.J. and Major Dunlap, flying to Cornelia's funeral. They flew to Albuquerque first, then nonstop into Nashville. Major Dunlap piloted, and Nancy and B.J. rotated copiloting so they could take turns napping during the all-night flight.

"It feels like a day for a funeral," B.J. said as they flew into Nashville.

Sure enough, there was spitting rain and a fairly brisk wind, and it didn't look like it was moving on anytime soon.

They headed into the airport office to make phone calls and find a hotel room. Once they found a place that could accommodate them, they borrowed a car and headed to the hotel to get cleaned up.

Nancy's head pounded, but there'd be no time for rest or real sleep. Once she and B.J. were trussed in their full WAFS uniforms, complete with skirts, ties, wool gabardine jackets, and brown leather pumps, Nancy dialed the number of Cornelia's family home to let Mrs. Fort know they'd arrived safely.

When Mrs. Fort answered, Nancy's emotions pricked. The woman sounded so much like Cornelia.

"I'm glad you've arrived safely, Mrs. Love," Mrs. Fort said. "Please come over to our home. Everyone would like to meet you."

Nancy agreed, and after hanging up, she turned to B.J. "Let's see if Major Dunlap is in the lobby yet." There was no delaying what was going to happen today, so there was no use hanging out in the hotel room any longer. "Mrs. Fort has invited us to her home."

The skin around B.J.'s eyes was tight, but she nodded. "I wish we could give them answers since that's what they'll be hoping for."

"Most likely." Nancy picked up her WAFS cap and gloves. "We might not have any new information to share with them, but we can at least tell them about their daughter's selfless service."

"Very true," B.J said, and it turned out they were absolutely right.

Nancy and her group were introduced all around to members and extended members of Cornelia's family. Major Dunlap had carried the boxes of Cornelia's belongings in through the side door, and the family would go through her things later, thankfully, since Nancy knew she couldn't bear to be around to see it. Packing them up had been heart-wrenching enough.

All eyes were on them as they sat perched on a couch, surrounded by vases of funeral flowers and condolences notes, when Mrs. Fort asked them to explain exactly how Cornelia's plane had gone down.

Nancy released a breath and looked at Dunlap, who nodded for her to answer.

"We don't have the official report yet." Nancy tried to keep her voice from quaking. It was hard to do because she saw Cornelia's features in the faces staring back at her. "We only know that there was a midair collision when Frank Stamme clipped her wing. Cornelia's plane couldn't recover, and it went into a dive."

No one seemed surprised at the information, but everyone was clearly upset. One relative was opening crying behind a handkerchief while her red-faced husband kept his arm about her shoulders.

"Did she have a parachute?" someone asked.

"Of course." Nancy had seen Cornelia wearing one herself. "She didn't bail out though."

"Why not?" another asked.

The questions kept coming, and Nancy tried to answer them as best as she could, but it was like sitting in the audience of a theater production—a tragedy—where everyone had their lines to deliver, but the most important person was missing: the leading actress. And everyone was waiting for her to walk onstage, but the minutes ticked by, and she never did. Emotion rose in the room, suffocating and heavy, and grief once again clawed at Nancy's heart.

Major Dunlap took over at some point, giving Nancy a reprieve. "The moment we receive the report, we'll notify the family," he said in a calm, assured voice. "We're very anxious to find out what failed in the mission and how it can be prevented in the future."

"It could have been prevented if Stamme hadn't flown into her," someone muttered.

Dunlap lifted his hand. "We don't know what happened. From all accounts, it was an accident. Let's not dish out blame until we have the official report."

Heads bobbed in agreement, but the pain in the room had become a sharp knife, cutting through everyone. When Nancy lost her brother, she'd endured myriad emotions. The pain over the loss of Cornelia was still fresh, still new, and even more so for her family. Nancy understood their shock and grief, and even when their questions were all answered, it would still take time to heal.

After Dunlap had answered the rest of the questions that were possible to answer, Mrs. Fort approached Nancy. "If you'd like to say a few words at the funeral, we can make room for it."

Nancy would have loved to say yes . . . but dread vibrated through her. Dread at losing her stoic battle of calm and breaking down in front of everyone. This day was about Cornelia and her family's loss, and it shouldn't be about how Nancy Love couldn't stop crying.

"I don't want to detract from the other speakers," she told Mrs. Fort quietly. "And I don't think I could put my feelings into words, but I want you to personally know that I miss her terribly. I loved her and loved her passion for our country."

Mrs. Fort's eyes filled, and she clutched at Nancy's hand. "I know one thing," she said in a quavering voice. "If she could have chosen a way to die, it would have been doing it in the service of her county, in an Army airplane."

Nancy wiped the tears falling onto her own cheeks and embraced Mrs. Fort. It was too bad that Cornelia was not eligible for military burial or honors and that the family wouldn't be allowed to drape her casket with an American flag. If anyone deserved the honor, Cornelia Fort did.

# CHAPTER THIRTY-THREE

"'P-47 cleared for takeoff.' I pushed the throttle to twenty-seven
hundred RPM's. The sudden power pushed me back against the seat
as I rolled down the runway. I was off in nothing flat. I had the flaps and
gear retracted as I passed over the end of the runway. That engine was
purring like a kitten as I climbed to altitude over the practice area at eight
thousand feet. I flew some basic maneuvers, shallow, medium and steep
turns. The stalls unnerved me, but I was amazed at the clean recovery."

—TERESA JAMES, JULY 5, 1943

*April 1943—Washington, DC*

Nancy knew she'd have to get back to reality soon enough, but she
hadn't expected it to be quite so soon. As everyone waited for the official
report on the death of Cornelia Fort, Nancy flew with Dunlap and B.J.
to Washington, DC, in the C-47.

B.J. took the opportunity to visit her former squadron mates at New
Castle.

Nancy was more than happy to see Bob, to feel his arms around her,
to be able to talk in person, especially since he'd be heading to England
on an ATC assignment soon. But then she was suddenly inundated with
policy changes coming in from Ferrying headquarters, and it cut her
time with Bob in half.

She might have been caught up in grieving over Cornelia, but the
directives arriving over the past couple of days from Washington, DC,
were getting more and more ridiculous. It was one thing to restrict female pilots hitching rides on bomber planes piloted by males, but it was
another to hand down the new regulation that a woman could no longer
copilot with a male pilot on bombers.

Nancy wanted to keep the WAFS free from reproach and scandal as
much as anyone, but the phone call from Del Scharr, who was heading

up the women's 3rd Ferrying Squadron in Romulus, set Nancy's blood boiling.

"Read it through again," Nancy said to Del, taking a seat at Bob's desk after pacing his office. "I'm going to write this down word for word, then take it to General Smith."

"You'll be going over Colonel Tunner's head if you take this to the chief of staff of the ATC," Del cautioned.

"Right." Nancy wasn't fazed. "Colonel Tunner had to have immediately approved these, or they wouldn't have gone out to you or any of the other squadron commanders."

She glanced at Bob, who stood by the door, arms folded, while he listened to her side of the conversation. As Del repeated the policy changes, Nancy's head ached more with each one. Four policy changes were being made. First, the women of the 3rd Ferrying Squadron would be allowed to only fly light trainer aircraft, which meant nothing bigger than primary trainers. This was a blatant rule made because of Cornelia's accident.

Nancy wrote it down, her teeth gritted together as her pencil scratched out the unbelievable words. This policy would mean that women couldn't transition into basic or advanced trainers or twin-engine aircraft. She'd literally been flying the C-47 for weeks.

"What else?" Nancy asked.

"Women will not be given assignments as copilots on bomber ferrying missions," Del said.

Nancy wrote that down as well. "Next."

"Women will not be allowed to transition on any high-powered single-engine aircraft."

Nancy bit back a retort. "Continue." She waved for Bob to come over to the desk. He crossed the room and leaned over to read what she'd written so far.

"In order to protect women's morals," Del said, "they will make their deliveries on alternate days from the male pilots."

Nancy wrote the words, the pencil becoming dark slashes on the paper.

"And finally, the women pilots are to be sent in opposite directions from the male pilots so they aren't even crossing paths."

Nancy wrote the last sentence with added force, nearly tearing the innocent paper. "Thank you, Del." She drew in a heated breath. "This should surprise me, but unfortunately, it doesn't. We've received a letter from ATC headquarters that women who are pregnant won't be allowed to ferry. In addition, women will not be allowed to fly one day before, through two days after, their menstrual cycle."

Del laughed.

Nancy wished she could laugh about it. But since it was a written directive going out to all commanders at the very moment she was on the phone with Del, Nancy couldn't feel the humor. Instead, she felt like she had a paper cut that wouldn't heal.

"Are you serious?" Del finally said.

"Yes." Nancy looked at Bob, whose jaw was like stone. She'd already shared her thoughts on this with him, and he couldn't fathom why there was this sudden bevy of regulations. "If this restriction stays in place, each WAFS will be grounded 8–9 days per month. And Esther Manning won't be able to fly at all." The woman was newly pregnant.

"I feel like we've gone back a hundred years in time," Del commented. "Like we're standing on a cliff we've already climbed a dozen times, and now the wind is forcing us off the edge once again."

"Exactly, and it's ridiculous. We aren't about to accept the ideology that women become hysterical while menstruating." When she hung up with Del, she faced Bob, and said, "How much do you value your relationship with Colonel Tunner?"

Bob's stoic expression didn't change. "Even if you weren't my wife, Nancy, I'd agree with you. I don't know why these directives were sent out. Colonel Tunner can worry about nursing his own bruised ego."

Nancy grasped his hand. "Thank you, Bob."

He squeezed her hand. "Don't thank me. This is about fairness and honoring the skills that you and the WAFS have developed through all the proper training. The WAFS shouldn't be treated so poorly. No one should."

"I have one more phone call to make," she said, dialing a number she'd memorized. "Then I'm going to call General Smith's office to make an appointment."

Betty Gillies answered the other end. "Nancy, how are you? Are you going to visit New Castle this time around?"

"I'm afraid not," Nancy said. "There's a bit of a stirring going on." After giving Betty the bare bones, Nancy was surprised when Betty didn't seem perturbed by the new directives.

"As far as I read it, and Colonel Baker reads it, each squadron can run their own team how they see fit." Betty paused. "Esther will be flying until, you know . . ."

Nancy frowned. "Is she quitting after she delivers her baby?"

"We haven't talked about that yet," Betty said. "What I mean is that Esther is going to be flying until she can't get the stick all the way back in the PT-19."

Nancy blinked. "Because of the size of her stomach?"

"Exactly."

Nancy felt some weight slide off her shoulders. "And Colonel Baker is all right with that?"

"He sure is." Betty paused. "He's changed his tune a lot around here since you had that talk with him."

Nancy let a small smile escape. "Glad I could be of service." She paused. "All right. I'm taking this to General Smith, so stay tuned for more updates. Hopefully ones with lessened restrictions."

After hanging up with Betty, Nancy felt better. She filled Bob in on the full conversation, but before she could move on to setting an appointment with General Smith, a knock sounded on the door.

Nancy rose from her chair as Bob crossed to answer it.

Tunner stood on the other side, a paper in his hand. "The report has come in on Miss Cornelia Fort." He glanced at Nancy, but it was all she could do not to glare at him.

She simply nodded, because she didn't think anything nice would come out of her mouth if she spoke. Bob took the report, then thanked him.

The instant the door shut on Tunner, Nancy was at Bob's side. "What does it say?"

He handed it over, and they read it together. Cornelia Fort had been exonerated of any blame in the accident. And Frank Stamme's actions had been ruled as an unfortunate miscalculation—an accident.

But most importantly, Cornelia wasn't at fault. Nancy grasped Bob's arm, feeling like her knees might give out. "I can't believe it. I mean, I *can* believe it, but I'm so relieved."

"Agreed." Bob settled an arm around her shoulders. "Cornelia deserves her name to be remembered with honor, in all things."

Nancy turned toward her husband and pressed her face against his neck. "I'm so happy for her family. A terrible thing to be happy about, but I know they'll find more peace this way."

"Yes." Bob kissed the top of her head. "They deserve that peace. Their daughter was never to blame."

"And the WAFS won't be blemished either."

"Exactly."

Even though Nancy was relieved with the news about Cornelia, she had another challenge to surmount. Bob's heading overseas would put him much closer to the battlefront. She wasn't thrilled about saying goodbye, but she also knew his meetings in England would only strengthen her case for women pilots in the US.

Her own meeting with General Smith had been hard to decipher. The man had listened to her carefully, taken notes, and seemed to agree with her. Or had he simply been diplomatic because they'd been face-to-face?

Her victory didn't come until weeks later, on April 17, when General Smith sent out an official response to Nancy's objections to the new regulations on women pilots.

She was back at Long Beach and called Bob immediately to report, then called Betty. "Listen to what General Smith has handed down," she told Betty. "It is the desire of this command that all pilots, regardless of sex, be privileged to advance to the extent of their ability in keeping with the progress of aircraft development."

Betty released a whoop. "Hallelujah! I'll bet Colonel Tunner is seething."

Nancy laughed. "Well, he's not speaking to me, that's for sure. Bob has kept me informed on that end. Colonel Tunner wasn't happy I went over his head with my complaints, but I couldn't wait for the cogs of a very slow machine to turn. Thankfully, General Smith agreed with me."

"As he should," Betty said. "As *everyone* should. Why would the US want to keep itself decades behind the ATA in Britain? We should be the most modern country in the world, yet our women have fewer rights and less respect than women in other parts of the world. Soviet female pilots are flying in bomber regiments, for heaven's sake. Not only that, but the Soviets also allow women to serve in their army as tank drivers, machine gunners, and snipers." She released a satisfied sigh. "Now we can transition to the bigger planes and do proper ferrying."

"Right. Each pilot, male or female, will progress according to their own skills. Not something prescribed by gender."

A moment of triumphant silence fell between them.

"Do you think that Cornelia's exoneration had something to do with this?" Betty asked quietly.

"Likely," Nancy said, equally subdued. "Although it shouldn't have had to depend on that, I know it helped, for better or for worse. The WAFS are accident-free so far—except for a few bent propellers."

"Correct," Betty said. "Now, does Bob know?"

"I called him before this—I woke him up," Nancy said with a laugh. "A bad habit of mine, but I guess he still loves me. Bob was glad General Smith didn't chop off my head."

Betty laughed too. "General Smith wouldn't be in his position if he were a loose cannon."

"True."

Another miracle came the following week, on April 26, this one from Colonel Tunner, who'd been very standoffish toward Nancy—but she'd remained firm in her beliefs.

"I have news," Nancy said, striding into the mess hall at the Long Beach air base, a file of important paperwork in hand.

B.J. and Barbara Towne looked up from their meals, their expressions expectant.

Nancy could hardly hold back her excitement. "Colonel Tunner has recalled the March 29 directives. Women can now fly when menstruating."

B.J. and Barbara both clapped, grinning.

Nancy held up a finger. "And if there's not a qualified WAFS to copilot, we can fly with a man."

"Someone had sense talked into him," B.J. declared.

Barbara pointed at Nancy. "I think we're facing the person who did it."

Nancy gave a modest shrug, then sat across from them with a coy smile. "Persistence doesn't always pay off, but in this case, it did."

B.J. raised her glass and tapped it against Barbara's.

"I know my husband was baffled," Barbara continued.

She was married to an AAF pilot, and she was newly pregnant. But she was determined to transition on the P-51 before she could no longer fit in the cockpit.

"Colonel Tunner has also created a pilot classification system," Nancy continued, setting the file on the table. "This way, pilots can be categorized by the types of airplanes we're transitioned on. Women and men will be classified equally according to the same qualifications."

B.J.'s eyes widened. "Smart move. Colonel Tunner has really done an about-face."

"True." Nancy folded her hands atop the table. "I think it's mostly that he's seen the proof for himself. Frankly, the WAFS are gaining respect everywhere. We're professional, fast, and don't take side trips when ferrying. Also, a male pilot doesn't need ferrying hours to qualify for overseas duty, so Colonel Tunner is handing more responsibility to the WAFS."

Nancy had heard plenty of stories of unfair treatment, though, especially at Camp Davis in North Carolina. The tow target planes the WAFS were flying had been redlined and were unreliable to operate. Engine failure, blowouts, broken instruments, and radios were all too common. Jackie Cochran had flown to Camp Davis to meet with the medical officer, who was requiring the women to have monthly medical exams, whereas he was not requiring the men to.

"In other words, the WAFS can now fly everything they've qualified on?" Betty asked.

"Everything." Nancy opened the file and tapped on the papers inside. "Every pilot will carry a classification card. It will state what you've qualified on. From Class 1, which is low-powered, single-engine, such as PT-17, PT-19, PT-26, and Cubs, to the Class II, Class III, Class IV, Class V, which are the biggest four-engine bombers and transports, and, finally, to Class P-I, which means special-class instrument rated, and this includes the P-51."

"Are you going for all the classes, Nancy?" B.J. asked.

Nancy's smile was slow. "Of course. It's my part in bringing this war to an end."

"That deserves another toast," Barbara said.

They might be toasting with only water, but since water was strong enough to carve through stone, it was genuine. There were other things to celebrate, too, such as the Allies' dominance over the Axis powers in Tunisia. Bombing raids were in full force by US pilots over Germany, and the Nazis had finally surrendered at Stalingrad—a major defeat.

But the hopeful war news was tempered by a phone call from Bob.

"Nancy, I have bad news," Bob said with softness. "General Olds has died of a second heart attack."

The words made Nancy's pulse still. She knew Olds had continued suffering from health issues since that heart attack he'd had the year before, which had led to his reassignment, but he'd returned to duty as a major general, serving in Davis-Monthan Field, Arizona.

"When?" she barely managed to say.

"Yesterday, on April 28. His sons were able to be with him in Tucson before he passed."

Nancy's eyes burned with tears, but she swallowed back a sob. "I'm glad his sons could be there. The WAFS wouldn't have happened without him." Somehow, life would continue to march on, even with the loss of those dear.

# CHAPTER THIRTY-FOUR

"I can hear a plane. . . . It's quite possible that somewhere up there, alone in the open cockpit of a trainer plane she is delivering, a girl is shivering in the wet wind, knowing she'll have to be alone and cold for another seven or eight hours. She's flying up there, a mile above the earth, so that some man may be released to fight for his country."

—OSCAR SCHISGALL, WRITING ABOUT
NANCY LOVE IN *THE CINCINNATI ENQUIRER*

*May–August 1943—Long Beach, California*

Nancy adjusted the straps of her parachute, then climbed into the four-engine B-24. Today, she was copiloting with Major Dunlap. She'd recently checked out on the B-25 twin-engine, medium-range bomber, the first woman to do so.

But this B-24 was a behemoth.

"Ready, Mrs. Love?" Dunlap asked.

"Ready, sir."

The sky seemed to part like a river as the B-24 jolted through the air, taking Nancy's heart to a new rhythm. Below, Long Beach became miniature, and the Pacific Ocean stretched out like a shimmering silver carpet.

Pride swelled within her. Pride and gratitude. Dents were being made on the warfront, and the news coming from both the European and Pacific Arenas was more promising than ever. The Allies had taken Tunisia, and German and Italian troops had surrendered in North Africa.

The WAFS were blooming. Betty Gillies had become the first WAFS to deliver the P-47 across the country. And Helen Mary Clark checked out on The Jug. There were currently at least a dozen more P-47s scheduled for delivery over the next few weeks, and the WAFS would be flying them.

So many changes were on the horizon. Nancy would be transferring to Cincinnati, Ohio, the newly designated Ferrying headquarters, on June 25. Tunner was insistent that Nancy be present, and she had agreed with him. They had twenty-three graduates from Cochran's flight school, bringing the number of WAFS to forty-nine. The new graduates would be split evenly among the four ferrying squadrons.

But first, Nancy was making a stop at Avenger Field in Sweetwater, Texas. She wanted to speak to the upcoming graduates of Cochran's program about what to expect when they started in the Ferrying Division. She asked Colonel Tunner to join her, now that they were back to tentative peace.

Not surprisingly, Sweetwater was in a heat wave, and the air was so humid, Nancy felt like she could drink from it. Practically the entire town had turned out, and the pomp included a marching band strutting along the open road, followed by the women in their uniforms, marching in tandem.

The graduation ceremony included short speeches by Cochran, Arnold, and Tunner, then Cochran's presentation of silver wings to each graduate. The graduates also sang, and after the formal ceremony, they all met together in a meeting room. Out of the sun and humidity, thankfully.

"I'd like to introduce Mrs. Nancy Love and Colonel Tunner," Cochran said to the gathered group of women.

Nancy surveyed each of the women in turn. Their eager expressions, their alert eyes, and their neat and professional appearances. Nancy was impressed. She felt an affinity toward these women already—they all had the same drive, the same passion, and the same dedication.

"Thank you, Miss Cochran." Nancy stood before the women after Cochran sat down. "It's a privilege to join you all today, and I look forward to seeing each of you progress to the Ferrying Division. At your assigned squadron, you'll have the same privileges as the officers. Plan on a week's indoctrination when you arrive. You'll learn how to file paperwork for each plane you deliver. You'll be on duty seven days a week, but you'll always be given some time off after each delivery to take care of personal affairs. Any questions so far?"

She paused as one of the women raised her hand and asked, "How long are the trips?"

"Depending on where you're based and the ferrying assignment, most trips are averaging 1,000 miles."

A few of the women murmured, exchanging glances.

"When you arrive at each base," Nancy continued, "you need to report back to your squadron leader so we have a record of where every plane is each day and each night."

Another woman raised her hand. "What types of ships will we be flying?"

"You'll start out on the PTs and BTs that you've checked out here," Nancy said. "Once you have 2,000 cross-country miles on a PT, you'll transition to the AT-6s and AT-17s. The speed of your progress will be determined by how fast you can learn and qualify on the bigger planes."

Nancy continued answering more questions, and overall, she was impressed with the upcoming pilots. Tunner also gave a short speech and answered a handful more questions. Overall, the Sweetwater trip proved to be only positive, and Cochran was perfectly cordial.

Once Nancy was back in Ohio, settled into her apartment and working at the Cincinnati air base office, she updated Bob.

"Well, you're closer to DC," Bob told Nancy over the phone. "We'll figure out a weekend when we can both get away." Bob was back from England, but she hadn't seen him nearly enough in the last couple of months.

"All right."

Someone tapped on her office door and opened it.

She looked up to see Colonel Tunner dressed in his flight suit.

His expression was harried. "I need to speak with you."

"Sure thing." Nancy returned to the receiver. "Bob, I'll call you later." She hung up and motioned for Tunner to sit.

"Sorry about barging in. This news can't wait."

"No problem." Nancy was grateful for Tunner's mighty change of attitude toward the WAFS Program, but his serious demeanor was making her nerves dance in warning. "What's going on?"

Tunner sat, then hissed a sigh. "Jackie Cochran has written a rather extensive letter to General Arnold with many demands, and it looks like things are going to fall into place according to her recommendations."

Nancy could only stare. "What does the letter say?"

"I don't have a copy, but I can give you the summary." Tunner leaned forward, his forearms propped on his knees. "Cochran pointed out that the ferrying group will reach nearly 1,000 women by the end of this year."

Nancy nodded. Her calculations had come up with the same result. Thus, her move to Ohio to manage things from a more central location.

"She's suggesting that before the women are militarized—"

Nancy opened her mouth to protest, but Tunner held up a hand.

"Before they're militarized under the Air Force, she wants their training and routines established so that it will be a natural transition."

Nancy bit her lip. It wasn't that she didn't want female pilots to have the option to become part of the Air Force—but focusing on two agendas right now, while they had plenty of battles to fight already, complicated things. "All right . . . I understand that. It's been Cochran's goal from the beginning. Why is this something urgent now?"

"Because . . ." Tunner drew in a breath. "Cochran thinks that because the Ferrying Program is headed this direction anyway, she should be made the director over the entire Women's Pilot Program."

Nancy didn't need it further spelled out. "Including the WAFS. Which would put me . . . where?"

Tunner linked his hands together. "I'm not exactly sure yet. I'm speaking to General Smith soon, then we'll have to meet with General Arnold."

"So quickly? Are things official now?" Nancy's stomach plummeted. Maybe she'd be relegated to a squadron leader. Cochran would shake up the entire system. Maybe even put in her dreaded relay routes. That couldn't happen, though, right? It would be like going backward. Many of the WAFS had proven their long-distance ferrying capabilities.

"Things are fairly official."

Nancy stilled the questions battling in her mind. "What does that mean?"

Tunner ran a hand over his jaw. "It means that General Arnold has created the Office of Special Assistant for Women Pilots, and Cochran has been named the director of Women Pilots."

Nancy leaned back in her chair. "What exactly does that mean for me at ATC?" She was repeating herself, but she was also trying to wrap her mind around these developments.

He puffed out a breath. "We're not entirely sure. It seems that Cochran's new position entails deciding where the women pilots will best be used, determining graduation standards, setting up rules of conduct, overseeing the women's welfare, outlining the militarization plans, and making visits to inspect the women pilots' living conditions."

Most of which Nancy was overseeing. Had she just lost her job? "Does ATC have any recourse?"

Tunner straightened. "Yes, of course. And I don't plan on having to explain ATC directives to Cochran every time I need to issue something."

Nancy smiled. She might not have been happy butting heads with Tunner previously, but she didn't mind being on his side now.

"We're going to assign you a new appointment," Tunner continued. "One that can't be interfered with, not even by Cochran."

Now they were getting somewhere, but still, Nancy wasn't looking forward to extreme changes or a difficult working environment with mounds of red tape.

"We'd like to give you the official title of executive for the WAFS, and you'd be on my staff, of course. You'd still be over the ferrying squadrons and their schedules. Cochran will be considered an adviser to the WAFS. We will regulate our *own* people at ATC."

"I accept," she said.

"Excellent." Tunner pulled a folded paper from his flight suit. "I've written up these duties, and if you agree, we'll make them official. The press is going to pounce once Cochran's position is announced, because ATC is going to announce yours too."

Nancy took the paper from Tunner, but before reading through it, she asked, "Does any of this have to be reported to the press? I mean, Cochran and I are on the same side in the long run. At least from my viewpoint. We both know Cochran is forwarding her agenda in every way possible—but since I have you at my back, I don't think we need to publicly air our differences of opinion."

"The press will be involved because General Arnold and Cochran are involved." He motioned toward the paper. "Read it, and tell me what you think."

Nancy read through the duties that Tunner had sketched out by hand. "Advise the Ferrying Division headquarters in the matter of how to delegate the WAFS assignments." She looked up at Tunner. "Agreed." She read the next lines. "Allocate which WAFS join which ferrying group. Supervise the introductory training and additional training on advanced aircraft. And finally, formulate the rules and regulations that govern conduct of the WAFS, as well as oversee the morale and welfare."

She met his gaze. "This is well-thought-out and what I'm mostly doing already."

Tunner folded his hands. "But now it's in a more official capacity that we'll include in our announcement."

"I don't have any additions."

"Excellent." Tunner rose to his feet and retrieved the paper. "I'll get you a typed memo soon. And I know I don't have to ask you this, but as a reminder, keep any comments to the press as innocuous as possible. We've been able to keep a lid on things for months, and I know that Cochran has been shutting down media at Sweetwater as well."

"I was planning on it." Nancy rose and shook Tunner's hand. They all wanted the program to stay on task and not be embellished or mini- mized in the newspapers. The press mostly portrayed the WAFS as glamour girls. Articles such as "Girl Pilots" published in *Life* had dispar- aged the dedication of women by reporting, "The girls are very serious about their chance to fly for the Army at Avenger Field, even when it means giving up nail polish, beauty parlors, and dates." As if the women cared about any of those things. They were giving up spouses, children, homes, and jobs. Not nail polish. Nancy steeled her emotions. "Thank you, sir."

"Thank you, Mrs. Love." He paused. "I know we haven't always seen eye to eye on some details, but what you've done for this program has changed our future. One that we can be proud of. Make no mistake that the WAFS have been instrumental in altering the tide of this war."

"It's been my pleasure." Nancy released his hand and stepped back. After he walked out of her office, she didn't move for a moment. Cochran would be taking on a much more prominent position in women's aviation now, and Nancy could only hope that the ripples would be small and that it wouldn't detract from the true intent of the WAFS mission.

Despite what Nancy hoped and what Tunner predicted, the media went into a frenzy once both announcements were made on July 5. *Newsweek*'s article was titled "Coup for Cochran," and under their photographs was the caption, "Miss Cochran and Mrs. Love: Which one bosses women flyers?"

When Nancy finished reading the article, she met with Tunner, plus General Smith on the phone. "This is ridiculous," Nancy said to Smith once he answered. "These articles are filled with half-truths and are taking the focus away from what the WAFS Program is all about by making it seem like Cochran and I are on the phone every day arguing over whose ideas are better."

"This will die down soon," Smith said in a tight voice. "I don't like the reporting either, but the media embellishes to get a more sensational story."

"I hate it," Nancy said. "If we can't trust the media, where can the general public get reliable information? If they're making my assigned duties into something newsworthy, then how are they twisting other news stories? We should be working, doing our jobs right now, instead of having these types of phone calls."

Smith's grumble came through the line. "Have you or Colonel Tunner spoken to Cochran?"

"Colonel Tunner spoke to General Arnold," Nancy supplied.

"Yes," Tunner confirmed. "Generally, Cochran doesn't seem bothered by the media reports."

This irritated Nancy, but she was tired of letting these articles weigh her down. Her job was busy enough. She had plenty on her plate, checking out on more planes and keeping the WAFS running smoothly. And she missed her husband. She didn't want this war as much as the next person, but nothing in her wanted to be in the middle of the circus that seemed to constantly lump her and Jackie Cochran's names together.

"I'm sure your office is too busy to deal with henpecking that's not even happening," Nancy told Smith. "Colonel Tunner is getting a promotion and will need to focus on that." Tunner's promotion was to brigadier general. More changes afoot.

Cochran was already taking her director position and putting plans into action. Nancy didn't particularly like them, but she was staying out of the decision that Cochran had made to redirect a group of graduates from Class 43-3 and send them to Camp Davis to be trained on towing gunnery targets.

Yes, the women could perform the duty, but Nancy didn't love the idea of highly trained female pilots becoming target practice for live gunfire by male combat pilots in training. But she kept her head down in the Cincinnati office because they were moving from four women's ferrying squadrons to six. In addition, she had determined that she would transition on every single plane that the WAFS would be assigned to fly.

But Nancy could no longer keep her calm when August brought another blow, this one impossible to gloss over. Cochran's next plan was approved. The WAFS Program and the WFTD classes in Sweetwater, Texas, would now combine to be named under the single organizational name of Women Airforce Service Pilots, or WASP.

No matter where the women pilots worked, or for which division, they would all be considered WASPs, starting officially on August 5.

The past year of building and creating and growing the WAFS Program would now be defunct in name and recognition.

Nancy decided she was taking a couple of days off. She called Tunner and told him, barely keeping her voice steady.

"I'm sorry, Nancy. I know this is a blow. It is to all of us. The WAFS was our brainchild, and now . . ."

When he didn't finish, Nancy felt a rising wave of anxiety. "What aren't you telling me?"

His silence spoke volumes, silence so dense she could have waded through it.

"Colonel Tunner?"

"The uniform is going to change too," Tunner said in a firm tone. "I suggested the Original WAFS keep theirs—the one you designed—to set them apart as the forerunners of the program. But . . ."

"But you were overruled."

"Yes."

"By Cochran, who has General Arnold's ear."

"Yes."

Nancy closed her eyes. "I don't want to know anything more right now. It can all wait. I'll be back in two days. I need to see Bob."

"Of course." Tunner spoke somberly. "Have a safe flight."

It wasn't too hard to find a plane to ferry, and when she landed in Washington, DC, later that afternoon, Bob was waiting at the hangar to greet her.

She gave him a fierce hug, then drew back. "Do I look like an old lady?"

His brows dipped. "What?"

"I feel like I've aged thirty years," she said, the tears building. "I know it's silly. I'm healthy and safe, and you're healthy and safe, but I want to go to our apartment, lock the doors, and never come out again."

Bob cradled her face with his hands, his blue eyes intent on hers. "Sweetie, none of this diminishes the program you've built. The WAFS are still the WAFS but with a new name. And I'll spend the next two days trying to convince you, but mostly, I want to feed you." He kissed her forehead. "You don't look older, but you're thinner. Come on, we're hitting up the nearest diner, and I want you to order anything you like."

# CHAPTER THIRTY-FIVE

"Last week came a shake-up . . . even the Air Forces weren't agreed on which of the photogenic female flying chiefs would outrank the other. The ATC maintained that Miss Cochran's job was merely advisory and not superior to Mrs. Love's executive post. But officials at Air Forces headquarters insisted that Miss Cochran had 'highest authority' over women pilots: 'If the Air Transport Command is not already aware of this, they will have to be made aware of it.'"

—*NEWSWEEK,* "COUP FOR COCHRAN," JULY 19, 1943

*August 1943—Cincinnati, Ohio*

"Can you believe it's been a year since the WAFS started, and now—" Nancy bit off her sentence. The hour was growing late, and she should head to her apartment and sleep, but her mind wouldn't shut off because of the news she'd received that day. She'd decided to give Bob a rest and had called Betty instead.

"And now we're the WASP," Betty said over the phone, irony in her words. "I went to bed a WAFS and woke up a WASP."

Nancy laughed, but it was a dry laugh. "I was hoping when I woke up that it had all been some sort of topsy-turvy dream."

"That would have been nice." Betty stifled a yawn. "Are the rumors true, Nancy? Is the uniform changing too?"

"Yes." Nancy closed her eyes for a moment. Brigadier General Tunner had briefed her, and she hadn't even reacted. She'd felt numb, but now, the more she thought about it, the more the irritation crawled along her skin like vengeful red ants. "Not only are we being called the WASP, but our WAFS uniforms will be obsolete."

Betty sighed. "You spent a lot of time putting them together—considering all the necessities—and getting things approved."

"I've been usurped by a fashion designer." Nancy rose from her office chair and walked around the desk. Through the window, the sun had set, and the Ohio sky glowed a brilliant magenta.

"What? Is Cochran now a fashion designer?"

It wouldn't have been entirely surprising, especially since Cochran had coined the brand "Wings to Beauty." "No, but she hired one from Bergdorf Goodman."

Betty didn't speak for a moment. "Are you joking, Nancy?"

"I wish I were." She paused. "The uniform would be fine for any other organization, but it's not the WAFS."

"What color?" Betty sounded dubious.

"Santiago Blue." Nancy drew in a breath. "It's a pretty dark blue, I'll give Cochran that. The blue will make up the wool gabardine jacket and skirt. The beret will match, of course. For flying, we'll have a battle jacket and blue wool slacks. In addition, we have two shirts—cotton for summer and flannel for winter. And a tan-colored trench coat. Gloves and shoes are black calfskin. All topped with a pair of silver wings."

"Sounds like something a cover model would wear in a magazine photo shoot," Betty mused.

"I haven't seen the uniform in person, but I'm wondering how long I can get away with wearing our WAFS."

Betty laughed. "I'm not planning on changing until someone gives me a direct order."

"It won't be coming from me."

"Mrs. Love, you still here?" Tunner tapped on her partially open door, and Nancy turned from the window.

"Yes, sir, I'm on the phone with Betty Gillies."

Tunner stepped into the room. "Excellent. I need to speak to you both."

"Of course." Nancy returned to her desk, and Tunner sat across from her. She set the receiver between the both of them. "Can you hear us, Betty?"

Her voice sounded tinny through the receiver. "I can."

Tunner steepled his fingers atop the desk. "Now, we have a situation in which I need you ladies' help."

Nancy wasn't sure how many more "situations" she could stomach. She drew in a breath and focused on Tunner.

"We're having trouble getting male pilots to ferry the B-17s over the Atlantic Ocean to the United Kingdom." The skin about his eyes tightened. "So, I thought, Why not have a couple of our girls show them how it's done?"

Nancy blinked.

"What?" Betty's voice came through the phone. "You want us to transition on a B-17 and fly to Europe?"

The edge of Tunner's mouth lifted. "I do. And it's not to make you ladies into some sort of spectacle for the media. You're seasoned and talented pilots. We're just setting the example."

Nancy was listening but not fully comprehending. "This isn't setting a speed record to Canada, like the WAFS did for the PT-26s. Or when Del Scharr checked out on the P-39 that the men were complaining about, thus proving anyone could take on the *flying coffin*. Scharr even wrote her own checklist." She paused. "This is across the ocean, sir. We'd have to . . ." Her mind jumped ahead through the many hoops. "We'd have to transition up the chain."

Tunner gave a curt nod and produced a paper upon which he'd outlined the process.

Betty couldn't see the paper, so Nancy read aloud. "Begin sandbagging in the B-25 immediately." Sandbagging was flying along with an instructor. Nancy had already checked out on the B-25, so Betty would be next. "Start Army instrument training and check out on the B-25."

She scanned the rest of the list. "You want us to check out on the BT-13, C-78, C-73, and then finally the B-17?"

"Exactly."

Betty seemed to have no reply from her end.

"This will take weeks," Nancy said. "We'd have to move our schedules and—"

"Drop everything else." Tunner straightened his shoulders. "Things like name changes to the WASP or uniform redesigns are the least of our concerns right now. The inter-office politics will eventually sort themselves out. We have a bigger frontier to conquer, ladies, and a war to win. The ATC needs to deliver the B-17s and their crews to the AAF squadrons in England. The B-17s are rugged and strong. Not only can they reach Germany and return again without fueling, but they can be ferried across the Atlantic without ships. They don't go down easily in a fight and can return our men home even if they're damaged. Saving lives is what will happen."

Nancy knew the specs of the B-17, its 103-foot wingspan and 74-foot length. The plane was powered by four Wright 1,200 horsepower radial engines, and it could fly 300 miles per hour at 30,000 feet.

Nancy released a slow breath. What would Bob say? He'd be supportive, but . . . it would be a lot. She and Betty would be making history, sure, but she didn't care about that. Nancy could see both the fire and the desperation in Tunner's eyes. He needed them to do this, and she knew she'd never have anyone better than Betty to undertake this task.

"Ladies," Tunner continued, "flying the B-17 on the Snowball route will light a fire under those men's wings."

Nancy knew that the Snowball route began in Gander, Newfoundland, or Goose Bay, Labrador, to Prestwick, Scotland. From there, on to England. It was bothersome that the male pilots were complaining when the deliveries were desperately needed. But even if the men weren't pushing back, this was an opportunity she couldn't pass up.

The momentum of the war continued to shift. In July, the Allies had landed in Sicily, leading to the German evacuation. The Allies had bombed Rome, and the British had completed a bombing raid on Hamburg. Mussolini had been arrested on July 25, and the Italian fascist government had crumbled. Marshal Pietro Badoglio seemed willing to negotiate with the Allies.

"I'll do it," Nancy said. "Betty can decide for herself—"

"I'm in too." Betty's voice rang out, loud and clear from the receiver. "What's first?"

The tightness around Tunner's eyes relaxed, and his mouth curved. "Well, ladies, first task is to get your vaccinations, including your first: a typhoid shot."

It turned out that Nancy called her husband that night anyway.

"Can I come?" Bob asked the moment Nancy filled him in.

"That would defeat the purpose," Nancy said with a laugh, although nerves were starting to take over as well. What had she agreed to?

"Fine, but I'm going to give you a lot of advice," Bob said, both amusement and pride in his voice.

"I wouldn't expect anything less from my know-it-all husband."

"I don't know it all."

"You sure act like you do," Nancy said.

The smile was evident in his voice when he answered. "I don't know when I'll see you again. Can you fill me in on that, Mrs. Love?"

"Come to Cincinnati," she said immediately. "I'll take you to watch the Cincinnati Reds play baseball at Crosley Field, and you know the beer is world-famous."

"You don't need to bribe me, sweetie. My best girl is there."

"Who would that be?"

"I think I need to show you a few things on the B-17."

"Sorry, Mr. Love. You'll be the student in this situation."

He laughed. "Can't wait."

Next, she called her parents. Her father answered, and she gave him a rundown of her assignment. "We're keeping things hushed for now, Daddy, so don't tell anyone except for Mother."

"I won't, my dear," he said. "People might wonder why I'm glowing with pride though."

Nancy smiled to herself. "You tell them you're happy because the weather is fine."

Her father chuckled. "You're remarkable—although you've probably figured that out by now. Everyone is so proud of you."

By "everyone," she knew he always referred to her brother as well.

"How's Mother?"

"She's busy with quilting most of the time," her father said. "Joined a ladies group. It's been good for her. Keeps their hands and minds busy—which we all need during this war as we wait for news."

Over the next few weeks, Nancy followed Tunner's outline, while Betty was doing her part in Wilmington, becoming instrument rated on the B-25. Nancy traveled to Romulus to earn her instrument rating on the BT-13, C-78, and C-73.

Then, in August, Betty and Teresa James flew a ferrying mission of P-47s to Fort Myers. The following day, Betty arrived in Cincinnati, meeting Nancy.

"Finally, I get to talk to my copilot in person," Nancy said, striding toward Betty as she walked into the hangar.

The two women embraced, then Nancy stood back. "Let's look at you."

Betty wore her full WASP uniform, and she did look smart. But it wasn't the colors of the WAFS, so the sight was bittersweet.

"Thought you might be wearing the WAFS uniform," Betty said with a smirk. "Didn't know what to pack."

Indeed, Nancy wore the WASP blues, too, but she still had the khaki WAFS uniform hanging pressed in her closet, ready to go at a moment's notice. "We have more urgent matters to deal with," Nancy said, linking her arm with Betty's as they walked to Tunner's office. "Don't need the media stirring up more rumors. We already have enough of their attention."

They headed into Tunner's office, where Captain Robert D. Forman waited.

"Betty, this is Captain Forman," Nancy said, making the introductions between the pair.

"Nice to meet you, Mrs. Gillies," Forman said, shaking Betty's hand. His eyes were friendly, his gaze perceptive, his hair a faded red. "I've heard nothing but good from General Tunner."

Betty smiled. "He said you're the best, and he only wants us working with the best."

"I'll try to live up to that," Forman said with a laugh. "But call me Red. Everyone does."

"All right, Red, what do you have for us today?"

"How about copiloting the B-17E?"

Betty grinned and glanced at Nancy. "Don't mind if I do."

"Come this way. I'll introduce you to her."

Nancy walked with the pair, her skin prickling with anticipation.

"Her official name is B-17E #41-2550," Forman continued. "But we call her the Flying Fortress."

Nancy and Betty would spend the next weeks with Forman, as mandated by Tunner. They'd be training on cross-country runs, which included night flying and night landing. Next, they'd become instrument rated and checked out on the B-17.

The following day, Nancy woke before the sun, happy she'd slept a few hours. Her mind was already thinking ahead to their flight workday of practicing landings and short distances with the B-17, then flying to Middletown about thirty miles north of Cincinnati.

Once she and Betty had a quick breakfast and suited up in their WASP flying outfits, they met Forman on the tarmac.

"We might have a bit of an audience today, ladies," he said as he walked them through the precheck. "The Aeronca Aircraft Corporation in Middletown is receiving the Army-Navy 'E' Award in honor of their production of war equipment."

Nancy had heard of the prestigious award. "Should we fly to another location?"

"Of course not," Forman said. "They'll love seeing the B-17 swooping in. We might make the papers though."

"That's nothing new when Nancy Love is involved," Betty quipped.

Nancy narrowed her eyes at her friend. "I'm not the one who asked for this assignment. If the men were doing their job . . ." She winked at Forman, and he returned a grin.

"We'll show Middletown how it's done," Forman declared. "Then they can spread the news."

"What does Aeronca build?" Betty asked.

"The L-3 liaisons and the PT-19s and PT-23s," Forman said. "But even more interesting is they build the elevators for the B-17."

"Ah, so this is all part of a plan?" Nancy asked. "Flying in for the ceremony?"

"Something like that."

# CHAPTER THIRTY-SIX

"It was a gala day for the citizenry of Middletown as well, for the entire town seemed to have turned out to pay tribute. The high-ranking Army and Navy officials plus an assemblage of leading lights in the aviation field—builders of the sky giants—plus an imposing list of invited guests added luster to the resplendent and decorative grandstand. A guest in the form of a Flying Fortress, which alighted on the field during the ceremony, was a messenger of additional good will."

—*AERONCA WING TIPS*, AUGUST 10, 1943

*August–September 1943—Middletown, Ohio*

The morning sun gleamed gold, and the sky boasted a clear blue as Nancy, Betty, and Forman finished the precheck for the B-17 flight to Middletown. Forman took the pilot seat, Nancy the copilot, and Betty below them in the navigator's station. If the fine, windless morning wasn't an endorsement from Mother Nature, then Nancy didn't know what was.

"Ready?" Forman asked.

"Ready." Nancy moved her earphones onto her ears and gave Forman a thumbs-up. She turned on the electrical switch to activate the hydraulic pump that would give oil pressure to the first engine. Next, she pushed the start-engine button, and the eleven-foot-seven-inch propeller jolted to life. In less than two minutes, all four engines were roaring, making it impossible to speak to each other except through their headset microphones.

"Throttle," Forman said.

Nancy grasped the engine throttles, and the bomber began to move slowly toward the end of the runway. Once they turned to face the entire length of the runway, she pressed the four throttles forward. Takeoff had begun, and the speed climbed on the airspeed indicator.

"Wait until it reaches 110 miles per hour," Forman said into her headset.

Nancy's heart thundered along with the four engines as the massive plane gained speed, and when it reached 110 miles per hour, she pulled back on the control wheel. "We're flying," she sputtered as the bomber lifted from the runway.

Forman chuckled. "Bring down the nose."

She pushed the control wheel forward now so that the nose of the B-17 would level out. The landing gear hummed into place, tucking into the belly of the plane.

The airspeed indicator continued to rise, and once they reached 135 miles per hour, the plane began to climb higher. The entire flight would be less than an hour.

"I'm closing the cowl flaps," Forman said.

"How high are we taking her?" Nancy asked.

"12,000 feet," Forman said.

Nancy looked over at him to see his grin. She moved one of the headphones off her ears, but the noise was nearly earsplitting. Replacing it, she said, "What's our approach?"

"We'll come in on a southwest approach," Forman said.

"Yes, sir." Nancy peered out the windscreen at the ground below—buildings and patches of ground growing smaller and smaller. Eventually, the meandering stretch of the Miami River came into view as it curved around the airfield. They'd be making a short-field landing in order to avoid the wires at the northeast end of the runway of Middletown, Ohio.

"Ready?" Forman asked. "Contact the tower to get clearance for landing."

Once Nancy got the tower clearance, Forman brought the aircraft in. From her viewpoint, Nancy could see the people waving, gawking, and raising cameras to snap photos.

"Go ahead," Forman said. "Wave to the crowds. Most of them have never seen a plane this large. I'll wait here."

Nancy raised her sunglasses and perched them on her helmet, then she looked over at Forman. "You don't want to get out? They're going to think I landed this thing on my own."

He shrugged his shoulders good-naturedly.

So Nancy climbed out of the plane and spoke to a few reporters. They knew her name, which impressed her, but she quickly corrected the idea that she was the only one flying the plane. After stopping at the restroom facilities, because there was nothing on the B-17 that worked well for a woman since it was too cumbersome to strip off her flight suit and use the chemical toilet, she headed back to the plane. A group of kids shouted and waved at her, so she waved back, smiling. Once she was back on the plane, she again sat in the copilot's seat.

"Let's get her in the sky," Forman said.

Nancy didn't think she'd ever take the thrill of flying a B-17 for granted.

A few days later, Betty accompanied them on the B-17 on a cross-country trip. Tunner had administrative business to attend to at the various stops, so he came along too. Forman piloted, and when they approached to land at Ludington, Michigan, the airfield was too short.

"I'm aborting." Forman retracted the landing flaps, applied full power, and pulled back on the yoke. They lifted above the airfield again. But the abrupt use of full power made engine number four detonate.

"Feather," Nancy said, her training instinctive as she felt the higher drag kick in.

Forman did so by turning the propeller blades so they pointed in the direction of flight, lessening the air resistance.

"Let's land her at the Traverse City airport," Tunner cut in. "It's the closest base."

"That's a Navy base," Forman said tightly. "They might not want the intrusion."

"Do we want to fly all the way back to Ohio on only three engines?" Tunner asked.

Forman's jaw tightened, but he turned the plane.

The air-traffic controller didn't immediately give them clearance, even when Nancy explained they were one engine down.

"I'm not going to circle," Forman told the control-tower operator. "I need immediate clearance."

Nancy glanced back at Betty, who was wide-eyed.

Finally, the controller came back on. "Cleared to land, but only if an emergency."

"We don't have much choice," Forman told the controller.

"Cleared."

As they landed, Nancy stared as several jeeps drove out to meet them. Inside were armed men—armed Navy men—she guessed by their uniforms.

"What's going on?" she asked, but no one seemed to have an answer.

"It's not like we're the enemy," Betty muttered.

Forman's conversation with the Navy commander was very short before he climbed back into the cockpit, his face as hard as stone. "They're demanding that we leave right away. On three engines. They claim they can't service the plane and that we need high-level security clearance to even be here."

"What's going on?" Tunner asked.

"Well, we won't find out now—maybe later," Forman said, his words like steel. "Where to next, Nancy?"

"The AAF base in Alpena should be able to handle the repair," Nancy said.

Forman nodded.

"Can we take off with only three working engines?" Betty asked, worry in her voice.

"This plane is built to survive worse," Forman said. "Didn't ever think we'd be flying this way over US soil though."

As Forman pushed the throttles forward, they gained speed, and once they hit 110 miles per hour, he pulled back on the control wheel. The Flying Fortress lifted, and Nancy felt relieved. The workmanship of this plane really was superior, and she now understood firsthand the desperate need to get them over to Europe.

Over the next days, Nancy finally checked out on the B-17, after the repairs were made in Alpena. She landed at multiple airports, and the following week, she began to transition on the B-17F. Her work included landing with three engines running, then only two.

She found that the B-17 was smooth in the clear sky, but it became clumsy when the weather turned bad. At 35,000 pounds empty and over 65,000 when filled with fuel and bombs, it was an intense physical experience to pilot this plane. Especially when they had to shut down one or two of the four engines and navigate from there.

It wasn't uncommon for Nancy and Betty to climb out of the plane, arms and legs quaking and their flight suits stained with perspiration. Betty was too petite to see over the control panel, yet she managed to keep the plane straight.

"Does the sun come up earlier each day?" Betty asked one early morning in Cincinnati when Nancy met her at the barracks. The cool summer air felt refreshing, but they were both missing out on sleep. "Or is it just me?"

"I think it's you," Nancy teased with a tired smile. "Let's get moving. We're not going to go through all this training on the B-17 and wear out before we can make a cross-country flight."

Betty gave her a salute, and they strode from the barracks. They began their morning run to the field, where they'd go through their routine of push-ups, sit-ups, pull-ups, and other calisthenic exercises. Because of how physically grueling flying the B-17 was, Nancy put together a memo to the WASP organization detailing the requirements for the physical strength training required to fly the bigger planes.

By the end of August, both Nancy and Betty were qualified and trained. They'd also taken on ferrying missions of delivering multiple B-17Fs, totaling twenty-four hours of ferrying time. The night before they left on the first leg of their mission that would take them across the Atlantic, Nancy called Bob with sobering news. "Did you read the papers about the Bloody Hundredth?"

"I did," Bob said, subdued.

On a mission to Schweinfurt–Regensburg, the Eighth Air Force Group, which included 376 bombers targeting the German aircraft industry, lost sixty bombers and had many more crippled. Losses happened all the time, but this felt closer to home since the crews were flying the same type of plane as Nancy.

"They're going to need replacements right away," she said.

"Yes," Bob agreed. "Your mission couldn't come soon enough."

He sounded so serious that Nancy had to ask, "You aren't changing your mind about all this, are you?"

"No," Bob said immediately. "It's difficult to see these kinds of setbacks. And to know you're going to be on the other side of the Atlantic soon. You have my letter of introduction to Major Atwood?"

"Yes, it's already packed in my B-4 bag." Bob's letter was written on official ATC letterhead and introduced Nancy and Betty to Major Roy Atwood, the executive officer of the ATC European Wing in London.

"Great," he said quietly.

Neither of them spoke for several moments.

"I love you, Bob."

"I love you, too, sweetie."

The next day, on September 1, Nancy and Betty flew a B-17F from Cincinnati to New Castle. Nancy wasn't entirely sure if she'd slept the night before—or maybe she had dreamed she was awake. Her mind had gone over every flying scenario she'd ever been in. A dull headache had formed, but she didn't have time for any distractions.

Her crew consisted of Betty copiloting at the moment, with 1st Lt. R.O. (Pappy) Fraser as navigator, radio operator T/Sgt. Stover, aerial engineer T/Sgt. Weintraub, and assistant aerial engineer T/Sgt. L.S. Hall. They were a solid team, and Nancy felt honored to be included with them—a part of history, really. A part of the war effort.

Once they landed in New Castle, they were outfitted with fleece-lined suits and oxygen masks that would be necessary for the North Atlantic crossing. They stayed overnight, and Nancy found herself facing a night in the BOQ 14 barracks. Memories flooded through her of how over a year ago, the WAFS had started in this place.

"We've come a long way since the Original WAFS," Betty said as they walked to the barracks together.

"We sure have," Nancy said. "I don't think I could have predicted any of this. Hoped for it, maybe."

"Just think, in two days, we'll be over the Atlantic."

Nancy smiled. "Sometimes it seems too good to be true."

Betty nudged her. "Look around you. This is all really happening."

Nancy finally slept that night, yet the feeling of trepidation persisted in the morning. Everything was moving forward as it should, but doubts bounced around in her head whenever she had a quiet moment. Not that there were many of those, surrounded by her crew. Next, they flew to La Guardia Airport in New York for an overnight briefing. Once they were again cleared, they headed to Presque Isle, Maine, to prepare for the flight to Goose Bay, Labrador, in Canada.

The Canadian government had given the US carte blanche to use the air base they'd built early on in the war. Landing in Canada scattered some of Nancy's spinning thoughts. She and Betty headed into one of the offices to make phone calls. Betty called her husband, then Nancy called Bob to update him on their progress. Finally, she called Tunner.

"Good to hear about your safe arrival," he said into the phone. "I heard the weather is keeping you grounded an extra day."

"Yes, sir," Nancy told him. "We should be clear tomorrow. These are fast-moving clouds."

"Excellent," Tunner said. "Safe flight tomorrow."

"Thank you." Nancy smiled over at Betty, who smiled back.

When she hung up with Tunner, Nancy said, "I guess we enjoy the rain until it's time for dinner?"

Betty stretched out her arms. "Suit yourself. I'm going to take a little nap, if you don't mind."

"I don't mind." Nancy wasn't going to attempt any sort of a nap, or she'd be wired again tonight. "I'll see you at dinner."

After Betty disappeared into their sleeping quarters, Nancy was tempted to call Bob again, but she called her parents instead.

"Hi, Daddy," she said as soon as her father answered.

"Are you on US soil or English?"

She smiled at the eagerness in his voice. "Neither. We have a weather delay in Canada. Should be flying out tomorrow though."

"We're praying for you, my dear."

Her mother's voice could be heard in the background, and her father said, "Oh, here's your mother. She wants to hear all about it."

Nancy nearly laughed. The less her mother knew about weather delays or the various scenarios that could affect a transatlantic flight, the better.

But her mother's voice was cheerful, excited even. "I don't think I'll sleep a wink while you're in that huge plane, flying over the ocean."

"It's really very safe, Mother," Nancy said. "We won't be over enemy territory or anything like that. We're only making an overseas delivery."

"I know," her mother said. "Your father has explained it all to me—more than once and answered my many questions. I can't quite believe my daughter is doing this—and with Betty too. It's remarkable."

When Nancy met Betty and the rest of the crew in the mess hall for dinner, their spirits were high. Maybe the delay had been good. It had mellowed everyone's nerves, and they could enjoy a quieter night together. The weather had already calmed.

"Looks like the heavens are parting and bestowing a perfect flight for tomorrow," Fraser said.

"Makes my job easier," Stover said. "I can radio the control tower without the static."

"Yeah, we don't want to overshoot Scotland," Weintraub deadpanned.

"I'll keep y'all on track," Hall said.

Stover clapped Hall on the shoulder. "Glad to have you on board. I feel peachy keen to be traveling with the two best pilots."

Nancy smiled, and Betty smirked. "That's right, boys."

"Mrs. Love?"

Nancy turned to see the AAF chief of Air Staff, General Barney Giles. He peered at her through his black-rimmed glasses, holding out a telegram. "This just arrived, and it's marked urgent."

Nancy took the telegram, a dozen thoughts running through her mind. Was there an emergency somewhere? Was everyone in her family all right? She'd just spoken to her parents. Maybe it was something with Bob. She opened the telegram, and as she silently read the words, her vision blurred, and all warmth drained from her face.

The message was from General Smith, and it included a second message from General Hap Arnold: "Just have seen message from General C.R. Smith, indicated that a B-17 with women crew will leave for England shortly. Desire that this trip be canceled, and no women fly transoceanic planes until I have had time to study and approve."

The telegram slipped from Nancy's hand as she rubbed at her temples. She felt sick to the center of her stomach. They'd put in so much work, and everyone was ready . . . Once again, gender had slammed down a barrier.

"What is it?" Betty asked, picking up the telegram and reading it. "This can't be true, can it?"

"Apparently, it is," Nancy gritted out. "General Smith's opening note makes that clear."

Betty's face flushed. "I don't understand, Nancy."

By now, the rest of their crew had passed around the telegram, their faces growing pale as well.

"They can't cancel in the eleventh hour," Fraser said, looking around the table. "Can they?"

"I don't know." Nancy stood from the table. "I'm going to call General Tunner and see what's going on."

"I'm coming with you," Betty said, standing.

The rest of the crew rose, pushing back their chairs in haste.

"Come with us, boys," Nancy said. "We might as well all hear this together."

The night sky was clear and cool as they headed to the office with a phone. Nancy called the office in Cincinnati, but she didn't expect an answer, so she called Tunner at home.

"I received a telegram from General Smith stating that General Arnold is canceling our mission," Nancy said tightly. "We're being replaced by a male pilot and copilot."

"Ridiculous," Tunner said. "You're both qualified, and General Smith authorized the flight."

"Evidently, he didn't run it by General Arnold, who seems to have more clout since he's in England right now." She tightened her grip on the receiver. "Can you find out what's going on? I'm here with my whole crew. We'll wait until you call us back."

The next hour felt like the longest of Nancy's life. She didn't dare call Bob because she wanted to keep the line free. And once she heard his voice, she was also pretty sure she'd lose whatever control she had over her emotions right now.

When the phone finally rang, Nancy jumped to answer.

"General Smith thought you were well on your way across the Atlantic," Tunner said. "Apparently, he didn't know about the weather delay."

"And?"

"And he sent a telegram informing Brigadier General Paul Burrows, the commander of the ATC European Wing, of your mission. General Smith also told Burrows to pass on the message to General Arnold about you and Betty flying the B-17 and how it would be the first instance of overseas ferrying of any type of military bomber with women serving both as pilot and copilot." Tunner drew in a breath. "General Arnold doesn't want women flying into a war zone."

Nancy didn't speak for a moment. Nothing that came to mind would be ladylike or polite or something she wanted to be remembered for. "It's final, then?"

"It's final."

# CHAPTER THIRTY-SEVEN

"Production was so heavy that we frequently had rows of P-51s
stored in the middle of the Long Beach Airport. If you got back
to base by noon, Operations sent you right back out that day.
You picked up the airplane and headed for Palm Springs so that
you could leave from there the following morning to ferry the
plane to Newark. If you got back to base later in the afternoon
you didn't have to go back out until the next morning."

—B. J. ERICKSON

*September–November 1943—Goose Bay, Labrador, Canada*

Morning arrived as it always did, but this morning, Nancy felt as
though her limbs had been weighed down with barbells. She didn't want
to move. She didn't want to face the day. But lying on a stiff cot all
morning wasn't going to do anyone any good. There were worse things
in life—much worse things—but for now, she wanted to wallow in her
own disappointment.

She gave herself five minutes, or maybe ten, and then she dressed
and left the barracks before the sun had a chance to change the color of
the sky. Her head was pounding both from disappointment and from
drinking her sorrows with Betty and the boys the night before.

Nancy had let everyone down. Even though Tunner had given her
and Betty the assignment, she should have known there'd be pushback from Arnold. There always was. She could blame Smith for not
informing the ATC European Wing from the start, but she should have
checked on that. It had been her mission, *her* assignment, after all.

As she walked about the airfield in the cool weather beneath a perfectly clear Canadian sky, she wondered if there would be a time in the
future when women pilots would be treated equally. Truly as equals and

not as some quota or concession. Would women ever be recognized for their full skills and talents and not be judged by gender?

After the phone call with Tunner the previous night, she'd sent everyone out of the office and called Bob.

He'd been upset, too, ranted and raved and cussed, his ocean of words rushing over her like a tidal wave. Of course he'd apologized, which had only made her feel worse.

"Call my parents," Nancy had told him. "I haven't the heart. They won't have to worry so much, though, so maybe that's one positive thing."

"It's so hard to believe the rug was pulled out in the eleventh hour," Bob had said, seething. "This should have been yours, Nancy. You're ready, and your crew is qualified."

"I know." She wished Bob were with her. She'd give anything to feel his arms around her right then. Her voice turned hollow. "Another time, maybe."

Not during the war, that she knew.

Now, in the predawn gray, she walked aimlessly, her heart plucking like a forlorn violin ballad. Eventually, she found herself heading toward the B-17; its massive form stood stoic in the dim light.

She stopped a dozen yards away and rested her hands on her hips. Looking up at the nose of the plane, she noticed a change since the previous night. Someone had painted "WAFS" and below that "Queen Bee."

Her crew had named the airplane.

Hot tears fell on Nancy's cheeks. It was a small thing but a heartfelt show of support. Nancy and Betty might not be piloting the plane overseas, but their spirits would be on that plane.

The air shifted, and a breeze stirred Nancy's hair. She remained gazing at the B-17 as the chill burned off the air and the rising sun softened the sky to an iridescent blue. A perfect flying day.

But instead of flying over the Atlantic, she and Betty would be traveling as passengers back to the US on a C-52A.

The next few days felt surreal, and somehow, they passed. Over the following weeks, Nancy had to tamp down her disappointment again and again. Ironically, Fraser had to bring back some of her personal belongings that had been left on the B-17. Nancy's departure had been so unexpected that she'd forgotten about her shoes, some papers, and the Mae West life preservers that belonged to her and Betty.

And on top of that continued disappointment, tragedy hit on September 23 when WASP aviator Betty Taylor Wood crashed her A-24 and didn't survive. Betty had married her Sweetwater flight instructor only six weeks earlier. When Jackie Cochran went to Camp Davis to investigate, she discovered sugar in Betty's gas tank, which explained the sounds of the engine surging, then cutting out—heard by those on the ground. Betty had been sabotaged.

The conversation Nancy had with Jackie Cochran was somber, but Cochran insisted on not making an official report to the AAF. She feared that it could put the whole WASP Program in danger. They all feared it.

Cochran continued pushing for the WASP to be militarized, but not under the WAC, which had been General Tunner's suggestion. Ironically, the holdup with Cochran was that she didn't like the WAC director, Colonel Oveta Culp Hobby. Nancy wasn't sure what exactly had come between the two women, but she didn't want to put herself in the middle of it.

Tunner filled Nancy in on a brief stop at her office. "Congressman John Costello of California introduced the bill to Congress yesterday."

Nancy knew exactly what this meant. "To militarize the WASP?"

"Yes, and it's on its way to the House Committee on Military Affairs for review."

"Is this good news or bad news?" Nancy knew her own opinion, and it usually coincided with Tunner's.

"We weren't consulted, of course; it's Cochran's baby. But I'm concerned that if the outcome has Cochran's name on it, things in the Ferrying Division will drastically change."

Nancy agreed, but there wasn't anything she could do about it except wait for the outcome.

In mid-October, Nancy received word that Cochran had sent a group of women from Class 43-6 and Class 43-5 to B-17 transition school at Lockbourne. Nancy decided it was a small victory since women pilots weren't needed to ferry the B-17. Qualifying to fly them simply gave the women more skill sets. And at the very least, Cochran had taken note of Nancy's and Betty's transition work, even though their flight had been canceled.

Nancy also took heart when B.J. Erickson flew orientation flights on the B-17 during October.

But in November, B.J. called Nancy and said, "There's a report circulating that the women learning to fly the B-17s at Lockbourne are the first women to fly the Fortress."

Nancy frowned. "How can such erroneous information be passed around? Everyone knows about Betty and me qualifying and putting in all those hours."

"Do you think it was Cochran?"

"I don't know." Nancy was tired of worrying about Cochran, but she wouldn't be surprised if something the woman said had been misconstrued and then not corrected. "I'll let General Tunner handle it. He owes me anyway. Oh, and Pappy Fraser wrote to me. Told me he's ready to join my crew anytime and says he'll be on board if we want to fly a B-29."

"Good man," B.J. said, amused. "Smart man too."

"You've been setting your own records," Nancy said. "The higher-ups are noticing." B.J. had successfully been delivering P-51s across the country in record time.

"The weather has been cooperating," B.J. said with a laugh.

"Still, it's no small thing."

And more WASP had checked out on the P-51. In fact, Carole Fillmore took one from California to New Jersey but had had to stop off in Athens, Georgia, because dusk had fallen. She'd called the Athens control tower to ask for permission to land, but no one had answered her. So she'd tried again but had again been met with silence. She'd circled the field and contacted the control tower a third time, asking for a radio check. Finally, the controller had answered: "Will the woman who is calling please stay off the air? We're trying to bring in a P-51."

Fillmore knew she was the only P-51 in the area, so she again asked for landing clearance.

The control tower repeated its message, this time shouting, "Will the woman who is calling please stay off the air! We're trying to bring in a P-51!"

Fillmore had run out of patience and said into her throat mic, "For your information, the lady who is *on* the air is *in* the P-51." Without waiting for an answer, she took the final approach and landed in the center of the runway at 120 miles per hour.

"Aw, that was beautiful," the operator drawled, changing his tune completely.

When Fillmore climbed out of the cockpit onto the wing, it was to an audience of dozens of cadets who'd gathered to see the P-51 for the first time.

Someone in the crowd shouted, "It's a girl!" The cheers started and hats waved.

When Fillmore had told Nancy the story, Nancy could only laugh, knowing those men would never forget the sight of Fillmore's dark-blonde hair blowing in the wind as she'd proudly stood on the wing of the P-51 Mustang.

After her phone call with B.J., Nancy passed along the message about the B-17 misinformation to Tunner. He promised to send the correction in a memo to the War Department's Bureau of Public Relations right away and to send Jackie Cochran a copy of the memo as well.

A bit of good news finally came when Air Staff in Washington recommended B.J. for an Air Medal for her performance on duty. But B.J. wasn't happy about being singled out.

"You've earned it," Nancy told her on the phone after the announcement was made.

"I'm doing my *duty*," B.J. said. "That's all. Just like any of the Original WAFS."

"Maybe you're right," Nancy said. "Although any recognition for a female pilot is a tribute to all of us."

B.J. released a heavy sigh. "That's a good way to view it, but I still think that it's not necessary."

"Smile and bear it?"

"Something like that," B.J. grumbled.

Nancy's disappointment over the botched transatlantic flight faded somewhat with more complications arising that took added attention. She shouldn't have been surprised when one of them at the forefront centered on Jackie Cochran, who'd sent out a new proposal to the AAF to appoint special assistants beneath her umbrella, calling them WASP establishment officers.

Tunner and James Teague spent a grumpy couple of hours in Nancy's office as they reviewed the regulations that Cochran had proposed.

"This will be in direct conflict with your management, Nancy," Tunner said as he tapped a pencil on the pages strewn across her desk. "Right now, the women pilots are assigned to a ferrying group at whichever ATC base is a good fit. The pilot groups serve under the correlating base commander. But Cochran's proposal puts another person in the mix."

Nancy rubbed at her temples. "Right. It means that the 'establishment officer' would be in the middle of every decision . . ." She read aloud from the proposal, "And they will represent the director of Women Pilots on nontechnical administrative matters, supervise conduct and morale, and maintain WASP discipline as well as report back the ongoings of the pilots to Cochran."

"All of which you already do, Mrs. Love," Teague cut in. "Except for reporting to Cochran."

"Correct," Nancy said.

"The new officers won't serve a purpose," Teague said. "Unless they're being spies and reporting on everything to Cochran. We already have an established military chain at the AAF, and our ATC has success-fully operated with the women's squadrons through the ferrying groups. Why add another layer of administration?"

"Exactly." Tunner sipped from his second or third cup of coffee. Nancy had lost count.

She wrote down Teague's words. "I'll include that in this draft."

Tunner leaned back in his chair. "You and Teague will have to go to Washington to get this polished and presented. It's too big to let slip through."

"Yes, sir," Teague said, then he looked at Nancy.

She didn't want to be distracted from her duties at the Cincinnati headquarters, but Tunner was right. This couldn't be pushed to the side.

Nancy's trip to Washington, DC, proved to be useful since the WASP regulation Cochran proposed to put herself in charge of all women flying for the Army was eliminated. Nancy felt relief at the re-sult since it meant that the ferrying groups would continue to operate as planned at a time when more and more pursuits were coming off the factory assembly line and needed to be ferried. Nancy had already put in orders earlier that summer to increase training for the women on cross-country travel and crosswind landing.

Tunner had also raised, or re-raised, the requirements that the WFTD graduates be qualified to deliver AT-6 planes. Cochran had re-duced required hours from two hundred to seventy-five, then all the way down to thirty-five.

Yes, they needed more pilots, but they needed *qualified* pilots. Accidents and mishaps among the newly graduated WASP were on the rise, and Tunner wasn't pleased. Neither was Nancy. There'd been too many ground loops, cases of overshooting and undershooting land-ings on runways, and flying in bad weather. In addition to Margaret Oldenburg and Cornelia Fort's deaths, six other WASP pilots had been killed in training or active duty. Jane Champlin had died when her in-structor Henry S. Aubrey had failed to go on instruments during night training. Kathryn Lawrence had been in training on a PT-19A and had been forced to bail out, but her parachute had failed to open.

Then Mabel Rawlinson had been killed at Camp Davis in North Carolina in an A-24 during a night training flight with her instructor. When a mechanical problem caused them to return to base, the landing gear had hit the tops of the pine trees, and the plane had dived and hit the ground. Her instructor had been thrown clear, but Mabel had still been trapped inside by the malfunctioning canopy when the plane had burst into flames.

Next, both Margaret Seip and Helen Jo Severson had been with their instructor Calvin Atwood in a UC-78 on a flight from Sweetwater to Big Springs to practice radio navigation. Both women had been flying under the hood to simulate instrument flying when Atwood had lost control of the mechanically failing plane. And, of course, Betty Wood's death had been due to the compromised fuel in her A-24. All the WASP accidents had been caused by issues out of the women's hands.

This only made Nancy more determined that the training for the larger planes not have any holes in it. Tunner had come up with a plan to have a designated pursuit school in Palm Springs, California, for both male and female pilots. Nancy worked with him to put together a list of fifty-six women ferry pilots to train there in a four-week program of learning to fly the P-47, P-40, P-51, and P-39. Things were well on their way, but Nancy had begun to receive disconcerting reports out of Dallas and then Wilmington from Betty Gillies.

"Colonel Baker's slowing things down," Betty complained over the phone.

Baker was either hot or cold toward the WASP, but Betty had been handling things fine for a long time, so this issue must be a bigger deal. "What's going on?"

"Three of us have checked out on the P-47, as you know."

Yes, Betty, Teresa James, and Helen Mary Clark were all actively ferrying the P-47s. "What is Colonel Baker doing, then?" Nancy asked.

"He's letting the women ferry the Fairchilds, of course, and the P-47, like I mentioned, but the Martin B-26 is off-limits," Betty said. "Colonel Baker says the B-26 is too important to the Men's Training Program so they need to be reserved for the men, and the women shouldn't be clogging up the time on those planes."

"Unfortunately, I'm not surprised," Nancy mused. "Do you want me to have General Tunner call him?"

"That would be appreciated," Betty said. "I think Colonel Baker's scared of you."

Nancy scoffed. "I'd call him, no problem, but he doesn't report to me, so he'd complain even more."

"Right." Betty paused. "Thanks, Nancy. How is everything else going?"

"I'm getting ready to head to Dallas," Nancy said. "Florene Miller says that some of the male instructors are thwarting flight checks at Love Field."

Betty blew out a breath. "Sounds like resentment toward the women pilots."

"Yes, and General Tunner wants me on the ground to figure out what's going on. They have plenty of airplanes to be ferried, so there shouldn't be anything slowing them down."

"Good luck," Betty said. "If you discover the magic word that changes the hearts and minds of those male pilot instructors, let me know."

Nancy laughed. "I will. I'm still battling against sexism on a couple of fronts, even though I'm mostly surrounded by supportive men."

The following day, Nancy arrived in Love Field. The first thing on her agenda was to meet with Florene Miller and Dorothy Scott. Florene was a dark-haired woman from Texas who'd been an instructor at the War Training Program in Odessa and Lubbock before joining the WAFS. Dorothy Scott had learned to fly while attending the University of Washington and had been working as a flight instructor in Pullman when she heard about the WAFS.

"I hate to pass on gossipy things," Dorothy said as they all sat together in Florene's cramped office.

"All rumors have a kernel of truth in them, right?" Nancy asked.

"Right, and Scottie hears more than I do," Florene said, reverting to Dorothy's nickname.

Dorothy cast a quick glance at Florene, who nodded. "All right. It's like this: rumors are flying around, and girls are guessing who's going to pursuit school and who isn't. Some girls are saying they don't want to go, so that throws everything into a confusion."

Nancy frowned. "Why wouldn't they want to go to pursuit school?"

"They've heard about the risks, so . . ." Dorothy bit her lip. "They're speculating on who won't live through it."

Nancy tried to tamp down her surprise but probably didn't do a good job of it. "Flying is always a risk. Do these women not understand that?" She knew the WASP losses were certain to scare off a few, but she was surprised that pilots who'd stuck with WFTD and graduated would feel that way.

"I think the women we're sending to pursuit school should be those who've already dedicated themselves to checking out on the A-24s and A-25s," Dorothy said.

"Good point," Nancy said. "What about the two of you? You're on the list. Will you accept?"

"Definitely," Dorothy said.

"Yes, me too," Florene added. "Which other Originals will be going?"

"Helen Richards, Gertrude Meserve, Nancy Batson, Helen McGilvery, and Barbara Donahue."

"It will be a reunion," Dorothy said with a wide smile.

Nancy knew it would be much more grueling than any reunion, but her pilots could handle the challenge. Over the next two days in Dallas, she met with the instructors and the base commanders in between flights and various duties. She informed them that they were all to follow the ATC and WASP regulations and she wouldn't allow obstructions for the women pilots to transition. Also, there wouldn't be any bootleg transitions, where the women were receiving instruction without it being cleared by the commander.

When Nancy returned to Cincinnati, there was hardly time to breathe before she received the stressful news that Florene had been in a serious accident but had come through unscathed.

"What happened?" Nancy asked Florene during the late Sunday night phone call. It was two days before the girls would report to pursuit school in Palm Springs.

"I took out the P-47 for some maneuvers in the afternoon, and haze thickened to the point that the tower told me to come in early." Florene's voice cracked. "My approach was directly into the sun, and the haze made visibility almost nil. I knew the utility lines were below me, but I didn't realize how close. I hit one of the utility poles."

Nancy's pulse hammered. This could have been so much worse.

"My plane shot straight up, then went into a roll," Florene continued. "The power line was severed and the radio communication killed, so the entire airfield went dark, and I couldn't hear anything. I continued to fly, circling the field since I couldn't see a darn thing."

Nancy wished she could block the imaginings of the horror that could have so easily followed.

"The commander ordered a bunch of jeeps to form a line and illuminate the runway with their headlights," Florene said.

"And that's how you landed?"

"Yes, and somehow, right side up."

Nancy winced. "Were you worried about that?"

"I worried about everything." Florene paused. "I'm still going to pursuit school, if that's all right with you."

Nancy wasn't surprised; she was also impressed. "If you're sure. You came through a dangerous forced landing, which is no small thing."

"Right," Florene said. "I wasn't sure if the commander was going to kill me or fire me, but he was so relieved I survived that he congratulated me."

Nancy laughed, more from relief than anything else.

"You deserve congratulations on keeping a cool head through it all."

"I'll take it."

# CHAPTER THIRTY-EIGHT

"Helen [Richards] and I are roommates, and there are eight of us girls with thirty-five fellows. We spent today getting passes and entrance red tape then went to town. I'm surely sold on Palm Springs for its warm sun, beautiful mountains and quaint shops in town. This is on my 'post-war living' list. Our barracks are two-by-four with outside plumbing (building adjoining though modern interior). No hot water and sand everywhere. Tomorrow we start flying. It will be dual in BC-1s (AT-6 type). Then in order, the P-47, 39, 40 and 51. We are divided in flights A and B, fly half day, school half day. I'm in A flight and must be on the line at 7:15 each a.m. We have to wear skirts at evening mess—dern it."

—DOROTHY SCOTT, LETTER HOME, DECEMBER 1, 1943, PALM SPRINGS

*December 1943—Long Beach, California*

"Safe travels, sweetie," Bob said over the phone as Nancy sat in the Long Beach office. "Watch out for the twin peaks of the San Jacinto Mountains. And say hi to everyone for me."

Nancy already had her bag packed for her flight to Palm Springs. She wanted to check out the pursuit school and wish everyone well, plus speak to Florene in person about the P-47 crash in Dallas. "I'm looking forward to seeing how it's all running. This will be the forerunner to future groups and normalizing women advancing to more powerful aircraft."

"Yes, General Tunner is brilliant."

Nancy waited.

"And you, too, of course," Bob amended, amusement in his words. "No one is more brilliant than my wife."

Nancy laughed.

Later that day, when she arrived in Palm Springs, she found a group of women pilots, including some of the Originals, who'd joined pursuit school: Dorothy Scott, Florene Miller, Helen Richards, Helen McGilvery, Nancy Batson, Gertrude Meserve, and Barbara Donahue were all at the same table in the mess hall.

"Good afternoon, ladies," Nancy greeted them.

Dorothy scooted her chair over to make more room. "Glad you could make it."

Nancy settled among them. "How's everything so far?"

"Well, our planes are painted in camouflage, so that's taken some getting used to," Gertrude said, her blue eyes rounded. "We've been told we have to wear skirts at evening mess, but at least the food is excellent."

Everyone laughed.

"You all have flights scheduled this afternoon?" Nancy asked the group.

"Scottie is going up in the AT-6 trainer with her instructor," Florene said, motioning with her fork toward Dorothy. "I'll go up after her."

"Great, I'll come out and watch the takeoffs and landings." This would be a good opportunity to speak one-on-one with Florene about her accident.

"I wrote all our complaints to my twin brother," Dorothy said. "I'm sure he'll appreciate the news. But mostly, I bragged about being here." She turned her smile upon Nancy. "Thank you for selecting me for pursuit school. It's such a privilege."

The other women voiced their thanks as well.

"It is pretty swell," Florene said with a huge smile.

The women continued to talk, catching each other up on recent letters from home and discussing war news about how the Italians had surrendered to the Allies in September, though the Germans had rescued Mussolini. In October, Italy had joined the Allies and declared war on Germany. And in November, the British had performed an air raid on Berlin.

"I'm ready to head out," Florene eventually said. "Who's coming?"

Nancy cleared the table with the others, and everyone dispersed. She walked with Dorothy and Florene to the hangar and shook hands with the instructor, 2nd Lt. Robert M. Snyder. Once Dorothy and her instructor had finished their precheck on the AT-6, Nancy waved them off, then turned to Florene.

"How are you doing out here? Any nerves when flying since your forced landing?"

Florene hesitated. "Not when flying in general, but I don't like to fly close to sunset, even if it's only circling the airfield. I guess my brain is telling me to take more precautions and not fly when it's extra windy or get stuck in the dark."

"I understand." Nancy looked toward the control tower that was busy giving planes clearance to take off and directing other planes to land. "The wind is light today."

"Yes, four miles per hour out of the northwest," Florene said. "Although there's a high overcast, it won't mess with visibility of the runway."

They watched Dorothy do takeoffs and landings with her instructor a couple of times in the AT-6. They continued to talk and watch the incoming and outgoing flights, including a P-39.

"There's Scottie again," Florene said. "This will be her final approach, then it's my turn."

Nancy spotted Dorothy's plane descending toward the runway. A form appeared behind her, higher in altitude but very close.

Nancy frowned and shielded her eyes. It was another plane, no doubt about that. "What's that P-39 doing?"

"Does he not see Scottie's plane right below him?" Florene said, panic sharp in her voice. "He's way too close."

Florene began to jog toward the runway, waving her arms, although there was no way the pilots would notice her.

Nancy ran after her.

Surely the tower had seen the close proximity of the P-39 and could warn it. But as Nancy ran, she saw what she never wanted to see. The P-39 collided with the AT-6, and the tail section of the AT-6 was severed.

Her heart jolted as she watched both planes veer off their courses, then plummet straight toward the earth. There wasn't far to go.

Her stomach lurched, and she stopped, staring in disbelief and horror. Florene had also stopped a few feet ahead of her.

Both planes struck the ground not far from each other in a terrible, gut-wrenching crunch. All hopes for a different outcome were shredded to bits.

Nancy began to run again. In the back of her mind, she heard jeeps and emergency vehicles, and seconds later, they roared past her toward the wreckage. Dark smoke billowed up from both planes, but still, Nancy and Florene ran.

Suddenly, the AT-6 containing Dorothy and her instructor burst into flames as the jeeps came to a stop near them.

Florene cried out and sank to her knees as the orange flames consumed Dorothy's plane. Nancy stood rooted to the ground, arms wrapped about her torso as horror vibrated through her. Perhaps Dorothy had bailed out? But Nancy knew there'd been no time. Both planes had been too close to the ground.

Maybe Dorothy had crawled out of the plane before it had burst into flames?

But as the terrible minutes crept by, there was no sign of any pilots having escaped. Nancy tasted ash in her mouth, and smoke seemed to burn through her lungs.

Others gathered around them in stunned silence, and Nancy helped Florene to her feet. Pulling Florene into her arms, Nancy really had no words of comfort. No words at all.

In one horrific instant, Dorothy was suddenly gone. She'd been so full of life, so excited about pursuit school, and so invested in making sure transitions were being done right and fairly.

Somehow, Nancy made it through the next couple of hours. All three pilots had died—Dorothy Scott, her instructor Snyder, and the pilot of the P-39. Nancy felt like she was living in a disturbing dream that she couldn't wake up from when she met with the commander of the base, who determined that the pilot of the P-39 hadn't seen the AT-6 below because of his banking altitude and the position of the low sun.

"Your pilot was not at fault," the commander told both Nancy and Florene. "I know that's a very small comfort, but I also have an idea of what the WASP pilots have been up against. The tower could see everything as it played out, and the warning didn't come fast enough. The P-39 pilot wasn't given clearance to land."

All very small comforts, but Nancy knew they'd be important in the days to come. Right now, she had a grieving squadron and a family to inform.

As she and Florene walked out of the commander's office, the velvety evening air made the entire incident feel surreal.

She turned to Florene. "How are you holding up?"

Florene paused in her step and dabbed her face with a handkerchief. Her eyes were rimmed red and her nose chafed and raw. "I can't believe it . . . I mean, I watched it, but it seems unreal."

"I know." Nancy dragged in a breath. "We need to notify her family. This will be difficult, but can you call her parents and her brother, Ed? You were her squadron leader and have spent the most time with her—I think they'd want to hear it from you."

Florene's eyes filled with tears again, but she said with resolve, "Of course. I'll do it."

Nancy set a hand on Florene's arm. "It won't be easy, but it's important. When I called Cornelia Fort's family, they were upset but also grateful that Cornelia had been doing what she loved. And, of course, it helped them to know that the accident wasn't her fault."

Florene sniffled. "I'll let Scottie's family know."

Nancy pulled her into a hug and held on tight for a moment. "We can do this. It's hard and shocking right now, but we also need to find ways to prevent this from happening again."

Florene drew away and wiped at her eyes. "The tower has already admitted to fault."

"Right, but I think the planes need to be more visible. An overcast day and a desert terrain makes the camouflage paint nearly impossible to see. Which is the entire point of camouflage, but maybe not for a training school."

That night, Nancy spoke to Bob over the phone with the lights off in one of the offices. That way, she could look out the window and see the gathered stars spread across the sky.

She'd been stoic for several hours, trying to hold herself together and make the decisions that needed to be made. But with Bob, she could cry and rant, and he'd be a sounding board, one not telling her to calm down.

"I can't believe that pilot didn't see her plane," Nancy said. "I mean, it happened, so it's possible, but the tragedy is completely senseless. A complete waste. Dorothy was such a lovely human being."

"I'm sorry you had to witness that," Bob said softly. "I can't imagine what that must have felt like."

"I think I was in shock," she said. "Florene too. It's like we saw the crash happening but couldn't fully comprehend it all."

"Do you want me to come to Palm Springs?"

"No," Nancy said, even though she wanted to see him more than ever. "I'm not staying past tomorrow. I've asked Florene to contact the family, and she'll be accompanying the body home."

"I can meet you somewhere else," he offered. "Name the place."

Nancy rubbed at her forehead, feeling a headache building. "Stay put. I'm stopping again in Dallas on my way back. We have more damage control to do. With nearly 300 WASP in operation now, we need to make sure all our hard work to get the women to transition to the pursuits isn't going to be compromised." She released a thready breath. "It sounds coldhearted, I know, but Florene's accident wasn't too long ago, and now Dorothy's." She closed her eyes.

"What can I do?" Bob asked.

"Just answer the phone when I call," she said. "I'm sorry it's so late tonight, but I guess you're used to me waking you up."

"I am, and it's not a problem." Bob's voice lowered. "You'll get through this. We all will. Dorothy was a victim of an accident. Nothing was her fault. She loved her job, and she probably wouldn't have changed many things about her choices."

"She was tickled to join pursuit school." She moved her gaze to the window and the silent stars there. "I wish that pilot had been flying a different route."

The next day, Nancy made her stop in Dallas, met with the commander to go over her agenda, then reviewed the reports on Florene's accident.

A couple of days after that, Florene reported to Nancy how everything was going with the funeral plans for Dorothy.

"Her twin brother, Ed, is a remarkable man," Florene said. "He acknowledged that a lot of American families are sacrificing for this war. And sometimes, we have to pay dearly."

Nancy's eyes filled, and she gripped the receiver tighter.

"Ed told me that his sister always wanted to be first in everything, and now she's also first in death." Florene's voice cracked. "He believes she's up there, first to lead the family into eternity. Waiting for everyone."

Nancy wiped at the tears on her face. "Thank you for sharing that. I needed to hear it." She drew in a breath. "I have to ask you, Florene, do you want to finish pursuit school?"

"Yes," Florene said without hesitation. "What happened to Dorothy shook me up, but it's part of the flying risk. We all know it, yet we all continue."

"All right, then. After pursuit school, you'll transfer to Long Beach," Nancy said. "It's the rule if a pilot washes out on an airplane."

"I understand. I'd be happy to work under someone else for a bit."

"B.J. will take care of you," Nancy said, her heart aching. They all took care of each other, and losing one of their own had left a hole.

"I've no doubt," Florene said. "I'm grateful to each of you. How did it go in Dallas?"

"There's a lot of work to be done," Nancy said. "But it's all necessary and will be good in the long run. I'm recommending that the transition department be much more thorough. Each student needs more technical training as well. I'm also going to make it clear that just because a woman becomes a WASP, she's not automatically qualified to advance to pursuit school."

"Agreed," Florene said. "Everyone should be judged on her own merits. That's what Scottie was pushing for too."

"Exactly. And if a student is borderline on the qualifications, she needs to remain in training until she can easily transition. But I'm also emphasizing that if a woman doesn't want to fly pursuit, she's not required to. Regardless, we're going to encourage the transition. Dallas has been struggling the most, but now we'll use that experience to set a higher standard for everyone."

"Thank you, Nancy, for everything," Florene said. "I don't think you get enough credit doing so much of the behind-the-scenes work. I'm sure you'd rather be flying like the rest of us."

"I'm flying much more lately than I have been," Nancy mused. "Mostly to pave the way. We're all contributing where we can the most."

It wasn't until the first training group of the six Originals and several of Houston's graduates finished pursuit school and began successfully ferrying the larger planes that Nancy finally felt the loss of Dorothy Scott had been honored.

# CHAPTER THIRTY-NINE

"We completed our checkout by the end of the third day (despite an engine fire during the first flight) and thereafter demonstrated our ship, Ladybird, decorated with a painting of Fifinella on the nose, at the very heavy bomber training base at Alamogordo, New Mexico. After a short time, the purpose of the flights had been achieved. The male flight crews, their egos challenged, approached the B-29 with new enthusiasm and found it to be not a beast, but a smooth, delicately rigged, and responsive ship."

—DORA DOUGHERTY

*January–March 1944—Cincinnati, Ohio*

Nancy paced her Cincinnati office as she waited for the WASP squadron commanders and their assistants to arrive for the meeting she'd called. The tide of the war was changing, and the push for militarizing the women was gaining traction. Changes were happening, and they were happening fast.

But today would be a hard day, for all of them.

The brisk clip of heeled shoes sounded from the corridor, and Nancy crossed to the doorway of her office.

As she watched the group of women walk toward her, impeccably dressed in WASP blues, pride swelled within her. Most of them were the Originals, women Nancy had served with for nearly two years now. Women she'd trusted and worked with and challenged and learned from.

She greeted each one as nerves thrummed through her. There weren't any other women on the planet who Nancy trusted more. She needed them more than ever. Would they rise to the challenge she was about to issue? No matter how difficult?

After everyone took the chairs Nancy had brought into the office, she said, "Yesterday, I learned that several of you took it upon yourselves to meet with commanders of various groups and push ahead an agenda that hasn't been approved by myself or General Tunner."

The faces looking back at her were a mixture of surprise and embarrassment.

Nancy folded her arms. "This meeting is not to reprimand any of you but to get everything out in the open. We need to communicate with each other, and we need to respect our superiors who have been tasked with running the Ferrying Program." She looked over at Betty Gillies. "Betty, can you fill everyone in?"

Betty's cheeks flushed, but she stood and faced the others. "First, I need to explain myself. We all know about the militarization bill, and we all know how long it's been in the works. There's always a delay. We also know that major changes are coming. American pilots are doing amazing things in this war, and the casualties have been a lot less than General Arnold projected. Which, of course, is excellent news. On the war front, American troops have infiltrated and are gaining ground in New Guinea, Italy, Burma, and the Marshall Islands, to name a few."

All heads nodded. Everyone read war news whenever possible.

Betty continued. "We didn't discuss militarization directly as WAFS, and we've been avoiding the subject as WASP. It's like we've all been tiptoeing around it. We're set on doing our jobs and not getting involved in the politics. But I wanted to change that, and I . . ." She cut a glance to Nancy, who merely motioned for her to continue. "I jumped ahead and took matters into my own hands."

The room went absolutely silent.

"I took B.J., Delphine, and Esther to Washington, DC, with me. We met with Jackie Cochran to find out her agenda. The meeting wasn't really productive, and we didn't get any definitive answers, but it was certainly an interesting two hours."

A few of the other women smiled.

"Then we met with the Navy—since they've made inquiries about the use of women ferry pilots."

Several women exchanged glances.

"Our next stop was the Pentagon, where we spoke with Brigadier General William E. Hall, who, as you know, is the deputy chief of Air Staff." Betty drew in a breath and met the wide-eyed stares. "I asked him how to go about receiving a commission in the Army of the United States as a service pilot. He was very supportive and said, 'By golly, if you can, that would solve all our problems.'"

No one moved for a long moment, until Avanell Pinckley asked, "So, you want to militarize under the Army and not the WAC or the Air Force?"

"Yes, that was the goal." Betty looked again at Nancy. "I couldn't find anything in the Army or AAF regulations that would prevent this. I hoped that this could happen without government legislation. It would also mean that the WASP could be militarized and kept out of the WAC. It was a plan I believed to be solid, but I executed it in the wrong way."

The air in the room seemed electric with curiosity.

Betty bowed her head and took a seat, so Nancy finished. "Unfortunately, I didn't know of any of this, or I would have deterred Betty." Nancy folded her arms. "We can't supersede the Arnold-Cochran plan, no matter how much we don't want to be militarized under Cochran's leadership. I had to order everyone back to their bases because although this grassroots effort was done with honest intentions, it put the base commanders in a tough spot." She took a chair and leaned forward. "The cost of this unauthorized trip has to be repaid, which I know that Betty and the rest of you involved intended to do anyway. But the bottom line is that the transportation requests weren't authorized in the first place."

B.J. lifted a hand. "I must also confess to something. I thought if I applied as a service pilot under my initials B.J. Erickson, I would get accepted. I've apologized to Nancy, but I owe an apology to everyone in this room. You've given me your trust, and I've violated it. Please accept my sincerest apology."

Heads bobbed around the room.

"We understand you all had good intentions," Nancy said. "Unfortunately, we received word that an official directive has been sent out by Air Staff Personnel, and it was clarified that only men could be commissioned as officers in the Army of the United States."

"So, we went on a wild goose chase, and it ended up backfiring," Betty said in a dull tone.

Nancy clasped her hands together. "A few positives came of it, despite things." Everyone looked at her with interest. "We discovered how supportive General Hall was of the idea, which will light a few more fires—in good places. Most importantly, no matter any of our personal feelings, we need to have a united front with Cochran. We need to pull together and fight on the same team. We can't allow the newspapers to pit myself and Cochran against each other. Nothing will get accomplished then. In February, Costello will reintroduce the WASP bill to Congress, and our reputation needs to be squeaky clean."

Since the Costello bill hadn't passed Congress but had instead gone into review by the House Committee on Military Affairs, then a subsequent amendment, it would soon be reintroduced.

Everyone in the room nodded.

"Early in the war, the RAF pilots were given three months to live," Nancy said soberly. "Once the US joined, the pilot casualties have only gone down. This means, of course, that the Pilot Training Programs are being cut back, and some of the men are returning home, in need of jobs."

Nancy didn't need to overexplain what that might mean for the WASP Program, which was another reason to push for militarizing the WASP.

After answering a couple of questions, she dismissed the meeting, but everyone stayed around to chat. She moved to Betty and gave her a long hug. When Nancy drew away, Betty's eyes were wet.

"You don't hate me?" Betty asked.

"I don't hate you," Nancy said. "I think what you did was brave but couldn't work for various reasons."

Later that night, she reported all that had gone on to Bob.

"You're doing a fine job, sweetie," he said into the phone. "The WASP need to remain unified and stay ahead of petty administration details."

"Yes, but why does it have to be so hard?" Nancy asked. "My teeth are getting smaller from gritting them so much."

"Stop reading the reports about Cochran."

Nancy scoffed. "If only it were that easy. I'm like a bee attracted to the honey."

"I understand that," he mused, "but what I want to know is, When will I see you again? I'm tired of these phone calls. I'm heading to the Pacific at the end of February, and I don't want to wait until after."

"We both have rechecks due, so let's meet and do them together."

"You're brilliant—have I told you that? Someplace warm, please?"

"Long Beach it is." Nancy was smiling by the time she hung up with her husband. She had to do a recheck on the B-17 to keep her qualification, and Bob had to do a recheck on instruments.

Seeing Bob was always too short of a reunion and was filled with other people and busyness. When February arrived, they met in Long Beach, and the stolen moments were sweet but only made her long for the war to end and to live once again in the same place with Bob.

Before seeing him off again, she told him of her plan to stop at Sweetwater on her way back to Cincinnati. The WASP Class 44-2 was graduating, and at the same time, B.J. would be receiving the Air Medal. General Hap Arnold would be in attendance as well as Jackie Cochran.

"You'll be brilliant, as always," Bob told Nancy, pulling her into a hug.

"Maybe I will, but I'm still anxious about it all."

Bob kissed the top of her head, his arms still around her. "What's your biggest worry?"

"That I'll snap and say something I regret." She sighed against him. "There's no reason to. I've literally lectured my squadron leaders to focus on our shared goals and rise above pettiness."

"There. You'll do that. You always keep your cool around others— why would this graduation ceremony be any different?"

"You're right." She lifted her face. "As usual."

Bob grinned, creasing the lines that had deepened about his eyes over the years. He was the same man, though, the same Bob.

"Cochran and I need to discuss the upcoming hearings," she said. "We'll be attending them together, with General Arnold."

"See?" Bob said, his blue gaze tender. "Everyone is on the same team now, and you'll keep emotions in check." He leaned down, and she let her eyes flutter shut as he pressed a kiss on her mouth—a kiss tasting of warmth and home.

"Be safe, will you?" she murmured after a moment. "I don't want any tragic phone calls."

"The same goes for you, sweetie."

The morning of March 11, 1944, dawned bright and clear. The Texas sky was a giant swath of blue coming in through the small window of Nancy's quarters at Sweetwater. She'd heard plenty of adventurous stories of the barracks living conditions, from how the women had to check their boots and pant legs for scorpions in the morning to the constant dust to the invasion of locusts. On the hotter nights, some women dragged their cots outside to sleep, and more than one rattlesnake had been found curled up on the cots in the morning, not to mention the crickets that joined them as well.

Nancy donned her full WASP uniform, adjusted the Santiago blue tie against the pressed collar, then pinned her beret into place. As a final touch, she added a swipe of Montezuma red lipstick. There would be plenty of photos today, and she needed to appear the official part. After graduation, she'd meet with Arnold and Cochran to go over Arnold's hearing statement.

It was good to see B.J., who looked elegant in her crisp WASP uniform, and Nancy kept her focus on her friend. Arnold pinned the medal on B.J.'s jacket lapel himself, and after the ceremony and the graduation speeches, Nancy congratulated B.J. once again. Then Nancy entertained some questions from the graduating WASP, after which she headed into Cochran's office.

Nancy greeted Cochran briefly, who nodded with a tight smile.

"Thank you for coming, both of you," Arnold cut in before there could be any more small talk. "Let's all sit." He motioned to the chairs, and Nancy settled in.

She thought of what Bob had said, and she forced her shoulders to relax.

"Let's jump right into it," Arnold said. "I'll be the only witness at the hearing, and I want both of you in full uniform at my side. Ethel Sheehy will also join us. We're familiar with the controversy that's been stirred up—pitting Mrs. Love against Miss Cochran—so we need to show a united front."

"I agree," Nancy replied. Ethel was the chief recruiting officer for the WASP, hired on by Cochran. Nancy glanced at Cochran, and though Cochran's shoulders seemed to stiffen, she didn't respond.

"Excellent," Arnold said. "Any questions from either of you?"

Cochran folded her arms.

Since Cochran didn't offer anything up, Nancy said, "I do have a question actually. What is the summary of the revised Costello bill?"

Arnold clasped his hands. "In general, that existing regulations hold out until the end of the war, so women will remain as flight officers or as students."

Nancy had no qualms about this.

Finally, Cochran had a comment. "Female flight cadets will be commissioned as second lieutenants in the AUS once they graduate from training."

This sounded fine to Nancy as well.

Arnold jumped in again. "The women will receive the same pay as the men in the Army. They'll also be entitled to the same benefits, rights, and privileges."

"According to their rank, of course, and length of service," Cochran filled in.

"Fair enough." Nancy drew in a slow breath and ignored the uptick of her pulse. Everything had been fine and cordial so far. "Is the hearing statement prepared? Can I read it?"

Arnold's brows twitched. "It's prepared, and you'll receive a copy of it later on." His comment was plainly dismissive. "Any other questions?"

Both Arnold and Cochran were gazing at her so intently that if Nancy did have more questions, she'd probably pass on them. As it was, the meeting had been very brief—much quicker and neater than she had expected.

"Thank you for giving me an idea of what to expect." Nancy stood and straightened her jacket. "I'll see you at the committee hearing."

Arnold and Cochran rose, and Nancy shook hands with each of them, then left the office. There was still plenty of daylight, and she planned to begin her trip back to Ohio.

The day finally arrived, and on March 22, 1944, General Arnold stood before the House Armed Services Committee, joined by Nancy, Jackie Cochran, and Ethel Sheehy—all wearing their WASP uniforms. Arnold spoke with directness and friendliness, and Nancy was impressed with how the committee seemed interested and open to everything he proposed.

When she called Betty later to report, Nancy said, "I never thought I'd say this, but General Arnold was brilliant. I understand now why he's in his position. He's respected for his opinion and authority. Also, having me, Cochran, and Sheehy flanking him, showing unified support, was perfect."

Betty laughed softly. "I never thought you'd compliment that man, but you're setting the standard once again."

"Now we need to avoid bad press," Nancy said with a sigh.

Maybe it had been a premonition, or maybe it had become second nature for Nancy to have her dealings reported on, but the newspapers lambasted the WASP bill. There were a few supporting opinions published, but Nancy felt furious when she read some of the articles. It seemed that everyone was complaining. Veterans' organizations wrote to Congress, saying that the women were taking jobs from the men. Male civilian flying instructors complained, and parents complained that their sons, who were aviation cadets, were now being transferred to infantry.

Since the ACAA WTS Program that trained the pilots had been terminated in January and the AAF had started its own pilot cutbacks, suddenly, WASP pilots were seen as a threat. The returning combat pilots still wanted jobs flying too. Which meant they wanted to take the utility pilot jobs and replace the women.

Between the laid-off flight instructors, the returning combat pilots, and the veterans' organizations, a full publicity campaign was growing, and everything was aimed at denigrating the WASP.

With Bob in Australia on assignment, Nancy spent a restless night, then hurried into her office early the next morning.

Tunner was already in his office, and Nancy wasn't surprised.

She tapped on his partially open door.

"Come in," Tunner said in a tired voice.

As she stepped into his office, she winced at the sight of his disheveled hair and red-rimmed eyes. If she hadn't known better, she would have thought he had a hangover.

"Did you even sleep last night?" Nancy said.

"For a short while." Tunner motioned to the chair on the other side of the desk. "I assume you read the evening papers?"

Nancy sat and gripped the bag she carried. "I did. I want to write a rebuttal and send it to every newspaper. I hate to have all the work that Costello did on the bill be completely wasted." She fully expected Tunner to have some argument, but instead, he surprised her.

"I've already started one. Well, several."

He slid the paper over to her. "Ignore the scratch-outs. It's rough."

Nancy scanned through the page. "This is good." She took his pencil and made a few notations. "Have you talked to General Arnold?"

"I called him first thing, even though it's early yet," Tunner said. "He has a concern that he didn't share with me before—he was the only witness who went before the committee. He thinks that demonstrates bias right from the start."

She hadn't thought of it that way before, but now she agreed with Arnold.

"Mrs. Love," Tunner said, becoming formal. "I've also spoken to General George. He's asking me to compile a comprehensive report on the WASP pilots and their job skills, responsibilities, and performance at the Ferrying Division. I will include input from the squadron commanders as well as pursuit school." He drummed his fingers on the desk. "If this escalates into an investigation, like we think it might, we want you to give the deposition."

# CHAPTER FORTY

"Aviation will soar ahead, though its progress between our
1903 flight and today still takes my breath away. Women
even fly military planes now! What kind of girl would want
to fly an experimental jet? A pioneer like me, maybe?"

—ORVILLE WRIGHT IN CONVERSATION WITH
ANN BAUMGARTNER, WRIGHT FIELD, OHIO, 1944

*April 1944—Cincinnati, Ohio*

Nancy hadn't been feeling well all morning, and she was about to
head out of her office to speak to Tunner when her phone rang. She
paused, debating, then finally answered it.

The man on the other end of the line said, "I'm calling from the
New Cumberland airport in Pennsylvania, on behalf of Evelyn Sharp. Is
this Nancy Love?"

Nancy immediately went on alert. She didn't know the caller, but
she knew that Evelyn had requested RON the night before because of
bad weather over the Allegheny Mountains. Nancy had just met with
her on April 1 in the Cincinnati office. Evelyn had checked out on the
P-38, and her assignment this week was to deliver a P-38J to Newark.
"This is Nancy Love," she said into the phone.

"Mrs. Love," the caller said. "I'm sorry to inform you that Miss
Sharp was killed this morning shortly after takeoff. Her plane's engine
went down, and there was no recovering."

A flash of disbelief shot through Nancy, hot and fast. "She didn't
bail out?" she asked in a whisper. How could this have happened to
sweet Evelyn? She was only twenty-four, one of the Originals, and one
of the brightest pilots.

"Unfortunately, there wouldn't have been time. She hadn't even
cleared the trees."

Nancy's mind reeled with questions. She needed as much information as she could get. This wasn't a time to crumple into a chair and block out the world. "Tell me everything you know."

As the airfield employee spoke, Nancy wrote notes so she'd remember them later and could report to Tunner. Her hand shook as she recorded the details, and her stomach felt like it had turned inside out. Apparently, when Evelyn had landed at New Cumberland, she'd mentioned that one of her engines had been giving her trouble. This morning, everything had seemed fine in the precheck, and she'd been cleared for takeoff by the tower.

Evelyn had taken off, and almost immediately, black smoke had begun to pour out from the left engine. The P-38 had gone into a stall, then the left wingtip had clipped a cluster of trees, and the plane had dropped. She'd been in the air for one minute.

After hanging up, Nancy took a steadying breath, her eyes hot with tears. She dialed the Wilmington office, and Helen Mary Clark answered the phone. She'd taken over for Betty Gillies when Betty had been reassigned to Farmingdale.

"Helen," Nancy said. "Are you sitting down?"

"I am," Helen said warily.

Nancy dragged in a breath. "Evelyn's been killed in a P-38." She spilled everything, her voice choking with emotion.

"Not Evelyn," Helen said with anguish. "Why would she fly with a problem engine? Or did they tell her it was fixed when it wasn't?"

"We'll get to the bottom of that later." The pressure in Nancy's chest only tightened. Evelyn had been set to take over as the commander of the new women's squadron in Palm Springs since the pursuit school had been moved to Brownsville, Texas. "We need to get Evelyn's body back from Harrisburg, then accompany it to her home in Ord, Nebraska. Probably by train. Can you assign Nancy Batson? I know she's in Farmingdale, waiting to take a P-47 over to Newark, but can you have her return to Wilmington immediately?"

"Of course," Helen said. "You don't want to be the one to take Evelyn to Nebraska?"

Nancy paused, her throat like a vice. "No. I can't." Now wasn't the time to confess that she still wasn't over the death of Cornelia Fort. She simply couldn't face another funeral. "We're taking up a collection to present to her parents. There'll be no money coming in from insurance or death benefits, as you know, since we're not militarized."

"I'll reach out to everyone," Helen said in a quiet voice. "I'm so sorry, Nancy."

"We all are."

After Nancy hung up the phone, she slammed her palm onto the surface of the desk. The pain of the action was muffled by the pain in her heart. Steeling herself, she rose and walked stiffly to the door, then headed to Tunner's office to let him know the latest tragedy.

Three Originals had now been lost.

After speaking to Tunner, the numbness had worn off. There was much to be done. And she still had to prepare for the upcoming deposition she'd be giving to the Committee on the Civil Service of the House of Representatives.

By the time she got to her apartment, her head was pounding, and her throat felt sore and swollen. She checked the medicine cabinet for some aspirin when she noticed a few red spots on her neck. Upon closer inspection, she found red spots on her upper arms and on her back. She realized she'd itched throughout the night and this morning without paying much attention to it . . . It had to be chickenpox.

Over the next two weeks, Nancy dealt with isolation due to chickenpox, fighting to not scratch herself raw and getting updates by phone from Nancy Batson about Evelyn's funeral. Nancy spent sleepless hours trying to combat the itchiness by writing long letters to Bob in Australia. She moved through the rest of her duties with a heavy heart as the newspapers continued reporting on the lambasting of the WASP bill.

The pilot shortage at the Ferrying Division, which the bombing of Pearl Harbor had instigated, couldn't be denied, so Nancy couldn't understand why the WASP bill was being so heavily criticized. The bill wouldn't go to the House until June, so Nancy hoped her deposition would make a difference.

The waiting felt agonizing, but thankfully, Bob was back in the US after his Australia assignment by the time the date of the deposition arrived.

"I'll come in with you," Bob said the morning of the big day. They'd been able to spend a few precious, short days at their apartment in DC together. "I'll wait in the lobby until you're finished. I want to make sure you'll be all right. It's so soon after Evelyn."

Nancy exhaled, blinking against the stinging in her eyes. "I'm doing this for all the WASP, especially for Evelyn, who literally gave her life for the program. Her family received no benefits for her sacrifice, and some of these families can't afford much." She reached for Bob's hand. "They can't use the excuse that we've negligently lost pilots in the program— we've lost some, yes, but even General Arnold has pointed out that the total casualties are much less than expected."

Bob squeezed her hand. "I can still come."

"I don't know if having you there would look good or bad. Good because my husband is supportive of his WASP wife. Or bad because you work for ATC, and they might think there's unfair favoritism going on."

Bob's forehead creased, but his gaze didn't waver. "I understand. I'll be the one pacing like mad behind closed doors."

"It's just a deposition, Bob." Nancy rose up on her toes and kissed his cheek. "I'm answering questions I could answer in my sleep." At least, that was what she kept telling herself.

Bob's hands moved to her waist. "You do talk in your sleep."

"Hardly."

"Okay, you mumble."

Nancy smirked, then she looped her arms around her husband's neck. "Have I told you that you're wonderful?"

"Not for a while." The edge of his mouth lifted. "Are you about to tell me now?"

"I am." She gave him a light kiss. "You're wonderful. But don't let it go to your head. We need fewer egos in the world."

Bob chuckled, then kissed her back. "Go get 'em, sweetie."

Nancy smiled, even though her pulse had started a low thrum. She'd be happy to refute claims of women pilots being favored over the men or that women were given better assignments or even that men were doing ground assignments while the women were flying the planes in their stead.

That Sunday morning in April was a busy one overseas. The morning news reported that the Soviets had driven out the final pockets of German resistance in Yalta. The British RAF flew air raids from bases in Italy, targeting Romania. And American warships in the Atlantic Ocean sank the German submarine U-550.

Less than an hour later, Nancy took her seat in the stark deposition room before the Committee on the Civil Service of the House of Representatives. Across the table sat the two male investigators for the Ramspeck Committee who were tasked with questioning her: Colonel McCormick and Mr. Shillito. Robert J. Ramspeck, who was a congressman from Georgia and a former deputy US Marshall, was the man leading the WASP investigation and the one who had formed the committee.

"Mrs. Love," Colonel McCormick began, "how would you rate the qualifications of the girls who graduated from the training school at Avenger Field?"

"The women are good pilots." She hoped the nervousness pulsing through her would settle down. "We follow the same regulations and qualifiers as the male graduates of the Training Command."

The stenographer typed her answers as Nancy spoke, and Nancy tried to ignore the tapping sound.

Mr. Shillito asked the next question, his gaze owllike through dark-rimmed glasses. "What is the policy on pursuit pilots?"

Nancy wasn't sure if such a simple question needed an answer, but she obliged. "We need pursuit pilots."

Mr. Shillito waited for more, but that was Nancy's answer.

McCormick spoke next, his dark mustache sporting a bit of salted gray. "Mrs. Love, what is the relationship between you and Miss Cochran?"

Nancy tamped down the frustration at the question, but she'd expected this line of interrogation, so she was prepared. "Miss Cochran oversees the administrative duties of the WASP, and I handle the operations side."

McCormick's expression didn't change, but there was a sternness there. "Would you say that you and Miss Cochran have conflicting opinions?"

Nancy chose her wording carefully. "There is no battle between us, sir."

Neither man appeared convinced, but they could believe what they may. Just because she and Cochran had differences of opinion didn't mean they were in some sort of *battle*. There was enough war going on in the world.

The next question from Mr. Shillito wasn't a surprise either. "Why do the girls want to be militarized?"

Nancy had heard many reasons over the past year, but they all narrowed down to a handful. "For recognition and protection. When a female civilian pilot arrives to pick up an airplane, she isn't always trusted and is sometimes viewed as a spy. Also, if the female pilots were militarized, they'd receive compensation and insurance for their families, as the male pilots do."

The stenographer typed away.

McCormick's next question was unexpected. "Off the record, Mrs. Love, how much do you think the uniform is worth?"

Besides the fact that the fabrics were good quality and a fashion designer had designed it under the tutelage of Cochran? "I have no idea, sir. I haven't taken an interest in clothing, as others might."

The men glanced at each other, then Shillito asked, "What items are issued? What are purchased?"

This was straightforward, at least. "The basic uniforms are issued," she said. "We're given two winter and two summer ones. All accessories are purchased by the women."

"How much are *you* paid?" Shillito pushed up his glasses.

"I'm paid $142.08 every two weeks."

"And the other WAFS?"

She thought it was interesting he said WAFS instead of WASP. "$250 a month. Overtime hours takes it to about $280." She didn't know why this needed to be asked in a deposition. Payroll was a firm detail, not an opinion.

"Mrs. Love," McCormick said next. "Which girls are competing for Air Medals?"

She had to tamp down a laugh as she remembered how B.J. had felt mortified to be awarded the medal. B.J. had been doing her job, no more than any other pilot had. "I have no idea what you mean, sir," Nancy said pointedly, although she was proud of herself for keeping calm. At least on the outside. "The Air Medal was awarded to Miss Erickson."

McCormick's mustache twitched. "How did Miss Erickson make those deliveries so fast?"

Again, Nancy suppressed a laugh. "Well, the weather was good, sir. Miss Erickson is a good pilot and a hard worker. She also had fast airplanes."

Neither of the men seemed amused.

The questions continued, and she had no trouble answering them. She only had to keep her mirth in check.

When the deposition was finally over, she was asked to sign the six-page document. She shook everyone's hands, including the stenographer's. Walking out of the office, Nancy held her head high, pleased with her answers. She had been direct. She hadn't faltered. And now it felt like a weight of stones had been lifted from her shoulders.

As she headed to her car, her step was light and her heart happy. Then she paused on the sidewalk. A young boy across the street shouted the most recent newspaper headlines: "Today has been declared Black Sunday! Massive number of US fighter planes lost!"

Nancy's pleasant mood evaporated in a blink. She waited for a passing car, then crossed the street. Paying for the copy, she stood a few paces from the newspaper boy and read the headlines.

The US Fifth Air Force division had successfully completed a bombing raid over Hollandia, New Guinea, but upon return, twenty-six planes had been lost in foul weather. The three squadrons of the 475th Fighter Group had lost more men in this single mission, due to weather, than it ever had in a combat mission.

Nancy's eyes burned, and swallowing became impossible. The war news was terrible every day, even when Allied forces prevailed. Why was this so different from any other news? Because it involved pilots and bad weather? A risk for every pilot?

Nancy folded the paper and continued to her car, her mind wandering to the men lost in those planes and the families who'd received the devastating news. War was truly a waste, for everyone. On the earth or in the skies, at home or abroad. Everyone was suffering some sort of loss, and maybe Nancy could be grateful that her brother had never been sent into combat. Hadn't ever endured the unspeakable.

By the time she reached the apartment and stepped into Bob's arms, she felt ready to collapse.

"Was it so terrible?" Bob asked gently, his hand slowly moving up and down her back.

"The deposition was fine. Partly ridiculous but mostly fine," she said, muffled against his chest.

"Then, what's wrong, sweetie?"

She drew away from him. "I read the newspaper—have you been listening to the radio?"

A line appeared between his eyebrows. "No, I've been on the phone a lot. What's happened?"

She pulled out the newspaper tucked inside her handbag.

Bob snapped open the paper and began to read as he slowly walked to the couch. Sitting down, he read the entire article, his face grave, before he looked up at her. "I can't imagine why they were ordered to fly into near-hurricane conditions."

"I can't either."

Bob's gaze moved over her. "Come here. Sit. I'll make you something to eat. What are you hungry for?"

Nancy joined him on the couch and leaned her head against his shoulder. "I'm not hungry. I want to sleep for a day or two. Is that possible? Can you take my calls?"

Bob's chuckle was soft, and he set his arm around her. "You can sleep as much as you want today, but tomorrow, I'm afraid we both have to get back to work."

She nestled closer to him. "I don't want to miss any of our time together, so I shouldn't sleep too much."

He pressed a kiss on the top of her head. "I'll feel better knowing you won't be flying back to Ohio in a catatonic state."

Nancy closed her eyes, breathing in Bob's familiar scent. "Don't think about moving. I'm comfortable."

Whether or not she would have actually fallen asleep would never be discovered because the phone rang. And rang. Bob finally answered, and it was clear he was speaking to Tunner. Bob looked over at her, as if asking her permission to hand off the phone.

"I'm awake," she said and rose on aching limbs. She answered Tunner's call and gave him a rundown of the deposition.

He congratulated her, but she felt no warmth from it. Her countrymen overseas were in a literal fight for their lives, and now her country was questioning the value of the WASP Program. Squirreling for nonexistent infractions. Shouldn't they all be working for a common cause and fighting for a common goal? Instead of asking petty questions about the cost of a uniform or if there was friction between herself and Cochran?

None of that mattered in the long run. Bringing the war to an end and stopping the senseless loss of life was what mattered.

As Tunner summarized his own findings for the report he was putting together, one thing stood out to Nancy. He'd found that the WASP pilots were logging in fewer hours than the male pilots. In addition, regardless of gender, all pilots in the Ferrying Division had been utilized. And the only reason a pilot wouldn't fly as much as another was due to which planes they were qualified to fly.

"And finally," Tunner said, "we've been canceling all leaves requested by Ferrying Division pilots because we're still in a pilot shortage."

"So nothing should be standing in the way of the WASP?" Nancy clarified. "We're still needed?"

"Definitely."

# CHAPTER FORTY-ONE

"I wish to express my appreciation for the loyal, devoted, and cooperative efforts which you have put forth in the interests of the Ferrying Division since 12 March 1942.... In all these tasks you demonstrated ability, good judgment and superior executive qualities. You have dependably and efficiently performed every assignment given to you. Your splendid service and your loyalty have been a source of deep satisfaction to me."

—LETTER TO NANCY LOVE FROM WILLIAM H. TUNNER,
BRIGADIER GENERAL, USA, COMMANDING

*April–November 1944—Orlando, Florida*

After Nancy said goodbye to Bob again, she headed to the Officer Training School in Orlando, Florida, on April 19—something Jackie Cochran had secured. Tunner had ordered Nancy to take part in the first class that included squadron leaders and other Originals: Gillies, Batson, Donahue, Erickson, Bohn, Miller, Batten, and Scharr. Nancy threw herself into studying the material on Army procedures, military discipline, chemical warfare, and more so she could set the standard and earn top scores.

But the media debates about the WASP bill followed her to Florida.

"You're going out to dinner with Cochran?" Bob asked over the phone one night, surprise filling his question.

"It's not just me," Nancy said. "Gillies and Bohn are coming too. Besides, Cochran flew in to meet the first officer class."

"Ah, that makes sense. Are you all right with that?"

"I'm managing," she said. "The others are grumbling a bit loudly, so I'll have to talk to them before dinner. But that's low on my list of worries. First, Representative Ramspeck is coming into town for a dinner meeting."

"Boy, oh, boy. Can I join that dinner?"

"I wish." Nancy blew out a breath. "He'll probably grill us on the WASP, you know, casual dinner conversation."

Her prediction turned out to be accurate.

Their dinner with Representative Ramspeck proved to be a quizzing game, with him asking questions about the WASP.

Nancy, at one point, said, "Have you not read my deposition, sir?"

"There's never too much information to be had," he said. "What's your favorite plane to fly, Mrs. Love?"

She didn't have to think about it since lately she'd been flying the A-20 and absolutely loved it. "The A-20 is very special," she said with a smile. "All these ladies are working on transitioning on the bomber here in Orlando."

Ramspeck's gaze cut to the other women at the table—Bohn, Batson, Donahue, and Erickson. "Is that right? Tell me about the A-20."

B.J. cleared her throat. "It's also known as the Db-7. An attack bomber with twin 1600-horsepower Wright engines."

Ramspeck took off his glasses and slowly cleaned them with his napkin, then put the glasses back on. "Is she fast?"

Nancy didn't like his tone, but she loved B.J.'s reply.

"She's smooth, fast, and has a ceiling of 25,000 feet. What's not to love?"

Ramspeck sat back in his chair, arms folded. "Sounds expensive."

Everyone politely laughed, but the undercurrent of tension only rose.

After calling Bob that night, Nancy determined that Ramspeck would say what he would to Congress, and there was nothing Nancy could do about it.

The dinner with Cochran the next night went smoothly, and nothing irritated Nancy about the woman. Nancy wondered if Cochran was playing nice because they were all in a holding pattern, waiting for the WASP bill to go through.

The Ferrying Division currently had 303 pilots, and the rest of the WASP graduates were filling other positions. But more graduates were coming, and they had to be assigned, either to the Ferrying Division or to Training Command. Those who had the most potential and desire were sent to pursuit school. The most in-demand job was ferrying the pursuit planes, such as the P-51, A-20, P-38, and P-61.

By the time Nancy and her ladies finished OTS training, the congressional meeting was fast approaching. On June 5, 1944, the Ramspeck Committee presented their compiled findings to Congress. The committee's conclusive report was that the WASP Program was unjustifiably expensive and unnecessary. Not only that, but the Committee also recommended that the WASP Program stop recruiting new pilots and that their training be terminated immediately.

No one was happy at the Ferrying Division. For Nancy, it was a blow, and she imagined it was an even bigger blow for Cochran.

Nancy didn't have time to nurse her wounds, though, because the war news dominated her thoughts. Perhaps the writing was on the wall, and she should have foreseen what was happening, but she and everyone else in the country were riveted to the news about the massive Allied assault into Normandy. On June 6, 1944, tens of thousands of paratroopers dropped out of more than 900 C-47 planes, in addition to 4,000 men arriving on military gliders, carrying supporting weapons and medical teams. And the advance on Nazi forces began.

The Allied forces outnumbered and outpowered the Germans in every way, so now it was only a matter of time before the Allies prevailed.

On June 21, Congress voted down the WASP bill, and militarization was denied.

The even bigger blow came when Tunner called Nancy into his office, where Teague was already seated.

"Close the door, please." Tunner clipped his words. He sat on the other side of his desk, shoulders stiff, hands steepled atop his desk.

Nancy shut the door and took a seat on the edge of a chair.

"General Arnold informed me that all recruitment and training of additional WASP will cease immediately," Tunner said. "No new classes will start after July 1, and those who are on their way to Sweetwater for Class 45-1 will be sent back home."

"What . . . what about . . . ?" She swallowed against her too-tight throat.

"The WASP are still needed," Tunner said. "You're not going anywhere."

But the foreboding had already started in Nancy's gut.

Every day, the blows kept coming, and all Nancy could do was watch the domino effect. Some hope bloomed when Cochran went to a meeting with General George and several others to plan out the future and submit recommendations for the WASP Program moving forward.

Then Tunner was assigned to command the India-China Division of the Air Transport Command. He'd oversee the supply chain to China across the Himalayas from India—the same route Bob had test flown a year and a half before.

Starting in July, General Robert E. Nowland took over as Ferrying Division commander. Most recently, he'd served as the commanding general of the 28th Flying Training Wing at George Field, Illinois, then as chief of staff of the ATC.

On August 1, Cochran finished her report and submitted it to Arnold, recommending that if the WASP couldn't be militarized, it should be deactivated. Cochran didn't want the WASP to become a division of the WAC, no matter what.

"The Ninety-Nines have started an initiative to get Congress to reopen the bill for reconsideration," Betty told Nancy over the phone. "Another group out of Sweetwater is petitioning as well."

Nancy wanted to feel encouraged, but the growing weight on her heart told her otherwise. She didn't have Bob to vent to since he'd left on a three-week assignment to South America for the ATC. With the bill being shut down, it felt like the women's pilot industry was moving backward.

"We're in the process of moving 123 women pilots out of the Ferrying Division," Nancy said. "Our momentum to get the WASP militarized is changing with the war successes. We're still ferrying bombers to be transferred overseas, but we're also ferrying the returned planes to the boneyard so they can be dismantled or repurposed."

"Are the rumors true that no more combat pilots will be trained?" Betty asked.

"That's what I've been hearing. Everyone wants the war over—no one more than me and you, I'm sure." Nancy absently twisted the phone receiver cord around her finger. "The men are starting to come home, but the returning pilots are demanding jobs on American soil."

"Of course they are," Betty said. "They should have jobs, but there should be room for both."

"Agreed."

Soon after the Allied troops retook Paris, the ripple effect meant that the WASP Program was further disabled. The rumors became true as civilian male pilots in the US were no longer being trained for combat and were instead transitioned to ferrying, replacing the women. The four-week WASP Training Program at the AAF School of Applied Tactics in Orlando was shut down in September.

And on October 3, Arnold made an announcement that rocked Nancy and her pilots to the core. The WASP would be officially disbanded on December 20, 1944.

Nancy spent the next couple of days in a numb daze, wondering if her heart was even still beating. She went about her duties as efficiently as possible only to return to her Cincinnati apartment alone. It was hard to push away the dejection during the dark hours of night. Bob kept telling her he was concerned about her, but she kept telling him she was fine.

Another blow came on November 25, when Hazel Ying Lee crashed her P-63 because the control tower in Great Falls, Montana, gave her mixed landing signals. Lee was only thirty-two years old. And like the other WASPs who'd been lost, Lee did not qualify for the honors of a military funeral. Her death was another devastating loss to the WASP community.

A small bright spot came when Bob lobbied for reassignment to Cincinnati and became the deputy commander of the Ferrying Division. It was a gallant thing to do, and Nancy didn't even know how much she needed him until he was there.

Her nights were no longer long and lonely. She curled next to Bob as the moon glowed through the window.

"It's both wonderful and terrifying," she murmured, happy to have her husband back, her cheek pressed against his chest. "The changing tide of the war seems too good to be true, yet all signs indicate a definitive Allied victory."

"There's still a long way to go," Bob said as his fingers trailed along her arm. "But you're right. Just like General Arnold pointed out, unless there are major combat losses in the air raid over Germany, pilots will continue returning home. And they'll be given the jobs the WASP are currently doing."

"I understand," Nancy said, "but it's surreal. We're being told that if the WASP continue, we'll be replacing men instead of releasing them. On that account, it softens the blow, but I still want to serve our country. General Arnold is basically giving us a couple of months' buffer so the men can get transitioned and qualified. He wants the WASP returning home by Christmas." She let her shoulders sag. "It's a nice thought—home for Christmas."

"It is a very nice thought." Bob's arm tightened around her.

"Then, why do I feel so positively bleak and like my feet are being pulled underwater? The war changing tides is what we have all been praying for, but until Germany and Japan surrender, the WASP can continue serving our country."

"What has Nowland said?" Bob's voice rumbled softly above her.

"He sent a letter of appeal to General Arnold, saying that it would cost more money to replace the WASP pilots and that he wants the women to be retained until the men can be fully trained. Then we'd be let go over a period of time."

"Ah, need I guess General Arnold's reply?"

"It was swift and stern, as usual," Nancy said, biting back her disappointment. "Nowland was informed that contrasting the reduced costs of keeping the program is not on the table for debate right now. The WASP are being disbanded because of a policy decision that benefits the

AAF. End of case, and no exceptions will be made. So, I'll be out of a job come December 20."

Bob's hand rested on her shoulder and squeezed. "Through it all, sweetie, you must see how much you and your ladies have achieved. You've ferried planes to where they need to be, making crucial deliveries under all kinds of conditions and restrictions. And you've single-handedly proven that women can fly larger planes successfully."

Nancy moved up on her elbow and looked down at him in the dim light. "I've done nothing single-handedly. You, Bob, are a major reason I've come this far and, consequently, the other WASP."

His fingers brushed the ends of her hair. "Thanks for the endorsement, but we both know you were a spitfire before I even met you."

She smiled and nestled against his warm skin. "Well, I had great parents and a daredevil brother who might have encouraged me a little too much."

He chuckled, the sound vibrating through her.

"I might go to the final graduation on December 7," she said after another moment. The WASP Class 44-10 would be the last to graduate from Avenger Field, and then it would be over. Done.

"I think you should attend," Bob said, encouragement in his voice. "I'm impressed those ladies are sticking it out even with the program being disbanded."

"They'll still be qualified pilots, but they'll have to make their own way without the WASP net."

"True, and attending will give you some closure."

"Maybe." Nancy wasn't quite sure if she wanted to be part of the graduation where she was certain that Arnold would offer platitudes that would probably never come to fruition. Yet she'd been part of the WASP from the beginning, so maybe . . . Would she be able to sit through the ceremony while her heart shattered?

# CHAPTER FORTY-TWO

"You, and more than nine hundred of your sisters, have shown that you
can fly wingtip to wingtip with your brothers.... The entire operation
has been a success. It is on record that women can fly as well as men. We
will not again look upon a women's flying organization as experimental.
We will know that they can handle our fastest fighters, our heaviest
bombers; we will know that they are capable of ferrying target towing,
flying training, test flying and the countless other activities which you
have proved you can do. This is valuable knowledge for the air age into
which we are now entering.... We will never forget our debt to you."

—GENERAL ARNOLD, DECEMBER 7, 1944,
GRADUATION SPEECH TO THE WASP CLASS 44-10

*December 1944—Cincinnati, Ohio*

From her Cincinnati office, Nancy read a transcript of the speech
General Arnold gave at the WASP Class 44-10 graduation. The speech
turned out to be very pretty indeed, but Nancy had decided not to attend. Maybe she should feel guilty for not being part of the graduation,
but in the end, she wasn't interested in being inundated with questions
about the demise of the WASP. Only time would tell if Arnold's words
of "we will never forget our debt to you" would prove to be true. Would
the world truly remember the WASP?

When she spoke on the phone to B.J., Nancy found herself cheering
up her friend, even though she felt the same despondency.

"There's no reason room can't be made for women pilots in the military," B.J. said. "How many planes do we need to fly, and how many
hours do we need to accumulate in order to prove ourselves?"

"I agree," Nancy conceded. "But it would be a constant fight if politics can disband the WASP. That tells me the rest of the country isn't
ready for women in the Air Force."

B.J. made a low noise in her throat. "I hate this. What are you going to do now? What can any of us do?"

Of course, this had been on Nancy's mind continually. "I'm going to keep praying that this war ends as soon as possible. I've been working on finding jobs for some of the ferrying pilots. Mr. Traylor from the Reconstruction Finance Corporation is in need of pilots to fly surplus warplanes to sales centers. Bob and I were talking about settling in San Francisco. We'll see what happens, but we're planning on selling the house in Massachusetts." She paused. "Maybe we'll have babies."

B.J. laughed. "I think there's going to be quite the baby boom."

Nancy smiled to herself. "Likely."

"I'm also trying to imagine what sort of kid you and Bob Love will produce," B.J. said with humor laced through her words. "The combination is going to be quite spectacular."

"Right back at you. How's your engagement going with Jack London?"

"Very well."

They both laughed.

"I'm going to miss you, Nancy," B.J. said quieter. "Oh, I know we'll keep in contact and all that, but it won't be the same."

"No." Nancy paused at the thought. "Not the same at all."

Her later conversation with Betty was much the same.

"Are you sincere about having children?" Betty asked, never afraid to ask delicate questions.

"Of course. My mother will be thrilled."

"Uh, I can't see your expression," Betty said. "This isn't about giving your *mother* grandbabies. It's about what *you* want."

Nancy coiled the phone cord around a finger. "I want children, I do. Bob does too—or at least, that's what he says, but we haven't talked much about it since Pearl Harbor." She hesitated. "I think something's wrong with me, and I need to see if I can even *have* children. We've been married for ten years and nothing. So I'm making a doctor appointment."

"Good, I'm glad you're doing that," Betty said. "Whatever happens is what's meant to be."

"You sound like Bob," Nancy said lightly. "Otherwise, Bob keeps talking about buying a sailboat once we find a place to settle. I guess we're living by water somewhere."

"It's about time," Betty said warmly.

"We'll have to wait until this blasted war has truly ended." Over the past few months, Finland and the Soviet Union had agreed to a cease-fire; the Allies had liberated Athens, which was currently under martial law; the Germans had surrendered Aachen, Germany; and the French had captured Strasbourg.

"What do you think about the Order of the Fifinella?" Betty asked. "Are you going to join?"

"I'm not," Nancy said, then quickly amended, "but don't feel obligated to follow my lead. The organization is a good thing. I . . . I just can't be a part of it right now." The Fifinella mascot had come from Walt Disney's design of a winsome lady gremlin mascot, and the organization would be a way for the WASP to stay in contact both professionally and personally. But how could she explain to Betty that she felt like she couldn't muster the energy or enthusiasm to join?

Clara Jo Marsh, staff executive at the headquarters of the Eastern Flying Training Command, had asked Nancy for a roster of the women in the Ferrying Division. Clara Jo wanted to keep the WASP women in contact and include them at the ATC WASP.

"When's your last flight as a WASP?" Betty asked tentatively. Gently.

"Two weeks." Nancy's eyes burned. It felt surreal to speak the words aloud. "Bea Medes and I will be picking up a C-54B from the Douglas plant in Chicago and delivering it to the West Coast."

"Excellent," Betty murmured. "Did you see Nowland's report on our numbers? By December 20, the WASP will have delivered 12,652 aircraft. That's three-fifths of all planes coming off the assembly line."

"And now the WASP are being disbanded." Nancy hated that she couldn't keep the dejection out of her voice, but Betty was her best friend and could read her like a map.

"We'll get through this somehow," Betty said when Nancy was usually the one with the pep talks.

After hanging up, Nancy felt reassured. It wasn't just her losing all that she'd built up; it was every woman in the WASP. They would forge ahead together, just as Betty had said.

The next two weeks felt surreal, and at the end of it, Nancy found herself standing in their tiny apartment kitchen while Bob made coffee. She was about to head out on her final flight for the WASP.

"Sugar today?" Bob asked, pouring coffee into two mugs.

"Two, please." Nancy leaned against the counter, watching her husband. The last few weeks hadn't been easy, and she knew she'd been quieter than usual. Thinking, processing, grieving. Yet Bob had been Bob through it all. Always taking care of her. Willing to listen to her complaining or ranting, day or night. He really couldn't get away from it now that they were living together again.

He wore his shirt sleeves, not quite dressed in full uniform this early in the morning. As he stirred two teaspoons of sugar into her mug, Nancy felt her eyes well with tears. Again. It was a daily thing now. Maybe once she flew her final mission, the tears would be easier to hold back.

"Here you are." Bob turned and held out the mug.

She accepted it gratefully and took a careful sip, although her heart was hammering and her fingers trembling.

Bob noticed. Of course he did.

He stepped close and took the mug again, setting it on the counter, then pulled her into his arms. "It's going to be all right, sweetie," he murmured against her hair.

For a moment, she breathed in the clean cotton smell of his shirt, felt the warmth of his skin, and found comfort in the steady thump of his heart. "Sometimes I think I'm sleepwalking. Is this all really happening? Are the WASP really disbanded?"

Bob's hand moved across her back. "It's really happening, but there's nothing for you or any of the women to regret. You've served your country so very well. Without you, the tide of the war wouldn't have changed so soon. Women working in the manufacturing plants, women mechanics building war planes, women delivering the planes to the air bases . . . You were the backbone."

Nancy wanted to take solace in her husband's words. They felt true on an intellectual level, but her heart still ached.

Eventually, she extracted herself from her husband's arms, finished her coffee, and made it to the base. Although her emotions felt numb, her brain was sharp as she did her flight precheck.

Her final flight as a WASP pilot was bittersweet, yet the two-day flight in the C-54B #42-72389 with Bea Medes as copilot was smoother than a summer pond. They didn't encounter any bad weather or mechanical problems.

Other Originals were also taking their final flights. B.J. Erickson's final flight was in a P-61 that she'd qualified on with other female pilots earlier that fall. She delivered the P-61 to Sacramento, then was taken by military transport to Long Beach.

"There are sixty-six new P-51 Mustangs at Long Beach," B.J. told Nancy over the phone on December 19—the final night before disbandment. "Brand-new, waiting to be delivered, but there aren't enough male ferry pilots to get them delivered in a timely manner. So, the P-51s are sitting there."

"That's happening all over," Nancy said. "Farmingdale, Buffalo, Niagara, Evansville, Dallas . . . We have 133 women who can fly pursuits, and all of them are going home tomorrow. I wish you were here at Wilmington with us for 'the last supper.'"

"Wait one more day?"

"I would if we could—tomorrow we're all clocking out."

Nancy was both looking forward to and dreading the final meal she'd organized with a smaller group—seven of the Originals, plus the rest of the ladies who served in the 2nd Ferrying Group at the New Castle Army Air Base. Where it all began.

When Nancy walked into the officers' club, Betty greeted her, decked out in her WASP uniform.

"You're over here, ma'am," Betty said with a smile.

"In the center at the head table?"

"Of course—you brought us all together, so that's where you belong."

Nancy shook her head, but she was smiling. She took her seat at the long table next to Betty. On the right, Nancy Batson, Helen McGilvery, and Gertrude Meserve Tubbs filled in the chairs. To the left sat Helen Mary Clark, Teresa James, and Sis Bernheim. And on down the line, the other women filled in the seats.

"I guess I'm giving the first toast?" Nancy asked, raising her glass.

The other women all laughed.

"I'd like to recognize the three Originals who are missing tonight . . . Cornelia Fort, Dorothy Scott, and Evelyn Sharp." Everyone in the room sobered. "And acknowledge the other thirty-five WASP killed in service to their country, most recently Mary Webster, who died on a UC-78 as a passenger on December 9. May we always honor their memories."

The women raised their glasses.

Other toasts were made, becoming longer and longer. Memories shared. Jokes told. Tears shed.

Nancy didn't know how long they'd been there, but she was in no hurry, not anymore. Tomorrow, she'd wake up unemployed.

"You should sleep with us in the BOQ 14 tonight," Betty teased, "for old times."

"I think I will." Nancy held up her wine glass. "I had one too many of these. The food was delicious though."

Nancy headed with the other women to their barracks, arm in arm, laughing at nothing. The barracks had been gussied up and decorated over the last two years, but even that couldn't disguise the stark living conditions. None of them had minded the simplicity though—they'd been happy to serve.

After Nancy and Betty had both changed into their night clothes, Nancy wandered the small space of Betty's room as Betty took down personal photos from the walls and packed them up.

"Remember this?" Betty said, holding out a photograph of the two of them standing in front of the B-17 Flying Fortress.

Nancy's heart hitched. "That's one of my all-time favorite photos of us." She paused. "I have something to tell you—but you must swear to secrecy."

Betty's brows shot up. "Of course. You know I'm like a vault."

"Over the past month, General Smith has been working on securing me a foreign mission."

Betty sat on the edge of her bed, her eyes wide. "Do tell, Mrs. Love."

Nancy settled across from her. "Despite General Arnold's stern command that as of tomorrow, no women will be allowed to fly for the AAF in any capacity, General Smith has written to General Tunner in Calcutta. They want me to fly the Hump and submit a report of my findings on what can be improved."

Betty grinned, and Nancy grinned back.

"When do you leave?"

"I report to the New York Aerial Port of Embarkation at La Guardia Field on December 27."

Betty clapped. "I know better than to ask if I can come along, but I'm green with envy."

"As you should be—I'd be green if it were you going."

"And Bob is supportive?"

"He seems to be," Nancy said with a shrug. "Maybe I'll hear about his worry later—but he's putting on a brave front now."

"I think he knew from the moment you both met that he could never hold you back," Betty said. "Even if he wanted to."

"I wouldn't have married him if he'd been that sort."

Betty smirked. "I guess it helps that Lt. General Stilwell is no longer commander of the CBI Theater."

"Definitely." Nancy winked. Lt. General Joseph W. Stilwell had a rule of no American women in the Pacific Theater, although there had been some exceptions anyway.

"Right." Betty made a motion to zip her mouth. "Your secret stays with me."

"Is that someone yelling outside?" Nancy moved to the window and parted the drapes. She stared in disbelief at the sight across from the barracks. Flames poured out of the windows of the officers' club—where they'd all been eating and drinking only a short time before. "The club is on fire," Nancy said in disbelief as Betty joined her at the window.

Betty gasped. "What in the world? We need to save it . . ."

Nancy turned and hurried past her, throwing open the bedroom door. Other women had gathered in the hallway, in various states of dress, wearing nightgowns or robes. They pressed toward the exit, spilling out into the cold night.

By the time Nancy stepped outside, the blaze had intensified.

Other airmen had joined in the watch, and a bucket brigade had begun.

"Let it burn!" Nancy Batson yelled.

A few people snickered.

"They have no use for the WASP anymore, so let it burn!" Batson repeated.

The bucket brigade slowed and soon stopped all together. People gathered in small clusters and watched it burn. Without drawing attention to herself, Nancy headed back into the barracks and gathered her WASP uniform. She returned to the blaze, then tossed her uniform onto the orange flames.

She didn't know if anyone had noticed or was paying attention, but she didn't care. She'd never liked the WASP uniform, and now she wasn't obligated to wear it any longer. There was no use for it. This would also be her goodbye to working with Jackie Cochran. Nancy wished her the best, but there was no need to extend their relationship, working or personal or anything else. Besides, Nancy would proudly wear her WAFS uniform for the India trip.

"A fitting end, is it not?" Betty said quietly, coming to stand next to Nancy.

"Going down in a fiery blaze?" Nancy asked, feeling the irony.

Betty slung her arm across Nancy's shoulder.

Nancy matched her movement, and together with Betty, she watched the dancing flames, half mesmerized.

Yet tears filled her eyes as she thought of another set of flames. Ones that had resulted from the bombing of Pearl Harbor—the event that had brought the US into the war—and now, the flames consuming the officers' club signaled the beginning of a new chapter in her life.

On one level, Nancy knew she had a demanding and eventful future to look forward to. The flight to India, more time with her husband, a chance to visit her parents, friendships to maintain . . . and a war to finish off.

With or without being a WASP pilot, Nancy would always be an Original WAFS at heart. And she'd continue to serve her country—wherever they might have her. She wasn't giving up. There were too many skies yet to fly.

# AFTERMATH

On December 27, 1944, Nancy Love reported to the New York Aerial Port of Embarkation at La Guardia Field, where she climbed aboard an ATC transport. Since there had been an order in place of no women allowed in the Pacific Theater, with the exceptions of WACs working as OSS staff in China, or at AAF headquarters in Calcutta, and Army nurses, Nancy's assignment had to be approved.

Once in Calcutta, Nancy found that many improvements were needed on the Crescent run. She flew a staff B-25 over India as well as the C-54 over the Hump route, otherwise known as the aluminum trail because of danger of high mountain peaks and extreme wind conditions. Nancy also piloted twenty of the fifty-hour C-54 flights from Calcutta to Honolulu. Once she filed her report of suggested improvements to General Nowland on February 9, 1945, her official Ferrying Division duties were over.

With the exception of the brief diversion of Nancy's trip, General Arnold's directive that "no women will be employed by the AAF in any flying capacity either as pilot, copilot, or member of a flying crew" stayed in effect until the 1970s.

Bob and Nancy moved to San Francisco after Nancy's release, but that was short-lived because in December 1945, Bob was elected as the president of All American Aviation, taking over for Richard C. DuPont. This took them back east again, where they purchased a home in Chester County, Pennsylvania. The couple bought two planes, a Vultee BT-13 and a surplus P-38. Finding that the P-38 was too expensive to fly, they sold it and instead bought a four-seater, single-engine Bonanza. On July 15, 1946, the Army Air Forces awarded medals to both Bob and Nancy for their service during the war—the first husband-and-wife duo to receive such an honor.

Nancy and Jackie Cochran parted ways without much of a relationship. Cochran was awarded the Distinguished Service Medal and Distinguished Flying Cross, and in 1948, she joined the US Air Force Reserve as a lieutenant colonel. This did not enact any flying status for women though—a measure that would not happen for women in the Air Force until 1976. In 1953, Cochran became the first woman to break the sound barrier. She was promoted to colonel in 1969 and retired in 1970.

In 1946, Nancy and Bob went to a Boston doctor who specialized in hormones, and it was discovered that Nancy had a blocked fallopian tube that could be remedied by surgery. The surgery was successful, and on August 1, 1947, Nancy delivered her first daughter, Hannah Lincoln Love. When All American Aviation went from an airmail service to a passenger airline and became All American Airways, the Loves moved to Washington, DC.

In 1948, Nancy received a letter from the vice chief of staff of the United States Air Force that offered her a commission as a lieutenant colonel in its Reserves.

The Love family continued to grow, and their second daughter, Margaret Campbell, was born March 22, 1949, and their third daughter, Alice Harkness, was born November 1, 1951. In 1952, the Love family moved permanently to Martha's Vineyard, Massachusetts, where Bob's sister, Margaret, and his widowed mother lived. Bob commuted to Washington, DC, each week, flying their Bonanza on Monday mornings and returning to Martha's Vineyard on Fridays.

Nancy and Bob loved being parents and included their daughters in their aviation and sailing life. They flew their Bonanza whenever they went off-island, hauling their "children, dogs, furniture, spare sails, marine parts, and assorted cargo" (*Nancy Love and the WASP Ferry Pilots of World War II* by Sarah Rickman, 243).

All American Airways became Allegheny Airlines, and Bob was the chairman of the board until 1954, after which he became the director. Once Bob didn't have to be in Washington, DC, five days a week, he turned his attention to sailing. Throughout the 1950s, Bob and Nancy entered sailing races along the East Coast. After Nancy's father died in early 1958, her mother moved to join the family on the island.

It wasn't until the 1960s that Nancy discovered that her head injury from falling out of the plane while attending Vassar had been more serious than anyone had realized. While boating with her family, Nancy was steering their *Gay Gull III* at Jonesport, Maine, and they hit an unmarked outcropping. Nancy was standing and fell forward, striking the boom crutch and splitting her face down the middle. She had plastic surgery to repair the damage to her face, but the X-rays revealed that she'd had an old skull fracture. The discovered skull fracture explained her many years of headache pain (*Nancy Love,* Rickman, 253–254).

Although life seemed idyllic, surrounded by family and summer visitors, who included many of the WAFS and WASP, such as Betty Gillies, B.J. Erickson London, and Alice Hirschman Hammond, sailing the coast, flying the family airplane, horseback riding, and holding lobster cookouts, Nancy struggled health-wise after her girls left the nest. The smoking she'd picked up during the war continued, and she battled depression, which she numbed with alcohol. Her family intervened, but her challenges continued, and in 1974, Nancy was diagnosed with breast cancer.

Nancy underwent a radical mastectomy in the spring of 1974, but unfortunately, the cancer returned in 1975. Still, Nancy put her energy into her daughter Hannah's wedding that would take place that fall.

In 1976, the Order of Fifinella organization, comprised of former WASP members, notified Nancy that she'd been named "Woman of the Year," and the award would be presented at their October reunion. Nancy's health went into sharp decline, and over the phone, she told WASP President Bee Falk Haydu, "All my life, I thought I'd go down in a blaze of glory in an airplane. Here I am hardly able to do anything at all." At 6:30 a.m. on October 22, 1976, Nancy Harkness Love died, on the same day that the WASP had gathered to honor her at their reunion.

Thirteen years later, in 1989, Nancy was enshrined in the Michigan Aviation Hall of Fame. Then in 1996, she was posthumously inducted into the Airlift/Tanker Association, the Michigan Women's Hall of

Fame in 1997, and the National Aviation Hall of Fame in Dayton, Ohio, in 2005—the ninth woman to receive such an honor. A statue dedicated to Nancy Harkness Love stands at the New Castle County Airport in Delaware.

Deborah G. Douglas said, "Love's plan for the WAFS, both in conception and execution, remains an important model for the integration of women into the military. . . . It was absolutely critical that both men and women believed that members of either sex had something to contribute. . . . The gender debate in the military has never been the same since. And that makes Nancy Love one of the more productive historical figures of the first half of the 20th century" (*Nancy Love*, Rickman, 274).

The WASP eventually won their militarization and veterans status in 1977, and in 2008, Nancy was inducted into the Pioneer Hall of Fame for Women in Aviation. In 2010, the WASP were awarded the Congressional Gold Medal. During the assembly at the Capitol on March 10, 2010, Lt. Colonel Nicole Malachowski, the first female pilot in the Air Force's Air Demonstration Squadron, said, "Today is the day when the WASPs will make history once again. If you spend any time at all talking to these wonderful women, you'll notice how humble and gracious and selfless they all are. Their motives for wanting to fly airplanes all those years ago wasn't for fame or glory or recognition. They simply had a passion to take what gifts they had and use them to help defend not only America, but the entire free world, from tyranny. And they let no one get in their way" (https://www.af.mil/News/Article -Display/Article/117355/wasps-awarded-congressional-gold-medal/).

NANCY HARKNESS LOVE WITH
A FAIRCHILD PT-19A TRAINER

ROBERT LOVE AND NANCY LOVE

NANCY LOVE AND BETTY GILLIES

NANCY LOVE IN A BOEING B-17 FLYING FORTRESS

# CHAPTER NOTES

## CHAPTER 1

The 1919 Orteig Prize that Raymond Orteig issued was an exclusive award promised to the first aviator, of any Allied country, who crossed the Atlantic Ocean in a plane in one flight. Specifically, from Paris to New York or New York to Paris. And the winning prize? $25,000 and, of course, plenty of fame (see *Fly Girls*, Keith O'Brien, 19). Several attempts were made, all ending in disaster. René Fonck narrowly survived a fiery crash that killed two of his crew members (22). Other pilots weren't so lucky, such as Charles Nungesser, a famous World War I pilot, whose plane never arrived in New York. It wasn't until twenty-five-year-old Charles Lindbergh, an airmail pilot from Minnesota, that the feat was finally accomplished in 1927 (25).

## CHAPTER 2

Following World War I, a plethora of trained pilots returned to American soil. Jobs such as airmail and passenger airlines were still years away, so the employment options for a pilot were limited. Barnstorming became popular as a way for a pilot to travel around the country, perform stunts, and offer rides in their plane. The Midwest was the biggest draw for these pilots because of the abundance of fields and barns. A wealth of affordable war surplus planes, ranging from $50 to $500 in price, only added to the commonality of barnstormers (see https://sandiegoairan dspace.org/exhibits/online-exhibit-page/barnstormers-take-to-the-sky).

## CHAPTER 3

Prior to the US issuing pilot's licenses, the only way to get licensed was through the Fédération Aéronautique Internationale, or FAI, which was based in Paris. In 1926, as a result of the Air Commerce Act, the US started issuing pilot's licenses. William P. MacCracken Jr., who was

the assistant secretary of Commerce for Aeronautics, received the first issued private pilot's license: Pilot License No. 1. MacCracken had offered
the honor to Orville Wright, but Wright refused, saying he didn't need
a federal license proving that he'd been the first man to fly. In 1927,
Phoebe Omlie was the first woman to receive a Transport License (#199)
from the Aeronautics Branch in the US (see https://www.faa.gov/about
/history/milestones/media/first_pilots_license.pdf).

## CHAPTER 4

After World War I, planes became safer and more durable, with
innovative metal parts replacing wood and canvas. Because of the increased capacity of 1920s and 1930s planes, pilots began breaking aviation speed and distance records. Explorers also had the benefit of traveling to previously impenetrable places, such as Antarctica. Airships grew
in popularity until the 1937 tragedy of the fire aboard the Zeppelin
Hindenburg. After that, the airships became less desirable. And, of
course, the successful transatlantic crossing by Charles Lindbergh became predecessor for international air travel (see http://www.1920-30.
com/aviation/).

## CHAPTER 5

When Nancy Love first started flying, radio communication was still
evolving. The Air Commerce Act was passed in 1926. This created more
developments in air commerce, navigation, establishing airways, and
developing safety rules (see http://avstop.com/history/needregulations
/act1926.htm). Before 1926, planes didn't have communication with
those on the ground since airway radio stations had only ground-to-
ground communications through radiotelegraph. The National Bureau
of Standards (NBS) set to work developing a ground-to-air radiotelephone system that spanned up to fifty miles. Improvements continued,
and in 1928, two-way radio communication stations were instituted
throughout the federal airways system. Commercial planes were then set
up with a radiotelephone transmitter and receiver, although the stations
could serve only one airplane at a time. The private planes still had to
rely on dead reckoning navigation. Then in 1929, the NBS introduced a

low-frequency radio range (LFR), or four-course radio range, which vastly improved radio navigation (see http://www.npshistory.com/publications /nhl/theme-studies/aviation.pdf, 84–85).

## CHAPTER 6

Aviator Johnny Miller was a self-taught pilot who became fascinated with planes at the age of four, and as a teenager, he began flying as a barnstormer. His career as a pilot included delivering airmail, setting a transcontinental record in a Pitcairn autogiro, competing in air races, flying for the US Marine Corps, and later serving as a jet airline pilot. For years, Miller wrote a regular column in the *American Bonanza Society* monthly magazine. Johnny continued to fly well into his nineties (see https://www.flyingmag.com/news-aviation-legend-john-miller -dead-102/).

## CHAPTER 7

Alice Hirschman Hammond and Nancy Love's friendship was a close one. In 1933, Alice won the first closed-course race for women in Michigan. She was a friend of Amelia Earhart, and after Earhart's disappearance, Alice proposed that a scholarship be developed to memorialize Amelia, which became the Amelia Earhart Memorial Scholarship Fund. During World War II, in 1941, Alice commanded the women's flying squadron of the Civil Air Patrol. Alice competed in sixteen of the All Women's Transcontinental Air Races, and she served as the president of the Ninety-Nines from 1951 to 1953. In the 1960s, she transferred to the Civil Air Patrol in Philadelphia, where she participated in search-and -rescue missions (see https://www.airzoo.org/enshrinees).

## CHAPTER 8

Nancy Love's premature gray hair came in as a streak near her forehead after her accident with John Miller in 1933 (see *Nancy Love and the WASP Ferry Pilots of World War II*, Sarah Rickman, 25). She suffered from frequent headaches as a result of the blow to her head, but it wasn't until the 1933 spring semester that she took time off from Vassar College.

CHAPTER NOTES

## CHAPTER 9

The Ninety-Nines was founded in November 1929 by Amelia Earhart and other women pilots in order to provide a supportive environment with the shared passion for flying. In 1929, there were 117 licensed women pilots, and ninety-nine of those joined the organization, which prompted the name of Ninety-Nines. Amelia Earhart served as the first president, and it quickly grew to become an international organization. Today, thousands of licensed women pilots are members throughout more than forty countries. Their primary focus includes educational programs, aerospace workshops, flight-instructor seminars, and other aviation programs. Ninety-Nines is headquartered on the grounds of the Will Rogers Airport in Oklahoma City, Oklahoma (see https://www.ninety-nines.org/).

## CHAPTER 10

Jacqueline Cochran first learned to fly in 1932 and, soon after, found that she loved air racing. She competed throughout the 1930s in multiple races, setting records, such as the world's unlimited speed record for women in 1937. Her second marriage was to the wealthy tycoon Floyd Odlum, who funded many of her campaigns, including Jacqueline Cochran Cosmetics. Cochran was close friends with Amelia Earhart and joined the Ninety-Nines, eventually becoming the president of the organization from 1941 to 43 (see *The Women with Silver Wings*, Landdeck, 47–48).

## CHAPTER 11

Jacqueline Cochran took her first flying lesson in July 1932. She was looking for a way to be a more effective traveling salesperson for a cosmetics company, and her future husband, Floyd Odlum, suggested she fly to her appointments. Floyd offered to pay for the lessons, and Cochran took it from there. One week after her first lesson at Roosevelt Field in Long Island, she soloed. She fell in love with the freedom and speed of flying. On August 17, 1932, she became number 1,498 to earn her private pilot's license. Earning her license in just six weeks attracted attention from the press, and Cochran's story made the *New York Times* (*The Women with Silver Wings*, Landdeck, 55–56).

## CHAPTER 12

By the time Nancy Love attended the Katharine Gibbs School, it was a well-established educational institution turning out executive secretaries. The secretarial school was founded by Katharine Gibbs, who, at forty-six years old, was left widowed and had not been included in her husband's will. She wanted women to have more employment opportunities, so she opened a school in Boston's Back Bay and on Park Avenue in New York City, where she hired teachers from MIT, Columbia, and Brown to teach part-time. Since twenty-six states had laws prohibiting married women from working, Gibbs targeted young society women and college sophomores. She did not allow Jewish women to attend. Her death came two months after her oldest son, Howard's, death by suicide. Gordon, her younger son, and his wife took over the operations and ownership of the school (see https://newenglandhistoricalsociety.com /katharine-gibbs-invents-modern-professional-secretary/).

## CHAPTER 13

During the 1916 polio epidemic, New York City was hit hard with the disease. Bob Love was one of those cases. Statistically, about 25 percent of polio victims died. By the end of the year, 27,000 cases had been reported, with 7,000 of them being fatal. New York City had 9,000 cases alone and around 2,000 deaths.

The full name of polio is poliomyelitis, or infantile paralysis, and it affected mostly infants or children. According to the New York State Department of Health website, "Polio is a viral disease which may affect the spinal cord causing muscle weakness and paralysis . . . enters the body through the mouth, usually from hands contaminated with the stool of an infected person. Polio is more common in infants and young children and occurs under conditions of poor hygiene."

The virus ran rampant in bigger cities, such as New York City, since sanitation was harder to manage. A vaccine wouldn't be developed until the 1950s (see https://blogs.baruch.cuny.edu/histmed3450/?p=95).

## CHAPTER 14

After World War I, the Air Service was reconfigured under the Army Reorganization Act of 1920. Flight training was set up in Texas, and other tactical divisions were set up at other locations. Then in 1926, the Air Corps Act changed the name of the Air Service to Air Corps. This act established the Office of Assistant Secretary of War for Air. "The Air Corps had at this time 919 officers and 8,725 enlisted men, and its 'modern aeronautical equipment' consisted of sixty pursuit planes and 169 observation planes; total serviceable aircraft of all types numbered less than 1,000" (see https://www.afhra.af.mil/About-Us/Fact-Sheets/Display/Article/433914/ the-birth-of-the-united-states-air-force/). The Air Corps Training Center was established in San Antonio, Texas. It wasn't until 1942 that another reorganization created "three autonomous US Army Commands: Army Ground Forces, Services of Supply (later, in 1943, Army Service Forces), and Army Air Forces" (see https://www.afhra.af.mil/About-Us/Fact -Sheets/Display/Article/433914/the-birth-of-the-united-states-air-force/).

## CHAPTER 15

During the 1930s, women worked at jobs outside the home more than any decade previous. By 1940, the number of employed women went from 10.5 million to 13 million. Most of the jobs the women held were clerical, educational, or domestic. The marriage rate declined 22 percent, so that meant more single women were looking for jobs. Despite the general public's sentiment against married women working, First Lady Eleanor Roosevelt lobbied with her husband for more women to work in political offices. Not surprisingly, women earned smaller wages and had fewer benefits than their male coworkers (see https://www.history .com/news/working-women-great-depression).

## CHAPTER 16

First Lady Eleanor Roosevelt was a major supporter of aviation and female pilots. In her "My Day" column, she wrote: "WASHINGTON, Tuesday—It was interesting yesterday at lunch to talk to Miss Cecile Hamilton about the problems of the woman aviator. Apparently, they may spend a great deal of money learning how to fly and never get a chance at a job. . . . There must, however, be possibilities for women pilots to be helpful" ("My Day," Eleanor Roosevelt, November 22, 1939, https://www2.gwu.edu/~erpapers/myday/displaydocedits.cfm?_y=1939&_f=md055430).

And then again in 1942, her column had a major impact:

> HYDE PARK, Monday—I have a letter from a gentleman who is very much exercised because our women pilots are not being utilized in the war effort. The CAA says that women are psychologically not fitted to be pilots, but I see pictures every now and then of women who are teaching men to fly. We know that in England, where the need is great, women are ferrying planes and freeing innumerable men for combat service. It seems to me that in the Civil Air Patrol and in our own ferry command, women, if they can pass the tests imposed upon men, should have an equal opportunity for non-combat service. I always believe that when people are needed, they will eventually be used.
>
> I believe in this case, if the war goes on long enough, and women are patient, opportunity will come knocking at their doors. However, there is just a chance that this is not a time when women should be patient. We are in a war and we need to fight it with all our ability and every weapon possible. Women pilots, in this particular case, are a weapon waiting to be used. As my correspondent says: "I think it is time you women spoke up for yourselves and undertook a campaign to see that our 3,500 women fliers, every one of whom is anxious to do something in the war, be given a chance to do it." Hence, I am speaking up for the women fliers, because I am afraid we cannot afford to let the time slip by just now without using them. ("My Day," Eleanor Roosevelt, September 1, 1942, https://www2.gwu.edu/~erpapers/myday/displaydocedits.cfm?_y=1939&_f=md055430)

## CHAPTER 17

Nancy Love was one of five women who Phoebe F. Omlie chose in 1935 to join the National Air Marking Program, which was part of the Bureau of Air Commerce. Other women included Louise Thaden, Helen Richey, Blanche Noyes, and Helen McCloskey, making them the first employees of a US government program planned and directed by an all-women staff and paid for by the Works Progress Administration. The program divided states into sections of twenty square miles. The name of the town or nearest town was painted on the roofs of the largest buildings at fifteen-mile intervals. If a building wasn't available, ground markers were created with bricks or rocks. The air markers created a way for private pilots to navigate since they didn't have radios. In an article Ellen Nobles-Harris wrote, she stated, "By the middle of 1936, 30 states were actively involved in the program, with approvals given for 16,000 markers at a cost of about one million dollars" (see https://www.ninety -nines.org/air-marking.htm).

## CHAPTER 18

The Society section of the local Battle Creek, Michigan, newspaper printed an account of Nancy Harkness and Robert Love's wedding, titled "Hannah Harkness, Hastings Woman Flyer, Is Wedded":

On January 11, 1936, in the First Presbyterian Church of Hastings, Michigan, Hannah Lincoln (Nancy) Harkness became the bride of Robert MacLure Love. The Rev. John Kitching officiated at the ceremony, which took place at high noon. A detailed account of the wedding can be found in an article in the Society Sections of area newspapers, which begins:

"The church was decorated with evergreen and variegated white flowers. The Wedding March from *Lohengrin* and Mendelssohn's recessional were played on the organ. The bride, who carried a bouquet of white orchids and lilies of the valley, wore a white satin dress made along princess lines, with a high cowl neck, long sleeves and train. She also wore a tulle veil, which attached to a small off-the-face cap. . . . Her matron of honor, Mrs. Robert B. Harkness Jr., of Lincoln, Massachusetts, wore an ankle-length gray crepe dress with an aquamarine sash and a gray velvet hat." (*Nancy Love*, Rickman, 39–40, taken from Battle Creek, Michigan, newspaper, Jan. 12, 1936)

## CHAPTER 19

Women weren't always allowed to enter air races, and in August 1929, the Cleveland National Air Races held the First Women's Air Derby. The race began in Santa Monica, California, and ended in Cleveland. The requirements to enter the race were to have 100 hours of solo flying, including twenty-five of those hours cross-country; a license from the Fédération Aéronautique Internationale; and a gallon of water and three-day food supply in their planes. Twenty women pilots entered the eight-day flying Derby. Fourteen finished, with Louise Thaden as the winner. Other notable races included the Women's International Free-For-All, the Dixie Derby, the Women's National Air Meet, and the Ruth Catterton Air Sportsman Pilot Trophy Race.

Sometimes, women were allowed to compete against men, for example, in the National Air Race and Transcontinental Handicap Air Derby and Frank Phillips Trophy Race. In 1936, women were allowed to enter the Bendix Trophy Race, in which Louise Thaden and Blanche Noyes won first place.

After World War II, air racing was rejuvenated by Ninety-Nines President Jeanette Lempkel. Races such as the first All Woman Air Race and the All-Woman Transcontinental Air Races (AWTAR) were born (see https://www.ninety-nines.org/women-in-air-racing.htm).

## CHAPTER 20

Louise Thaden, as close friends with Amelia Earhart, shared her final conversation with Earhart before she embarked on her round-the-world flight:

In January of 1937 I flew to California. Circling Union Air Terminal at Burbank I landed, taxiing toward Paul Mantz's hangar, to see A.E.'s twin-engine Lockheed. I could just see the top of her head as she leaned forward in the cockpit. Pushing on the brakes and opening the throttle of my Beechcraft I pulled up with a thunderous roar wing to wing with the "Flying Laboratory."

"Look here," I said to her, "You've gone crazy on me. Why stick your neck out a mile on this round-the-world flight? You don't need to do anything more. You're tops now and if you never do anything you always will be. It seems to me you have everything to lose, and nothing to gain. If you fall in the drink all you have accomplished during the last nine years will be lost. You know as well as I do it's a hazardous flight over oceans, jungles and thousands of miles of uninhabited country."

She laughed. "Come over here." We sat down on the edge of the rubber lifeboat which was inflated for test. "You're a fine one to be talking to me like that. Aren't you the gal who flew in last year's Bendix with a gas tank draped around your neck?"

"Yeah," I said, "but that's different. I was over land with a chance of walking out."

"Listen," she answered, "*You* can't talk to *me* about taking chances!"

"Well all right Amelia, I give up, but just the same I wish you wouldn't do it."

We sat in silence for a few minutes, each thinking our own thoughts.

"I've wanted to do this flight for a long time," she said finally with unusual seriousness.

"I know you have."

"I've worked hard, and I deserve one fling during my lifetime."

"But Amelia . . ."

"If I bop off you can carry on; you can all carry on. But I'll be back." And she grinned.

"But Amelia!" I said in grim hopelessness, "You're needed. And you know as well as I do no one could ever take your place."

"Oh pshaw!" she said jumping up, brushing dust off her slacks. "I have to run. Will you have dinner with G. P. and me?"

"Sorry," I said. "I'm expected in town. What flowers shall I send for you?"

"Well, water lilies should be appropriate shouldn't they?"

In silence we walked to the car. "You know all the things I'd like to say," I said.

Tanned hand on the door handle, blonde sunburned hair blowing in an off-shore breeze, she turned toward me. "If I should bop off," she said, "it will be doing the thing I've always wanted most to do. Being a fatalist yourself you know The Man with the little black book has a date marked down for all of us—when our work here is finished."

Nodding, I held out my hand. "Goodbye, and all the luck in the world!"

Perhaps it is because I have known Amelia for so long that I find it difficult to draw a word picture of her. Perhaps that is why it is impossible adequately to describe her stanch fineness, her clear-eyed honesty, her unbiased fairness, the undefeated spirit, the calm resourcefulness, her splendid mentality, the nervous reserve which has carried her through exhausting flights and more exhausting lecture tours.

As many another I have often speculated on death and life hereafter. Eternal life, I think, is a life so lived that its deeds carry on through the ages. A. E. has carved a niche too deep to ever be forgotten. She will live. So I have said no farewell to her. As she invariably ended letters to me, so I say to her, "Cheerio!" (see "A.E."—A Postscript, *High, Wide and Frightened*, Louise Thaden, 150–152).

## CHAPTER 21

By August 1941, the British Air Transport Auxiliary (ATA), a civilian organization set up during World War II, was ferrying military aircraft from factories to airfields, which freed up pilots for combat roles. The women's section of the ATA flew Tiger Moths, but they soon changed to allow women to fly more types of aircraft, including Hurricanes, Spitfires, Lancasters, and Flying Fortresses. During the war, the ATA pilots delivered more than 309,000 aircraft. Eventually, the ferry aircraft were loaded with guns so they could defend themselves against German aircraft during ferrying deliveries (see https://www.kenleyrevival.org

/content/history/women-at-war/air-transport-auxiliary#:~:text=The%20
first%20eight%20women%20were,Patterson%2C%20and%20
Winifred%20Crossley%20Fair).

## CHAPTER 22

The Lend-Lease Act was passed on March 11, 1941, and allowed the United States to lend or lease ships, planes, or other war supplies to Allied nations—or those who were aligned in the defense of the US. For nearly a year, leading up to the signed Act, debates raged about whether the US could maintain neutrality while sending war supplies to other countries. British Prime Minister Winston Churchill requested help from President Roosevelt after Britain lost eleven destroyers to the German Navy. Although Roosevelt had promised in his 1940 presidential election campaign to keep America out of the war, that all changed when the Axis powers continued to gain ground. Secretary of War Henry L. Stimson summed up his argument in favor of the Act by saying, "We are buying . . . not lending. We are buying our own security while we prepare. By our delay during the past six years, while Germany was preparing, we find ourselves unprepared and unarmed, facing a thoroughly prepared and armed potential enemy" (see https://www.archives .gov/milestone-documents/lend-lease-act).

## CHAPTER 23

When the Japanese military launched their surprise attack on the US Naval base at Pearl Harbor, it sent America headlong into World War II. The attack on Pearl Harbor killed 2,403 US military personnel, including sailors, soldiers, and civilians. One thousand one hundred seventy-eight people were wounded, and 129 Japanese soldiers were killed. This set off a chain reaction around the world, and Allied countries declared war on Japan. On December 8, following the Japanese attack on Pearl Harbor, the US Congress nearly unanimously approved Roosevelt's declaration of war on Japan. The single, opposing vote against the declaration of war was by Representative Jeannette Rankin of Montana, who said, "As a woman, I can't go to war, and I refuse to send anyone else" (see https://www.history.com/topics/world-war-ii/pearl-harbor).

## CHAPTER 24

While working at the ATA in England, Jacqueline Cochran experienced the trials of war firsthand. In her book, *The Stars at Noon*, Cochran shared her experience: "Bombing of London was heavy in those days. The Battle of Britain was on. The sky at night was full of flashing planes, searchlights, and antiaircraft fire accompanied by the incessant sound of the sirens and the explosions of bombs. One night just before I left England the biggest raid of all was on. My house seemed to be in a sort of grandstand position and I got out of bed, wrapped a blanket around me and sat on the front steps. It was a long fight. The panes in my windows were broken from nearby bomb explosions. A house went to pieces a block up the street and then another hit came just a block below me" (113).

## CHAPTER 25

Teresa James, who became one of the original WAFS, was well qualified at 2,200 hours of flight time. Meeting Nancy Love for the first time at New Castle, Teresa observed: "This Base is new and not at all what I had expected an Army Base to be. Buildings and roads are under construction and mud is knee-deep all over the place. I don't know what I expected, probably old red brick buildings with ivy clinging all over. . . . Nancy Love is everything I thought and more! Beautiful, capable and charming. Wish she would show up right now. Twice already she has put me at ease, and I could stand it again" (*The Women with Silver Wings*, Landdeck, 25).

## CHAPTER 26

Teresa James received a telegram on September 6, 1942, inviting her to join the Ferrying Program. Signed by Nancy Love and Colonel Robert Baker, the telegram read: "Ferrying Division Air Transport Command is establishing group of women pilots for domestic ferrying. Necessary qualifications are high school education, age between 21 and 35, commercial license, 500 hours, 200 horsepower rating. Advise commanding officer Second Ferrying Group, Ferrying Division Air Transport

Command, Newcastle County Airport, Wilmington, Delaware, if you are immediately available and can report at once at Wilmington at your own expense for interview and flight check. Bring two letters recommendation, proof of education and flying time" (*The Women with Silver Wings*, Landdeck, 11).

At a petite five foot one, Betty Gillies mastered the P-47 in early 1943 and observed, "It really was no problem fitting myself in the airplanes. I sat on a cushion, which with the parachute, put me up plenty high. And the only real long-legged airplanes were those for which I had the blocks. I could use a cushion behind me quite well in all but the P-38, the P-47 and the P-51. In those cockpits, the gunsights were too close to my face if I used a cushion behind me. The blocks Grumman made up gave my legs the length I needed. Grumman also made me a gadget to turn fuel valve in the P-38" (*The Originals*, Rickman, 140–141).

## CHAPTER 27

Sacrifice was a normal and expected part of any war, and the Gillies family was no different. Betty Gillies's husband, Bud, was exempt from the draft because of the work he did with Grumman Aircraft. Betty also wanted to do her part. Because her mother-in-law agreed to care for the children, Betty was able to serve by flying for the WAFS. In her words: "It was hard to leave Bud and the kids, but we managed to keep in close touch and see each other from time to time. TDY [temporary duty] at Farmingdale [1943–44] was a joy to me because then I could RON [remain overnight] at home. I loved flying and I was, and still am, very patriotic" (*The Originals*, Rickman, 51).

## CHAPTER 28

In Betty Gillies's diary, she wrote about her experience when she first arrived at New Castle and saw the BOQ barracks: "As I remember, my reaction to the physical properties of the base was mainly AWE! The huge airport with the fantastic flying machines scattered about. Our quarters were rather drafty. My room was on the north-west corner and one could see daylight through several of the cracks. But I loved it! BOQ

14 was right in the center of the base and next to the Officers' Club, which we were privileged to enjoy" (*The Originals*, Rickman, 56).

## CHAPTER 29

After Catherine Slocum left the WAFS Program, the remaining squadron consisted of Nancy Love, Betty Gillies, Cornelia Fort, Aline "Pat" Rhonie, Helen Mary Clark, Adela "Del" Scharr, Esther Nelson, Teresa James, Barbara Poole, Helen Richards, Barbara Towne, Gertrude Meserve, Florene Miller, Barbara Jane "B.J." Erickson, Delphine Bohn, Barbara "Donnie" Donahue, Evelyn Sharp, Phyllis Burchfield, Esther Manning, Nancy Batson, Katherine "Kay" Rawls Thompson, Dorothy Fulton, Opal "Betsy" Ferguson, Bernice Batten, and Dorothy Scott. Soon to join were Helen "Little Mac" McGilvery and Kathryn "Sis" Bernheim. Even though Pat Rhonie left early on, she is still counted among the Original squadron of twenty-seven (*Nancy Love*, Rickman, 97–98).

## CHAPTER 30

Once the WASP pilot training was moved to Sweetwater, Texas, the Pilot Training Program was divided into a two-phase system. During the 23 weeks of training, the trainee had 115 hours of flying and 180 hours of ground school. Their training also included "military training including military courtesy and customs, Articles of War, safeguarding of military information, drill and ceremonies, Army orientation, organization, military correspondence, chemical warfare and personal affairs" (*Those Wonderful Women*, 369). Ground school included "mathematics, physics, maps and charts, navigation, principles of flight, engines and propellers, weather, code, instrument flying, communications, and physical and first aid training" (369).

## CHAPTER 31

It wasn't until November 25, 1942, that newspapers in America began reporting that over two million Jews had been murdered. Up until then, US State Department officials considered the mass extermination of the European Jews only a war rumor. In response to learning that the deaths had indeed occurred, December 2 was declared an international day of mourning. And on December 17, Allied governments, including the United States, Great Britain, and the Soviet Union, released a "Declaration on Atrocities." Although this declaration condemned the cruelty toward the Jews, there were no plans for rescue efforts made (see https://encyclopedia.ushmm.org/content/en/article/the-united-states -and-the-holocaust-1942-45).

## CHAPTER 32

Every WASP death was a tragedy, but Cornelia Fort's struck Nancy's core since Cornelia was an Original and she'd survived the Pearl Harbor attack by dodging a Japanese bomber. About that fateful December day, Cornelia said, "I jerked the controls away from my student and jammed the throttle wide open to pull above the oncoming plane. . . . He passed so close under us that our celluloid windows rattled violently, and I looked down to see what kind of plane it was. . . . The painted red balls on the tops of the wings shone brightly in the sun. I looked again with complete and utter disbelief" (*Fly Girls*, P. O'Connell Pearson, 31).

Cornelia was a strong advocate for freedom, a belief she carried with her into the WASP Program. Before her death, she wrote, "As long as our planes flew overhead, the skies of America were free and that's what all of us everywhere are fighting for. And that we, in a very small way are being allowed to help keep that sky free is the most beautiful thing I've ever known" (Pearson, 95).

## CHAPTER 33

The pilot classification list is as follows:

Class I—qualified to fly low-powered, single-engine airplanes (PT-17, PT-19, PT-26, Cubs)

Class II—qualified to fly twin-engine trainers and utility planes (UC-78, AT-9)

Class III—qualified to fly twin-engine cargo/medium transport planes and on instruments (C-47, C-60)

Class IV—qualified to fly twin-engine planes in advanced categories, such as attack planes, medium bombers, and heavy transports (B-25, A-20, A-24, A-25)

Class V—qualified to fly the biggest airplanes, four-engine bombers, and transports (B-17, B-24, B-29, C-54) and able to deliver them overseas

Class P-i—qualified to fly single-engine (P-51, P-47, P-40, P-39, and P-63) and twin-engine (P-38 and P-61), high-performance pursuits or fighters. The small "i" after the P denoted instrument rated. (See *Over the Hump*, Tunner, 27–28.)

## CHAPTER 34

The *Newsweek* article titled "Coup for Cochran," with the caption, "Miss Cochran and Mrs. Love: Which one bosses women fliers?" beneath their photographs, read in part: "Last week came a shake-up . . . even the Air Forces weren't agreed on which of the photogenic female flying chiefs would outrank the other. The ATC maintained that Miss Cochran's job was merely advisory and not superior to Mrs. Love's executive post. But officials at Air Forces headquarters insisted that Miss Cochran had 'highest authority' over women pilots: 'If the Air Transport Command is not already aware of this, they will have to be made aware of it'" (*Nancy Love*, Rickman, 130).

## CHAPTER 35

In order to fulfill more duties with women pilots, Jacqueline Cochran sent a selection of those who graduated from Class 43-3 to Camp Davis, where they'd enter training for towing gunnery targets (see *Nancy Love*, Rickman, 132). WASP aviator Betty Jane Williams said, "We were basically used as target practice. We flew target sleeves behind our planes so ground troops could practice firing live ammunition at a moving target. A couple of times they almost blew me out of the sky." Other duties included test-flying refurbished planes to see if they were ready to return to service (see https://www.dailynews.com/2022/05/28 /thank-you-to-the-wasps-unsung-women-pilots-during-world-war-ii -who-served-and-died-for-freedom/).

## CHAPTER 36

In Nancy Love's B-4 bag, she carried a letter written by her husband. Bob's letter was written to Major Roy Atwood, executive officer of the ATC European Wing in London, and it was supposed to be an enthusiastic introduction (see *Nancy Love*, Rickman, 142):

*They should arrive in Prestwich presently, and due to the shortness of time will bring this letter. I have known these people for a good while and they are thoroughly competent as pilots, as well as having a background in aviation activities. They are being sent to perform a certain number of liaison with the ATA and other agencies interested in the ferrying of the aircraft to the UK.*

*I am sure you will find these two personalities pleasant, if not unusual, in that they arrive as they did, and sincerely hope you will give them your highly accredited effort in showing them around.*

*Very sincerely yours,*

*Robert M. Love*

*Colonel, G.S.C.*

*Deputy Chief of Staff*

*P.S. Incidentally one of them is my wife and the other a good friend.*

## CHAPTER 37

Nancy Love's disappointment over the canceled B-17 transatlantic mission didn't fade. Years later in 1955, she wrote, "I had always wanted to fly a B-17 and wondered if I'd be capable of handling an airplane of that size. . . . We started for Prestwick, Scotland, with a crew of three enlisted men and a lieutenant navigator. This dream was shattered for us when we were held overnight by weather in Goose Bay Labrador. Someone high up, who apparently disapproved us of in particular, heard about it and stopped the flight. Betty and I, raging and frustrated, were sent ignominiously home, while a male replaced us as pilots. That disappointment is still with me though later I managed to fly around the world, about half of the trip as a pilot" (*Nancy Love*, Rickman, 146).

## CHAPTER 38

WASP aviator Iris Critchell remembered how the P-51s took ferrying precedence over most of the other aircraft in the urgency to get them delivered overseas: "The P-51s were such a high priority, in the fall of 1944 after we delivered to Newark, we no longer were allowed to detour and pick up a P-39 or P-40 on the way back to Long Beach. Instead, we were under orders to return to base immediately on the airlines or military transport the fastest way possible. At the Newark airport where we landed, the harbor was right there. The ships were pulled into the slips where they waited for our airplanes. We'd land the P-51 where the men were ready to load the aircraft onto the ships. Sometimes they were in such a hurry, they'd start to pull it by the tail to be loaded—with us still in the cockpit! They wanted them on their way to England or Italy as fast as possible" (*Global Mission*, H.H. Arnold, 358–359).

## CHAPTER 39

Delphine Bohn, who was the commander of the 5th Ferrying Group's women's squadron in Dallas, didn't hold back on her opinion of how stressful it became toward the end of 1944, knowing that the WASP Program was going to be disbanded: "Even the female of the human species began to wilt, to lose energy and strength. There was a greatly evident lack of all vitamins. We were subjected to debilitating psychological pressures! The questions of militarization or non-militarization and with whom as primary director were wrapped round with and buried in too much desire for personal glorification by too many people. Also, there were too many questionable decisions to be made as to our own grading of various female abilities and disabilities, inclusive of flight" (*Nancy Love*, Rickman, 211).

## CHAPTER 40

Nancy Love shared this story of her first C-54 delivery with another WASP as her copilot: "The plane was to be delivered to American Export Airlines, and was the first DC-4 to be assigned to them. So the chief pilot and high officials were at the field at 1 p.m., waiting. They had never had such big ones before and were much impressed by the size of the plane. They hurried aboard, walked up the long passenger aisle, opened the front cockpit door with expressions of triumph and welcome on their faces. They stopped in a sort of frozen shock as their minds finally grasped the fact that the two happily grinning pilots were women! Without a word, they turned and walked out again" (Mardo Crane, "The Women With Silver Wings," Part One, *The 99 News*, Special Issue 1978).

## CHAPTER 41

WASP member Marie Muccie fondly remembered the huge military zoot suit she wore when first in training. When the bill to militarize the WASP in 1944 was turned down, Marie realized that society wasn't ready to accept women fully into the military and be given the same duties as men. She clarified, "Opponents of the bill say we Wasps were not under military discipline. They must be kidding. We received the same training as the male Air Force Cadets. The US Army Air Corps issued orders for all military missions. We flew all the same type of military aircraft from small trainers to bombers. . . . By offering official recognition of our part to help win the war would mean a great deal to us. It would be like the US government saying, 'Thank you for a job well done.' We earned it, we deserve it and we did do a good job" (*Fly Girls*, Pearson, 167–168).

## CHAPTER 42

Despite the devastation that Nancy Love felt over the disbanding of the WASP Program, she reached far into her network to line up jobs for the women pilots. In one such case, she wrote to Mr. Traylor of the Reconstruction Finance Corporation about possible available jobs: "I am very anxious to see these pilots given an opportunity to utilize the flying skill they have acquired in the service, since they have worked hard and conscientiously for the Army, and now find themselves without jobs. . . . If you will advise me as soon as possible of your requirements, I will advise the WASP Squadron leaders at our Ferrying Groups, and can assure you that they will select highly qualified pilots upon whom you can depend" (*Nancy Love*, Rickman, 214–215).

Following is the full list of the 38 WASP who died. Overall, 27 WASP were killed on flying missions. The rest died in training crashes or as a result of malfunctioning equipment (see https://cafriseabove.org /wp-content/uploads/2021/10/Women-Airforce-Service-Pilots-Killed -in-Service.pdf).

# IN TRIBUTE TO THE 38 WASP WHO DIED IN THE SERVICE OF THEIR COUNTRY

## IN ORDER OF DEATH DATE

**T: Trainee**
**A: Active duty**

Margaret Sanford Oldenburg (T) July 29, 1909–March 7, 1943

Cornelia Fort (A) February 5, 1919–March 21, 1943

Jane Dolores Champlin (T) May 14, 1917–June 3, 1943

Kathryn Barbara Lawrence (T) December 3, 1920–August 4, 1943

Mabel Virginia Rawlinson (A) March 19, 1917–August 23, 1943

Margaret June "Peggy" Seip (T) June 24, 1916–August 30, 1943

Helen Jo Anderson Severson (T) November 2, 1918–August 30, 1943

Betty Taylor Wood (A) March 1921–September 23, 1943

Virginia Caraline Moffatt (A) May 31, 1912–October 5, 1943

Mary Elizabeth Trebing (A) December 31, 1920–November 7, 1943

Dorothy E. "Scottie" Scott (A) February 16, 1920–December 3, 1943

Marian J. Toevs (A) May 13, 1917–February 18, 1944

Betty Pauline Stine (T) September 13, 1921–February 25, 1944

Frances Fortune Grimes (A) 1914–March 27, 1944

Evelyn Sharp (A) October 1, 1919–April 3, 1944

Marie Ethel Sharon (A) April 21, 1917–April 10, 1944

Mary Holmes Howson (T) February 16, 1919–April 16, 1944

Jayne Elizabeth Erickson (T) April 14, 1921–April 16, 1944

Edith "Edy" Clayton Keene (A) December 19, 1920–April 25, 1944

Dorothy Mae "Dottie" Nichols (A) September 26, 1916–June 11, 1944

Marjorie Doris Edwards (T) September 28, 1918–June 13, 1944

Gleanna Roberts (T) January 11, 1919–June 20, 1944

Lea Ola McDonald (A) October 12, 1921–June 21, 1944

Bonnie Jean Alloway Welz (A) June 22, 1918–June 29, 1944

Susan Parker Clarke (A) August 5, 1918–July 4, 1944

Paula Ruth Loop (A) August 25, 1916–July 7, 1944

Bettie Mae Scott (A) July 26, 1921–July 8, 1944

Beverly Jean Moses (A) December 21, 1922–July 18, 1944

Mary E. Hartson (A) January 11, 1917–August 14, 1944

Alice E. Lovejoy (A) August 15, 1915–September 13, 1944

Marie Michell Robinson (A) May 23, 1924–October 2, 1944

Peggy Wilson Martin (A) February 8, 1912–October 3, 1944

Marjorie Laverne Davis (T) December 22, 1922–October 16, 1944

Jeanne Lewellen Norbeck (A) November 14, 1912–October 16, 1944

Gertrude "Tommy" Tompkins-Silver (A) October 16, 1911–October 26, 1944

Hazel Ying Lee (A) August 24, 1912–November 25, 1944

Katherine "Kay" Applegate Dussaq (A) March 14, 1905–November 26, 1944

Mary Louise Webster (A) June 30, 1919–December 9, 1944

# SELECTED BIBLIOGRAPHY

Arnold, H.H. *Global Mission*. Blue Ridge Summit, Pennsylvania: Military Classics Series, TAB Books Inc., Harper & Row Publishers, 1949.

Cochran, Jacqueline. *Jackie Cochran: An Autobiography*. Rufus Publications, 1987.

Cochran, Jacqueline. *The Stars at Noon*. An Atlantic Monthly Press Book, 1954.

Douglas, Deborah G. *American Women and Flight since 1940*. Lexington: University Press of Kentucky, 2004.

Keil, Sally Van Wagenen. *Those Wonderful Women in Their Flying Machines: The Unknown Heroines of World War II*. Fourth Direction Press, New York, 2000.

Landdeck, Katherine Sharp. *The Women with Silver Wings*. Crown, New York, 2020.

Nathan, Amy. *Yankee Doodle Gals: Women Pilots of World War II*. National Geographic Society, 2013.

O'Brien, Keith. *Fly Girls: How Five Daring Women Defied All Odds and Made Aviation History*. Houghton Mifflin Harcourt, 2018.

Pearson, P. O'Connell. *Fly Girls*. Simon & Schuster Books for Young Readers, 2018.

Rickman, Sarah Byrn. *Nancy Love and the WASP Ferry Pilots of World War II*. University of North Texas Press, 2008.

Rickman, Sarah Byrn. *The Originals: The Women's Auxiliary Ferrying Squadron of World War II*. Braughler Books, second edition, 2017.

Smith-Daugherty, Rhonda. *Jacqueline Cochran: Biography of a Pioneer Aviator*. McFarland & Company, Inc., Publishers, 2012.

Thaden, Louise. *High, Wide, and Frightened*. Red Kestrel Books, 2019.

Tunner, William H. and Booton Herndon. *Over the Hump: The Story of General William H. Tunner, the Man Who Moved Anything Anywhere, Anytime*. New York: Duell, Sloan and Pearce, 1964.

# DISCUSSION QUESTIONS

1. Before reading this book, what did you know about female aviators' WWII service?

2. What do you think drove Nancy Harkness Love to stay persistent in pushing for a women's aviator ferrying program despite all the setbacks and red tape?

3. Why did it seem so complicated and sometimes difficult for the female pilots to gain experience and respect from their male peers?

4. What do you think was at the core of the continual conflict between Nancy Harkness Love and Jacqueline Cochran?

5. What did you notice about the difference between the men who supported women aviators (such as Nancy's brother, father, and husband) and the men who kept putting up roadblocks to prevent progress?

6. Why do you think the United States was so slow to utilize female aviators when their closest ally, the United Kingdom, began recruiting female pilots as early as January 1940?

7. Do you agree with the decision most of the Allied powers made to keep women pilots out of combat? Contrast that with the Soviet Union's all-female aviation regiment that flew bombing missions against the German military.

8. What do you think about Congress turning down the WASP bill for militarization in 1944, while other groups, such as the WAC, WAVES, and SPARs, were granted military status in the 1940s?

9. The generational perceptions and differences between Nancy Love and her mother come through in the story in several scenes. What generational differences do you see in your families?

10. Nancy Love burned her WASP uniform at some point after the ferrying program was disbanded. For plot purposes, I put it into the final scene, but what are your thoughts about her actions, knowing how much time she dedicated to the WAFS/WASP program?

# ACKNOWLEDGMENTS

Researching the well-lived life of Nancy Harkness Love was a privilege. I'm very grateful for many expert readers who combed through scenes in order to make the details solid. Thanks to author Chalon Linton, who was able to give me feedback on military details. Thanks as well to author Julie Wright, who found ways to enhance Nancy's character. My daughter Kara, who was relegated to being my sounding board since she is also a pilot, came with me on a couple of field trips in search of specific information. One of those locations was the National WASP WWII Museum in Sweetwater, Texas.

We also visited the Hill Aerospace Museum in Roy, Utah, and met Lieutenant Colonel (Ret.) Carl William Shepard Jr., who graciously agreed to read the flying scenes in the book. His additions and clarifications were valuable, and I appreciated his time. My agent, Ann Leslie Tuttle, continues to be a champion of my stories, and she's always generous with her time and feedback. Thanks to Ilise Levine, who helped me brainstorm and gather information about female aviators who have remarkable histories—there were a lot, so it took some vetting.

I'm grateful for Shadow Mountain Publishing and their support of my work. Thanks to the remarkable team, which includes Chris Schoebinger, Heidi Taylor Gordon, Lisa Mangum, Derk Koldewyn, Troy Butcher, Amy Parker, Ashley Olson, Haley Haskins, Callie Hansen, Jinho Song, and editor Samantha Millburn—whose talented and thorough editing made the manuscript shine. A special thanks to Lorie Humpherys for her proofreading extraordinaire.

Many thanks goes to several friends and authors, specifically Jen Geigle Johnson, Rebecca Connolly, Allison Hong Merrill, Mindy Holt, Taffy Lovell, Julie Daines, and Jennifer Moore. My family continues as a major support of my writing career. Thank you to my parents, Kent and Gayle Brown, and my father-in-law, Lester Moore. And of course, thanks to my husband, Chris, our children, Kaelin, Kara, Dana, and Rose, son-in-law, Christian, and our grandson, Ezra.

My final thanks goes to Sarah Byrn Rickman, whom I hope to meet one day. She is the leading scholar of the Women Airforce Service Pilots (WASP), and I own most of her nonfiction books. Her research on the female aviators of the 1940s is not only comprehensive, but she has also captured the lady flyers' hearts and souls.

## Also by **HEATHER B. MOORE**

Based on the true story of the free-spirited daughter of Queen Victoria.

Based on a true story. Inspired by real events. A riveting and emotionally gripping novel of an American soldier working as a spy in Soviet-occupied East Germany and a West German woman secretly helping her countrymen escape from behind the Berlin Wall.

Based on a true story, this gripping WWII novel captures the resilience, hope, and courage of a Dutch family who is separated during the war when the Japanese occupy the Dutch East Indies.

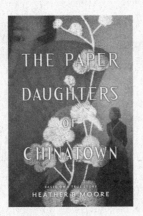

Based on true events, *The Paper Daughters of Chinatown* is a powerful story about a largely unknown chapter in history and the women who emerged as heroes.

Based on the true story of two friends who unite to help rescue immigrant women and girls in San Francisco's Chinatown in the late 1890s.

Available wherever books are sold

SHADOW
MOUNTAIN
PUBLISHING